Wicked HEART

THE HEARTS OF SAWYERS BEND
BOOK FIVE

IVY LAYNE

GINGER QUILL PRESS, LLC

Wicked Heart

Find out more about the author and upcoming books online at www.
ivylayne.com

Contents

Also by Ivy Layne

THE HEARTS OF SAWYERS BEND

Stolen Heart

Sweet Heart

Scheming Heart

Rebel Heart

Wicked Heart

Wild Heart

THE UNTANGLED SERIES

Unraveled

Undone

Uncovered

THE WINTERS SAGA

The Billionaire's Secret Heart (Novella)

The Billionaire's Secret Love (Novella)

The Billionaire's Pet

THE BILLIONAIRE CLUB

Prologue

SAVANNAH

He was out there again, skulking around the kitchens of Heartstone Manor in the middle of the night. None of the kids at school would believe it.

Finn Sawyer, the undisputed king of our high school, cooking? For fun? No way.

Watching him bent over a copper saucepan, his dark hair falling in his eyes, I wished with desperate rage that I'd told his secret before he'd told mine.

Now it was too late.

If I said anything now, everyone would think I was lying in revenge.

The more I thought about what he'd done that day at school, the more I wanted to bash him over the head with that copper saucepan. I hated no one on this planet as much as I hated Finn Sawyer.

The day he'd transferred to the local high school, he'd become the bane of my existence. Before that, no one cared that I lived in the big house. I was the daughter of the house-keeper, a townie, just like everyone else. I'd made it clear early on that I barely interacted with the Sawyers, and everyone pretty much forgot I had anything to do with them.

Then Finn got himself expelled from Laurel Country Day, and even his father's generous donations hadn't been enough to convince the school to take him back. Setting fire to the headmaster's office tended to make school administrators cranky. Coming into our rural public high school from an elite prep school like Laurel Country Day should have been hard for Finn. After all, he didn't know a soul except for me, and by unspoken agreement, Finn and I pretended to be strangers.

It wasn't an act. Not really. We might have slept under the same roof, but I could count on one hand the number of conversations we'd had. Prentice Sawyer did not encourage chit-chat between the family and staff. I might have been young, but I knew enough about life to understand how it was.

My mother had a good job. She worked her ass off, but Prentice Sawyer paid her well, especially considering she didn't have to worry about room and board. I love Sawyers Bend, but it's not exactly bursting with jobs. If I got my mother fired, we'd go from comfortable to desperate in a heartbeat. Which was the only reason I hadn't bashed Finn with that copper saucepan. Yet.

He flicked the whisk in lazy swoops, his t-shirt stretching across his back as he leaned over the pan and drew in a long breath, savoring the rich scents of vanilla and cream. He was so absorbed that he hadn't noticed me lurking in the dark hall leading to our small apartment off the kitchens.

This wasn't the first time Finn had snuck into the kitchens late at night to cook. His relationship with the family chef was an anomaly in Heartstone Manor. He'd pestered Chef Guérard to teach him to cook for years until the chef had agreed to a single lesson if Finn would promise never to bother him again. I don't know what Chef Guérard saw in Finn, who was only fourteen at the time. It must have been something extraordinary because he never argued about teaching Finn again, even though he knew he'd be fired if Prentice ever found out.

I'd seen Finn during his lessons a few times, barely recognizing him as the boy who ruled our high school with disdain and sullen apathy. With Chef Guérard, he was all intense focus, seeming to absorb the chef's instructions into his very cells.

That wasn't the Finn I knew from school. Another kid might have been bullied after transferring from his cush private school to our rural public one. Not Finn. In the perverse way of teenagers, he rose to the top of the social hierarchy powered by the sheer force of his indifference. He slouched around school, sullen and sneering, impervious to anything the other kids might throw at him.

On his third day, two boys in his class jumped him behind the gym, thinking to teach him a lesson about the pecking order. He'd pummeled them both, walked away, and never said a word to anyone. That was all it took. Within two weeks of his transfer, he'd become the bad boy every girl swooned over and every boy wanted to be. Ugh. I tried to pretend he didn't exist.

Until recently, it had worked out fine. He ignored me. I ignored him. Problem solved. Until today. Today, Finn Sawyer ruined my goddamned life, and, for once, I had something to say about it. Stepping forward, I left the dark of the hall for the dim light of the main kitchen.

3

"Why did you do it?" I demanded, keeping my voice low so it didn't carry down the hall and wake my mother.

Finn's shoulder jerked a fraction of an inch, the only sign that I'd surprised him. Then, with a careless flick, he tossed his hair off his forehead and shrugged.

"What do you mean, why? I was bored."

He was bored? That was all he had to say? *He was bored?*

"Why do you hate me so much? We barely know each other. I've never done anything to you!"

With another flick of that dark, shiny hair, he turned his attention back to whatever he was whisking in that stupid copper saucepan. "It wasn't about you. You don't have to take everything so personally. I was bored, and it was fucking funny. You should have seen the look on your face."

I ground my teeth together, hurtled back to that afternoon in the cafeteria when I'd passed Finn's table carrying my lunch tray.

I heard one of Finn's asshole buddies ask, "Is she a hot fuck? I know she plays the good girl, but that rack is fuckin' sweet."

Finn had leaned back in his chair and shrugged, noting that I'd slowed to hear his answer, already reminding myself that I couldn't beat him over the head with my lunch tray.

Then he said it. "Savannah? Hell no. She's gonna be a virgin till the day she dies. Trust me, she's a complete prude. It's the fucking Sahara in that cunt. Don't bother wasting your fucking time."

Then he'd slashed me a look with those green eyes, a vivid mossy emerald I'd never seen on anyone else. I'd recoiled at what I saw there—equal parts amusement and vindictive pleasure.

"You did it because it was funny?" I struggled not to

scream. The last thing I needed was my mother waking up to see what was going on outside her door.

Another shrug. "Yeah. Obviously. It was fucking hysterical. I thought Murphy was going to cry. He was practically salivating at the idea of getting in your pants."

"Murphy's a pig," I shot back, "but my prom date dumped me because of you. Now the whole school thinks I'm a dried-up prude who'll never put out."

Finn slanted me a look under his thick lashes. "You *are* a dried-up prude who'll never put out, so really, I wasn't lying. I was just saving Murphy the time."

"Do you know how long I saved up for that prom dress? And it's not like I can go with someone else. No guy in school will go anywhere with me now," I wailed in furious despair.

Looking suddenly far older than his years, Finn flicked off the burner under his saucepan and turned, crossing his arms over his chest. He leveled that deep green gaze at me. "That's the kind of guy you want to take you to prom? The kind that's only looking to get laid? If anything, I did you a favor."

"You made me a freaking social pariah, you dickhead. And you get to head off to college and start over. Meanwhile, I'm stuck here for another year, and I'm never going to get another date. They all think you're the fucking king of the universe, and if you say I'm a dried-up prude, it might as well be gospel."

"Not really my problem."

That was it. That was one more smart-ass comment than I could take.

I lunged forward, smacking him hard across the face, my hand burning at the impact. Finn didn't even flinch. He placed his palm flat on my chest and pushed me out of reach.

He didn't shove, just gently but firmly moved me out of his way. That pissed me off even more.

"I am not a dried-up prude! And I do not have the Sahara in my—" I didn't have a problem with swearing, but I couldn't bring myself to say that word to Finn. Never mind that he'd said it in front of the whole freaking cafeteria.

He dropped his arm and studied me, his green eyes appraising, glowing with amusement. I was getting very tired of being the butt of Finn Sawyer's latest joke.

"You sure you're not a dried-up prude?" he asked with a lift of his chin. "Prove it."

I tossed my hair back over my shoulders, setting my hands on my hips so I wouldn't slap him again. "What kind of moron do you take me for? *Prove it?* Fuck you. You're the last person I'd ever—"

Finn's hand shot out, closing over my arm, yanking me toward him. His mouth hit mine with fury, his palms coming down on my cheeks, holding my face still.

I was too surprised to stop him. Then I didn't want to.

He kissed me like he wanted to consume me, his mouth raw and rough and hungry. My lips opened under his, my mouth, my body. All of me wanted to kiss Finn Sawyer.

He smelled of vanilla and sugar, of decadence and the dark. His lips were sweet, his tongue stroking, demanding and cajoling until I was pressed to him, my head tilted back, one hand clutching his t-shirt at his waist, my head spinning. I didn't remember him backing me up to the big table in the middle of the kitchen.

I should have stopped when his hands closed over my

hips and he lifted me to sit on the edge, making a place for himself between my knees.

I should have stopped when his hand slid under my shirt, his rough palm sliding up my ribs, fingers curling around my back, his thumb grazing the side of my breast through my tank top.

I'd never been kissed like this. My knees clamped his sides, holding him close, until his hand dropped to my hip, dragging me almost off the edge of the table, close enough for the thick bar of his erection to grind into the growing heat between my legs.

Fuck the Sahara, I could feel how ready my body was, my breasts tight and swollen, pressing against his chest, that callused thumb stroking, stroking until I wanted to beg. He never stopped kissing me. He didn't press me back to the table, didn't try to strip off my clothes. Just kissed me until I was liquid in his arms, ready to do anything for more of Finn Sawyer.

I don't know what would have happened if we hadn't heard it.

A door shut somewhere. Maybe my mother getting up to use the bathroom in the middle of the night or one of the family coming downstairs. Neither of us stuck around to find out.

All that delicious liquid heat evaporated in an instant. I shoved Finn back and leaped off the counter, bolting for the door.

His mocking voice chased me down the hall. "Like I said, a complete prude."

My body hummed with a desire I'd never known before as his cruel words sliced through me.

I thought I hated him after that scene in the cafeteria, but now I knew what hate really was. Knees trembling, body aching with unfulfilled need, I escaped into the only space that was mine.

Our small apartment was dark and quiet, my mother still asleep. Splashing cold water on my face, I tried not to look at myself in the mirror. The glimpse I caught was enough. Swollen, red lips, my gray eyes too bright.

What had he done to me? How could I have let Finn Sawyer kiss me like that? How could I have—

I was not going to think about it. I tried to go to sleep, but I couldn't stop the merry-go-round in my brain. I lay awake until the sun came up. When I finally gave up on sleep and crept into the kitchen for some juice, I found a small white ramekin of crème brûlée in the staff refrigerator, topped with a card that read, *Sahara*.

I took out the ramekin, turning it in my hand. The crust of sugar was perfectly browned. Even through the chill of the fridge, I could smell the night before. Vanilla, sugar, and Finn. The memory hit me like a freight train—the heat of his body, his rough mouth. His hands on my hips, pulling me closer, so close our bodies were almost one. Almost.

A sticky mess of emotions assaulted me. Desire. Regret. Fury. Humiliation. I pitched the delicate porcelain cup into the trash, wincing only a little as it shattered.

If I never saw Finn Sawyer again, it would be too soon.

I almost got my wish.

Less than a year after that night, Finn Sawyer disappeared off the face of the earth.

It would be ten long years before I saw him again.

And I'd been right.

It was still too soon.

Chapter One

FINN

10 YEARS LATER

I paused outside the door to the main kitchen of Heartstone Manor, hugging the shadows, waiting for my shot. For a little bit of luck. For the exact right moment to set it all in motion.

Inside the kitchens, organized chaos reigned as the cook raced to get dinner plated and served. Mrs. Bailey called out to April, the day maid who helped her with the dinner service. April called back from somewhere out of sight, her words rushed.

It was past time to plate the salad and arrange it in the dumbwaiter for its trip up to the formal dining room. I checked my watch. They were running three minutes behind. Mrs. Bailey's head was probably about to explode. I pictured Savannah upstairs, tapping her foot in irritation as she waited for the salad course to arrive, ready to be served to the family.

My family.

I should have been in the dining room with them,

awaiting my meal, arms crossed over my chest, a surly expression on my face. That was my default these days. A throwback to high school. Angry. Sullen. Wishing I was anywhere but here, trapped in Heartstone Manor, just like I had been all those years ago.

In this moment, I didn't care about any of it. I didn't care about my family, my father's will, the late dinner.

None of that was important. I was a man on a mission, and the mission was the only thing that mattered. I held my breath, listening, waiting for my chance, my tool of sabotage burning a hole in my pocket.

My ears tracked the movement in the kitchen, my eyes only able to catch quick glimpses through the door. A mutter reached my ears, and every muscle strung tight in anticipation.

"Where is that girl? We have to get these salads upstairs."

I edged closer and risked a peek into the kitchen just in time to see the wide back of Mrs. Bailey disappear into the small room containing the dumbwaiter, her hands loaded with salad plates. This was it.

I had no idea where April was, but I did know she'd be back any second. She hadn't gotten distracted and wandered off. Savannah did not employ slackers in Heartstone Manor. With a quick glance to make sure the kitchen was empty, I dashed to the stove and the pot of soup simmering over the largest burner, a soup tureen filled with steaming water close by.

In a flash, I dropped a sugar cube into the soup. Risking one more second to let it dissolve, then another to give the soup a quick stir, I disappeared from the kitchen as silently as I'd entered.

In the hall, I headed left, away from the kitchens and

Mrs. Bailey. Passing the open door to the prep kitchen, I heard a cabinet shut and picked up my pace. It had to be April, maybe grabbing something she'd prepared earlier or a garnish she'd forgotten.

Spinning to my right, I ducked into the gym, peering around the doorframe to see April head back toward the kitchen, something leafy and green filling her hands. I stayed where I was, waiting for her to turn into the kitchen before I sprinted the rest of the length of the hall.

Taking the steps to the first floor two at a time, I was glad I had to cross the main level to reach the dining room. I needed time to wipe the smug grin off my face, to calm my racing heart. I didn't want anyone to see, to guess that I was up to anything other than the usual—sulking around Heartstone Manor and ignoring my siblings.

I strolled into the dining room as I usually did, sliding into my chair between my older sister Avery and my younger sister, Parker. Both of them shot concerned looks my way, but neither said anything. From across the room, Savannah Miles slanted me a cool look.

Not a thing about that look was unprofessional.

I still felt the slice of it.

Savannah had hated me for years. By the time I got what I wanted, she'd hate me even more. I could live with that. I had to. I had a mission, and no one was going to derail me. Not even the formidable Savannah Miles.

Savannah slid a salad plate in front of me and slipped away, taking her position just inside the door of the butler's pantry, unobtrusive and alert, as she always was. I tried to hide the exuberance fizzing through my veins. The rest of them might miss it, but Savannah wouldn't. She didn't miss much. I didn't need her to get suspicious and figure out what I was up to.

To get what I wanted, I had to get rid of Mrs. Bailey without getting myself kicked out of Heartstone Manor. It was the thinnest of lines—be annoying enough to drive off Mrs. Bailey, but not so annoying Savannah would have me booted from my home.

My oldest brother Griffen had made it very clear. If it came down to a dispute between a Sawyer and Savannah, Savannah would win.

It's not that Griffen cared more for our housekeeper than he did for his family. It's more that Sawyers did not have a good reputation for treating staff with respect. At least not during my father's reign. I'd always heard my grandfather and great-grandfather had been true gentlemen. Something they clearly hadn't passed down to Prentice Sawyer.

No woman on staff had been safe from Prentice except for Miss Martha, Savannah's mother. He hadn't laid a finger on her for the same reason Griffen was protecting Savannah. Heartstone Manor had needed Miss Martha in her time, and it needed Savannah now. Without Savannah, everything around here would grind to a halt. She hadn't been willing to take on the job unless Griffen promised she wouldn't have to deal with a new generation of Sawyers preying on the staff.

So far, our generation of Sawyers didn't seem to take after our father. Except for our cousin Bryce, but Griffen had taken care of him the first time he'd cornered a maid and tried to get handsy. According to our father's will, Griffen couldn't throw Bryce out of the house for the next five years, but he could encourage the maid to press charges for assault, something he'd made it clear he'd support wholeheartedly. I still hadn't decided how much Griffen took after dear old Dad, but the way he'd stuck up for Kitty was a point in his favor.

I took a sip of wine and picked up my fork, stabbing a crisp leaf of lettuce, my chef's soul withering at the aroma of vegetable oil drifting up from the plate. Bottled dressing. I fought the urge to sneer and roll my eyes. *She has one job*, I bitched in my head. *It takes three minutes to whisk up a decent vinaigrette, and she's serving us ranch from a bottle?*

Shit like this made it hard to feel guilty for annoying her into quitting. I didn't know what Griffen was paying her, but I'd noticed the staff was more than happy to be working here. In this, Griffen wasn't like our father, treating staff like they should be grateful just to come to the big house every day. The current staff had health insurance and vacation time. Mrs. Bailey had to feed sixteen of us three times a day, but breakfast and lunch were usually a buffet set up on the sideboard. She had plenty of time to make dressing from scratch. She didn't because she was either lazy or unimaginative. My guess was both.

I thought about the sugar cube I'd dropped into the soup, and a warm glow filled my chest. Such a small thing, that sugar cube.

The added sweetness wouldn't be noticeable in the tureen of soup. The sabotage wasn't in the sugar. It was in the drop of liquid I'd let soak into the sugar before secreting it in my pocket. Bitrex. The most bitter substance on earth. Usually added to cleaning products so children wouldn't drink them, only a teaspoon was enough to taste in a swimming pool. I'd diluted it and still only used a drop. That drop would be more than enough to put my plan in motion.

I'd come back to this house swearing I'd never cook for my family, that I'd never again darken the door to Heartstone's kitchens.

It had taken me too long to understand that Heartstone's kitchens were exactly where I needed to be.

In my defense, being back here was really fucking with my head. I'd hated this house by the time I left. I'd hated my father. Hated being a Sawyer. Hated my older brothers. Hated school. Hated this town. I'd hated everything and everyone but my sisters, Miss Martha, and Chef Guérard. During my teens, Miss Martha had commented more than once that I'd been such a sunny child, sweet-tempered but overflowing with mischief. Most of which got me into trouble.

Then I hit middle school, and everything went to hell. She and I both knew it wasn't puberty that turned me into the entitled little shit I became. It was my mother. And my father.

Darcy Sawyer had been love and light and everything good in my world. And then she died, leaving us all adrift. Lost. At the mercy of Prentice, our not-so-loving father. The father who saw me only as collateral. The father who left me for dead. So yeah, back then I hated pretty much everyone.

The only thing I cared about had been cooking. Not much had changed. And the only place in this house I'd ever felt at home was the kitchens. As a child I badgered the family chef to teach me. Chef Guérard refused. Repeatedly. For years. Eventually, he gave in. One lesson, he promised, if I'd swear never to darken his door again. After that one lesson, he gruffly ordered me to return the next day, adding, "Don't get caught." I hadn't.

We both knew what would happen if Chef Guérard had been caught talking to me, much less teaching me to cook. I knew what he was risking, but I couldn't let it go. I needed to know what he knew. Needed to understand.

He risked his job to teach me and later saved my life when I ended up homeless at nineteen, abandoned by my family and left for dead. He gave me a new life to replace the one I'd been born into. I'd taken the chance he offered me and dove in headfirst. I would never return to Sawyers Bend. Never.

Famous last words. Six months ago, my father was murdered. Couldn't have happened to a better guy. The family lawyer hunted me down and suggested I return for the reading of the will. I almost didn't come. Even after all these years, I couldn't forget. Wouldn't forgive.

Fuck my father. I hadn't let him control me for the last ten years. Why would I start now? After a few days, curiosity got the better of me. I came back to Sawyers Bend and stood with my siblings at our father's grave. I half expected him to rise from the coffin, refusing to succumb to something as mundane as death. He hadn't. The funeral had been oddly ordinary for one of the undead. Family only. No media. All very normal, except that our brother, Ford, was in jail for our father's murder.

I hadn't seen Ford in ten years. He'd done some pretty shitty things in his day, including orchestrating Griffen's exile and marrying his fiancée and later, joining our father in trading my life for a business deal. But I still couldn't believe he'd shot our father. For one thing, if Ford wanted to kill Prentice, he wouldn't have been caught. He sure as hell wouldn't have been stupid enough to stash the murder weapon in his own closet. No one believed he did it, but the evidence said otherwise, and he remained in prison.

Ford's arrest was my first surprise in coming home.

The reading of the will was the second.

I hadn't expected my father to leave me anything. Once upon a time, he had the option to save my life with a handful of cash. He said I was a bad investment. I was shocked to find out he'd left us all trust funds—with a few stipulations.

To inherit, we each had to live at Heartstone Manor for the next five years, allowed to leave for only two weeks a quarter. And we had to be good little boys and girls for Griffen. My father had exiled Griffen when I was thirteen. They'd never spoken again. To everyone's surprise, Prentice had left him everything. The company. The house. Control over our trust funds. But no cash.

My father had been wily. My guess? He assumed Griffen would dip into our trusts for ready cash, draining us dry while he ran the company into the ground. Goes to show Prentice didn't know everything. Griffen hadn't told us how much was in our trusts—I wasn't sure he knew himself—but he'd sworn he wouldn't touch them. Instead, he'd been working his ass off, along with his wife, Hope, and our brother Royal, to grow the company into more of a powerhouse than it already was.

I wasn't close to my siblings. Until a few months ago, I hadn't spoken to Griffen since I was thirteen. None of them knew where I'd been for the past decade or what I'd been doing. Not really.

I didn't know how I would survive living in this house for the next four years and six months, but I thought there was a chance Griffen wasn't going to steal my inheritance.

That didn't mean I couldn't fuck it up on my own. There was that second clause, after all. The one about being a good little boy. Being good has never been my forte. I was a raging asshole through most of my teens and early twenties. In the last few years, I'd gotten my inner asshole under control. Mostly.

I was a decent human being these days. Most of the

time. Dropping that sugar cube in the soup had been a dick move. Driving Mrs. Bailey into quitting was not the act of a nice guy.

I'm self-aware enough to know when I'm being an asshole, and while I was mostly good these days, this plan to take over the kitchens was like a trip back to see the old Finn. The Finn who'd set the headmaster's office on fire to get kicked out of school. I'd had a plan back then too. And it had worked. Just like this one was going to work.

Chapter Two

I crunched the last bit of salad, biting back a smile as I watched Savannah open the dumbwaiter to reveal the steaming tureen of soup.

I did feel bad about what I was doing to Mrs. Bailey. She wasn't the worst cook in the world. She just wasn't the best. Or more than halfway decent. But she was a hard worker and reliable. She'd find another job. Another kitchen. I just needed her out of this one. This kitchen was mine.

Here's the thing that really makes me the asshole.

I could have told Griffen I wanted to take over the kitchen after the last cook quit. By then I'd already been drawn back, stealing into the kitchens in the dead of night to cook, shuffling in the dark, moving in near silence so I wouldn't wake Savannah and Nicky. I'd loved those kitchens as a kid. They were the only place I felt like me. The only place in this entire fucking town where I had real roots.

With every night I snuck in, the need grew. I wasn't a kid anymore. I was a man. This wasn't Chef Guérard's kitchen anymore. And it sure as hell didn't belong to Mrs. Bailey. It was mine. It had always been mine. If I had to be in Heartstone Manor, I needed to be in the kitchens. Needed it like I needed food and sleep. Like I needed to cook. It was an itch under my skin, this need. So deep, so true, it was more than a little terrifying.

I could have gone to Griffen and asked to take over the kitchens. I'd thought about it. All I had to do was walk into his office and say I wanted to claim the kitchens. I'd have to cook for the family, sure, but the trade-off was worth it. The kitchens would be mine. My territory. My space. Mine. I hadn't known how much I needed that until the idea fully formed in my mind. The depth of my want left me unsteady.

I couldn't just ask Griffen. What if he said no? The thought was intolerable.

I didn't need to ask. I had a loophole. After I'd annoyed Mrs. Haverty into quitting, Griffen had sworn that if I drove away another cook, I'd have to take over the job myself.

Drive away another cook? I could do it in my sleep. By the time I realized how much I needed to be in the kitchens, I already had Mrs. Bailey on the ropes. She'd objected to my midnight visits, complaining that I moved things. I didn't use her supplies, cleaned up after myself, and was gone by the time her day began. But I touched the paper towel holder one time, and it was too much. The second time she accused me of hiding the salt—I didn't—and she convinced Savannah to ban me from the kitchens.

Not that it stopped me. It was bad enough I had to share the space with Mrs. Bailey. The idea that she could ban me from the kitchen I'd grown up in was not worth considering. I continued to ignore the ban, and Mrs. Bailey continued her tantrums. She always knew when I'd been in her space, making up lie after lie to turn Savannah against me. As if Savannah needed any help. She disliked me enough on her own. For good reason, unlike Mrs. Bailey.

I'd thought my invading what Mrs. Bailey saw as her territory might do the trick, but so far she was hanging in there. She'd underestimated me. Tonight's dinner was going to push her over the edge, and I was going to enjoy every minute of it.

Savannah rounded the table, clearing our salad plates. Only a few more minutes. I watched Savannah set the last of the salad plates in the dumbwaiter and ladle soup into the first bowl. She glanced up and met my eyes, hers narrowing as they locked on mine. I grinned, unable to resist poking at her.

There was something about Savannah Miles. She'd always gotten under my skin, even when we were kids. That sunrise hair, those cool gray eyes. The sheer competence of her. If you didn't think competence was sexy, you hadn't met Savannah Miles. The woman could do anything. Throw her an impossible task, and she'd take a few notes, disappear, and come back with the impossible made possible.

After years in high-pressure kitchens, I appreciate anyone who can get shit done with minimal fuss. I'd never say it out loud, but Savannah was better at running Heartstone Manor than her mother had been. Miss Martha had been the housekeeper here as long as I could remember. Savannah had grown up in Heartstone Manor, always there, elusive, not one of us, but not entirely separate. Now she was running the place.

Rolling the linen-covered serving cart close to the table, Savannah began to serve the soup. My gut tightened, and my foot bounced under the table. I was ready to go, vibrating with anticipation. Across the table, my brother Royal lifted a spoon to his mouth.

Holding my breath, I pretended to fill my own spoon, blowing on the hot soup to stall. Someone else had to taste it first. Royal closed his lips around the spoon and swallowed. Immediately, his lips pursed, his forehead wrinkling, eyes squinting as he yanked the spoon from his mouth, staring at it in confusion.

"What's wrong?" his girlfriend, Daisy, asked from beside him. She peered into her soup bowl before dipping in her own spoon and taking a cautious taste. Her face twisted in revulsion. "That's foul," she said under her breath, shooting a quick glance around the room.

At the head of the table, Griffen shot out a hand to cover Hope's, stopping her from picking up her spoon. "Don't. I don't know what it is, but the soup is—" He stopped, swallowing, scrunching up his face as if trying to force the bitter bite of the soup from his mouth. "Savannah, would you take the soup back down to the kitchen? I'm sure it was an accident, but it's inedible."

"Of course," Savannah answered, smoothly collecting full bowls from around the table, her expression serene. Until she got to me. Leaning in to take my full bowl, her breath warm against my ear, she hissed, "What did you do?"

I raised my eyebrows. "Me? Nothing." I lied without remorse. "How could I have done anything?"

Savannah's eyes narrowed into slits, her high cheek-bones flushed in anger. I loved looking at her when she was mad. All that fire made my heart beat harder.

A scrap of humanity shoved through my exhilaration as I remembered that Savannah was the one who was going to have to clean up my mess. Mrs. Bailey was going to flip her shit. That was the point of the whole exercise. I'd never ruin food for fun. But I knew I wasn't the one she'd yell at. Even if she knew I'd been responsible, Mrs. Bailey would never dare to yell at one of the Sawyers. She'd yell at Savannah, who worked her ass off and hadn't done anything but stick up for Mrs. Bailey. It was unfair. I was such an asshole.

I should just march into Griffen's office, say I wanted the job, then go apologize to Savannah for being a complete dickhead and making her job harder.

I wasn't going to do that, but I could do one thing for her. Reaching out, I snagged her wrist with one hand, stopping her from leaving. "Ask Mrs. Bailey for some milk chocolate. Not dark chocolate. Milk chocolate. It'll counteract the bitterness so anyone who tried the soup can get their taste buds working again."

Savannah gave a sharp nod, her eyes so squinty I was surprised she could see to push the full serving cart from the room. Griffen was watching me, his own eyes hard. I did my best to look innocent, grabbing a roll from the basket in front of me and buttering it with great attention to detail.

I should just tell him I wanted in the kitchens. Since he'd been home, Griffen had been the big brother I remembered. Kind. Patient. Our father had trapped him here with the will, setting it up so that if Griffen didn't stay, there wouldn't be anyone to run the company. Most of the town would have gone under without a Sawyer to sign their paychecks.

My brother Ford, practically Griffen's twin, had been running Sawyer Enterprises with our father at the time of the murder. But since Ford was in jail for shooting Prentice, Griffen was the town's only option.

When I was thirteen, our father had exiled Griffen for trying to undercut a business deal. Six months ago, Prentice had dragged him back, yoking him with an entire town. And

Griffen had stayed. He'd married Hope, his childhood best friend, and devoted himself to saving this family. I had every reason to believe he'd let me take over the kitchens if I could work up the nerve to ask.

That I couldn't do it was arguably insane. I'd spent the last decade working in professional kitchens, letting every kind of verbal abuse roll off my shoulders. I'd worked for chefs with god complexes who berated their staff nonstop. I'd done some yelling of my own, and I was a long way from the days when a cutting word from my father burned itself into my soul. Anyway, Griffen didn't yell.

So many times I'd thought about opening the door to that office, the office that had been my father's, standing in front of the desk where he'd so often sat and asking for something I wanted—something I needed.

I couldn't do it.

I shot back in time to standing there with my father sneering at me, telling me to get the fuck out and stop wasting his time. To the last words I ever heard him speak. "I don't give a fuck what you do with him. He's worth nothing to me."

I wanted to believe that the Griffen sitting at the head of the table was the same brother I'd known as a kid, but I'd been away a long time. So had Griffen. I didn't know him now, and he didn't know me. Trust had to be earned, and I wasn't fool enough to think I could trust Griffen just because I wanted to.

Until Prentice had exiled him, Griffen had been the perfect protégé. Just like Ford. And the last time he got the chance, Ford had left me for dead. With all that stacked up, I'd be an idiot to trust Griffen.

I wasn't asking anyone for anything. Especially my family. Once, they'd left me to die. All of them. My father.

Ford. Royal. They were all old enough to have known. Old enough to have done something to bring me home, to save me from the hands of kidnappers ready to trade my blood for cold hard cash. And not one of them had.

So yeah, I wasn't going to ask them for anything.

I wasn't going to ask anyone for what I wanted.

I was going to take it.

Chapter Three

FINN

Standing in the dark kitchen of Heartstone Manor, I turned in a slow circle, evaluating my options. The way Mrs. Bailey had organized this kitchen was insane. The space had no flow. It was anti-flow. Her prep area was divided, half of it in another room entirely and neither near the gas range. Her pantry was a jumble of bags and boxes, nothing labeled or airtight. At least it was clean. Not as clean as it should be, but sanitary enough that I wasn't afraid to eat.

How could she work like this? Didn't she have any pride?

My hands itched to empty every cupboard, bare every shelf, and put everything back in a way that made sense. Efficiency is paramount in the kitchen. How Mrs. Bailey managed to produce a decent meal with this setup was beyond me. Then again, her meals were mediocre at best, so I shouldn't be surprised.

I glanced to the far-right corner of the kitchen and the dark hall that led to the tiny apartment Savannah shared with her young son, Nicky. I was used to being quiet in the kitchens late at night. It was one thing to sneak in and not get caught, another to wake either Savannah or Nicky. They both needed their sleep, and I had no doubt Savannah would make me pay if I woke her up.

That meant the kind of reorganization I wanted to do was out of the question. I couldn't move heavy copper and cast iron cookware quietly enough to ensure Savannah's sleep wasn't disturbed. I'd have time for that later. When the kitchens were mine. For now, I'd have to settle for driving Mrs. Bailey slowly, subtly crazy.

I started by sliding open the drawer that held her small kitchen tools and emptying it as silently as possible, setting everything on a dish towel so the metal didn't clank. I swapped the contents of that drawer with another, this one filled with pot holders and other kitchen linens.

Next, I moved her basic spices, the ones she used so often she didn't put them away. They went under the sink, replaced by random, more exotic flavors from the pantry. Coriander seed, turmeric, star anise. Nothing Mrs. Bailey had used since she'd been at Heartstone. She was a salt and pepper cook. With liberal use of shortening. Don't get me started on her obsession with shortening.

I made my way around the kitchen, striking where she'd feel it most, moving and hiding the things she used every day. Basics. Her sponge was in the huge commercial fridge. Her favorite cooking knife secreted among the measuring cups.

I had to be creative. I couldn't sabotage the food at every meal.

I was long past hating my siblings. None of us were close, might never be, and I didn't know them well enough to like them, exactly, but I didn't hate them. And Hope was a million months pregnant. We all knew she'd had morning sickness for most of her pregnancy.

I'd sat through enough meals watching Griffen coax her to take one more bite, worry creasing his forehead as she tried to swallow, her face drawn and a little green. Now that she could eat, I wouldn't be the one to ruin it for her. The soup had been bad enough.

The looks on their faces had been priceless. Damn, that soup was disgusting. I'd make it up to all of them. Later. After I got rid of Mrs. Bailey.

Deep in the night, I snuck from the dark kitchen, falling asleep only after setting my alarm to go off before sunrise. Mrs. Bailey got in early. I wasn't planning to miss the show when she realized what I'd done.

I slept better than I expected, waking minutes before my alarm went off. Showing up to the gym before dawn wasn't overtly suspicious. I didn't hit the gym every day, and not often in the early morning. I'd been a night owl for years, used to closing down the restaurant kitchen late and heading out with my staff to hit a bar before tumbling into bed hours after midnight.

Since returning to Heartstone Manor, I'd had trouble sleeping. Too much on my mind, too much unsettled in my heart, and not enough to do. I had five years to sit around and wait. Not a great situation for a guy like me. I need work to keep my brain busy. I needed the kitchen, the demands of time and chemistry and everything happening at once.

Despite how I'd spent my teen years, I didn't enjoy sitting around sulking. I'd done enough of that since I'd been home.

I needed action.

Once I got rid of Mrs. Bailey, I'd have all the action I could handle.

For now, I woke in the night far too often and ended up either invading the kitchens or here, in Heartstone's ancient gym, running on the treadmill until the demons keeping me awake shut the fuck up.

At the moment, I was walking instead of running. Boring, so boring, but at a run, the treadmill was too loud to overhear anything from the kitchen. I didn't have to put up with it for long. Fifteen minutes into my walk, I heard the first rumble of sound. I checked my watch. Six thirty. Took longer than I'd thought it would. Or I'd missed the early grumbles as Mrs. Bailey realized, drawer by drawer, that something was very wrong in her kitchen.

The rumble of sound was followed by a shriek. And another. I shut off the treadmill and paced to the gym door, close enough to listen, but out of sight from the door to the main kitchen. I wanted to hear, but I didn't want to get caught.

"Savannah!" Mrs. Bailey howled. "Savannah!"

I winced. She sounded like she was about to lose it. She shouted for Savannah until I caught a scuffle of feet and heard the low tones of Savannah's voice, set to soothe. She was good at that. Not good enough. I edged closer, ears tuned for her words. All I caught was, "Mrs. Bailey, take a deep breath. I'm sure it's not that bad."

She kept going, her voice pitched lower, a non-distinct murmur, followed by another screech that included the words *I know he—*

I didn't have to ask who the *he* was. Mrs. Bailey knew who was after her. But unless the security team had wired the kitchen with cameras, they couldn't prove it was me. Not that they needed proof. All they needed was Savannah's word, and Griffen could solve the problem by getting rid of me.

Or I could solve the problem by asking him for what I want. Like an adult.

I tried that idea on, trying to picture it in my head as I had so many times. And as it did every time, the picture twisted, Griffen's face morphing into my father's. I could hear his scornful laughter, the sound of his voice as he called me a pussy and said he'd never let a son of his in the kitchen. I wasn't a servant, and I wasn't a woman, so what did I need with cooking?

Everything. I needed everything.

As a teenager, I'd only known there was something mystical in the alchemy of cooking. Now that I'd spent a third of my life in professional kitchens, I understood that it was more than magic, more than science and art married with the necessity to nourish the body. It was life.

If I asked and Griffen said no, I'd have to leave. I couldn't stay if he turned me away as my father had. I knew I could find a job somewhere in town if I needed to scratch my itch that badly. Hell, I could buy a food truck. I didn't have enough cash to set up the kind of place I'd dreamed of running, but I was far from broke.

No, the problem wasn't getting in a kitchen; it was getting into Heartstone's kitchen. If Mrs. Bailey had settled for having me banned from the kitchens, I might have tried the more mature route of asking Griffen for what I wanted. Maybe. But then she'd started lying to Savannah, telling her I'd snuck in and ruined supplies, or moved things, any number of sins that weren't mine. Did I defy the kitchen ban? Abso-fucking-lutely. Did I leave that kitchen exactly the way I found it? Minus the food I'd cooked and left for anyone who wanted a bite? Also yes. Until the night before,

I'd never done a thing but cook and clean up after myself. Mrs. Bailey had earned this, even though I knew she'd never see it that way.

The voices in the kitchen faded away. I waited a long moment before retracing my steps to the treadmill and restarting my workout, this time at a brisk jog. I was ten minutes in when Savannah strode through the door, her face set, gray eyes as hard as granite.

I tried a charming smile. Sadly, Savannah had always been immune to my charm.

Letting the smile drop, I paused my workout, pulling up my t-shirt to wipe the sweat from my face. Taking a long drink from my water bottle, I lifted one finger to indicate she should wait, knowing it would annoy the shit out of her. I shouldn't annoy Savannah. Especially since she could have me thrown out at any moment.

I couldn't help myself. She was just so pretty when her cheeks flushed and her eyes sparked. I hadn't been this reckless, this self-destructive, in years. Control and ambition had gotten me through the last decade. Six months back at Heartstone and I was poking at Savannah like I was sixteen again.

"What's up?" I asked, one eyebrow raised in a smirk. She rewarded me with a flex of her jaw. She was trying not to yell at me. I was an asshole who was complicating her life, but I was also a Sawyer. Help did not raise their voices to the family. Ever.

Except Savannah wasn't *help*, and I was an asshole. All the same, I was willing to bet she wouldn't dare raise her voice to me. I was wrong.

"What the hell do you think you're doing?" she began, her gray eyes spitting icy fire, voice a shade higher than a polite volume.

"I don't know what you mean." I drank again, keeping my eyes on hers, using all my willpower not to laugh. It's not that I was underestimating her. Savannah would get rid of me if I pushed her to it. She was a hardass. Totally. That just made me want to poke at her more. She fucked up my sense of self-preservation. Completely. That fizzy feeling in the blood that I got when I was up to trouble? Just talking to Savannah was enough.

"You know exactly what I mean," she shouted back, wisps of hair curling wildly around her face, a strawberry blond halo. I wanted to reach out, tug a curl and see if it sprang back the way I thought it would. I didn't dare. She'd probably bite my hand if I got too close.

I kept my mouth shut, watching her to see what she'd do next. As she often did, Savannah surprised me.

Letting out a long sigh, she deflated, all her righteous anger draining away as quickly as it had flashed to life. "What do you want?" she asked grudgingly.

I wished it were as simple as that. Who knew? It might be. Could I tell Savannah what I couldn't bring myself to admit to Griffen?

I opened my mouth, the words at the tip of my tongue. *I want the kitchens.* So simple. All I had to do was ask.

My mouth snapped shut. I couldn't. I trusted Savannah. Why? I didn't know. Maybe because she hadn't gotten me kicked out of the house yet, even though I'd given her plenty of reasons to get rid of me. Maybe because she'd always been fair, even when I was a massive prick. If I could tell anyone, I thought it might be her.

I'd never know, because I was keeping my mouth shut. I was too close to getting Mrs. Bailey to quit. To claiming my kitchens. I couldn't mix up the plan this late in the game.

Bullshit. I knew it even as the thought crossed my mind.

I was the master at improvising. This wasn't about the plan. No, this was about Savannah and not wanting her, wanting anyone, to see that soft mushy spot inside of me. The part of me that needed back in those kitchens, needed to claim them, to make my mark on this place, on this house. On my family.

I was barely ready to admit to myself what it meant to be back here, to want the kitchens for my own. I wasn't going to admit it to Savannah.

"Are you trying to make me crazy, Finn? I have enough to do to keep this place from falling down on us without running interference for you with Mrs. Bailey. Can't you find someone else to annoy? Go pester Griffen."

I just lifted an eyebrow and took another drink of my water. I didn't want to pester Griffen. I wanted to pester Mrs. Bailey until she quit and left the kitchens to me.

"You know what's going to happen if she walks out, don't you?" she persisted. "Griffen wasn't kidding. You said the last thing you wanted was to cook for your family."

I *had* said that. And it *was* the last thing I wanted. Until it wasn't. But I couldn't say that to Savannah. She'd probably smack me. I was perverse enough to wish she would. Doing my best angry teenager, I jerked up a shoulder and curled my lip. "I don't want to cook for them," I lied.

Head shaking, she said, "I don't understand you, Finn."

I shrugged, dropping the act, and grinned at her. "I don't understand me either. So far, it's working for me."

Savannah opened her mouth, likely to shout at me again, when her phone beeped. Pressing her lips together and sending me a glare, she checked the screen. Whatever she saw drained the blood from her face.

Tapping the screen, she unlocked the phone and scrolled, reading a text. I couldn't see the words from my angle, but it was a long one. She blinked at the screen, time stretching, her eyes flashing with emotion. Grief, fear, confusion. She wobbled on her feet. I took her arm, squeezing to get her attention.

"You okay?" I asked, the humor gone. Something was very wrong. Savannah didn't get upset when she was working. Except when she yelled at me. Otherwise, she was implacable—endlessly efficient and effective. Not emotional. Not hysterical. The way the breath jerked in her lungs, I knew she was about to be both.

"Hey," I urged, jostling her arm to get her attention. "What's wrong? Who is that?"

Savannah shook her head slowly. "My mother-in-law. Oliver's mother. Nicky's grandmother."

I assumed Oliver had been her husband. "Is she okay?"

"She— I guess. She doesn't say. I haven't heard from her in so long. I didn't think she'd—" Savannah drew in a slow breath and let it out, her gray eyes dazed.

I stepped into her, slinging an arm around her shoulders in a gentle hug. Whatever was up with that text, it had thrown her completely off her stride. Nothing threw Savannah Miles off her stride. She was unstoppable. I squeezed her shoulders, bringing her back to earth.

"What does she want?"

"Hmm?" Savannah was still looking at her phone, though the screen had gone dark.

Another squeeze, and she lifted her face to mine, her gray eyes clouded and distant. I'd put my arm around her in comfort. That was all. Comfort.

It had been years since I'd been this close to Savannah.

I'd forgotten so much. I'd made myself forget. The way we fit. How good she smelled. The way her mouth moved under mine. Fuck. Not the time for that particular trip down memory lane. Not the fucking time.

Still holding her, I asked again, "Savannah, what does she want?"

She let out another long breath. "She wants to see Nicky. She said she misses him." Lifting one shoulder in a helpless shrug, she said, "I don't know how she can miss him when she hasn't asked about him in two years."

Doing the math, I had to ask, "Not since your husband died?"

"She blamed me. She didn't handle it well." Savannah gave a huff of a laugh, abrupt and sharp with bitterness. "She lost it, said it was all my fault for being a bad wife. I wasn't patient enough. I pushed him too hard. I was cheating on him and Nicky wasn't his, even though he looks exactly like Oliver. She tried to ban us from the funeral, and afterward she ordered me to stay away from her family. She said she'd get a restraining order if I didn't."

Savannah lifted a hand, palm up. "I was grieving and angry at Oliver for dying on me and trying to figure out how to work and raise Nicky by myself. I couldn't handle her stuff too. So I did what she asked and left them all alone. I haven't heard from any of them since we buried Oliver." She heaved in a breath, her eyes swimming with tears.

Alarmed, I pulled her into me, wet heat running down the side of my neck as her tears spilled over. Shit. Her breath shuddered in and out, hitching, every muscle in her body locked tight as she fought for control. Even as she tried to get it together, she softened against me, her forehead warm on my neck, one hand gripping my t-shirt.

I dared to stroke her back, trying to soothe. Soothing wasn't my default. I could piss her off in a heartbeat, but this? I would have bet I was the last person she'd trust with her pain. I would have been wrong. She melted into me, tears slowing, breath evening out under the gentle stroke of my fingers up and down her spine.

I could have stood like that all day. Before I got used to it, Savannah jerked back, scrubbing under her eyes with her palms, her cheeks bright red as she gathered her dignity around her in a cool cloak. "Please stop annoying Mrs. Bailey, Finn. I'm begging you."

I lifted a hand and bopped her on the tip of her nose with one finger, my nerves sparking at the flare of temper in her eyes. So much better than tears. "No, Savannah, you aren't begging me. Not yet. But you will."

Her gasp of outrage filled my soul.

Water bottle in hand, I strolled from the gym, finally feeling like my life was moving in the right direction.

Chapter Four

SAVANNAH

"That's it! I can't take it anymore!"

I quickened my pace down the hall to the kitchens. I knew that voice. Mrs. Bailey, our cook. The only cook we'd managed to keep for more than a few months. A low rumble answered back, the words indistinguishable. I didn't need to hear them. I knew that voice too. If Finn Sawyer drove off another cook, I was going to kill him. For real.

What the hell had he done this time? I knew he snuck into the kitchens late at night to cook. That little habit hadn't changed, even after all his years away. But he didn't use Mrs. Bailey's supplies, and he left the kitchens clean, so I let it go. I also knew he hadn't done half of the crap she accused him of. I'd let that go too. I'd banned him from the kitchens. That was the best I could do. If this was about those damned spices, I was going to . . .

I forced myself to take a deep breath as I rounded the door to the main kitchen. Empty. Following my ear, I turned left and came to a stop in the doorway of the pantry attached to the kitchen. Finn stood with his arms crossed over his chest, a mulish expression on his face, staring down at Mrs. Bailey, who glared at him with undisguised hatred.

"What did he do?" I asked, wishing for the thousandth time that Finn Sawyer hadn't come home after his father died. Why couldn't he have stuck with his disappearing act? Oh, yeah, the will and all that Sawyer money.

No one knew exactly how much was in the trusts Prentice Sawyer had left to his children, except maybe Griffen and the family attorney, but Prentice had been a billionaire. A pittance to him would still be quite the inheritance. Finn would have been a fool to walk away out of spite. Finn was a lot of things, but never a fool.

Mrs. Bailey let out a grunt and turned her back on Finn, eyes glittering as they landed on me. "He was in here again, rearranging my spices. He threw half of them away! More than half. And look at that!" She threw her arm up at an empty space on a shelf above her head. I raised my eyebrows and waited.

"My shortening," she wailed. "He threw out my shortening! How am I supposed to work like this?"

I turned to Finn, who glared at Mrs. Bailey, completely unrepentant. He shrugged. I resisted the urge to punch him. I hated that shrug.

"Please tell me, Finn, why did you throw away Mrs. Bailey's supplies?" I marshaled every ounce of professional restraint I had. Finn had always gotten under my skin, but I had a job to do, and I wasn't going to let Finn Sawyer get in my way.

"Her spices were shit. Old, stale, and half of them were fake. Cheap discount store stuff. She should have more pride than to cook with that crap. And I'm not getting into the shortening. This isn't the fifties. I know we're in the South, but we have access to local grass-fed butter. What the fuck are you doing with shortening in our kitchen?"

"Watch your language," I cut out, one eye on Mrs. Bailey and her round, flushed, furious face. Finn and I towered over Mrs. Bailey, but what she lacked in height, she made up in width. In the few months I'd known her, she was a calm presence in the kitchen. Capable, organized, and a decent cook. She was kind to the staff and never missed a day of work. A delight to manage. Never late, never gave me a hint of trouble. And now she was going to quit.

I could see it coming, in the rising red in her face, the huffs of indignation. Attacking her shortening was one step too far. Mrs. Bailey was going to blow. I made a last-ditch effort to derail her.

"I'll have him banned from the kitchens. From the whole lower level. I'll personally replace everything he threw away."

Her dark eyebrows drew together. "You already banned him from the kitchens. Didn't keep him out. I don't have to put up with this. His insults. His interference. The sabotage."

"Please, Mrs. Bailey, just let me work this out. I know we can—"

The shake of her head sent dread spiraling through my stomach. No. She couldn't. She couldn't leave me with him. We all knew what would happen if Finn ran off another cook.

With genuine pity in her eyes, she said it. "I'm sorry, Savannah. You're a good girl, but I can't do it anymore. I quit. You can mail me my check." Her hands went behind her back to undo the strings on her apron.

"Please, Mrs. Bailey—" I begged. It was no good. Shoving the apron at me, she fled.

I whirled to face Finn. "You're going to pay for this." Without waiting for his response, I stormed out. I'd been dreading this day since the first cook had quit.

Finn followed behind. "You going to tattle on me?"

I didn't respond. We both knew exactly where I was going. To the only person who could make Finn pay. The only problem was that the punishment would be just as miserable for me as it would for Finn.

When Prentice Sawyer died, I'd been at a low point. A few years before, life had been perfect. I had a great career. A wonderful husband. A beautiful baby boy. Faster than I would have thought possible, I lost my husband, then my career. Nicky and I ended up back in Sawyers Bend, sharing the tiny spare room in my mother's cottage while I waited tables and wondered what the hell had happened to my life.

Then Prentice died, and Griffen came back to Sawyers Bend. The day he showed up at my mother's cottage looking for help, I barely recognized him. Ten years older than me, he'd been a stranger when we'd lived under the same roof. I was twelve the day Prentice exiled him, but I'd always remembered him as kind. Nothing like his father.

So much had changed, but not that. Where Prentice had been cold and cruel, Griffen was warm and kind. When he offered me the housekeeper position at Heartstone Manor, I'd jumped at it. While I was torn on the subject of the Sawyers, I'd always loved Heartstone Manor. No one, except my mother, knew the Manor like I did. I'd spent most of my life there, going mostly unnoticed as I explored and discovered Heartstone's secrets.

For reasons no one understood, Prentice had let the house go in the years before his murder. The day Griffen hired me, I'd walked into a disaster. Dust, cobwebs, half the rooms were empty, and the rest hadn't been cleaned in far too long. I'd had two days to prepare the place for the entire Sawyer clan to move in. It seemed like an impossible task.

I'll never forget the swell of pride when Griffen and his new bride walked into a house transformed. Heartstone wasn't back to its original condition—we had months of work before we'd get there—but I'd turned it from derelict to inviting in forty-eight hours, proving to everyone that I was more than up for the task of running Heartstone Manor. In the months since, I hadn't stopped, ruthlessly organizing and improving until I had the house running like a well-oiled machine.

Except for the kitchens.

From the start, Finn had been a burr under my skin. Feeding sixteen people plus staff three times a day took coordination and attention to detail. Two of my best traits, but I am not a cook. I'd managed for the first few days, but the position was a full-time job on its own.

My first cook quit when someone tried to murder Griffen and she'd been caught in the crossfire. Understandable, though unfortunate. I'm not sure how long she would have lasted, even without the attempted murder. Finn had already been haunting the kitchens, complaining about the food and demanding work space.

He'd run off our second cook, Mrs. Haverty, over a hollandaise sauce that was too tart. I still don't know how their argument had escalated into Mrs. Haverty quitting over a sauce, but Finn had talked smack and the next thing I knew, she was grabbing her purse and telling me to put her check in the mail. Just like Mrs. Bailey.

I was going to kill that son of a bitch. I skidded to a halt in front of Griffen's office door, taking a second to get myself together. Griffen would be furious. Sucking in a deep breath, I got myself under control and raised my hand to knock on the door.

"Come in," a deep voice answered. I swung open the door and strode into Griffen's office, Finn tight on my heels.

Griffen smiled when he saw me, his eyes warming. Beside him, his wife, Hope, gave me a smile of her own. In unison, their gazes moved over my shoulder, Hope's narrowing in concern, Griffen's in aggravation.

"What happened?" he demanded, his eyes locked on his younger brother.

Hope let out a sigh. "Mrs. Bailey quit?" At my curt nod, she shook her head. "The spices?"

I nodded again. "And shortening. He threw away her shortening."

Hope choked on a laugh, her hazel eyes glinting with amusement as they landed on Finn. "I hope it was worth it."

Standing, she braced her hands on her lower back, the curve of her pregnant belly throwing her off balance. With a shake of her head, she leaned down to press a kiss to Griffen's cheek.

"I'm going to let you handle this one." Passing me on her way to the door, she reached out to squeeze my arm. "Come find me when you're done in here." I nodded again, my teeth clenched tightly so I wouldn't scream.

"Griffen," I started, desperate to stop what I knew was coming. We'd all been here before. Griffen had told Finn what would happen if another cook quit.

Griffen stopped my words with a look. He was the best boss I'd ever had, but he wasn't a softy. His gaze was granite as it settled on Finn. "I assume you know what this means?"

I glanced at Finn, standing beside me, his arms crossed over his chest, his jaw tight. "You've made it clear."

"I'll give you the rest of today to get organized," Griffen

said. "Starting tomorrow, I'll expect you in the kitchens. A full breakfast and dinner every day but Saturday. A light lunch depending on who's home. You'll have to work with Savannah on your budget."

I tried not to let my dismay show. Griffen paid me to keep the house running, and that included feeding the residents of Heartstone Manor. His eyes shifted to me, softening with a hint of remorse. "If you have any trouble with him, let me know."

Finn let out a low rumble beside me. I resisted the urge to look at him. "I will. It'll be fine," I assured Griffen. It was my job to make it fine. Finn Sawyer was not going to get in my way. I wouldn't let him.

Griffen's eyes flashed between the two of us. "Finn? Are we clear? Savannah handles the staff."

"I get it," Finn ground out. "Savannah is in charge of the staff. If she fires me, you kick me out of the house, and I lose whatever Prentice left me. Do I have that right?"

Griffen's expression was completely neutral. "You do. Can you handle it? You made it through the army. You should be able to follow the rules well enough to stay on Savannah's good side."

Something twisted in Finn's face at that comment. Why? Was it the mention of the army? Of staying on my good side? I hated that I wanted to know. The easiest way to survive this would be to stay as far from Finn as possible. Difficult, considering I lived behind the kitchens. But I'd manage. I had to.

"I have a few conditions," Finn said, his emerald eyes hard.

Griffen raised an eyebrow and waited.

Chapter Five

SAVANNAH

" **I** need a starter budget to replace the spices in the pantry and get some tools to reorganize."

"How much?" Griffen asked, eyes narrowing on Finn. I don't think he'd expected a shopping list to be one of Finn's conditions. Neither had I.

Finn named a number that wasn't low, but wasn't unreasonable.

"Fine." Griffen's eyes flashed to me, and I nodded, making a note. "What else?"

"I'm not serving at the table. I stay in the kitchens."

Griffen digested that demand slowly before saying, "Fine. Anything else?"

"Savannah doesn't serve dinner either. We can train Kitty or April to handle dinner service, or you can all serve yourselves."

"I can serve dinner," I insisted, knocked off balance. What did it matter if I served dinner to the family? Someone had to do it. It was part of my job.

Griffen stopped my protest. "Humor me," he said

before switching his attention back to Finn. "Why don't you want Savannah serving dinner?"

Finn didn't look at me when he answered. "Savannah's day starts before dawn. The family isn't finished with dinner until after seven-thirty. Savannah misses having dinner with Nicky every night and doesn't officially get a break until it's almost his bedtime. That's bullshit."

Griffen looked poleaxed. I could feel the same expression of blank shock on my own face. Mind reeling, I snapped my mouth shut. Finn was always around, in the gym, in the halls, leaving us random treats as the only evidence of his late-night kitchen invasions. We rarely spoke; when we did, it was always to fight. I hadn't thought he was paying any real attention to me.

Griffen processed Finn's bizarre request faster than I did. Raising an eyebrow, he asked me, "Would you prefer to skip the dinner service and eat with Nicky?"

I didn't answer right away. I was usually forthright with Griffen. It should be easy to tell him the truth. Yes, I would absolutely prefer eating with my son over working in the dining room.

I loved this job—for the most part. Living on-site and having Nicky close by was ideal. I saw him more than I would if I worked full time in an office, but I missed our dinners together, and the dinner service was boring. I tried to grab a snack before, but most days I ended up starving, watching everyone else eat while I waited to grab a plate when they were done.

Finn's eyes flashed to me, and he gave an impatient grunt. "She doesn't want to work the dinner service, but she'll have an allergic reaction if she admits something might be too much for her to handle."

I narrowed my eyes at Finn, imagining I was one of

Nicky's superheroes who could blast laser beams from my eyes. He'd be ashes at my feet. Instead, I ground my teeth, torn between appreciating his uncharacteristic thoughtfulness and being irritated at his presumption. I could ask for a change in my duties if I needed one. I didn't need Finn Sawyer to step in for me.

But you wouldn't have asked, would you? Not in a million years. Because Finn is right. You're incapable of refusing a challenge.

Damn him. I would definitely lose my job if I murdered Finn. He was an asshole, but Griffen was attached. Fine. Letting out a short breath, I gave Griffen my most professional smile. "I can handle the dinner service, but if I have the option, I'd prefer to end my day before dinner and eat with Nicky."

"Done." He shot an appraising look at Finn. "And I'm embarrassed Hope and I didn't think of it sooner. We got used to you working long days when we were trying to get the house functional. But things are running smoothly." A considering pause. "Smoothly enough," he corrected, accounting for the regular power outages and ongoing plumbing issues. "You need a break."

"I appreciate it," I said. I turned my head to meet Finn's amused gaze, my next words clearly forced through gritted teeth. "Thank you for the suggestion."

Finn grinned back at me. He knew exactly how annoying it was that he was the one to do me this favor. That was twice now. First that hug when Oliver's mother had texted, and now this. I should be grateful, but this was Finn. Even when he was being nice, I wanted to smack him.

Turning back to Griffen, he said, "Everyone can get their own lunch today, but I'll have something for dinner tonight. It'll be basic, but better than ordering pizza."

"All right," Griffen answered, a curious light in his eyes as he studied his younger brother. Finn squirmed the tiniest bit under that look.

"Are we done here?" he demanded, his chin lifting, dark hair sliding across his forehead.

Griffen nodded and watched Finn stalk out of the room. Turning to me, he sat back in his chair, his head tilting to the side as he looked at the ceiling. "Is it just me, or did he seem less pissed off than he should be?"

I crossed my arms over my chest, trying to think through the annoyance clouding my mind. Eventually, I nodded. "I've never been good at guessing what's going through Finn's head, but I thought there'd be more pushback." Good. More diplomatic than saying I expected he'd throw a raging tantrum.

I found myself asking, "Do we know he can handle it?" It had been bothering me ever since Griffen had threatened him with the job if he ran off another cook. Griffen raised an eyebrow, and I continued, "He said once that he went to culinary school and that he'd worked as a cook, but—" I shrugged, a little embarrassed to admit the truth to Griffen. "I assumed he was lying. It was back when everyone first came home. He was arguing with the cook, and I figured he made it up to get under her skin."

"Fuck. Hope told me about that. I meant to ask Finn about it, but then someone shot at me. Twice. And we had that car accident, and Hope was pregnant—" Griffen shook his head. "I completely forgot."

Sitting back, he considered the problem. "The way he talks about food when he's complaining, I have a feeling he knows what he's doing. The few things he's made that I've tasted have been great."

"Very true," I agreed. "But making a plate of cookies or a

pot of chili doesn't mean he can handle the planning and cooking for the entire household three times a day."

Griffen let out a murmur of agreement. "We'll see how it goes. I'm sorry, Savannah. I meant what I said. If he gives you any trouble, let me know."

"I will," I said, knowing I wouldn't. Not unless I had to.

His gaze lingering on the door Finn had left open behind him, Griffen let out a sigh. "He's never been easy, but I'm not going to give up on him."

"I'll keep him in line," I promised, mentally kicking myself. How exactly was I planning to keep Finn Sawyer in line? I had no idea. He was going to be underfoot, working steps from my door, all day and into the night. I wanted to squeeze my eyes shut and cry. I was going to have to get over it.

Finn Sawyer had screwed up my life when we were kids, and he'd been irritating me nonstop since he came home, but I would not let him run me off the job I loved. Griffen's next words only strengthened my convictions.

"Before you go, you should know Hope and I are looking for a nanny. Someone who can help with the baby, as well as pick up the slack on child care. Between Nicky and August, we could use an extra adult around here running herd on the kids. While we're interviewing people, your mother agreed to step in."

"Really? She didn't say." A genuine smile spread across my face. I'd missed my mom since Nicky and I moved into the Manor. I loved my job, but the days were long, and I rarely found myself in town, too busy with my list of never-ending projects at Heartstone.

"We called her this morning. She's going to come by after school gets out, and she'll stay through dinner."

"I don't mind keeping an eye on the boys during

dinner," I said truthfully. Nicky was mine, and August was rarely trouble.

"I know, but it's not your job to watch the kids."

"It's too much," I said in a rush. "On top of school—"

A flush hit my cheeks. Griffen had surprised me with the news that he was paying the tuition for Nicky to attend Laurel Country Day along with Scarlett's boys. I could have said no, but I hadn't. I wouldn't deny Nicky the chance for a stellar education out of pride. But a nanny? That was too much. I was the housekeeper, not a member of the family.

"It isn't too much," Griffen countered. "And we've missed having Miss Martha around. She said she didn't want the job full time, but she'll step in until Hope and I find someone."

I only nodded in agreement, my throat tight. Clearing it, I asked, "Is there anything else?"

Griffen looked like he wanted to add something, but after a moment he just shook his head. "Hope wanted to talk to you." His lips quirked in a smile, eyes warming at the mention of his wife. "She wants to decorate for Halloween."

"It was on my list," I assured him. "I'll go find her now." With that excuse, I escaped, trying not to think about Finn downstairs taking charge of the kitchens, stamping his presence all over my domain.

The rest of the day was filled with an unending list of tasks, some fun, some not so much. I helped Kitty and April with a guest bathroom we were hoping to put to use again sometime this century. Scrubbing a bathtub wasn't my favorite way to spend the afternoon, but it let me check in with Kitty and April about taking over the dinner service. It turned out they were both happy to work a few hours longer for an appropriate raise in salary, and I was thrilled to cross serving dinner off my list of responsibilities. I owed Finn a thank you, even knowing it would burn as it crossed my lips.

Hope looked contrite when I finally caught up with her. "I wish I'd thought of taking you off dinner service. Why didn't you say anything?"

Her simple question struck me dumb. Why hadn't I mentioned it? I was comfortable with Hope. I considered her a friend, not just my employer. So why hadn't I asked? The truth was a barb under my skin. Slowly, I said, "I think Finn was right. I don't like admitting when my plate is too full. I like to think I can do everything."

Hope laughed and reached out to give my shoulder an affectionate squeeze. "I should probably scold you for not knowing your limits, but not knowing your limits is how you work miracles. And I know you thrive on challenges. But don't forget to take care of yourself while you're taking care of the rest of us."

"I'm working on it," I said, knowing it was a lie. I was great at taking care of everyone else. Myself? Not so much. But that was my problem, not Hope's. I snuck a look at her face and knew she'd caught my lie. She let me get away with it, but I had a feeling she was storing it away for later.

"Are you going to survive with Finn in the kitchens?"

"Survive?" I looked up at the ceiling, trying to decide between honesty and diplomacy. This was Hope, so I went with honesty. "One of us will survive. Not sure which one it'll be."

Hope laughed. "At least the cottage will be ready in a few weeks. That'll give you some space. And we'll all be eating better, so that's something."

"Mrs. Bailey's food wasn't that bad," I protested.

"It wasn't," Hope agreed. "But it wasn't Finn's cooking.

That chili he made last week? It was worth the acid reflux. Oh my god, it was so good."

I harrumphed, but Hope was right. It had been amazing. Hope had been suffering from acid reflux her entire pregnancy, even after the morning sickness backed off. Chili would not normally be on her menu. But we'd woken one day the week before to find an ancient crock pot full of chili on the kitchen island set to warm, a basket of freshly baked rolls beside it. Even Mrs. Bailey had eaten a bowl. Good didn't describe that chili. Divine. Life changing. And that didn't get to his baking.

"So, Halloween?" Hope asked.

"How crazy do you want to get? I found boxes of old decorations in the attic. I thought I'd go through them and use what I can. Then we can take a look, and you can decide if you want more."

"Sounds perfect. Thanks, Savannah."

"Anytime," I answered and headed off to unpack the boxes of decorations in the attic. I remembered some of these decorations from my childhood. Fake stuffed ravens with bendable claws. Garlands of black ivy run through with fairy lights. Gauzy ghosts hung from fishing line. Paper maché pumpkins I thought the Sawyer kids might have made in school ages ago.

I was almost finished decorating the front hall when it was time for dinner. I'd avoided the kitchens almost all day. My mother was down there. She'd shown up with the kids mid-afternoon and disappeared downstairs with them for a snack.

Nicky had been so excited to see her, I'd barely rated a hug. That was okay. My mom was one reason I'd come home after Oliver died. The job market wasn't great compared to Richmond, but I needed my mom, and Nicky needed his grandma. Those two had always been tight.

April had volunteered to handle the dinner service. With a cheeky grin, she said she had her eye on a new pair of earrings she'd seen in town and could use the extra cash right away. I arrived in the kitchens for dinner, not sure what to expect. Standing in the open doorway to the main kitchen, I stared, jaw dropped.

How had Finn managed so much in one afternoon?

Chapter Six

SAVANNAH

"It looks great, doesn't it?" my mother asked, beaming at Finn. She'd always liked him, the traitor. I inspected the room and gave a grudging nod, not quite meeting Finn's eyes.

"It does look good," I agreed before lifting my wrist to make a point of checking my watch. "Dinner should be heading up in two minutes."

Finn had plates set up along the length of the island, silver covers sitting behind them. There was no food in sight, but the kitchen smelled heavenly. Cheese and meat and spicy tomato. Lasagna? My mouth watered.

With a smug grin, Finn said, "It's under control, boss. Salads went up just before you walked in. When April gives me the signal, I'll start plating the main course. Then we'll have dinner in here."

We'll have dinner in here? *We?*

Crap. I hadn't thought about eating dinner together. Every night? Of course, every night. Where was Finn supposed to eat if he wasn't in the dining room with the family? Here, in the kitchen with the rest of us. My mother looked thrilled. I was not. Trying not to slouch into my chair like a sulky teenager, I took a seat beside my mother. "Nicky and August?"

"In Nicky's room, doing something with those cards they both like. Apparently, there was some serious trading going on at school today."

"Hmm." I was too distracted by the changes in the kitchen to say more. Finn hadn't changed everything, but what he'd done had impact.

The Heartstone Manor kitchens were divided into multiple rooms. When the house was initially built, there'd been the pastry kitchen, the rotisserie kitchen, and the scullery kitchen, all branching off the main kitchen, as well as assorted pantries. The small apartment off the main kitchen that Nicky and I lived in had once been the staff dining room, Nicky's bedroom the staff pantry. As modernization had taken over the house, the need for so much staff had declined, and the staff dining room had been turned into living quarters, the staff dining table incorporated into the main kitchen.

I'd always loved the main kitchen, cozy despite its vast size. The lower level had a Gothic vibe due to its rough stone and exposed metal pipes, but the main kitchen was bright and open, with large rectangular windows set high in the walls.

A massive cast iron and enamel stove, shipped from England not long after the turn of the previous century, took up a chunk of one long wall. More modern commercial convection ovens and a gas range took another chunk. A long butcher block island divided the room.

On the opposite wall from the stove and ovens, deep counters ran the length of the room, interrupted by a wide farmhouse-style sink. Most of the washing up was done in the scullery kitchen, with its even bigger sink and commercial dishwashers, but the farmhouse sink was big enough for any washing up that had to be done while cooking.

In the few hours he'd been in charge, Finn had markedly improved the room's flow. The island had been cluttered since our first cook had taken over. Now it was cleared of everything, just as it had been when Chef Guérard had ruled the Heartstone kitchens. Beneath the island, a shelf ran its length, now neatly organized with wire baskets, filled with what, I couldn't tell.

The previous cooks had used the old staff dining table as a prep area, despite it being across the room from the stove, range, and ovens. Finn had relocated the prep area closer to the largest pantry, the refrigerator, and the cooking space, leaving the dining table free to be put back to its intended use. Someone had taken the time to find placemats. A small pewter vase filled with wildflowers sat in the middle of the table.

"Did you set the table?" I asked my mother in a voice too low for Finn to hear.

She shook her head. "It was like this when I got here. He fed the boys a snack—apples and peanut butter, tea, and a cookie—and reset the table when they were done."

I stared at my mother, speechless. Finally, I murmured, "He made them tea? Afternoon tea?"

My mother smiled, glancing over to watch Finn as he peeked in the oven at something that sent a wave of buttery garlic into the room. I hadn't realized how hungry I was until I got here. If dinner tasted half as good as it smelled, maybe I wouldn't murder Finn. Maybe.

He'd fed the kids snacks and tea? At the table, like civilized humans? I tapped my fingers on the table, lips pressed together, avoiding my mother's eyes and watching Finn. He looked down at his phone and shoved it in his pocket. Swiftly, he pulled a huge metal baking pan from the oven and carried it to the island, cutting generous portions of lasagna and plating them carefully, garnishing each with a double leaf of basil. Faster than I would have thought possible, he had every plate ready for the trip to the dining room. Finn was stacking the covered plates to carry to the dumbwaiter when my mother nudged me.

"Go help him," she ordered.

I wanted to argue. My feet were sore, I was exhausted, starving, and my lower back hurt. I could have killed a bar of chocolate. I knew what that meant. My period was due in a few days, and I was about to hit maximum crankiness. I did not want to help Finn. Even if his lasagna did smell divine. Even if I would have jumped to help anyone else.

My mother tipped her head down and gave me her best mom glare. Sighing, I stood and crossed the kitchen to Finn. "How can I help?"

He shot me a surprised look, then jerked a shoulder in one of those shrugs I hated. "I've got it."

Shifting impatiently, I lifted my chin toward the dining table. "I can't go sit back down. My mom will yell at me."

Finn's grin lit his green eyes. "Miss Martha always liked me best."

My eyebrows drew together. "Don't be smug. Just tell me how I can help."

"You can start loading these plates in the dumbwaiter while I get the bread ready."

I nodded, carrying a stack of covered plates into the pantry that held the dumbwaiters, going back and forth until all the plates were loaded. "Do you want to try to fit the bread in here or send it up without and do the bread in a second trip?"

"Got it," Finn said from behind me.

I turned to find him holding a woven basket lined with linen napkins filled with several loaves of toasted, buttery garlic bread. Trying not to think about how hungry I was, I moved out of the way, going to the other dumbwaiter and unloading the salad plates from the first course. "Want me to put these in the scullery?"

"Yeah. I'll get to them later."

By the time I had the salad plates in the scullery, Finn had sent the last of dinner up. Rather than serving us, he set out a line of crystal dessert bowls. Placing an ice cream scoop on the island by the dessert bowls, he finally turned his focus to our dinner. "You can go tell August and Nicky to wash their hands."

I did, finding the boys sprawled across Nicky's bed, August's blond head beside Nicky's dark one, two binders filled with pages of trading cards open in front of them. "Dinner time, boys," I said. "Let's get those hands washed."

August popped up and headed to the bathroom, saying, "Thanks, Miss Savannah. I'm dying of hunger."

"I thought Finn gave you guys a snack?" I nudged Nicky to get up.

Nicky rolled over and looked up at me. "He did, but that was so long ago. Like hours and hours."

Leaning down to nuzzle my nose against his, I kissed his cheek. "Then you'd better get those hands washed so you can get some lasagna and garlic bread. It smells so good I almost ate Mr. Griffen's dinner before I sent it up."

Nicky giggled at that idea, giving in to my not-so-gentle nudges and rolling off the bed. "I don't like lasagna," he said, as he always did when confronted with foods that weren't mac and cheese, chicken fingers, or pizza.

"That's okay," I said easily. "I'll eat yours."

"Then what'll I have?" Nicky asked.

"I'm pretty sure I saw some onions and brussels sprouts in the pantry. Mr. Finn said he could make those if you didn't like lasagna."

"Gross, Mom!" Nicky shrieked, dashing into the bathroom and joining August at the sink.

Dinner was the best lasagna I'd ever had. I won't even mention the garlic bread, which tasted even better than it smelled. Or the strawberries Finn made for dessert, tossed in a sweet balsamic syrup, warmed, and served with vanilla ice cream. Simple and delicious. I hated to admit it, but Finn was a genius in the kitchen.

Stomach full, I left Finn the dishes without a twinge of guilt and ushered Nicky into our small apartment. My mother had headed home, and I had packing to do. What I really wanted was sleep. I was always like this right before my period. Tired, achy back, cranky, and dying for chocolate.

Changing into leggings and an old sweater, I considered the neat pile of packed boxes in the corner of the living room and the equally neat pile of flat cardboard ready to be built into more boxes. I hadn't thought I had so much to pack. The soft sounds of Nicky's favorite show drifted in from the bedroom as I sank onto the lumpy sofa, tired eyes drifting around the room.

I'd deal with it tomorrow. Or the next day. Parker had texted to say the appliances would be delayed—again—and the cottage wouldn't be ready for a few weeks. I had time, and my back was killing me. Across the room, tucked into an alcove, my bed beckoned. The same twin bed I'd slept in years ago.

Back then, my mother had claimed the single bedroom, and I had the twin bed. I could have done the same with

Nicky, but I didn't want to feel trapped in the bedroom after Nicky went to sleep. This way I could tuck Nicky in and enjoy a tv show or music without worrying about waking him.

I couldn't wait to move to the cottage. It had been tucked into the woods, a very short walk from the side entrance to Heartstone Manor, almost as long as the Manor itself. Over the years it had housed a variety of staff, ending in my day with the elderly groundskeeper. He'd retired around the time I left for college, and Prentice allowed my mother to move in. I stayed there a few times over the years, in the small room that would be Nicky's. But the cottage of my college years bore little resemblance to the one we were about to move into.

Griffen and Hope had taken one look and declared that it had to be renovated before we could live there. Honestly, it wasn't much worse than the apartment off the kitchens we currently occupied, and it was far bigger. Space. My own bedroom. A full kitchen that was all mine. A real living room. I would have taken it as it was, but Griffen had offered his sister Parker the job of renovating it, along with the equally run-down gatehouse Hawk lived in, and she'd run with it.

Parker had turned the place into a gem. The floors were refinished, the kitchen brand new. She'd juggled the budget to afford a gas fireplace in my bedroom. It wasn't just going to be nice; it was going to be amazing.

I sighed. One box. I'd pack one box, get Nicky tucked in, and pass out. After I ate my secret stash of chocolate. Plan made, I stood, wincing at the pull in my back and the throb beginning between my temples. My period was usually okay, but the PMS was always a bitch. Literally.

Just one box and I'd call it a night.

Chapter Seven

SAVANNAH

I put on some music and got to work, packing summer clothes we wouldn't need in the next few weeks and setting aside things Nicky had outgrown. I made it through two boxes before the alarm on my watch went off. Nicky's bedtime. I headed into the bedroom to get Nicky in his jammies and introduce him to his toothbrush. He went with only minor grumbles, telling me about the trades he'd made with August and the cards August's brother Thatcher had promised to trade him.

Thatcher, Scarlett's oldest, was thirteen, teetering between young man and child. Old enough to eat with the adults, young enough to trade cards with August and Nicky. He was a good kid. They all were. And soon we'd have a baby in the house.

I pulled the covers over Nicky's shoulders, listening with half an ear and wondering how easy it would be to get my hands on the baby once he or she showed up. Considering how excited everyone was, I'd have to get in line. My hand settled over my abdomen before dropping to my side, fatigue dragging at me.

Oliver and I had planned for three. By now I'd thought Nicky would have at least one sibling. Instead, it was just the two of us. The way things were going, that wasn't going to change.

Nicky was enough. Of course he was. He was my world. I didn't need a partner or more children. I had Nicky, my mom, and an odd kind of extended family in the Sawyers, who treated me more like one of their own than like part of the staff. I didn't need more.

Most of the time, reminding myself of everything I had made me feel better. Tonight, it was going to take more than a pep talk. Tonight it was going to take the chocolate I'd been craving since my back had started aching that afternoon. Closing Nicky's bedroom door behind me, I went to the galley kitchen in the corner of the living room, reaching for the cabinet above the refrigerator and feeling around for the bag of candy I'd hidden there.

A crinkle of plastic met my questing fingers. Dragging it out, I stared uncomprehendingly at the crumbs of chocolate inside. Empty? I thought back to the last time I'd raided my stash. I'd groped for the bag in the dark and shaken out one foil-wrapped chocolate. It must have been the last one. Throwing the bag in the trash with more force than necessary, I tried to think. I'd been looking forward to that chocolate for hours. The idea of giving up and going to bed was untenable. Tears welled in my eyes, and I gave a huff of impatience. Cranky and weepy. Fucking PMS. I'd rather just have my period.

There was chocolate in the pantry. I'd given it to the family after that awful soup. The rest of it was still there. Or it should be. Only one way to find out. I creaked open the door at the end of the hall and peeked into the dim, empty kitchen. Finn had left the light on over the stove, casting a warm glow over the room.

The kitchen was immaculate, the counters wiped clean, Finn's tools for breakfast neatly arranged on the island. A whisk and a mixing bowl. Pancakes? Waffles? My mouth watered. I needed that chocolate. Poking around in the partially reorganized pantry, I came up empty. I could just go to bed without. I was a grown woman. I didn't need chocolate. All that sugar and caffeine weren't good before bed anyway.

Forget that. There had to be something in here. Somewhere.

Leaving the pantry, I crossed to the refrigerator, giving a sharp tug on the heavy door. It swung open after a brief protest to reveal organized shelves of food. In a million years, I never would have pegged Finn as a neat freak, but everything I'd seen in the kitchen said I'd been wrong. Right there on the bottom shelf were two precise rows of glass dishes, each one filled with something that looked a lot like chocolate.

Taking one, I shut the door and grabbed a spoon from the drawer, the bittersweet scent of chocolate teasing me. The first bite had my eyes closing in bliss. The dark chocolate was decadent, the sweet just balancing out the bitter, a hint of orange giving each bite depth and the most divine fragrance. Everything in me sighed with happiness.

"You do realize you're eating tomorrow's dessert?"

My eyes fluttered open, Finn's voice weaving through my chocolate haze, warm and amused. He was close, only feet away, watching me in the dark, his lips curved in a half smile.

I should apologize. Heat flushed my cheeks, but no words left my mouth. Finn paced closer, reaching out to pluck the delicate glass bowl from my hand along with the spoon. I took a step back. Not enough.

"I—" That was all I got out. Finn popped the spoon in my mouth, his eyes heating as my lips closed around it, the dense, decadent chocolate melting on my tongue, my senses drowning.

"Chocolate Pots de Crème. One of the first things Chef Guérard taught me."

Another step closer. Another spoonful sliding between my lips. I jolted as my back hit the cold metal door of the fridge. My eyes tracked up to Finn's, his gaze shadowed in the dim light.

Finn fed me another spoonful. Then another. I let my lids fall shut, cutting off my sight, savoring, avoiding Finn's eyes that saw too much, even in the dark.

Glass clicked on wood. My eyes flashed open to see Finn turning back to me, the empty dish on the island, his hands free to close over my hips, pressing me to the refrigerator at my back. Despite his hold, I could have moved.

I could have.

I didn't.

I watched him, his head dipping to mine, his mouth at my ear.

"You smell like chocolate," he murmured. "I wonder how you'll taste?"

I would have sworn I hated Finn Sawyer. He was the last man I'd ever want to kiss. Once was more than enough.

I was a liar. I didn't think I wanted Finn to kiss me, but when he did, I didn't want him to stop.

I thought I'd forgotten what it was like. It had only happened that once, so many years ago. I'd built it up in my head, the overblown emotions of a teenage girl making that kiss into something it wasn't.

I'd been wrong. About everything.

Finn's hands closed over my hips, pinning me to the cold metal door, and his lips traced my jaw, sending shivers feathering over my skin. Lungs tight, I parted my lips for a breath, and he was there, his mouth on mine, tongue stroking.

The last time, he'd demanded. This time he seduced. Still, it was the same. I drowned in him, head tipping back, my mouth seeking his. I wasn't aware of lifting my hands, sinking my fingers into his hair, opening to his kiss.

He surrounded me, and I let him. A whimper reached my ear, and I realized it was me. Finn's hands slid from my hips, one arm wrapping around my waist, dragging me closer, the other slipping beneath my sweater, the callus of his palm a delicious scrape up my side. Strong fingers closed around my bare breast, the heat of him scalding. My body was beyond my control, my hips rolling into his as I rose on my toes, kissing him back, feasting on his mouth, arching my back to press my breast into his hand.

Abruptly, he stepped back, taking me with him. I would have lost my balance if not for the arm around my waist. My feet left the ground and I was sitting on the island, just like I had ten years ago, Finn between my spread legs, his mouth on my neck, nipping and biting as my head fell back, offering him everything.

He shoved my sweater up, baring my breasts, filling his hands, and lowering his head. Bracing myself on my palms, I leaned back, eyes closed, sinking into the spiky bliss of his mouth sucking, pulling, teasing, the pleasure so sharp it almost hurt. My body had been in stasis, so long untouched I'd forgotten what this felt like. Maybe I'd never known. I didn't remember it being like this, so much sensation my brain spun. All I could do was feel.

The heat of his breath, the fierce suck of his mouth on my nipple, the silk of his thick hair sliding across my skin. My legs circled his waist, drawing him in, the length of his erection so hard between my legs, my ancient leggings no barrier against him. Every nerve in my body strung tight, and I was floating in sensation. Instinct drove me to rock into him, rolling my clit against the firm pressure of his cock, the fabric between us irrelevant. The rush of pleasure was more than I could take.

Finn's mouth found mine, and I lost myself in the kiss, rocking into his hard length, gasping for breath against his lips as pleasure built with every press of his body to mine. His groan rolled over me like a wave, and his hands closed over my hips again, yanking me tight to him. The grind of his body into mine sent me flying. His mouth swallowed my cry, his lips feathering over my cheek, down my jaw, as I sobbed for breath, heart hammering in my chest. I hung there, someplace out of time, anchored only by Finn's hands on my hips, the rough heat of his jaw against my cheek, his breath harsh in my ear.

"Savannah," he breathed, my name barely formed. "Savannah, fuck." His lips moved, skating down the side of my neck, his teeth sinking into the tendon there, biting down just enough to send another bolt of sensation shooting through me. I jolted against him, feeling him move, taking me with him. My feet touched the ground, and my eyes fluttered open. In the dark of the hall outside my door, I couldn't see more than the shape of him, taller and broader, looming over me in the tight space.

I opened my mouth, but nothing came out. Were we going to—? Had he—? I had. He hadn't even gotten my clothes off, and I'd come hard enough to scramble my brains. Did he think—?

Lips brushed mine, the softest caress in the dark, before he was moving away. "Sleep tight, Savannah."

He was gone. I stumbled down the hall in the dark, closing the door behind me. What had just happened? I headed straight for my bed, avoiding the bathroom. I knew what I'd see there. Swollen lips. Eyes too bright, dazed with shock and lust. Just like ten years ago.

Falling into my bed, I dragged the covers up and stared at the ceiling, thoughts spinning in my head, warring with the heavy, sweet fulfillment suffusing every cell in my body. Worries tried to shout. What had we done? What did it mean? Would it happen again?

I snorted at that last thought. As if whatever had gone down in the kitchen had just *happened*. Like I hadn't been right there with him, kissing Finn back like my life depended on it, grinding my body into his until I came in an orgasm unlike any in memory. I hadn't started it, but I'd had every opportunity to end it. And I hadn't.

I should think about why. About what I was going to do next. Fatigue tugged at me, my body liquid, more relaxed than I'd been in years.

I didn't care about why. It didn't matter.

It wouldn't happen again.

Definitely not.

Pushing away my spinning thoughts, I rolled over, tugging my pillow into my arms, a smile curving my lips, and let sleep pull me under.

Chapter Eight

SAVANNAH

The thump of rock music woke me, pounding down the hall and through the door, dragging me out of a deep sleep. I blinked into the dim room, my brain taking far too long to join my pounding heart. What the hell was that? Who was—

The day before flooded back.

Finn. It was Finn, who had driven off Mrs. Bailey and taken up residence in the kitchens just outside my door. Ugh. And apparently he liked to start the day by blowing out his speakers.

Flopping onto my back, I squinted at the screen on my phone. Two minutes before my alarm. I couldn't even be pissed off that he'd woken me up early. Also, I grudgingly admitted, he had good taste in music, even if it was way too early for anything to be this loud.

The twinge in my back reminded me my period was about to start, which brought me right back to Chocolate Pots de Crème and that kiss. That orgasm.

"Nope. Didn't happen." My voice scratched my ears, rough and still thick with sleep. I rolled to my feet, shuffling to the bathroom for a few more minutes of privacy before I woke Nicky.

Staring at my puffy, flushed face in the mirror, I squinted, then got to work brushing my teeth.

Didn't happen. Yeah, right.

Was that how I was going to play this? Just pretend nothing had happened?

Yes. Absolutely. Because the alternative—going out there and facing Finn like a mature adult, having an actual conversation about those heated, sweet moments in the dark —was impossible.

My soul shriveled at the idea that he'd make fun of me. What if he acted like he'd been doing me a favor?

Or worse, what if he thought it was going to happen again? Which it most definitely could not. Ever. Never ever.

He was family, and I was staff. That alone was reason enough.

Plus, he was Finn. Finn Sawyer, my lifelong nemesis. The worst possible candidate for a booty call. No candidate at all for more than that. Not that I wanted more. I had enough on my plate with Heartstone Manor, and raising Nicky, and dealing with the reappearance of my mother-in-law. I didn't have room for more.

What about that kiss? That orgasm?

Never mind both of them. So what if no one had ever kissed me like that? Except Finn, ten years before. Never mind that I hadn't had an orgasm like that since . . . Since never, if I was being honest. Oliver and I had a satisfying sex life—before he lost interest. He'd lost interest a long time before he died.

Was I just going to forget how Finn made me feel? In a flash, I considered my options. Considered what would happen if we did that again.

No. Not happening. It would not end well, and I didn't have the bandwidth to deal with the fallout from sleeping with my boss's rebellious little brother. Not happening. End of story.

I turned my attention back to my ever-present to-do list. I had to prepare for the day and get Nicky ready for school. By the time I had my hair pinned up and my uniform on, Nicky was awake, leaning in the doorway of the bathroom. "Mr. Finn likes loud music."

"It seems he does," I said, ruffling Nicky's hair and pointing him in the direction of his waiting toothbrush. "Get to work on those teeth. I'll get your uniform, and we'll see what he has for your breakfast."

Nicky's morning routine was much faster than mine. Teeth brushed, he pulled on the navy pants and polo shirt all the boys wore to Laurel Country Day this time of year. I ran a brush through his hair after he pushed his head through his shirt, and he was ready, minus his sneakers. I located those along with his backpack, and we emerged into the kitchens to find Finn loading the dumbwaiter with shiny silver chafing dishes for the buffet upstairs.

"Waffles," he grunted. Jerking his head to the kitchen table, he said, "Your breakfast is waiting when you get the first shift settled."

I answered with a nod, ushering Nicky ahead of me into the hall toward the stairs to the first level. While Nicky and August usually ate in the kitchen, breakfast was the exception. With everyone on different schedules, it was easiest to set up a buffet in the dining room rather than feeding the early diners in both the kitchen and the dining room.

Kissing Nicky on the top of his head as I gently pushed him to his chair, I went to unload the dumbwaiter and get the buffet ready before anyone else showed up. When

Griffen and Hope arrived a few minutes later, I had the chafing dishes set up with waffles, sausages, eggs, and biscuits. I set out carafes of hot coffee and one of tea, scanning the room to see what I was missing. Nothing. Hot syrup and a bowl of cut fruit went beside the waffles. My stomach growled.

Pounding feet announced August and Thatcher, who spilled through the dining room door in a rush, Thatcher calling over his shoulder, "It smells so good, Tenn!"

"Waffles!" came August's shout of agreement. The two of them fell on the buffet like starving animals.

Tenn strolled in behind them, sending me a grin. "I hope Finn made enough. These two are ravenous. As usual."

I hovered for a few minutes, making sure everyone had what they needed and Nicky didn't drown his waffles in a vat of syrup. A perverse part of me was annoyed at how happy everyone was with Finn's breakfast.

Mrs. Bailey's breakfasts had been just fine. Waffles were waffles, right? But then I spied Hope taking a second bite. I hadn't seen her tuck into breakfast like that since she got pregnant, and I tried to let go of my annoyance. It was good she was eating, and even though Finn had been responsible for this meal, if the result was that Hope kept some food down, I'd take it. Part of it was probably just the natural progression of her pregnancy easing up on her morning sickness, but I had to admit, it was also the waffles. They did just look that good.

I was about to find out for myself. "I'm headed downstairs. If anyone needs anything, let me know."

I held up my phone before tucking it in my pocket. The house had an elaborate system of bells to alert staff to the needs of the family, but it was designed for a much larger staff than we had these days. Griffen and I had decided on a simple messaging app we'd customized for our purposes. Everyone living in the house and on the staff had the app, and we essentially texted to communicate. So much simpler than running every time the bell rang.

Griffen waved me off, his mouth full, and I went, both my stomach and my hormones dying for my own plate of waffles. The buttery maple scent in the air was making my head spin.

Finn was chopping something when I got there. His green eyes flicked to me, then to the covered plate on the table beside an insulated carafe of coffee. I braced for him to say something. Anything.

He turned his attention back to the cutting board, and I sat, nonplussed. He wasn't going to say anything? Not a sarcastic comment? No lascivious offer? He was just going to stand there and chop?

My stomach rumbled again. What was wrong with me? It had to be PMS. Finn wasn't talking. Finn was working and staying out of my way. Wasn't that what I wanted? Then why was I so annoyed?

Because this was Finn, and if I was being honest with myself, I'd never been rational when it came to Finn.

Letting out a sigh of defeat, I lifted the cover on my plate and drew in a long breath. Heaven. The waffle was perfection, golden brown, crispy on the first bite, steamy and tender in the middle. Perfectly sliced fruit, one scrambled egg, and a single square of chocolate.

I eyed that chocolate with suspicion. What did it mean? No one upstairs had chocolate. Was he making a sly comment about the night before? Was he just being nice?

Stop it! I ordered myself. *It's a piece of chocolate. Eat it. Don't obsess over it.*

Easier said than done, but I did my best. Pulling out my phone, I ate as I reviewed my to-do list for the day.

- Coordinate with April on the guest bath.

- Set a time to meet with Tenn and Scarlett about the wedding.

- Find more Halloween decorations.

- Get Parker a list of contractors qualified to work in the Manor.

- Assess the next target in the guest wing.

The list went on and on. The bulk of my day was spent rushing all over the Manor, just keeping the place running. A house like Heartstone should have had a full staff, but with Prentice's killer still out there and multiple murder attempts on more than one Sawyer, security was tight. Very tight. So tight the staff comprised me, Kitty and April, Billy Bob, Hawk, and now Finn.

Hawk was both head of security and our groundskeeper. He had his own staff of security rotating through the estate. Finn seemed to have food handled, so at least I didn't have that back on my plate. Billy Bob, brothers so joined at the hip they shared a name, were assigned to Parker and her renovation projects.

With only Kitty and April to clean the vast Manor, I ended up picking up the slack. Most of my long-term projects, like the guest wing bedrooms and collecting the historical documents scattered around the house, ended up put off in favor of the endless loads of laundry, ironing, vacuuming, polishing, and everything else it took to keep Heartstone going.

One day we'd be able to hire more staff, and I could dig into the fun stuff. For now . . . I scanned the list again. Today I was going to hit the guest wing and try to corral Tenn and Scarlett into a meeting on the wedding.

Everything else could wait. I knew both Scarlett and Tenn thought Christmas Eve was ages away, but not in the world of wedding planning, even for an intimate family wedding. It was the first week of October. December was a blink away.

Something occurred to me. Before I could think better of it, I called out, "Finn!"

His head rose, and he let out a grunt of acknowledgment that reminded me of a teenage Finn. I had to hide a grin. Clearly, Finn was not chatty in the morning.

"Mrs. Bailey was going to handle the menu for the wedding."

Finn stilled, eyes raising to the ceiling, moving from side to side as if a menu were printed on the stone above his head. "I've got it."

"But you're a guest," I protested. It was his brother's wedding. He shouldn't be stuck in the kitchen. And a wedding was a formal event, even if it was small. Could he handle that?

"Just the family?"

"And Scarlett's parents," I added. "West too. And Daisy's grandmother. My mother."

"So, just the family."

"Yes," I agreed, my chest squeezing as his assumption settled in. 'Just the family' wasn't only the Sawyers. Not anymore. That felt nice. Better than I thought it should.

Finn nodded and turned for the pantry. "I've got it."

I had no idea what that meant. Surely he didn't already have a menu in mind. How did he *have it*? "Okay. Here's the menu we worked out." I pulled up the menu on my phone and followed Finn to the pantry.

Taking the phone, he scanned the menu and shoved it back at me. "What part of this did Tenn or Scarlett ask for?"

I looked at my screen. "Tenn wanted filet as the main course, and Scarlett requested the oysters for one of the appetizers. Everything else was Mrs. Bailey's idea."

Another grunt. "This is shit." He turned his back on me, his disgusted mutter including something about stuffed mushrooms.

"You're going to come up with another menu?"

I thought the sound he made was a 'yes.'

Just to annoy him, I said, "I'll let you know when we're having the next wedding meeting so you can be there."

"I'm not going to any *wedding meetings*," he called after me, as if I was dragging him to his own execution.

"Yes, you are," I called back, escaping the kitchen before he could say anything else.

Chapter Nine

SAVANNAH

The next few weeks unfolded in the pattern of that first morning. Loud music before dawn. Breakfast on the table like clockwork, that single piece of chocolate set out only for me. A rush of hours flying by, filled with work and enough surprises that I barely had time to think about how much I didn't want to kiss Finn again.

The burst pipe in Sterling's room had taken me a full week to sort out.

The electricity going out in Hawk's gatehouse and the subsequent fight to get him into a room at the Manor while I begged the electricians to work us into their packed schedule. Hawk hadn't wanted to move into the Manor, claiming that sleeping on a camping cot with the mice was just fine if it meant he didn't have to put up with the family.

We knew it wasn't personal. Hawk just wasn't a fan of people, in general. He'd tried to stay put, insisting the cold didn't bother him, but Griffen refused, staring Hawk down until he gave a grunt that reminded me of Finn and finally surrendered. I installed him in the smallest functional guest room at his request, and aside from some minor grumbling and an outright refusal to eat with the family or in the kitchen with the rest of us, he'd settled in nicely.

As we moved further into October, fall settled over the mountains, bringing apple season and trips to the orchard that ended in smiling faces and sticky fingers. I finished decorating the house for Halloween. I took Nicky into town for his costume, a bright yellow catlike creature from his trading card game, all the while keeping one eye on Finn for trouble, and another on my phone, trying not to wonder when my former mother-in-law would pop up next.

Both remained suspiciously silent for most of October. It was my mother-in-law who broke first.

A few days before Halloween, I sat at the kitchen table going over notes from our last wedding meeting, pulling items for a new to-do list while Finn worked at the island doing something complicated with a potato, music blasting as usual. I didn't mind. He had good taste in music, and the pounding beat helped me focus. I was the de facto wedding planner, and despite everything else I had to do, I was enjoying the hell out of it.

I'd tapped Royal for help with contacts and equipment. Running the Inn at Sawyers Bend with Tenn meant that Royal had access to everything from florists to catering supplies. Once upon a time, Heartstone Manor's lower-level storage room had been filled with everything needed to host royalty at a moment's notice.

These days I had to scrounge to find extra place settings. I wondered if Prentice had sold off the dinnerware at the same auctions he'd used for the missing art. So far I didn't think Griffen's investigator had found any receipts that revealed where the sets of vintage porcelain were. My mother didn't know either. All I had were empty shelves where the Flora Danica and Royal Doulton should be.

Even so, we were in good shape. Griffen had gotten ordained from a website and would be performing the ceremony, which would be in the library. Even though I'd just finished putting up the Halloween decorations, I couldn't wait to start decorating for Christmas. It had been years since anyone had a real Christmas in this house. Not since Darcy had died.

I was determined to fill Heartstone Manor with cheer. We had children in the house again, one of them mine. And sometime between Thanksgiving and Christmas, we'd have a baby. A family holiday was exactly what we needed.

I penciled in a note to get real fir garlands for the front hall banister. I'd string the lights myself. It would be worth the extra trouble to have the scent of Christmas filling the house.

"Did you talk to Hope about Thanksgiving?" I asked absently, raising my voice to be heard over the music.

"What about it?"

I glanced over to see Finn scrolling on his tablet, making a list on a Post-it stuck to the island.

"The menu. Did you talk to Hope about it?"

"She said I'm in charge," he said to his tablet, his tone clearly saying that any other option was ridiculous.

Finn take input on a menu? Absurd.

He'd accepted a few suggestions on the wedding menu from Tenn and Scarlett, only because it was their wedding. Otherwise, he'd made it very clear to everyone that outside input was not welcome. I wasn't sure if his intention was to be ornery, but no one cared. Not even me. Everything that came out of Finn's kitchen was delicious.

My phone chimed with a text. The blood drained from my face when I saw the name on the screen.

Lydia Harris. My mother-in-law.

Hand shaking as I lifted the phone, I tapped the screen. Up popped the blue bubble.

> Savannah, I know you're carrying a lot of guilt, but don't you think it's time you stop punishing us? I want to see my grandson. I think it's best if you join us for the Thanksgiving holiday. If you aren't willing to give me that much, then send me Nicky. He deserves his grandmother.

I let out a long breath, reaching for my coffee cup with an unsteady hand. I stared into the empty mug, not registering anything. Heart pounding, I struggled to put my thoughts together.

Why did she always do this to me? I was Savannah Miles, for fuck's sake. I could do anything. I laughed in the face of crisis. I could solve any problem. How did one sixty-eight-year-old woman make me shake? Did she really think I'd send her my six-year-old son?

"What is it?" Finn asked, pouring a stream of hot coffee into my mug.

I drank, scalding my tongue, grateful for the burn that shocked me back to myself. Reading the text message one more time, I turned my phone face down on the table before I gave in to temptation and chucked it across the room.

His green eyes hard as they landed on my phone, Finn pressed, "Your mother-in-law again?"

I nodded. Finn studied my face, watching, I thought, for some sign I was going to break down.

I wasn't.

"I'm not going to cry all over you again. She took me by surprise that time. I knew she'd try again. It was just a matter of time."

Finn leaned back against the butcher block island and

raised his own coffee mug, taking a slow sip. "What does she want?" he asked, eventually.

"She wants Nicky."

"She wants to visit Nicky? Or she just wants Nicky?"

"That's the million-dollar question." I stared into my coffee.

"What did she say?" Finn sounded only vaguely interested, but I wasn't fooled. If Finn wasn't interested, he wouldn't bother to ask.

I wasn't sure if I wanted Finn in my business. I wasn't going to hand him a weapon to use against me. But this wasn't high school. And he wasn't that boy anymore.

More than anything else, I could use a sounding board. I didn't want to lay this on my mom. For one thing, she'd unequivocally be on my side. An excellent quality in a mother, but I could use an impartial opinion. Finn and I weren't friends. We weren't family. And he wouldn't hesitate to tell me if I was being an ass.

I read him the text message.

Finn let out a low whistle. "She's good. Just the right amount of accusation, and bringing what Nicky deserves into it." He took another sip of coffee, his eyes on me.

I fought the urge to squirm.

"Are you guilty?" he asked.

"No." I didn't have to think. I'd given everything I had to save Oliver, and it wasn't enough. It never would have been enough. Not when he didn't want to save himself.

Finn only raised an eyebrow.

I didn't have to explain. Didn't have to tear open this wound. I didn't owe anyone that. Especially not Finn.

I found myself saying, "She blames me for Oliver's death."

Finn waited, pressure building inside me as the silence dragged on. Finally, it all spilled out.

"She was fine the whole time Oliver and I were dating and when we first got married. A little intense about her firstborn baby boy, but she was okay. Then when Nicky was born, she went a little nuts. Always hovering, telling me what to do, endlessly criticizing everything I did. Formula was better. I absolutely couldn't send him to daycare. He should sleep on his stomach."

I lifted my mug and sipped, the coffee washing away some of my bitterness. "She had an opinion on everything. She was furious when I went back to work, but I liked my job, and I'd worked hard for it. She was even more furious when I enrolled him in a preschool between Oliver and my offices instead of letting her watch him. But we didn't agree on anything—food, nap schedules, potty training. I think that was the beginning of the end between us. When I chose the preschool over her."

"Where was Oliver in all of this?" Finn asked, an edge to his words.

"At the bottom of a bottle of Vicodin." I wasn't sugar-coating it anymore. I'd wasted too much time covering for Oliver.

When Finn just looked at me, I continued. "He loved mountain biking. A few months after Nicky was born, he had an accident. Went over his handlebars on a downhill and shattered his collarbone."

I barely remember that time. Nicky still wasn't sleeping through the night, and Oliver needed constant care. Those months had passed in a haze of fatigue, my heart swinging from the joy of Nicky to terror as Oliver fell further and further away from me.

"Lydia moved in. Oliver's mother. I was grateful for her

help, but in the end—" The backs of my eyes prickled, but I didn't allow them to form into tears. No. I was done crying for him.

"He was taking too many pills. I tried to stop him. His doctors wanted him to switch to ibuprofen, but Oliver said the pain was too much, and Lydia backed him up. It took months longer than it should have, but eventually he was functioning again. He got off the pills, and Lydia went home."

I fell silent, caught in memories. I'd hoped once Lydia was gone, Oliver would jump into parenting with me. We had this amazing little miracle of a baby, and he'd missed most of his first year.

Looking back, I'd never been lonelier than the first two years of Nicky's life. Hoping, always hoping things would change. Hoping I'd get my husband back. Hoping he'd be the father he'd always planned on being. But I wasn't telling Finn that part. I could barely think about it, even after all this time.

"And then?" Finn prompted.

"And then he had another accident on his bike. His collarbone again. There were multiple surgeries. More pills. So many bottles of pills."

I sighed. I still flinched when I saw an orange bottle with a white cap. I hated the sight of any prescription bottle. They'd stolen my husband, one little white pill at a time.

"At first they were his pills, prescribed by his doctors. When they refused to give him any more, Lydia took him to her orthopedist, who wrote him prescriptions for a while. And then there weren't any more prescriptions, but the pills kept coming."

"So she enabled him, and he OD'd?" Finn's face was blank. No compassion. No judgment.

It was exactly what I needed. I was so tired of the pity, of the stares.

"He got some pills laced with too much fentanyl. I warned him. After doctors started clamping down on opiate prescriptions, demand on the street increased, and fentanyl started getting into everything. His tolerance had gotten so high, and he wasn't careful." I gave a helpless shrug. "He'd pop a few pills, not even really knowing what they were, and then he'd have a bourbon. Then another. One day he had one too many, and he didn't wake up."

I jolted when Finn dropped into the chair on the other side of the table, bracing his forearms on the surface, his eyes heavy with understanding. "I know all about that shit. I lost a good friend the same way. Fucking fentanyl."

"I'm sorry," I said, knowing how useless those words felt. I'd heard them so many times. But they were all I had to offer, so I said them anyway.

Finn nodded his acceptance. "There are drugs everywhere in kitchens. Fast-paced, tons of pressure. Coke and amphetamines to keep you sharp, then something else to take you back down. Alcohol, pills, heroin." He sat back and crossed his arms over his chest. "I lost more friends to heroin than anything else."

"You?" I asked, even though it was none of my business.

Finn's mouth quirked in a smile that was somehow sheepish and devilish at the same time. "Not for long. When I started, I was too scared to try anything. I needed my job. Then, when I knew I could find work and I realized no one cared what I put up my nose or in my veins as long as I got the job done, I tried everything. You knew me back then." He gave that shrug I wasn't hating as much as I used to. "I'd do anything. My roomate got into heroin big time. It was cheap, and his girl dumped him, and he got sucked in."

"Did he—?" I didn't have to finish the question. None of this fit with the picture I'd had in my head of Finn as a cook.

"I don't know. I got out of there. The place we worked was a pressure cooker. Everyone was on something. The head chef was a psycho, but he'd built a reputation for the place, and it was enough to get me an offer for another restaurant with a chef I wanted to work with. I left and didn't look back. I'm glad I was there, though. I learned a lot about the job and what I want from it. And what I don't."

Changing the subject, he said, "I'm assuming your mother-in-law doesn't see her own part in all of this."

I laughed. "You mean her part as the long-suffering perfect mother who's never done anything wrong, ever? The mother who remembers begging me to get him in rehab while I was shoving pills down his throat, but conveniently forgets that she's the one who got him so many of those pills? According to her, I might as well have shot him."

"So why do you seem scared? Hurt, I can see. She was your mother-in-law. She enabled your husband's addiction and then blamed you for her actions. But why are you scared?"

I drew in a breath. I hated being scared. I'd rather be angry. But Finn was right. I was scared.

"Don't tell me you aren't scared, Savannah. I can see it all over you." He leaned in, his eyes intent on mine. "You let her make you cry. No one makes you cry."

His words sent strength flooding through me, restoring everything Lydia's text had drained away. I was a badass bitch, goddammit. And wasn't it funny that Finn sounded like he liked that about me?

"I don't know exactly why I'm scared," I admitted. "Maybe it's that she's been out of the picture for so long, and now she's popping up out of nowhere and demanding to see Nicky."

"Are you going to let her?" Finn asked.

Shaking my head, I said, "I don't know. I should. She's his grandmother. But the idea makes me nervous, and I don't know why."

Finn gave me a skeptical look. "I don't buy that. I think you're trying to logic yourself out of something your gut already knows. Why don't you trust her?"

I let out a huff of air. He was right. I did know. "She tried to take Nicky from me once, before Oliver died. After Oliver was recovering from the second accident, she suggested I quit my job and be Oliver's full-time caretaker and Nicky could live with her. I—"

I cut off, not sure I could bring myself to say what I was thinking. I'd never put it into words before, not even to my mother.

Finn waited until the words tumbled out.

"I always wondered if she already knew we'd lost Oliver and was hedging her bets with Nicky."

"You think she wanted Nicky to be her do-over baby," Finn said.

"I do." As soon as I put it into words, I knew I'd been right. "Oliver had a younger brother, but Lydia was never fixated on him the way she was on Oliver. Sometimes I wondered if she remembered she had another son. Everything was always about Oliver, and then Nicky."

"How did you stop her?"

"I—" Another confession was ready to tumble from my lips. Why was I telling Finn all of this? Why him and not my mother? Or Hope? Or anyone else on the planet other than Finn Sawyer?

Maybe I just needed to get it out, because the words

were there before I could stop myself. "I was going to divorce him. I found a lawyer, and we were working on a custody proposal. She helped me make it clear to Lydia that she wasn't getting Nicky."

Finn's mossy green eyes sharpened, and his fingers tightened on his coffee mug.

"Lydia doubled down on caring for Oliver, which was fine with me at that point. I had my hands full with a toddler and my job. I couldn't handle a husband who refused to get better, who seemed determined to float through life until those pills got the better of him."

Finn picked up his empty mug and stood. He loomed over me, and I braced, raw and vulnerable, not sure if he was going to kiss me or say something snotty. He did neither.

Leaning in, his breath warm on my cheek, he squeezed my shoulder and said, "You need to talk to a lawyer."

I watched him go, stuck where I was, my head spinning. Why didn't he ever do what I expected? And why was I starting to like it?

Chapter Ten

FINN

"Nicky, stop. You can't go to school today." Savannah sounded exasperated and apologetic at the same time. The odd mix of tones made sense when I heard Nicky.

"Mom, it's not fair." I almost didn't recognize Nicky's voice. He sounded older, his words low, gravelly, and somehow thick. Goopy. A bone-shaking sneeze, followed by a prolonged, choking cough. Ugh. That explained the goopy sound. Until I came home to Heartstone Manor, I'd never realized how many germs the little monsters carried around. So much snot when they got sick.

Another sneeze and a cough from Nicky.

"Mom, please," he begged. "I'm okay. I promise I'm okay. Please let me go." His scratchy voice hurt to hear, getting louder as he made his way down the hall to the kitchen.

"Oh, honey." Savannah's voice was heavy with apology, lagging behind him. "You can't go. It's cold and damp, and you're running a fever."

"But, Mom, it's Halloween. I can't miss Halloween. I'm

gonna be Pikachu!" His voice cracked on the last word before dissolving into heavy sobs. Shit. I rubbed the heel of my palm against my chest. It must have been killing Savannah to tell him no. Even my withered heart ached at the sound of Nicky's tears.

August and Thatcher, Scarlett's boys, had spent the last week fighting a cold, both recovering in time to be back at school a few days ago. Nicky was the last to get sick. Yesterday, it hadn't been much more than a sniffle. It looked like things had gotten ugly overnight.

I remembered Halloween at his age. Sawyers Bend went all out for tourists and residents alike, with every business on Main Street hosting trick-or-treating. The Inn threw a bash that included a bonfire, apple bobbing, and a haunted maze. Halloween was one of the few bright memories I had from growing up in Sawyers Bend. Now Nicky was going to miss it, just when he was old enough to really enjoy it.

"You can't go to school, sweetheart. You're too sick." Savannah said. It sounded like she'd stopped halfway down the hall.

"There's a Halloween party in my class!" Nicky protested. "Pizza and candy bags and there's gonna be games. I can't stay home. I want to show everyone my costume."

I caught the faint rush of Savannah's sigh. "I'm so sorry, baby. Even if I was willing to send you to school, which I'm not, one look at you and they'd send you to the school nurse. Even if you could hide your sneezing and coughing, she'd take your temperature and call me to come get you. It's against school policy to send you in with a fever. I'm so sorry, but there's nothing I can do."

Nicky hiccuped out a sob, muffled as I imagined

Savannah hugging him. "Come on," she said. "Let's get you a hot shower. After, I'll make you some tea and toast, and we'll figure something out about tonight. Okay?"

"Want a bath," Nicky grumbled, his voice fading out as their door closed at the end of the hall.

My eyes flicked to the clock. Savannah was running late, undoubtedly due to Nicky's illness. I gave my breakfast prep a quick look, checked the clock, and shot her a text.

> I heard Nicky. Poor kid. Stay with him. I'll handle breakfast.

A minute later, my phone chimed with a simple

> TY

I tried to ignore the squeeze in my chest at her slight sign of gratitude. Why did I care? Fuck, this woman was going to kill me. I hadn't laid a hand on her since that one ill-advised kiss weeks ago, but I'd thought about it. Fucking hell, I'd thought about it.

That moment in the dark, the flush of guilt on her face from stealing the dessert. She'd been irresistible. It had seemed so simple. What was a kiss? It was nothing. Just a moment in the dark between two consenting adults. I'd had no clue how quickly it would spin out of control. It had gone too far, and all I'd wanted was to push it further.

Even I was smart enough to know that taking it further was a very bad idea. We were acquaintances. Coworkers. Sometimes mortal enemies. None of those descriptions included kissing in the dark. Not to mention everything else I wanted to do to her in the dark.

I reminded myself of my vow to keep my hands to myself. Savannah wasn't some throwaway one-night stand.

The fact that I couldn't stop thinking about that kiss was all the evidence I needed that anything more was a bad idea.

But this wasn't about me. This was about Nicky. And Nicky, I'd learned, wasn't just a small appendage of Savannah's. He was his own little person, and a pretty cool one at that. Not a lot of whining or shrieking. Polite yet rambunctious. A smart-ass, but only enough to make his mother laugh. All in all, a decent little guy. Not one who deserved to have his Halloween ruined with an ill-timed cold. I couldn't do anything about his virus, but I could bring Halloween to him.

With ideas for a substitute Halloween brewing in the back of my mind, I got breakfast set up in the dining room, making the briefest of appearances. Just long enough to settle the chafing dishes in place and light the fuel pots beneath. I texted Griffen to let him know Nicky was sick and I was handling the breakfast service. I already knew he'd take it from there. If I was trying to slack off, he'd be on my ass, but covering for Savannah when Nicky was sick? No problem.

When Savannah emerged from their small apartment, her cheeks pink, loose red curls already spinning free from her bun, I had a plan.

"He has a costume?" I asked. At her blank look, I remembered she couldn't actually read my mind, no matter how much it sometimes seemed like she could. "Nicky. For Halloween. He has a costume?"

"He, um, yes. Yes, but he can't—"

"Yeah, I got that. I heard him hacking up a lung. I have a plan, assuming he's allowed out of bed."

"Sure. For a while, but he can't go—"

"Outside," I finished for her. "I got it. It's cold, damp,

and he's sick. I have it covered. Can you get him in his costume before dinner? Around four?"

"I can, but what do you mean you have it covered?" She was staring at me as if she'd never seen me before.

Was it that out of character for me to do something nice? Maybe. But I tried not to take offense. I wasn't here to make friends. Plus, if she'd been paying attention, Savannah would have noticed that I went out of my way for the kids more often than I did for the adults in the house. I didn't think of myself as a kid person, but Nicky, August, and Thatcher were cool. And anyway, kids are generally more trustworthy than adults. At least in my experience. None of them had ever failed to pay a kidnapping ransom and kicked me out of the house when I was too young to know how to adult. Unlike my father.

It was possible I had some issues to work out.

"I've got it covered," I said again. "Trust me."

Savannah gave me a long look with her sharp gray eyes before she left without another word. I didn't have time to wonder what she was thinking. I had a Halloween to plan.

As soon as I had breakfast cleared and finished the first stage of lunch prep, I checked the pantry for the ingredients for the marshmallow rice cereal squares and brownie bites I was already cooking up in my mind. After the last few weeks of making the kids afternoon tea, I knew all their favorite treats. Nicky was a sucker for marshmallow squares, anything brownie-related, and homemade apple cider. I had what I needed for the cider and the brownie bites, but I wanted orange food coloring for the frosting, and we were completely out of marshmallows thanks to the hot cocoa I'd made them over the weekend.

I had enough time for a quick trip into town before lunch. Before I left, I had two stops to make. First, I headed back up to my room in the family wing. The family wing of the Manor was a mix of two-room suites and single rooms. I had one of the single rooms, though I couldn't complain. More than spacious, it had a sleeping area with the same antique double bed I'd had as a kid, a desk area, and a sofa with an ancient tube TV that hadn't worked in at least a decade.

Every time I stepped into my room at Heartstone Manor, I was thrown back in time. My room was frozen in my senior year of high school, right down to the pictures tacked on the corkboard over my desk. I no longer recognized most of the faces there. Some high school parties, a few from a field trip to Sliding Rock, all of us sunburned and smiling. I couldn't remember being that young. Would I have valued those years more if I'd known how short my time was before everything changed? I'd never know. That sunburned, smiling kid was long gone. I wouldn't know how to get him back, even if I wanted to.

I could have redecorated when I moved back in. My sister Parker was renovating the cottage and gatehouse for Savannah and Hawk, respectively, and she was good at it. Amazing, actually. She'd been focused on the cottage so Savannah and Nicky could have more space as soon as possible, and I couldn't believe the transformation.

I'd only been in there a few times over the years, but I remembered faded paint and water stains on the ceiling. Now it looked like the after pic on one of those home renovation tv shows. I also learned she knew how to stretch a budget. Parker could have redone my room in her sleep. So why was I still living in this frozen monument to a past I hadn't liked that much while I was living it? I wished I knew.

I shoved a pile of laundry to the floor to reveal an old

trunk stuffed with the remnants of childhood that I hadn't been able to part with as a teenager. Sitting cross-legged on the thick carpet, I and opened the lid, the smell of cedar washing over me, bringing a wrenching ache to my chest. The last time I'd opened this trunk, I'd been another person. That kid had been an asshole, but he'd been innocent and so fucking young.

At the top was a Laurel Country Day sweatshirt with a graphic of a football on the arm. I'd never been much of a football player, but I liked being on the team. I dug past the sweatshirt, finding a certificate from some debate club thing. Debate club? I didn't remember doing debate club. The truth was, I didn't have clear memories of most of my childhood. When I left for my freshman year of college, I hadn't planned to come back. I thought I'd stay on campus during breaks, cut my father out of my life, and start fresh. That hadn't worked out exactly as I thought it would. For one thing, unless you were an international student, campus was closed during holidays.

Then there was that endless, miserable summer after my freshman year. Living back under my father's roof had been worse than I'd imagined. I tried to get a job cooking in town. One word in the ear of every restaurant owner in Sawyers Bend, and I was effectively unemployable. When I tried to get a job in Asheville, he took away my car.

According to Prentice, either I worked for Sawyer Enterprises or I didn't work at all. Since he wasn't planning on giving me any cash, not working wasn't an option. To Prentice's disgust, I ended up working on the grounds crew at the Inn. I'd enjoyed both the job and my father's impotent frustration. If I'd known what that little rebellion would cost me, I might have taken the office job.

Chapter Eleven

FINN

It hadn't occurred to me that I could leave. For one thing, I wanted to go back to college. At nineteen I'd been stuck in a merry-go-round of hating my father, performing for him to get what I wanted, then hating him all over again, even more than before.

The merry-go-round ground to a halt on spring break of my sophomore year in college.

I'd jumped on a plane to Cancun with some fraternity buddies and a vague plan involving tequila and hot girls in bikinis. Exactly what every guy dreams of for spring break. Except mine had ended in terror, pain, and the death of the life I'd known.

The second night of the trip, I got a little too drunk in a bar on the beach. Par for the course for spring break. But instead of waking up face down on the beach or half on top of a beautiful girl, I'd come to in a bare concrete room, my hands cuffed behind me, a black bag over my head, and a splitting pain behind my eyes.

All the arrogance I've acquired in the years since still can't match my nineteen-year-old self. Even in that dark, cold room with a bag over my head and my hands cuffed behind me, I'd been so sure that being a Sawyer would save my ass.

Being a Sawyer was how I ended up in that concrete room to begin with.

And more than that, being a Sawyer was worth absolutely jack shit when the man with the checkbook declined to write the check that could have bought me my life back.

I'd never gotten over that betrayal. It was a miracle that I survived. By the time I made my way back to civilization and a phone, I knew better than to call my father for help. For anything.

I remembered vividly the fear and pain of that moment, the fists and flashing lights. Knowing, for the first time, that I was on my own.

I stared into the cedar-scented trunk with blind eyes, back in that cold concrete room, replaying the last time I ever heard my father's voice. He'd told my kidnappers, "I don't give a fuck what you do with him. He's worth nothing to me."

Was that why my father had spent so many years trying to sire so many kids? So that when push came to shove, he could write one off and still have a pile of heirs to fall back on?

And now, since the bastard was dead, I'd never know what his reasoning had been. Why he and Ford had thrown me to the wolves. And Hope? She'd worked closely with all of them. Had she known? I wanted to believe that she hadn't, but I didn't know. Not for sure.

We never made amends. I wasn't sorry I'd missed my chance to talk to him one more time. What was there to say? It's not like Prentice Sawyer would have apologized. Hell would have frozen over first. Even if he had, I had nothing to say to him.

I don't know if he ever looked for me. Obviously, he told some bullshit story about me running off to join the army. Maybe the rest of them believed him. Maybe they didn't. It didn't matter. For me, that moment—my father saying I was worth nothing to him—was the end.

I never went back to college. Never went back to Sawyers Bend. Never spoke to my father, or any of them, again. I wrote Prentice one final letter months after it was over, telling him to go to hell. I doubt he cared.

I'd made my own way. If I had nothing else, I had the knowledge that I could do it again if I had to. I was stuck here for five years if I wanted my inheritance. Well, by now, it was more like four and a quarter years. A little over four years stuck here with my family, stalling my career for the uncertain promise of a payoff. It was possible there was money in the trust my father had left me. That might be enough for me to open my own place, on my own terms, without investors.

Maybe.

But then again, maybe there was nothing.

Maybe Harvey and Griffen were having a good laugh at the rest of us playing good little boys and girls to get our payday when there was nothing for us to inherit. Knowing my father, I'd give good odds the trusts were empty. That would be just like him, to get us to spend five years dancing to his tune for the promise of a payout that didn't exist.

I didn't want to think Griffen was in on it. I wanted to believe he was the Griffen I remembered. But even if he was still that Griffen, it didn't mean our father hadn't been playing him right along with us.

I sat back on my heels, holding a Lego Batman I'd built

when I was not much older than Nicky. Savannah was giving Nicky the childhood I never had. No one would ever throw her kid away. She'd die first. So would Miss Martha. Savannah didn't have the wealth I'd grown up with, but she was giving Nicky something worth far more than money. Love. After my mother died, love was in short supply at Heartstone Manor.

I had to ask myself, why was I here? I survived the last decade with ruthless pragmatism, working my ass off to learn and to keep a roof over my head, putting in long hours doing whatever I was told in whatever kitchen would hire me. I never made a bad bet because I always bet on myself, so why was I here?

Why was I giving up five years of my life? Five years I could spend building my resume and making connections that would serve my goal of opening my own place. That path was probably a hell of a lot better than hanging around here hoping Prentice had left me enough cash to make my dream come true. If I were being honest, the idea of using his money to fund my restaurant made me a little sick.

Which brought me back to the question that lingered in the back of my mind, haunting me. Why was I still here?

I set the Lego Batman aside and pulled out a green plastic army man. Once there'd been over a hundred. Now I had only a handful. I loved playing with these when I was a kid, setting them up on a carpet with Tenn, having mock battles for hours. There'd been a tank that went with the set, not much bigger than the army men, but we thought it was the coolest. We fought over it all the time. Whoever ended up with the tank always won the war.

Maybe that was my answer. Maybe this was my last chance to see if there was anything here for me. For better or worse, this was my home. These strangers were my family. Maybe it was worth five years to see what we could make of that.

I didn't know if I could forgive Ford for the part he played in my kidnapping. Back then, he'd been so tight with our father. I couldn't believe he didn't know. But Royal and Hope? They could have gone either way. The rest of them had been too young for me to think they'd been involved.

Griffen hadn't even been here. And my father never told my sisters anything. Didn't they deserve a chance?

I couldn't decide, which was pretty much what the last few months of sulking had been about. Now that I was back in the kitchens, grounded in a place that felt like mine, I was starting to wonder if I was sticking around for more than the money.

I set the army man aside and dug deeper in the trunk, my fingers sliding around a translucent red yo-yo, scuffed on the edges. I'd been a master with this yo-yo when I was ten. It was probably too big for Nicky's hand, but I could teach him how to use it.

At that thought, I gave a startled look at the small pile of treasures I'd accumulated. The Lego Batman, the army men, the yo-yo. A Rubik's Cube. A Chinese finger trap I used to torture my younger sisters. Was I really going to give these things to Nicky?

On one hand, they were just cheap bits of plastic that wouldn't be worth over twenty-five cents at a yard sale. On the other hand, these were the best pieces of my childhood. Didn't I want to hang on to them?

Not now, I slowly realized, the certainty growing in my chest. I didn't need this stuff. I had the kitchens back, the one place that had truly brought me peace back in those days. And Nicky was a good kid. If he didn't appreciate this stuff, if he left it all lying around, forgotten, I could always take it back later. But I didn't think that was going to happen.

I rooted around in the trunk for a few more minutes and didn't find anything else I thought Nicky would like until I happened on the one thing I knew would make his head spin. He, August, and Thatcher weren't the first kids to get obsessed with their trading card game. In fact, it had been huge when I was his age. And I had a card that was almost impossible to find. My prized Pikachu card would be the surprise at the end of my scavenger hunt. I couldn't wait to see Nicky's face when he saw it. It was a little beat-up, but I didn't think Nicky would care.

Gathering everything I'd found, I closed the trunk and headed back downstairs. One more stop, then I'd run to town for supplies. I couldn't pull off trick-or-treating by myself.

I stopped outside the door to the office, raising my hand to knock, hesitating out of habit. I'd always hesitated to knock on this door. Most of my life, this had been my father's office. My least favorite room in Heartstone Manor. A summons here could only mean trouble. At least, for me.

I remembered the bonfire we built the day we learned Ford had pled guilty to Prentice's murder. Griffen had lost it, turning his fury on the office itself, tearing down the trophy animals Prentice had hung on the walls. Royal added the heavy curtains and the stuffed bear head, Griffen tossing Prentice's portrait on the top with a manic grin on his face. I'd rolled out the ornate leather desk chair our father had loved, a wide smile stretching my mouth as I watched it burn.

My stomach twisted as I recalled what had happened after that. I'd lied to Griffen. About being in the army. About coming home. Why hadn't I just told him the truth about the last ten years? Why confirm our father's lie about the army and imply I'd been back to Sawyers Bend since? I'd wanted to force some kind of confession from Griffen, but it hadn't worked. Maybe because he had nothing to confess. Maybe he was exactly what he seemed to be. I still couldn't make myself believe that. Too much baggage and too many years apart.

I couldn't tell you the last time Griffen and I had an actual conversation. Since I'd been back, we didn't spend much time hanging out. I knew that was mostly on me. Too many years away from my family. Not that my exile was my fault. But even with our limited interactions since I returned six months ago, it bothered me that I couldn't trust my read on Griffen. He seemed like the Griffen I knew as a kid. He acted like that, Griffen. And he sure as hell was nothing like our father.

But I still couldn't bring myself to trust him. Trust takes time, and we hadn't had enough of that. Gritting my teeth, a tight knot in my chest, I knocked.

"Come in," Griffen said, his voice muffled by the thick door. It swung open smoothly to reveal Griffen, Royal, and Hope, their eyes locked on their respective laptop screens, deep in conversation. Standing at the door, I cleared my throat. The three of them looked up, Griffen's eyes widening in surprise.

"Finn," he said, his voice more than a little cautious. "Everything okay?"

"Yeah, but no. You talked to Savannah?"

Hope sat up straight. "Not since she texted to say Nicky was sick and you were covering breakfast. Is she okay? Did he get worse?"

"I don't think so. It sounds like the same thing August

and Thatcher had last week, but Savannah laid down Mom Law. No trick-or-treating."

"Tough," Royal said, shaking his head. "Cold out there, though."

"What can I do for you?" Griffen prompted.

I hesitated, not sure Griffen wouldn't laugh at my idea. My father would have.

"I'm going to run into town and get supplies to make some of Nicky's favorite treats and get some candy," I said, the tight knot in my chest loosening at Griffen's nod of agreement. "I thought he could put his costume on before dinner and go around knocking on doors in the Manor. Would you guys be up for that?" I directed that at Hope and Royal. "Could you answer your doors and hand out candy? I'm doing a scavenger hunt downstairs too. I don't know what else. I haven't figured it all out yet."

My mind was racing, putting together ideas of things I would have liked at Nicky's age. There'd been no fun in this house back then, but there could be now.

Griffen raised an eyebrow. "Absolutely. That's a great idea." Throwing a glance at Royal, he said, "You guys going to be around?"

"Definitely," Royal said with a grin. "You should stop by the bakery when you're in town and see what Daisy and Grams have for Halloween. Daisy's been making truffles lately, and she said something about a special design for Halloween."

I nodded as Hope said, "So there's us, and Royal and Daisy. Tenn and Scarlett will be out trick-or-treating with August and Thatcher, and Quinn and Sterling will still be at work. I don't know about Avery."

"Avery has an event at the brewery tonight, so she won't

be here," Royal supplied, "but I bet Aunt Ophelia and Claudia would love to play trick-or-treat."

The knot in my chest dissolved completely. Not only were they willing to play along, they seemed into the whole plan. We were going to give Nicky the best Halloween we could manage, considering he couldn't leave the house. "Cool. I'm headed out to the store now. Be back in an hour or so with candy and stuff."

"Sounds good," Griffen agreed. I was about to make my escape when he added, "Finn? This is a great idea. Thanks."

I felt my shoulder jerk in an involuntary shrug as I ducked out of the office and headed to my car. The warmth in Griffen's expression as he thanked me was so far outside my expectations that I had no clue how to respond. A part of me was still waiting for Griffen to be Prentice or Ford. All business, no heart.

Maybe Griffen really wasn't anything like them. Maybe, possibly, things were going to be different. I wasn't sure I was ready to think about that.

Chapter Twelve

FINN

I went a little crazy when I got to town. I hit the grocery store first and picked up what I needed for the marshmallow squares and the brownie bites, but the candy situation left much to be desired. Everyone else in Sawyers Bend had gotten here first, cleaning out the candy aisle in preparation for trick-or-treating. I found a few packs of Smarties and some lollipops. Not what I had in mind.

It probably didn't matter. Nicky was in kindergarten. Candy was candy. He'd be fine with Smarties and lollipops, but I couldn't seem to stop myself. I liked the kid, and being sick on Halloween was the worst, on top of having to watch his friends go out and trick-or-treat without him. Hoping Daisy and Grams had something resembling candy, I headed for Sweetheart Bakery on Main Street.

Sweetheart Bakery was a mainstay in Sawyers Bend. Most of the town agreed that Daisy and Grams were the best, from the perfect chocolate chip cookie to custom cake design.

Royal was an unlikely match for the town baker, but he

and Daisy had crossed paths a few months ago when she stopped a saboteur from dumping cockroaches in the Inn's ventilation system. They'd been inseparable ever since. Royal had good taste. Daisy made a mean cookie and was as sweet as anything that came out of her kitchen. I had to admit; I was partly inclined to like Royal just based on Daisy. She wouldn't have fallen for an asshole, and an asshole wouldn't have had the good judgment to hang on to a woman like Daisy.

My brain immediately went to Griffen and Hope. Hope had always been kind. Shouldn't that mean I could trust Griffen?

The answer was a resounding no, because Hope always had a soft spot for Griffen, even when we were kids. I knew she was in love with him; it was all over her face every time she looked at him. He seemed to feel the same way about her, but that didn't mean he deserved her. The Hope I'd grown up with would have put up with a lot of shit from Griffen before she fell out of love.

And even if Hope and Royal were good people, it didn't mean they hadn't known about the kidnapping and left me to die along with Ford and our father.

Though I had to admit, that was seeming less and less likely. Surely one of them would have said something by now if they knew the truth. The story about me dropping out of college to join the army hung over all of us.

The only people who knew it for a lie were those who knew the truth about the kidnapping. And so far, Griffen, Royal, and Hope were doing a great job acting like they thought it was the gospel truth. I'd even pressed the lie the day of the bonfire, and Griffen hadn't pushed back. They could be playing a long game or not know how to broach the subject, but my gut said they were in the dark. Which left the real question—when was I going to tell them the truth?

That was a problem for another day. Today was for Nicky. The scent of vanilla and sugar hit me as I pushed open the door to Sweetheart Bakery, decorated in orange and black streamers hung with black bats. A stuffed witch who looked a lot like Daisy's Grams stirred a cauldron on the table in the corner.

Daisy wasn't in the front of the bakery like I'd expected she would be when I walked through the door. Instead, her grandmother stood behind the register, her long silver braid pulled in front of her shoulder and a welcoming smile on her face.

She sent me a friendly wink. "Finn Sawyer, you're the last person I'd expect to see in here. Daisy tells me everything that comes out of your kitchen is just magnificent. And she says you give her a run for the money when it comes to baking."

The compliment settled in my gut like a slug of hot chocolate, drawing a smile to my face. "I don't know that I'd go that far, Mrs. Hutchins. I'm not bad when it comes to baking—I have to be good to hit my sweet tooth—but you and Daisy have something special."

"Well, that's certainly true. Still doesn't answer my question. What brings you in today? Did Savannah send you for some of our ginger molasses cookies? They're her favorite."

"Good to know," I murmured as I filed that tidbit away for later. "I need an edge when I get on her nerves. Why don't you pack me some of those cookies?"

She chuckled and started gathering them into a small white bag.

"But I'm really here for Nicky," I said. "He has that cold that's been going around, and he has to skip trick-or-treat."

"Oh, that poor boy!" she said. "What a time to be sick."

"He's pretty miserable," I agreed. "I'm doing an at-home trick-or-treat and scavenger hunt. It's not the same as going out with the bigger kids, but at least he gets to put on his costume and get some candy. I have the stuff to make his favorite marshmallow squares and brownie bites, but the store was out of any decent candy. Royal said Daisy had been working on some chocolates. Can you help me out?"

Mrs. Hutchins beamed with pride. "You came to the right place. Daisy got it in her head she wanted to add a confectionery section, and she's been making truffles and some other goodies." Crossing to the other side of the counter, she stopped behind a case of handmade truffles, chocolate-covered pretzels, and peanut butter cups.

"This looks amazing," I said, throwing out my backup idea to hit the drugstore for candy. Royal was right; Sweetheart Bakery had exactly what I needed. If I'd had time, I could have made some of this myself, but I had a scavenger hunt to arrange, not to mention lunch and dinner to get together. This was perfect.

"Pick me out whatever you think Nicky would like."

A few minutes later, she handed me a box stuffed with sweets and named a price I knew didn't cover even a quarter of what she'd packed in there. I tried to protest, but Daisy's grandmother shook her head firmly. "You tell Nicky to come in and see me the next time his mama or Miss Martha brings him into town. I'll have a cookie and a cocoa with his name on it."

"I'll tell him," I promised, hefting the box under my arm. Mrs. Hutchins had definitely gone overboard. I couldn't say a thing, considering the huge batch of marshmallow squares and brownie bites I had planned. And I couldn't bring myself to care.

As I drove home, I wondered when was the last time I did something for someone else with nothing to gain for myself? It shamed me to say that I couldn't remember. I'd been the center of my life for so many years, first out of sheer self-preservation, then out of habit. I made food for people all the time, but that was for a paycheck. My professional pride and satisfaction in my work was for me.

This whole trick-or-treat thing was for Nicky, and damn, it felt good to do something just because it would make Nicky smile. Because he was a good kid in a crappy situation. I knew my last-minute trick-or-treat and scavenger hunt wasn't the same as going out on Halloween with his friends. It wouldn't be as good as the bonfire at the Inn, but it would be better than nothing.

At the least, I had everything I needed to get him his sugar fix. Back in my own kitchen, I unloaded my haul, mixed up the marshmallow squares, and got the brownie bites in the oven.

Savannah lifted a hand in a wave as she rushed past me, disappearing down the hall to her apartment. As she opened the door, I caught the sound of Nicky's wet, hacking cough. He sounded like shit. Poor kid. He was getting shafted on the best holiday of the year. I couldn't stop hearing the tearful misery in his voice as he begged Savannah to let him trick-or-treat. I couldn't erase the pain in her voice as she'd told him no.

She'd done the right thing. The Mom thing. I'd never really appreciated that aspect of being a parent. The hard parts. I didn't have much in the way of good examples. Not since my mother died.

This Halloween plan wasn't just for Nicky. Savannah

loved her son, and I heard how hard it had been for her to tell him he couldn't go. Not that this was for her. Neither were those cookies I'd brought home. I could badger Daisy for the recipe and make them myself, but I wasn't going to.

Why would I? It's not like I could barter cookies for sex.

Could I? Not likely, and I wasn't interested in sex with Savannah, anyway.

God, I was a liar.

I was very interested in sex with Savannah; I just wasn't doing anything about it.

I wanted to. I'd kissed her on an impulse—the way I did most things that didn't have to do with cooking. She was gorgeous. Always had been, even before she hit puberty and grew all those lush curves I wanted to get my hands on.

Even when she was a little kid, she'd been beautiful. Her wild, sunset curls paired with those cool gray eyes. Fire and ice. And she'd had a mouth on her as a kid. Not enough to cause trouble, but enough to let everyone know she wasn't to be messed with.

Savannah was smart and passionate. And in the dark, the flush on her cheeks when she'd tasted her stolen dessert had been magnetic. I hadn't tried to stop myself. I'd grabbed her and kissed her, and fuck, it had been worth it. Feeling her come, the sweet, sharp gasps in my ear, her body writhing against mine. That had not been what I expected. Not at all.

I'd come within a breath of fucking her right there on the island. I did not need my conscience to tell me that was a bad idea. Not because she could have me kicked out of Heartstone Manor. Because this was Savannah. She was not the kind of woman who fucked her employer's brother, whom she was also supervising in our shared workplace.

With a spurt of shame, I remembered what I'd said

about her all those years ago in the cafeteria. *It's the fucking Sahara in that cunt.* God, I'd been a dickhead. What a shitty thing to say about a girl who'd never done a fucking thing to me. I just couldn't stand the idea of an asshole like Murphy touching her. Thinking about her. So, I'd made sure no one gave her a second look.

All these years later, I still felt bad about it. There was no way I was going to treat her like she was just a convenient body this time around. I owed her better than that. Anyway, my gut said she wasn't the kind of woman who fucked around, not at work, not at all. Which had me wondering how long it had been for her.

No, no, don't go down that path. Do not think about it.

Because I had a sneaking suspicion that I was the first man to give her an orgasm since her husband had died. And I did not need that thought in my head.

Come on, my evil side whispered in my ear. *You can't let a woman like that go unsatisfied.*

Shut up, I ordered myself. My evil side had been whispering things like that in my ear since the moment she left my arms and disappeared down the dark hall to her little apartment, the sound of her orgasm fresh in my ear.

The issue wasn't sex. The two of us would be brilliant at sex. No question about that. But, bottom line, I was almost positive Savannah was not a casual kind of woman. There wasn't a thing in her life she approached casually. I couldn't make myself believe the exception would be sex with me.

I had it on good authority that I was the crappiest of partners. I tried it once, the whole girlfriend/love thing. In my midtwenties, once I'd settled into a good job at a high-end restaurant in France. I was close to happy for once, learning, making friends, with enough in the bank to pay my rent. After the way the prior few years had gone, that was close to heaven.

Marie had been a sous chef at the restaurant across the street. One night, over a few bottles of wine, I fell in love. She was gorgeous, with dark hair she wore in punky spikes and huge blue eyes with the longest lashes. Her saucy French accent made me crazy with lust. Overflowing with talent and the temper to go with it, she entranced me. We spent eight blissful months cooking and fucking and drinking. I could have stayed with her forever. Then she dumped me.

I'd been as heartbroken and devastated as a self-centered twenty-seven-year-old could be. She said I was selfish. That my job and my ambitions always came first. She hadn't understood when I went after and got the job she'd been working toward. Hey, this was a meritocracy, right? Let the best chef win and all that. It had never occurred to me that she'd be pissed. She loved me, didn't she?

Looking back, I could see it all with crystal clear clarity. Marie had been right to kick me to the curb. Everything had always been about me, and she deserved more than that. She deserved a partner who could put her first. That wasn't me. That would never be me. I'd been raised by a selfish asshole, and the years spent trying to keep myself alive had honed that same selfishness in me.

A good partner had to be able to put the other person first, and I couldn't do that. I could be a decent guy, sure. Hooking Nicky up with a fun Halloween was nice. I wasn't a monster. But one act of kindness didn't make me a good partner. Just like Marie, Savannah deserved that. A man who could put her happiness first. God knows her husband hadn't. I wasn't going to be one more man who used her strength and didn't give back.

I was good for orgasms and food. That was it. If she wanted something casual, I was here. God knows I was willing. Something more than casual was not on my radar.

I didn't think it was on hers either. Savannah wasn't looking for a boyfriend. Even the sound of it didn't fit. *Boyfriend.* What were we, seventeen?

I wouldn't seduce her. I could. That's not arrogance. That's reality. She came apart in my arms from little more than a kiss. What she needed was a good, hard fuck. All she had to do was ask.

I wasn't holding my breath. Savannah was the most disciplined woman I knew. If I was hoping she'd break before I did, I wouldn't put the odds on me.

That was fine. I had more on my mind than Savannah Miles. Like finishing my plans for Halloween.

Chapter Thirteen

FINN

I barely saw Savannah all day. She spent as much time as she could in her little apartment with Nicky, who coughed and sneezed his way through the hours. Every time I saw her, she was pouring another glass of juice or scrubbing her hands under hot water.

I didn't blame her. Nicky was great, but at the moment, he was spewing germs everywhere he went, which made this trick-or-treat and scavenger hunt possibly a bad idea. I'd asked, and his costume had a full-face mask, so I figured that would be good enough.

Not long after four, I headed upstairs with my assembled bags of goodies for our trick-or-treat volunteers to hand out. Griffen, Hope, and Royal were still in the office. I handed Griffen their bag of treats, saying to him while glancing at Hope, "You should hand these out. I don't want him to sneeze on Hope and get her sick."

Griffen's eyes clouded. Hope immediately shook her head. "I'll be fine." Shooting Griffen a look, she nudged his shoulder with her own. "I'll be fine. This isn't the first cold that's gone through the house since I've been pregnant. Though hopefully it's the last."

Hope rubbed one hand over her very swollen abdomen. Not much more than a month left. Pretty soon, the big day would be up to the baby. I didn't want to think about that. Hope was tall but slender, and that baby was anything but. Lately, I wasn't sure how she could get up once she sat down.

Griffen opened the Halloween-themed gift bag I'd grabbed at the grocery store and peered inside. "Nice," he commented.

Royal did the same. "You stopped by Sweetheart. Did you save a truffle for yourself? Daisy does things with chocolate . . ." He stared at the ceiling with a knowing grin. "They're seriously good," he finished, still grinning.

"Daisy's Grams was generous, so I snagged a few for myself and Savannah." I hadn't had a chance to give Savannah hers yet. She had her hands full with a sick kid and her regular heavy workload. Griffen wouldn't mind her taking it easy when Nicky was sick, but Savannah would mind.

"Give us ten minutes," Griffen said, "and we'll head upstairs."

My spur-of-the-moment Halloween plan hadn't taken the whole day, but on top of handling meals and planning shopping for the week, it had been a busy day with still more to get done before it was over.

I threw a "Thanks," over my shoulder as I headed for the front hall and the stairs to the second level. Miss Martha met me on my way.

"I wasn't going to come by today," she said. "With August and Thatcher already at the Inn helping Tenn with the Halloween party and Nicky sick, but Savannah told me your plan when I called earlier, and I thought I could pitch in."

"That would be great. I'm just headed upstairs to talk to Aunt Ophelia and Claudia. I can definitely use you up there." I looped an arm through hers. "Have you seen Nicky yet? He looked awful this morning, and he was miserable about Halloween."

"It was very sweet of you to step in. He's looking forward to whatever you have up your sleeve. As long as it involves candy."

"Oh, it definitely involves candy," I assured her, leading her up the stairs to the second level. "It's not Halloween without a sugar overload."

Since no one else from my generation was home from work at this hour, Miss Martha and I headed to the guest wing to find my Aunt Ophelia and Parker's mother-in-law, Claudia, playing cards in the sitting room of Ophelia's suite.

Aunt Ophelia had moved in shortly after Prentice died. Actually, she'd moved in the second Savannah had her suite functional. According to Miss Martha, Prentice had stopped entertaining guests a few years before he died. Sometime after that, something had gone wrong with the electrical and plumbing in the guest wing—maintenance was never-ending in a house like this—and Prentice had just . . . let it go.

As much as he'd loved Heartstone Manor, I couldn't understand why he hadn't rushed to stop the decay of his beloved home. In the months since his death, none of us had found the answer. It had taken Savannah weeks to get things working in the guest wing again.

Once there were lights and running water, Aunt Ophelia arrived, accompanied by a truckload of trunks and her son Bryce. We didn't mind Aunt Ophelia. She was flighty and a little oblivious, but she'd always loved us kids. Our cousin Bryce, we minded. My siblings and I had our differences, but we were united in our hatred of our cousin Bryce. He'd been a spoiled little shit as a kid and was even worse as an adult. Until recently.

After almost getting her killed, Bryce had saved Parker's life—or tried to, which gave him a little grace. But not much. He left town shortly after we were sure Parker would be okay.

The whole scene had been nuts.

Parker, my younger sister, was always perfect. Always well behaved. Always did what she was told.

But perfect Parker, who never put a foot wrong, had served divorce papers to one of Claudia's sons and was currently living with the other in Heartstone Manor. I would have thought Claudia would be furious, but she'd been thrilled.

By all accounts, Claudia had loved her younger son, Tyler, Parker's first husband. Unfortunately for her—and for Parker—it turned out Tyler had been batshit crazy.

Aside from abusing Parker for most of their marriage, something no one had known about, Tyler had gone off the rails the day Parker decided she'd had enough and filed for divorce. Tyler hadn't liked the idea of divorce. Especially after Claudia cut him off financially. She loved her son, but she also loved her daughter-in-law.

Tyler had decided he'd rather be a widower than a divorced man and set about trying to kill both Parker and his brother Nash. With them dead, he was convinced his mother would have to put him back in the will. Who else would she have left but her devoted son Tyler?

We'd all learned that Nash had been head over heels for Parker since the day they met—at her wedding to Tyler.

Nash had bided his time for years, keeping his distance. The second Parker dumped Tyler, Nash had been there to help her pick up the pieces.

My guess was that the Claudia I knew was a shadow of her real self. Tyler was dead, killed by Hawk to save Parker and Nash, and Claudia was grieving. Tyler had been insane, but he was also her son, and despite his horrible faults, she loved him. A week after Tyler's death, she came to Heartstone Manor for a visit and never left.

No one was eager for her to go. Both Nash and Parker loved her. They got edgy every time the subject of Claudia going anywhere came up. For her part, I think Claudia needed her family around her.

Aunt Ophelia, who'd been at loose ends since Bryce left, loved having another woman her age in the house. It helped that they'd bumped into each other socially over the years and had always liked each other.

Claudia and Ophelia had fallen into an instant camaraderie, spending their days playing cards and gossiping, drinking tea, and going for walks around the still barren gardens or heading into town to shop and, as they put it, stretch their legs.

Claudia and Aunt Ophelia greeted Miss Martha more like a long-lost compatriot than as a former housekeeper, and their easy, affectionate welcome made something in me relax. I still wasn't used to so much friendliness in Heartstone Manor. Griffen, Hope, and Royal always seemed at ease when they worked together, happy to be in each other's company. Aunt Ophelia had welcomed Claudia, and they in turn treated Miss Martha like a close friend. I hadn't expected any of it. For so long, Heartstone Manor meant competition and isolation. Loneliness. Betrayal. But that was my father's house. Apparently things had changed.

I watched Miss Martha with Claudia and Aunt Ophelia, waiting for a break in the conversation so I could give them their instructions before I went to get Nicky and Savannah. I didn't think Miss Martha spent that much time with Ophelia and Claudia, but there'd been a few afternoons I sent up a tea tray and gave the kids and the ladies their tea together in the sunroom.

Aunt Ophelia had declared that the boys needed to learn some manners. I suspected Ophelia and Claudia both wanted grandchildren, but were willing to settle for a crew of sort-of grand nephews.

The women must have hit it off because they'd asked to have tea together regularly since that first experiment. Their openness to Miss Martha still surprised me. I was too used to my father's disdain for anyone he considered staff. I liked that the rest of the family didn't share his attitude.

Maybe they were taking Griffen's cue. Griffen treated Miss Martha like a surrogate mother. Definitely not like a member of staff. When I thought about it, it was the same way he treated Savannah. Not that he treated Savannah like a mother. More like a sister or something. It made sense, I guess, since she'd been a kid when he left, just like me.

"Let me see what you've got there, Finn," Aunt Ophelia said, shaking me out of my mental wanderings.

I handed both her and Claudia their trick-or-treat bags filled with goodies. "Oh, you got some of Daisy's truffles!" Claudia noticed.

"Am I the only one who didn't know about Daisy's truffles?" I asked.

"She popped by the other day when she got back from the bakery and had tea with us," Aunt Ophelia explained. "She has a hand with chocolate."

"I'll say," Claudia agreed. "Those champagne truffles

were divine. We have to go to town tomorrow and pick up some more."

She and Claudia smiled at each other before Ophelia continued. "Wonderful idea," Aunt Ophelia said before looking back to me. "I didn't mean the candy. I want to know what that is." She pointed to the scavenger hunt map in my hand.

"Oh, yeah. So we have the trick-or-treating upstairs, and whoever's at the last door will also have a map." I held up the map drawn with bright colors and clues I hoped weren't too obvious.

"Finn Sawyer, what have you done?" Miss Martha exclaimed, plucking the map from my hand and examining it. "This is wonderful!"

I shrugged, suddenly uncomfortable. "I'm not much of an artist, but I hid some things downstairs. I thought it would be fun since he doesn't get to do the apple bobbing or the haunted maze or any of the other stuff."

"You're a very kind man," Miss Martha murmured.

I shook my head, keeping my opinions to myself. What Miss Martha didn't know wouldn't hurt her. If I started in on all the reasons I was a shithead, she'd only disagree. Miss Martha had always liked me. God knows why.

If she knew the things going through my head about her daughter . . . But she didn't, and she never would. She'd probably murder me in my sleep. I didn't want to lose one of the few allies I had around here.

"What a sweet idea," Claudia exclaimed, beaming up at me.

"Let me see that," Aunt Ophelia demanded, holding out a hand.

Miss Martha gave her the map and turned to me. "Nicky's going to love it, Finn."

I shrugged, wanting to squirm under the eyes of the three older women staring at me, brows raised.

"You always were a clever boy, Finn. And a sweet one," Aunt Ophelia said, sending me a beaming smile. Claudia and Miss Martha nodded, smiling along with her.

"Nicky will be thrilled," Claudia added. "You've saved Halloween."

I actually felt the heat of a blush hit my cheeks. Okay, that was enough of this. I was going to have to throw a head-chef-style tantrum or something just to get my equilibrium back.

It wasn't a big deal. I was sliding the kid some candy and giving him an excuse to wear his costume. I wasn't a saint or anything.

I wasn't *sweet*, for fuck's sake. I'd never been *sweet*. I'd been a pain in the ass as a kid. Claudia hadn't been around, but Aunt Ophelia and Miss Martha knew the truth. I'd been in trouble all the time.

Didn't they remember?

I'd been kicked out of Laurel Country Day for setting the headmaster's office on fire.

I wasn't *sweet*.

I didn't have the heart to remind them I was still the same Finn they'd always known. Anyway, it was time to get Nicky and get things moving along. I still had to feed everyone after we gave Nicky his Halloween adventure.

Clearing my throat, I said, "Yeah. Anyway, Nicky's going to head up in a few minutes." Turning to Claudia, I asked, "Do you mind going back to your room? So he has more doors to knock on."

"Of course," Claudia agreed.

"I'll be in the empty room next door," Miss Martha added, holding up the scavenger hunt map. "Have

Savannah text us when you're heading up the stairs, and we'll all go to our assigned locations."

"Thank you, ladies," I said and backed out of the room, distinctly uncomfortable with their approving smiles and compliments. This was definitely my last good deed for a while. My reputation couldn't stand another episode like this one.

Chapter Fourteen

FINN

Downstairs, I found Nicky and Savannah outside the kitchen. Nicky's face was flushed and his nose was red, but for the moment, it wasn't dripping snot. That was a win in my book.

"How's the fever?" I asked. Savannah let out a sigh as she zipped the back of Nicky's bright yellow Pikachu costume.

"Lower, but still there," she said.

"No school tomorrow!" came Nicky's muffled voice from inside the costume. The costume covered him from head to toe, the mask sewn into a matching hood that zipped to the full, fuzzy yellow costume. Good for germ spread, but it had to be warm in there.

"You look awesome, little man," I said. "You look exactly like Pikachu."

"I love Pikachu," Nicky said.

I could relate. I loved Pikachu when I was his age, and I had a box full of cards upstairs to prove it. I hoped he would like the one I picked out for him. We headed out the door.

Savannah looked up and gave me a wobbly smile, dark

circles under her eyes. "Thanks, Finn. He's really excited. This is definitely making up for, you know, everything else." Clearly she didn't want to mention the festivities at the Inn and the fun Nicky was missing.

"Long day?" I asked with a nod and a faint smile.

"Yeah. I had a lot planned, and then, you know, little guy here." She rolled her shoulders as if trying to shed the weight of fatigue dragging her down. I imagined she hadn't gotten much sleep, given the way Nicky'd been coughing and sneezing most of the day. Still, the smile she sent Nicky was gentle and warm with love.

"Everyone wants their mom when they feel like crap," I said.

"Don't I know it? Pretty much the reason I'm back here," Savannah said.

"Speaking of Miss Martha, she wants you to text her when we hit the stairs so they can get into place."

Savannah pulled her phone from her pocket, murmuring, "We can see Griffen and Hope first, give the others an extra minute to get to their rooms."

We went straight ahead to the top of the staircase. The master suite was the only one in the central part of the house, and it took up most of the floor. Nicky hesitated before raising his hand to knock, looking over his shoulder at his mother, though I doubted he could see her well through the eyeholes in the mask.

"Go ahead, buddy," I said. "Give it a good hard knock."

Nicky did, his tiny fist barely making an impact on the thick wooden door. It swung open a moment later. Nicky stared at Griffen in silence. I nudged him in the back and stage whispered, "Trick-or-treat."

With a giggle, Nicky repeated after me. "Trick-or-treat, Mr. Griffen."

Hope opened the door wider and smiled down at Nicky, staying further back, out of the range of germs, probably to keep Griffen from putting her in a bubble for the rest of her pregnancy.

Leaning down, she said, "Nicky, that costume is amazing. Good taste. I'm not going to tell you not to eat all this at once, because I'm sure your mom will handle that. Happy Halloween!"

Griffen handed Nicky the bag filled with candy. Nicky opened the bag and gasped with delight. "Thanks, Miss Hope! Thanks, Mr. Griffen!"

Savannah smiled at both of them. "Thank you both so much."

"Any time," Griffen said with a smile of his own. "We didn't really do anything. This one was all Finn."

They all looked at me with that same approving expression I'd gotten from Aunt Ophelia, Claudia, and Miss Martha. It took everything I had not to squirm. I was not used to being the good guy. I didn't think I liked it.

I mean, the excitement in Nicky's voice, his giggle, all that was fucking awesome. Absolutely. Especially after hearing him cry that morning. That part made me feel like the fucking king of the world. But my siblings and the mom generation looking at me with gentle approval? That was just weird. It didn't fit the person I knew I was. I think I was Nicky's age the last time I got those looks from anyone, especially anyone I was related to.

We followed Nicky back to the head of the stairs and to the guest wing, guiding him first to Ophelia's door, where she ooh'd and ahh'd and made much of his costume and how great he looked.

Then to Claudia, where he got the same treatment. Finally, his arms loaded with orange bags stuffed with candy, we hit the empty room Miss Martha was in. She took Nicky in with a broad smile and said, "Pikachu! You didn't tell me Pikachu was going to be here! I can't believe Nicky's missing it!"

Nicky giggled again, the sound catching in his throat and ending in a cough, then rolling back into a giggle.

Savannah nudged him in the back. "Pikachu, what do you need to say?"

"Oh! Trick-or-treat!" Nicky said, his voice weird. I wasn't sure if he was trying to pretend he was Pikachu or if it was messed up from all the coughing.

Miss Martha handed Nicky his bag. "You have one more surprise," she said, handing over the map I'd made. My drawing was really unimpressive. Good thing Nicky was six.

"What's this?" Nicky asked, studying it.

Both women looked at me. I cleared my throat. "It's a scavenger hunt. Downstairs. See?" I leaned down and pointed to the beginning of the dotted line on the map. "You start here. Can you guess where that is?"

"The bottom of the steps?"

"Exactly," I said. "You start at the bottom of the steps, then you go to the first spot there." I pointed to the location of the first clue. "Follow the clues and see if you can find the prize at the end."

"What's the prize?" Nicky asked, bouncing on the balls of his feet.

"Well," I drawled, dragging out the word. "If I told you, it wouldn't be a surprise."

Nicky took off with a screech of glee. Miss Martha followed us out. "I'm going to help Kitty get set up for the dinner service so you two can watch Nicky do the scavenger hunt."

I started to protest, but she shook her head. "You spent so much time putting this together. You should get to watch."

I won't say I didn't appreciate it. I definitely wanted to see Nicky's face when he found the prize at the end of the scavenger hunt. I wasn't entirely sure he would think it was as cool as I did, but based on his costume, I had a feeling it would be a hit.

We caught up to Nicky at the top of the stairs, and I tugged him back in the direction we'd come from. "You want to take the elevator?"

"Yes! Yes!"

Generally, the kids in the house were forbidden to use the elevator, for a million excellent reasons. This one was an upgrade from the one we'd had when I was a kid. Much safer, but kids still weren't allowed to touch it.

Nicky followed us in and squeezed between us. The mask definitely made it hard for him to see. "Can I do the buttons?" he asked, his hand hovering at his side, ready to press.

"You can do the buttons," I agreed. "But first, do you want to take that mask off? You're going to need your eyes for the scavenger hunt."

A hard shake of his head. "It's not a mask. I'm Pikachu!"

Savannah bit her lip to stop a laugh, her gray eyes sparkling with amusement.

"Yeah, got it. You just remind me of Nicky, so I forgot," I said, not bothering to hide my smile. Seeing Halloween through Nicky's eyes was something new. It was impossible to be jaded in the face of his pure and honest excitement. For the first time since I'd been a kid myself, Halloween felt new. Thrilling. Maybe this was why people had kids.

Nicky pressed the button for the lower level, going stiff

as the elevator lurched into motion. When I pushed the door open, he headed for the base of the stairs with another shout of glee and studied the map, surreptitiously tugging his mask into the right alignment so he could see what he was looking at.

Fortunately, he headed off in the right direction toward the pantry April had been in the night I'd ruined the soup. I didn't keep much in there these days. Not like Mrs. Bailey had. It was mostly overflow—extra bags of flour, sugar, rice, canned goods. Staples I didn't need on a daily basis.

Nicky hunted around, finally locating the green army man on the second shelf, along with a small card that had a hint for the next location on the map. I'd drawn the map in a vague approximation of the lower level, but there were far more doors in real life than there were on the map. Without the clues, Nicky couldn't tell which doors he needed to open. But, considering he was six and also in kindergarten, I'd made the clues pretty straightforward.

Nicky stared at the map, thinking out loud. "I don't . . . Cuz there's no medicine down here, Mom. But, I don't know, because medicine isn't balls anyway, but—"

Resisting the urge to give him a hint, I bit my tongue, liking that I could follow his reasoning, especially considering the confusion on Savannah's face. The answer clicked in Nicky's head, and he took off like a shot, headed straight for the gym and the neat stack of medicine balls that had been in the corner as long as I could remember. Tucked behind them, he found the yo-yo.

And so we went on, Nicky nailing almost every clue, with only a few hints from me, until he ended up in the scullery. Even in the dimming light from the windows, I noted with pride that every surface in here sparkled. I was too well trained to leave behind a dirty dish or countertop.

Nicky turned in a slow circle, looked back at the clue again, and when the answer sparked in his mind, he lurched for the faucet. From behind it, he drew a slightly beat-up Pikachu Pokemon card.

"It's a Pikachu!" he shouted, "But I've never seen this one." His voice trailed off in confusion.

"It's a, uh—" I cleared my throat. "It was mine when I was your age."

Savannah turned worried eyes to me. Under her breath, she said, "Finn, you can't. I mean, that must be valuable."

"It's not," I said, just as quietly. "Not the way you mean. It's a little too beat-up to be worth real money. It's sentimental, but it's just rotting away upstairs, and I figured Nicky would appreciate it."

I shifted under the concern in her gaze, suddenly wishing I was anywhere else. Didn't I have dinner to finish? I wanted to pass the card off as no big deal, but Nicky's reaction was clear. The card was a big deal, and we all knew it.

Still, we didn't have to make a thing about it. Couldn't I do something nice without everyone freaking out?

"Oh, man, this is so cool." Nicky turned the card over, studying every detail. "August is gonna be so jealous." He turned his face up to me, tugging at his mask until his eyes slid into view through the mask. "I'm not trading this one, Mr. Finn. No way. This one I'm keeping forever."

He threw his arms around my waist in a tight hug. I dropped my hand to give him an awkward pat on the top of his fuzzy yellow head before giving in to the urge to squeeze his shoulder. "You're welcome, Nicky. Now, uh, listen, don't eat too much of that candy right now. It won't feel good on your throat."

"I won't," he shouted, running out of the room and back

toward the main kitchen, probably to tear off his mask and dive into the bags stuffed with candy.

That had been easy. I'm not saying parenting is easy. The circles under Savannah's eyes would have told me it wasn't, even if I couldn't guess for myself. But making Nicky happy? Saving his Halloween? No big deal. A few hours of my time, and in return, I got that huge smile and that hug.

From my end, it was well worth it, and that tugged at me. It wasn't that hard to make a kid happy. So why had no one ever bothered with me? After my mother died, I disappeared into the background. Prentice had been done with parenting, and there hadn't really been anyone else. Miss Martha loved me, but she wasn't my mom, and we'd both known that if she showed any of us too much attention, Prentice would have gotten rid of her. In his world, family and staff did not mix.

Back then, the only time anyone showed me any attention was when I was causing trouble. Was it any surprise I'd grown into an asshole of a teenager? I'd always thought it must have been too hard, too much work to bother with me. Watching Nicky run through the kitchen, I had to face the uncomfortable truth that it really wasn't that hard to give a kid some attention. All it took was someone willing to go just a little bit out of their way. When it had come to me, no one had cared enough to put in the time. Savannah's voice pulled me from memories I'd just as soon forget.

"Finn, that was, uh— That was really sweet of you. I appreciate it." Savannah sounded at a loss for words for the first time in her life.

I shifted, avoiding her eyes. There was that word again. *Sweet*. Ugh. "Yeah, it's fine. It was just, you know, he was so upset about missing Halloween, and I didn't— I just wanted to help out."

"You did. This was, uh, this was amazing. I, um, thank you. Really."

You could have cut the awkwardness with a knife. Suddenly, the scullery was far too small for two people. A little insane since we used to have a staff of four in here back in the day, but never mind. It was way too small for Savannah and me.

It was bad enough for the others to call me sweet. Hearing it from Savannah? No. She was the last person who should ever think I was *sweet*. Given the way I'd treated her when we were kids, she shouldn't be able to get her lips to form the word *sweet* if it was aimed in my direction.

I needed to get back into the kitchen, where everything made sense.

"I'm, uh, I'm gonna finish up dinner. I got something for you from Sweetheart Bakery. From Daisy's Grams. It's, uh, it's on the kitchen table."

I couldn't seem to get a word out without tripping over it. The whole trick-or-treat thing left me feeling weird. The second Nicky saw that card, I knew my instincts were right. Nicky knew exactly how awesome it was, and that was fucking cool.

But the rest of it—everybody acting so proud, with their soft looks and gentle smiles. It's not what I was used to, and I wasn't sure I liked it. On top of that, Savannah being awkward and, fine, me being all awkward . . .

I stopped myself. Why was I being awkward? What was my problem? It wasn't a big deal. Nicky was a cool kid, and he was sick. I did him a favor. Nothing for everyone to get all worked up over. I rolled my shoulders, watching as

Savannah fled the scullery. She strode through the kitchen, slowing when she saw the bag of chocolates from Sweetheart Bakery on the table. She lifted it, unfolded the top, and took a deep breath.

I could almost smell the rich chocolate, sugar, and a hint of vanilla. Ever since the night I'd kissed her, all it took was a scent of chocolate to bring me right back to the feel of her under my hands. Her gasps, the heat of her kiss.

Okay, I'd rather go back to awkward. Hadn't I decided that wasn't going to happen again? I'd definitely decided that wasn't going to happen again.

She folded the bag closed and looked at the second, larger bag. Lifting it carefully, she opened it and smiled a secret smile. Mrs. Hutchins had been right. Savannah loved those ginger molasses cookies.

Gathering her booty in her arms, Savannah hurried down the hall after Nicky, probably ready to get him out of that costume and back into bed. Without his stash of candy.

I watched her go with an odd sense of loss.

Which didn't make any sense. I should be glad everything had gone well. Nicky was happy, and he was out of my hair in time for me to finish dinner on schedule. What more did I want?

Nothing. Everything was exactly as planned. Right?

Right.

Wishing I believed myself, I returned to the kitchen and got busy with my dinner prep.

Chapter Fifteen
SAVANNAH

"No, Finn, you mind your own work. I've got this," my mother said, shooing Finn away as if he were a pest. The side of Finn's mouth quirked, and he shook his head but didn't protest.

"Just give me a second, Miss Martha, and I'll be out of your hair." He added a sprig of rosemary to the roast in front of him, checking something, the seasoning maybe—I don't know, I'm no cook—before he slid it in the oven. I tried not to look at his butt when he leaned over, but really, could anyone blame me? It was a fairly spectacular ass as asses went.

It was one of the bonuses of working at Heartstone Manor. There was no shortage of attractive men. So much eye candy. Not that I wanted to date any of them. And not that it would have been the slightest bit appropriate if I did. This was a home. It was my home, in a way. It was also my place of employment. And I did not need to complicate my life like that. But I could look all I wanted.

Looking was free.

I caught my mother's eyes on Finn's ass and almost

kicked her under the table, but I didn't want her to know I'd noticed her noticing. She was my mom, but she was still a woman, and Finn had an ass worth looking at.

"I'll get tea together," I said. "We can have a quiet one before the boys are home from school."

"No," my mother said, rising. "I'll get tea together. You sit. Put your feet up."

"Mom—"

"Savannah, if anybody knows your workload, it's me, and on top of that, you're moving tomorrow, and Nicky's just barely over his cold. Sit, put your feet up. I'll bring you some tea and a snack."

I sat. She was right. It had been almost a week since Halloween, and, like most kids, Nicky had bounced back quickly. I'd somehow escaped getting sick, a fact I was extremely grateful for. Moving was stressful enough. I did not want to do it with a cold.

On his way out the door, Finn added, "There are some ginger molasses cookies in the breadbox. Daisy's recipe. Or as close as I could get."

"Really?" I couldn't help asking.

"Really," Finn confirmed. "I'm trying to crack it. Let me know how close they are."

"Daisy wouldn't give you the recipe?"

"She might, but I don't want to ask. I think I can figure it out on my own." At my confused look, Finn said, "We have a friendly competition going on. I'm trying to figure out her ginger molasses cookies, and she's determined to deconstruct those pear tarts we had last week. She swears she's almost there with the tarts."

"Mmm, those pear tarts were delicious," my mother said, preparing a plate of treats that included the ginger molasses cookies.

I was a sucker for those things. So moist and soft, with the rich mineral sweetness of molasses, the crunch of the sugar sprinkled on top, the warmth of the ginger, and just enough of a bite from . . . something. I didn't know what it was. That was for Finn to figure out. All I knew was I could live on those cookies.

Finn disappeared through the door to the kitchen, leaving us alone. My mother carried the tea tray to the table, setting cookies out on individual plates while we waited for the tea to steep. It still struck me sometimes how we'd flip-flopped our roles. For most of my life, she'd run this house, as at home in this kitchen as the family chefs. Now that was my job. And while she'd always be my mom, I'd become a mother myself. Somewhere along the line, she'd also become my closest friend.

Taking the seat opposite me, she sat back, smiling as she took in the kitchen. In my mind, she didn't look a day older than she had when I was Nicky's age. I knew that couldn't be true, and there was more silver in her strawberry curls than there had been years ago, maybe a few more lines around her gray eyes, but she was still active, still vibrant. Still sharp as a tack.

"I have to admit," she said, "I had no idea Finn could handle a kitchen like this."

I'd been thinking the same thing. When he was given the job, I'd balked partly because I thought I'd be stuck working next to a jerk all day. But the other part was worry that he'd double my workload. It was one thing to be able to create a delicious dish. His midnight kitchen invasions had proven that he could cook. Running a kitchen that serves three meals a day to a household as large as ours requires a skill set above and beyond merely cooking well. A skill set Finn appeared to have.

"Me neither," I agreed. "We knew he'd worked as a cook at some point. I guess we thought that's what he did in the army. Though now I'm not so sure about that. Griffen mentioned the army, and Finn was weird about it."

"And you haven't asked?"

"No. I don't know. I feel uncomfortable prying, I guess."

Why hadn't I just asked him? It's not like we didn't see each other here and there all day, every day. It seemed too personal, and I was wary of getting too personal with Finn. It wasn't a good idea.

I'd been spending far too much time trying not to think about that kiss. The kiss that hadn't been repeated, no matter how much I wished it had. And how much I knew I shouldn't.

My mother poured the tea. I lifted my cup, letting the steam disguise the faint pink I could feel on my cheeks just from remembering that kiss. I had to be careful. My mother saw everything.

Almost as if she was reading my mind, or part of it, she said, "You know, now that things are steadier here, once you and Nicky move into the cottage, you'll be settled. You still like the job?"

"You know I do. I love Heartstone Manor and working for Griffen and Hope—"

"Is nothing like working for Prentice," my mother finished for me. With a fond, maternal smile, she went on, "I think Griffen is a throwback to his ancestors. They were gentlemen through and through. I never pictured Hope as the mistress of Heartstone Manor. Mostly because she was such a shy, quiet thing as a child. But now I couldn't imagine anyone better. They run a good household, and it's lovely to see them together."

Almost in a whisper, I confessed. "I can't wait for the

baby. I don't want another one of my own. Not any time soon. My hands are full." I laughed at my understatement. "But sometimes, someone else's baby is the best. All the snuggles, none of the three a.m. feedings. And so much more sleep."

My mother nodded. "Exactly. And you have time for another down the road if you decide that's what you want."

"Any word on the nanny search?" I asked. I knew my mother had been helping Hope with interviews.

"Not so far. We had a good candidate, but she couldn't pass the security checks. There was an ex-boyfriend who'd had some trouble, and it wasn't clear exactly how ex he was. We're still looking. We have someone promising coming in tomorrow."

Mentally, I crossed my fingers. I still wasn't sure how I felt about the nanny watching Nicky, but for Hope's and Griffen's sake, I wanted them to find someone before the baby got here. None of us had realized how difficult the search would be.

"What I was going to say," my mother continued, "is that you're settled. You have a home, and I'm so glad it's near me this time, even though I know you loved Richmond. You have a job that you love. Nicky likes school. Maybe it's time to start dating. You're too young to be alone for the rest of your life." She raised her eyebrows in a quick, silly wiggle before taking a delicate sip of tea.

"Absolutely not," I said.

"Savannah, honey—"

"Just no, Mom." Raising a hand to stop her protest, I continued. "I love you, and I know you're saying this out of love, but no. I just— I don't know, just the thought of going on the apps trying to figure out which way to swipe? What to wear? What to say?" I shook my head in a firm negative.

145

"I want to enjoy feeling settled before I shake things up again. Dating is too much right now."

"I'm not buying that, Savannah," she said, with that mom tone that told me I wasn't going to weasel out of this conversation. "You can figure out anything you put your mind to."

I sighed. "It's not just that, Mom. It's just—" I searched for the right words. "I don't think I have it in me to be a good partner right now."

"Are you still grieving Oliver?"

"No," I said, so firmly that I realized it was true. "I think a part of me will always grieve Oliver," I explained. "I loved him. And the way he faded away, the way he left us hurt in a different way than if he'd gotten sick or been hit by a car. I'll always grieve the man I married, but this isn't about Oliver. It's just . . . I don't know. I don't think I have it in me to be a good partner right now."

I picked up the ginger molasses cookie and broke off a piece, nibbling and thinking. My mother sipped her tea and waited. I'd always loved that about her. She was full of advice, but she always knew when to wait for me to get my thoughts together. Finally, my messy tangle of emotions coalesced into words.

"I love my work," I said. "I love having you nearby and being able to spend more time with Nicky. I love my life right now. Even when it gets crazy and stressful and exhausting. I love the challenge, and I love being in charge. Plus, when the hell would I have time to date somebody?"

My mother raised one eyebrow and took another sip of tea before she said, "You make time, Savannah."

"Well, what if I don't want to?" I challenged. I'd spent so many years doing things for other people. Oliver. Nicky.

People I loved more than life. People I wanted to take care of. But when was it time for me?

"I guess I just don't want to make time for someone else, you know? That's what a partner is—someone you share your life with, and I guess I don't want to share." I paused, letting the words fade. They were true, and being selfish felt right. More right than it ever had before.

"Honey," my mother said, her voice gentle, something in her tone putting me on guard. "This isn't about finding a husband, or even a boyfriend, but—" She huffed out a breath of air. "It's been a long time for you. And everyone needs affection."

"I get plenty of affection," I protested.

"Savannah." She drawled out my name in a sigh, rolling her eyes. "I'm not talking about affection from me or Nicky."

Did my mother just tell me I needed to get laid? This must be what it feels like when your brain explodes. Even though we'd just admired the same ass, this was not the advice I needed right now—especially not from my mother.

Chapter Sixteen

SAVANNAH

"Mom, are you talking about sex?"

Her teacup clicked against the saucer. She picked up a mini vanilla scone left over from tea the day before, smoothly swiping raspberry jam over the top and adding a dollop of clotted cream.

Before she took a bite, she said, "Savannah, you're human. You need food, sleep, exercise, mental stimulation, love. And yes, you need sex."

She popped the scone in her mouth, leaving me staring at her, dumbfounded, my jaw hanging open. Had the very proper Miss Martha just told me I needed sex? Were we really going to talk about this?

"Eat the rest of your cookie, sweetheart," she said.

I broke off a piece of the cookie, savoring the sweet molasses and warm ginger as my mind reeled. "Mom." I sucked in a breath and decided to stop beating around the bush. "If you're talking about orgasms, I can handle that myself." I ended in an almost whisper. We were alone in the kitchen, but there were a lot of people in this house, and you never knew when someone might come in.

"Anyway," I pressed, "You're one to talk. You weren't exactly dating up a storm when I was growing up."

"Maybe not," she agreed in a crisp voice. Her Miss Martha voice, as I thought of it. "I didn't date much when you were young, but that didn't mean I lived like a nun either."

Her words hung in the air between us as she took another dainty sip of tea. Wait, what did that mean? She hadn't lived like a nun?

"Mom, who were you—" My hand shot up, stopping her in case she was actually going to answer. "Never mind. I didn't ask. I don't want to know. I really don't want to know."

Oh god. Now my brain was racing through all the men my mother might have had a friends-with-benefits relationship with when I was a kid. And truly, the list was endless. She knew everyone in Sawyers Bend and more than a few people in Asheville. And what did any kid really know of their parents' personal lives?

Like any child, I'd been wrapped up in my own life. If my mother said she had to run out to the store or had a book club meeting, it's not like I would have pushed for more detail. *Okay, whatever, Mom. See you later.*

The idea that some of those times she'd been out on a booty call was just . . . *Holy shit.*

I put down my teacup, tilted my head to the side, and gave her a long look. She was only fifty-eight, and she'd always been a good-looking woman. Even as a kid, I knew that. Thick strawberry blond hair, a little redder than mine, and slightly less curly. Clear, gray eyes with long, thick lashes that were killer with a swipe of mascara.

I'd gotten my build from her: tall, with broad shoulders, a small waist, full hips, and, as they used to say, an ample bosom. We both dressed it down for work—a curvy figure is not the best asset as a housekeeper, especially when Prentice Sawyer owned the house you were keeping. She kept him far away from me as soon as I'd hit puberty. I knew exactly why, and I had always been grateful for it.

I'd had my own issues when Bryce moved into Heartstone, though Griffen had made it clear he had zero tolerance for that kind of crap. He'd told Bryce, but that asshole had taken one look at my tits in my modest uniform, a uniform I'd chosen myself, and had gotten grabby. I reported the incident to Griffen, as I promised I would, but my knee in Bryce's nuts had solved the problem before Griffen needed to.

Yeah, my mom wouldn't have trouble finding a man, not today and not two decades ago. She probably had no shortage of men willing to fulfill her needs.

I shook my head. I was done thinking about my mother and sex. I was glad she wasn't lonely, but no. I made a stab at ending the conversation. "It's just not on my radar right now, Mom. Maybe, I don't know, maybe later. Maybe I'll—"

I didn't know what to say. Maybe I'd meet someone? I didn't even want to look. I just wasn't interested, and I didn't see that changing any time soon, but I knew she wouldn't accept that as my last word on the topic.

"Savannah, life is happening without you." She shook her head, and the sadness in her eyes pinched my heart. I didn't want her to be sad over me. I was fine. "You have so much to offer. I don't like seeing you alone like this. Now that you've got your feet under you again—"

"But Mom," I tried again, "I'm not alone. I have you and Nicky and Hope, plus Parker and the rest of the Sawyers. I have a job that I love, and I'm about to move into that adorable cottage that Parker's turned into a perfect gem. It's hard to believe it's the same place you lived in when I was in college. Everything is great. Can't I just coast for a while and enjoy this before I shake things up again?"

My mother's cool hand covered mine, her fingers curling around my own. She squeezed, and I wished there wasn't a table between us so I could hug her.

"Of course you can, honey," she said. "I just want you to be happy. I'm not trying to push you into anything you're not ready for. Just keep it in mind, all right? There's a whole world out there. You don't have to spend the rest of your life by yourself."

"I'll keep it in mind," I lied.

I wasn't going to keep it in mind. Not the dating part, at least. I meant what I said. I didn't have it in me to be a good partner right now, and I didn't want to share myself that way. Didn't want to make room in my life for someone else's needs.

Things were just calming down around here. Especially, though I hated to admit it, since Finn had convinced Griffen to change my schedule. Now that I was done with my workday at dinnertime, it felt like I had a normal life again.

Well, a normal life that included armed security and frequent murder attempts on various Sawyers, along with ongoing plumbing and electrical issues in the Manor. But that was all normal around here. Normal didn't mean boring. And once Nicky and I were settled in the cottage, coasting for a while sounded just about right.

I didn't want to date. Dating felt like work, but the idea of a booty call tugged at me. Interesting, but complicated. Who would I even call?

Finn! My body screamed in answer.

Oh, hell no.

Then I thought about the last really good orgasm I'd had. And it had not been of my own devices. Because that fucking kiss had been a hell of a lot more than just a kiss. My cheeks burned, but at least this time I didn't have to worry. My mother wouldn't suspect the flush on my cheeks. She'd think I was just embarrassed about talking about sex with my mother, which I was. Ridiculous, considering I was a grown woman, and so was she. I could talk about booty calls with my mother.

No, I could not. And I could not think about a booty call with Finn.

Sex with Finn was a terrible idea. Disastrous.

But is it? Is it really? He made you come in less than five minutes. No one's ever done that before.

My body had definite opinions about Finn, and all of them were positive. Eager. Ugh.

My body could shut the hell up. The rest of me would have to handle the fallout from any bad decisions my body made, and I wasn't up for that. I broke off another piece of cookie, determined to keep my brain firmly in charge of my hormones. It didn't help that now my favorite cookie reminded me of Finn. I'd have to get over it. Finn was off the table, and I sure as hell wasn't giving up my favorite cookie.

"Have you heard from Lydia?" my mother asked, changing the subject. Seconds before, I would have sworn I'd gladly talk about anything, as long as it wasn't sex. Anything except my mother-in-law.

"Not in the last few days. I'm trying to ignore her."

"Do you think that will work? I recall Lydia being very focused when she wants something."

"So diplomatic," I said into my teacup, avoiding my mother's gaze. *Very focused* was a nice way to put it. Sighing, I set my teacup on the table. "What else can I do? I don't want to let her into our lives, but she is Nicky's grand-mother. I feel like I owe her more than this, but then I remember how things ended, the things she said after Oliver died, and I can't stand the idea of reaching out or letting her see Nicky."

"Have you talked to Harvey about this?"

"No. I don't need a lawyer," I said.

My mother shook her head. "If she keeps pushing, and you don't want to give her what she wants, you may need his insight."

I nodded, hoping that would close the subject. It's not that I thought she was wrong. I just didn't want to go there. Not yet. Hopefully not ever. I guess I was hoping Lydia would find something else to fixate on and leave us alone. A likelihood that was becoming more and more improbable with every text. Fortunately, my mother knew when to leave some-thing alone and changed the subject to one that didn't make me want to run for the room with my hands over my ears.

"I forgot to tell you," she said, "I brought over some things from my place I thought you might want in the cottage."

"Really? I thought I got everything when we moved out."

"You did. These are family things. A blanket your grandmother crocheted, that painting we bought at that flea market when you were little—you know, the one you like of the stream and the woods, and a few other bits and bobs."

"Oh, Mom, are you sure?" I'd loved that painting the instant I saw it at the flea market when I was Nicky's age, and I loved it still. In it, the familiar landscape of a moun-tain stream had appeared misty and full of dreams, straight out of a fairy tale. Hanging that painting in the cottage would make it home.

"Of course. I want you to take a little bit of home with you to your new place. I put the box in my car. We can get it when—"

"I'll bring it over for you." Finn's voice cut in on my left, startling me. When had he come back into the room? Had he . . .? No, there was no way he'd heard our earlier conversation. Unless . . . Oh my god. Had he been lurking in the pantry or the scullery?

That was the problem with the kitchen. It was not the ideal place for a private conversation. It was a huge open room, so I could see who was in here, but there were too many doors. Not to mention the hallway. There were so many places he could have been lurking.

Scanning his face for any hint he'd heard our conversation, I said, "It's okay. I'm going over there later."

Finn ignored me and looked at my mother. "Is it in your car?"

She beamed at him. Traitor. "In the back seat. It's two boxes. The doors are unlocked. Thank you, Finn."

He sent her a smile so bright my eyes almost watered. Damn, he was handsome when he wanted to be. "Anything for you, Miss Martha." He flicked a glance at me, his grin slightly less blinding. "I have a few kitchen things to bring over for you, anyway."

He walked back out, carrying the notebook I guessed he'd left on the kitchen counter.

"What kitchen things?" I called after him.

Finn ignored me. I held back the annoyed grunt in my throat, although I was now positive he hadn't overheard. He wouldn't have been able to resist teasing me if he had.

"I always knew he'd grow up to be a good one," my mother said with a warm smile.

"What made you think that?" I asked wryly. "He wasn't exactly a good one in high school."

"He had a tough row to hoe, Savannah. Losing his mother so young, and you knew his father. That man had no business raising children. Especially not one as sensitive as Finn." She shook her head with a fond smile. "But when he was Nicky's age, a sweeter child I never knew. When Darcy died, she took the light out of this house, and I think she took a bit of Finn's heart with her. Then Prentice was such a royal ass afterward. I did my best, but it's not the same."

I let out a long sigh. She was right, as usual. Finn hadn't had an easy time growing up in this house.

"You know," I said, "I was so angry with Oliver by the time he died, but it didn't make it any easier. All that anger, and his death still broke my heart. But Prentice? He could have had everything, and I don't think there's a single person who wishes he were still here." I considered what I'd said. "Except Ford."

My mother nodded in agreement, her lips pursed. "Knowing Ford, I'd guess he doesn't so much wish his father hadn't died as he wishes he wasn't in prison for the murder."

"Probably true," I agreed. According to what I'd heard, Ford had spent a lot of years drinking Prentice's Kool-Aid. But even he'd woken up at the end. Prentice never had.

Chapter Seventeen

SAVANNAH

Not long after my mother left to run a few errands, I realized I had a few minutes free and grabbed another load of our things to bring over to the cottage. I was barely out of Heartstone Manor before my arms began to ache, loaded down with far too much. I'd been ambitious and optimistic when I grabbed the box of odds and ends, stacking more odds and ends on top. A winter coat, some rain boots I was almost positive Nicky hadn't outgrown, and a collection of scarves I'd shoved in a winter hat.

At this point, halfway to the cottage, the scarves were slithering out of the hat, and one boot was jammed in my armpit. If it fell, I'd have to put the whole mess down and start over. Not a big deal, maybe, but it was the principle. I am one of those people who has to bring in all the groceries in one trip. It felt like I'd been carrying things from the Manor to the cottage for weeks. If a little extra piled on top cut out a trip, I was all for it. I didn't think Nicky and I even had this much stuff.

The cottage was only a few hundred feet from the

Manor, down a winding gravel path through the side lawn. Hiking the box higher, I sped up, ignoring the renegade boot as it thumped to the ground. I'd go back and get it later.

Now that moving day was so close, I was impatient to fill my new home with our things. To be settled. I hadn't felt settled in a long time. Maybe not since before Nicky was born. Not since Oliver's first accident. I missed that feeling of belonging. Of laying my head on my pillow at night, knowing I was home. Safe. Happy.

Only a few minutes' walk from the side door of the Manor, the cottage felt like it was in another world. Oliver and I had a nice house in Richmond, a new build in a new development. It had been pretty, and we'd put in some nice upgrades, but it had lacked charm and character. I'd realized only once I'd moved out that growing up in Heartstone Manor set a high bar for charm and character.

The cottage was smaller than our home in Richmond had been. It might even be smaller than my mother's place in town, but it had loads of charm and tons of character, especially now that Parker was finished with it.

Tucked into the trees at the edge of the lawn, the cottage was a two-story stone building with a steep roof and a front porch that ran the width of the house. While the inside had needed a ton of work, the exterior had been almost perfect, except for the sagging porch.

The stone was local, shot with veins of light gray and brown, giving the cottage a warm, inviting feel. The deep green front door and trim on the windows and porch echoed the surrounding woods, and I always thought it looked like the cottage had grown there rather than being built by human hands.

My mother had lived there after I'd left for college. Back then the outside had been just as charming, but the inside had been dated and worn. Scuffed floors, an ancient kitchen with cabinets that hung at an angle and never closed all the way. Leaking pipes, stained sinks, drafts, and fireplaces that didn't work.

Parker had wiped all that away with her endless to-do lists and hours of scrubbing. I never would have guessed Parker and I had so much in common, but the first time I saw one of her lists, I knew we were meant to be friends.

Months before, after she left her husband, Parker asked Griffen for a job. On the road to divorce and without a job or any money in the bank, she told me she expected Griffen would put her to work in the Inn. She never expected him to throw the Manor renovations in her lap.

Married right out of college, Parker had never held a regular job. She'd certainly never picked up a hammer or paint bush, much less planned a renovation. Griffen must have seen something Parker hadn't, because Parker managed the job as if she'd done it a thousand times before.

Once I saw her at work, I wasn't surprised. She was organized, meticulous, methodical, and had a great sense of style. She was also willing to learn anything she didn't know. That woman knew how to find a tutorial on the internet like a librarian.

I'd been surprised to find she also knew how to get the most out of a tight budget. Not a skill I'd think a Sawyer would have, especially one who'd been married to a Kingsley. They weren't quite as wealthy as the Sawyers, but it was close. Still, somewhere along the line, Parker had learned to squeeze a budget until it screamed. I certainly benefited. The cottage was a showpiece. A beautiful little gem. And it was mine.

I shivered with excitement. I was going to have my own bedroom again. It had been so long. First sharing with

Nicky at my mother's house, then sleeping on the same twin bed I'd used as a kid out in the living room of the house-keeper's apartment. Without my own space, everything felt temporary.

Now I'd have my own room. With a door that shut. And locked. No more Nicky getting his fingers in my face cream because it was the right color to finish his fingerpainting masterpiece. And a real closet instead of a rack in the living room. As far as I was concerned, Parker was a genius. She'd taken out the tiny sewing room upstairs and converted it to a small walk-in. Even better, she'd given me a fireplace.

Even with the unexpected electrical expense and plumbing problems that had popped up, Parker had managed to find room in the budget for a gas fireplace upstairs to supplement the wood-burning one on the first level. I'd had a lot of dreams for a home, but a fireplace in my bedroom was a decadence I never imagined.

On top of that, my bathroom was a dream. Parker had worked some kind of magic on the vintage but stained fixtures. Now everything was gorgeous, gleaming white and chrome. I actually had a slipper tub in my bathroom. Nicky's bathroom and the powder room on the first floor were small, but they were equally pristine and would be just fine for us. Two and a half bathrooms for only Nicky and me was a heck of a lot better than the ancient bathroom we were sharing in the housekeeper's apartment.

Years ago, when Heartstone Manor had been run by an army—footmen and butlers, ladies' maids and parlor maids —that space had been the staff dining room and housekeep-er's office. While modern technology meant we'd never again need that many people working in the house, eventually we'd expand the staff. I hoped.

So, now that she was finished with the cottage, Parker's

next project was the gatehouse, despite Hawk's protests. Griffen had lured Hawk away from Sinclair Security with the promise of yard work, of all things. Apparently, Hawk loved gardening, and the grounds of Heartstone Manor desperately needed someone who cared. After the old groundskeeper retired, Prentice hadn't replaced him, and by the time we'd all moved in, the weeds and ivy had taken over.

The first time I met Hawk, I'd taken one look at his stern expression, his broad shoulders, and muscles on top of muscles, and I thought Griffen was pulling my leg. This guy liked to garden? He looked like he caught bullets with his teeth for fun. But the few times things had been quiet and I spied him working on the barren garden beds, his face had relaxed into something that almost looked like peace.

Hawk liked to be on his own. He wasn't an ass about it, but I could tell he didn't like being around people more than he had to. My guess was that he thought if the gatehouse remained a disaster area, with sketchy plumbing, mice, and no electricity, no one would dare to invade his domain.

Griffen had overruled him and Parker backed Griffen up, eager to get her hands on the stone gatehouse with its high ceilings and tall windows. I knew that as soon as she had the gatehouse sorted, she planned to turn her attention to upgrading my former abode, the housekeeper's apartment, turning it back into a space for the staff to meet and take a break.

Weaving through the trees at the edge of the woods, I passed a guard in a dark uniform, heading back to the security room in the Manor, I guessed. I nodded in his direction, my hands too full for a wave.

Someday West, our police chief, would figure out who

killed Prentice. I remained convinced it wasn't Ford, despite the evidence to the contrary. Not that Ford didn't have motive. Practically everyone who'd known Prentice had motive to kill him. But the Ford I knew was far too intelligent to shoot his father and then hide the gun in his own closet. If he was going to kill Prentice, he wouldn't have gotten caught. Ford wasn't my favorite person on the planet, but he didn't deserve to rot in prison for a crime he hadn't committed.

I was holding on to the hope that West would find the real killer, Ford would come home, and we wouldn't have security crawling all over the estate every day. We'd be able to hire staff without them passing a Pentagon-grade background check.

I sighed as I thought of the latest nanny candidate. The security checks were making it extremely difficult to find someone. This latest one had a stepfather with a gambling problem, so she'd been crossed off the list. Hawk and Griffen had no room for weakness. If someone could be compromised, they didn't cross the threshold of Heartstone Manor. Hope had another few candidates on the line before we ran dry. I really hoped one of them would work out. A nanny would make all our lives a little less hectic.

My arms about to tear out of their sockets, I reached the cottage. I climbed up the porch steps, loving how the new boards didn't sink under my weight. Another thing Parker had fixed. Well, for that, I knew she'd had Billy Bob's help. Billy Bob was actually two people, Billy and Bob, brothers so close they shared a name. People started calling them Billy Bob years ago, and it stuck.

They were distant cousins of mine and were the original jacks of all trades. Whatever you needed done, Billy Bob could either do it or knew who could. I couldn't have put the Manor back together without them. Over the last six months, they were here more than they weren't, quietly fixing problems and moving on to the next. Today they were repairing trim work in the guest rooms we hoped to put back to use. Tomorrow, they'd help me move before going back to work in the Manor.

Bracing the box on my hip, I let the rest of the stuff slide to the porch. I'd get it in a minute. As soon as I put the box down. Though my arms ached, I still stopped in the door-way, inhaling deeply, savoring the faint scent of fresh paint as I took in my new home.

Chapter Eighteen

SAVANNAH

The first floor of the cottage was mostly open, a long rectangular room the width of the house that we'd use furniture to divide into a sitting area arranged around the wood-burning fireplace and a dining area between the sitting area and the kitchen.

Parker had repaired the chimney and fireplace, refinished the floors, and almost completely redone the kitchen. Every room in the cottage shared a similar style: dark oak-paneled wainscoting along the lower half of the walls and creamy white walls above. With dark beams cutting across the ceilings, it was both elegant and cozy. Only the bathrooms were different, done in floor-to-ceiling vintage white subway tile.

Parker had painted the cabinets in the L-shaped kitchen a lovely sage green and had managed to score me white marble countertops cut with lines of silvery gray. We'd gotten lucky there—Parker told me that clients of the countertop guy ordered the marble counters and then changed their minds. The cottage's measurements were a perfect match. I loved every inch of those countertops.

I dumped the box on one of my perfect, gorgeous counters and went back to the porch for everything I'd dropped, going back down the path to retrieve the fallen boot. Once inside again, I shut the door behind me and turned around, trying to picture it with furniture. I couldn't quite place it all in my head.

Hope, Parker, and I had scoured the Heartstone attics, stuffed with decades of furniture that was no longer in use but too valuable to throw away. It was a treasure trove. We'd set aside a couch and two armchairs that Parker had recovered. I'd have a dining table, chairs, a twin bed and dresser for Nicky, and a beautiful antique oak bed with matching dresser and mirror for my bedroom.

In the late afternoon light, my chest swelled, my nose prickling, as my eyes went damp with tears. It wasn't just that I had this beautiful new place to live.

It felt like home. For the first time in so long, I was home.

I hadn't known how much I needed that.

This was my place now, and I couldn't think of anywhere I'd rather be. Heartstone Manor certainly wasn't where I planned to end up. When I left Sawyers Bend for college, I'd been sure I was never coming back here. Not for good. If you told me I'd feel fulfilled by taking over my mother's job as housekeeper, I would have laughed in your face.

But that was before, when Prentice had been in charge. It was a different house now. A different family without Prentice.

I loved my job, which was a realization that still surprised me. I knew I wanted it when Griffen offered the position. It had seemed a hell of a lot better than waiting tables. Definitely more stable and lucrative.

I'd known I would like it. I'd known I could do it. But I hadn't known I would love it or feel challenged and excited when I woke up every morning. But I did, and now I had this jewel of a cottage for my own. It felt like a gift, knowing the time Parker had invested, how Griffen, Hope, and Parker insisted Nicky and I have a nice place to live. So different from Prentice, who'd never given a thought to my mother or me as long as Miss Martha did her job and I didn't get in his way.

Logically, I knew that, as my employers, Griffen and Hope needed to keep me happy. Running Heartstone Manor wasn't easy, and their housekeeper wasn't just a housekeeper. I worked with Harvey, the family lawyer, to make sure everyone was following the terms of the will. Every one of Prentice's children, and Hope, had rules to follow if they wanted to inherit.

They had to live in Heartstone Manor for five years, sleeping in the house every night, absent for no more than fourteen days each quarter. Griffen's and Hope's requirements were even more strict. It would be almost impossible for them to find someone capable of both running the house and passing the more stringent security checks required of anyone charged with enforcing the will.

When it came to Griffen and Hope themselves, I wasn't that cynical. They needed me as much as I needed them, and this cottage wasn't a bribe; it was a gift. It was because they wanted me to feel at home here. A tear of sheer happiness ran down my cheek. I swiped it away with a grin. I was at home. Finally.

I walked down the hall to peek at the powder room beside the storage closet opposite the kitchen. At first, we all thought it was another closet. Someone had piled boxes and buckets of old paint around and on top of the toilet and corner sink until the fixtures had disappeared. Now we had a perfect little powder room, which meant Nicky didn't have to share the small bathroom beside his bedroom with me or any guests.

I continued to wander, loving how the freshly painted creamy walls contrasted with the dark wainscoting and beams. Past the kitchen and powder room, Nicky's room was off a short hall behind the kitchen. No bed in here yet. Light streamed through the window, brightening the space. The room was small, but the ceilings were high. I already had visions of getting him a raised bed when he was older, something that let him put a desk or couch beneath so he could have space for both sleeping and hanging out. For now, it was plenty big enough for a six-year-old.

Turning back to the kitchen, I spotted the box next to the stove and folded back the flaps to see it was one of the boxes my mother had brought over. I pulled out a framed picture of a cartoon bear and a little boy holding brightly colored balloons. I recognized it immediately as the picture my mother had bought for Nicky when he was a baby. Behind it was the painting of the mountain stream I'd so loved as a child. Holding it up against the wall, I couldn't wait to hang it. The dreamy quality of the forest stream perfectly fit the cottage. I dug further and found the crocheted afghan my grandmother made me so many years ago, along with a needlepoint pillow she'd stitched when I was a child.

Miss Martha always knew. I'd been through some tough spots in my life, but I'd always been lucky to have my mom. She was the best. And she knew what made a home. Griffen and Hope giving us this place, Parker putting so much of herself into the renovations, it all meant so much. But these things were so much more than mere belongings. They were part of my family history. Love passed down through generations.

I folded the afghan carefully, thinking I might hang it rather than putting it on the couch where Nicky could spill juice on it. Or maybe I'd bring it upstairs and put it on the end of my bed. I could decide later. Closing the flaps to the box, I noticed an old-fashioned plastic milk crate on the floor, filled with small appliances.

My eyebrows knit in confusion before I remembered Finn's comments earlier. This must be what he was talking about. I opened it, curious. Half of the crate was taken up by a stainless steel countertop toaster oven. Perfect for everything from toasting bread to reheating a slice of pizza or making a quick batch of chicken nuggets. I'd had one of these in Richmond, but it hadn't made the move. Beside it, I found a handheld mixer. I wasn't sure I'd use that, but it was nice to have. The final item was a pretty stoneware crock that would look good on the counter, pre-filled with gently used matching spatulas, ladles, and other cooking utensils.

I crossed my arms over my chest and stared down at the milk crate. Finn was being thoughtful again. I couldn't quite figure him out. He'd been the villain for so much of my adolescence, then my outright enemy after the stunt that had lost me my prom date—or any date ever again as far as high school was concerned. I'd hated him for that for so long it had become a habit more than anything else.

This man, who gave my son Halloween when he was sick and sad, who thought to stock my kitchen with things I needed, who always put a piece of chocolate on my break-fast plate when he didn't do that for anyone else—this man was not that obnoxious, entitled high school kid I'd hated. And I had no idea what to do with that.

Knuckles rapped on the front door, startling me out of my thoughts. It opened inward as the knocker let themselves in. A dark head came into view, followed by broad shoulders in a familiar dark blue t-shirt. Finn. Of course it was Finn.

He kicked the door shut behind him, and I noted he was carrying a box—and not a packing box. Something that looked new.

"When I dropped off the other stuff," he said, "I noticed you didn't have one of these. Consider it a housewarming gift." He plopped the box on the counter to reveal a high-end drip coffeemaker.

My eyes flashed wide. First, he was right; I didn't have a coffee maker and hadn't had time to think about getting one. And I needed coffee in the cottage. Never mind that I'd be heading to the Manor almost as soon as I was awake. I still needed my own coffee.

And second, this was a really nice coffee maker. Not just because it was an expensive brand, but because of the design. The main section was a traditional drip into a glass carafe, but on the side, it had a travel mug and a smaller drip brewer for making single-serve coffee to go. It was the perfect coffee maker for a woman who dashed around in the mornings but still wanted her caffeine fix. It was incredibly thoughtful.

"It has a timer," I said stupidly, running a finger over the list of features on the box.

"Yeah," Finn said, shoving his hands in his back pockets. "You can set it up before you go to bed and have the coffee waiting for you when you get up." He shrugged one shoulder. "You should really grind the beans right before you brew it, but . . ." He blew out a breath, his hair flying out of his face.

I couldn't help but smile. "I probably shouldn't tell you I buy my coffee already ground."

The look on his face made me laugh outright. Finn tried to hide his horror, but he couldn't manage to wipe it from his face. Shaking his head, he said, "I'm just going to forget you said that. I should have gotten you the kind with the grinder built in."

"No!" I slapped my hands over the box. "It's mine now, and I'm keeping it. It's perfect." Swallowing, my voice a normal volume, I finished, "Uh, thanks. Really, this was so thoughtful."

"No big deal." His eyes skipped away from mine, that shoulder jerking in another shrug.

We were being weird again. What was wrong with us? Was he being weird because he overheard me talking to my mom about sex? No. I was just paranoid. Maybe it was just me being weird. I pretended to read the side of the coffee maker box, waiting for the mood to shift back to something normal.

I was used to arguing with Finn. We'd done tons of that in the six months we'd both been back at Heartstone Manor. This awkwardness that had sprung up since Halloween was something else, and I didn't like it. At least when we were fighting, I knew where I stood.

Finn ran a hand through his hair, forging ahead. "Yeah, like I said, I noticed you didn't have one, and I know you like your coffee."

"I do," I agreed. He sounded normal again, which was easier to handle. "Honestly, I haven't gotten around to

thinking about what I need in here. Parker and Hope have
been so generous with the furniture in the attics. I think
they have this whole place decorated, so I didn't want to
buy anything until I knew for sure what I didn't have. And
now you've taken care of so much of the kitchen."

Finn straightened, shoving his hands in his back pockets
again. It was almost like my pointing out his thoughtfulness
was making him uncomfortable, although why someone
would go out of their way to be nice and then be annoyed
when people said thank you was beyond me. "Did you want
to pick more stuff out yourself?" he asked. "I didn't think
about that."

I shook my head immediately. "No, I don't. I really
don't. Maybe at some point, I'll want to redecorate my own
way. Maybe. But right now that just seems like another big
long to-do list, and I'm more interested in everything we still
have to do in Heartstone. We're finally making progress
bringing the house back, and I'd rather focus on that than
make decisions about decorating." I thought about it and
wrinkled my nose. I did not have time to drive around
looking at paint samples or furniture or whatever.

"Anyway," I finished, too aware of how close we were.
"Now that I know how good she is at it, I'd just ask Parker
for help. I think it's going to look great once she has it
set up."

"Parker was always good at that," Finn said, his voice
soft. "Before our mom died, she and Parker redecorated
Parker's room so she could have a room she could grow into
instead of a little kid's room."

"I didn't know that," I murmured, touched by the
thought of Darcy and Parker working on the project
together, Darcy knowing her time was running out. I was
only nine when she died, the same age as Parker, and I still

remembered how thin and pale Darcy had been. And how much she'd loved her children. "Parker's room is gorgeous. Knowing her, I can believe she decorated it, even as young as she was. Parker's always had great taste. So did your mom."

Finn cleared his throat and gave a jerky nod. I should change the subject. Finn never talked about his mother. Except he'd brought her up.

Weird.

"Anyway," I babbled, "Decorating is covered, but I totally forgot about coffee. Which is not like me. So thanks again. That was really cool of you."

"Yeah, like I said, I know you like your coffee."

We stood there staring past each other for what felt like an eternity, but was probably more like ten seconds. Finn jerked a fraction of an inch, as if prodded. His chin popped up, and he said, "I have to get back to the kitchen. Is there anything you need moved around over here? I'm crap when it comes to decorating, and I don't know what to do with a hammer, but I can lift heavy things."

"No, I'm fine. I—" Before I could finish my denial, I thought of the boxes I'd stowed in the hall closet that I really wanted upstairs.

I'd asked Billy Bob to bring them over but hadn't said where to put them. When I tried to move them myself, I realized they were too heavy. In this, my sensible side beat out my ambition. The last thing I needed was to tweak my back, considering I spent most of my day on my feet.

"Actually, there are two boxes in the hall closet. I'd love if you could bring them upstairs, if you've got a minute."

"No problem." He was gone in a flash, seconds later calling down, "Where do you want them?"

"Anywhere in the bedroom," I shouted back. I could

sort out what to do with the contents once Billy Bob moved the furniture over the next day.

Finn jogged back down the stairs after bringing up the second box, saying, "I put them in the closet so they wouldn't be in the way when Billy Bob brings the furniture over tomorrow. It won't take long. Everyone is pitching in. We figured if we all put our backs into it, it wouldn't take more than a couple of trips."

I stopped, stunned. "What do you mean, everyone?"

"You know, everyone." Finn gave me a look like my brain was slow. "Billy Bob, me, Griffen, Hawk, Royal, and Tenn. Parker will direct traffic. Griffen banned Hope. He's afraid she'll try to lift things."

"She probably would," I agreed, "Though I'm not sure she can carry much with that baby in the way."

"True," Finn laughed. "I'll get out of your hair. I'm just going to unpack these things and grab the milk crate back. I use them in the pantry," he said, setting the remaining contents on the counter.

Turning with the crate in one hand, we slammed right into each other—a hazard of avoiding eye contact with the other person in a small space.

I rebounded off Finn's solid body, every cell in mine waking up at the contact with all that long, hard muscle. I swear the man radiated heat or pheromones or something, because the second I got this close, every part of me perked up.

I froze in place.

This was the part where I was supposed to step back and give him room to leave the kitchen.

Yep, any second now. I was going to step back and get out of the way.

Definitely not going to inch forward until my breasts made full contact with his chest.

Definitely not going to look up and meet those deep, mossy green eyes.

This was not a good idea.

That was the last thought I had before I raised up on my toes to meet his mouth in a kiss.

Chapter Nineteen

SAVANNAH

Finn's lips touched mine, and I couldn't imagine how we'd done this a month ago and never done it again. Finn Sawyer's lips were possibly the best thing that had ever touched me. Firm and strong, he controlled the kiss in all the right ways.

I reached for him, my fingers diving into his thick hair, holding him close, my tongue stroking his. I could hear my heart pounding furiously, my halting gasps for breath as I tried to kiss him deeper, longer.

He fit against me like he was made to match my body. Finn was taller, broader—not easy traits to find at my height, with my build, but, oh, the way he surrounded me, one hand holding the back of my head, the other at my waist, those long, strong fingers sliding to hold my hip, curving down to close around my ass.

Oh god, I should stop. I should step back. Go back to the Manor. Do something. Anything. Anything other than raise up further on my toes and press myself harder against him.

I tore my mouth from his. I swear it was to tell him we

couldn't do this anymore. But instead, my lips found the side of his neck. Salty heat. I bit down on the corded muscle just enough to drag a groan from his throat. I had a moment to remember that we were completely alone. The boys weren't yet home from school, and everyone who might wander by was occupied elsewhere.

Then my toes left the floor, and I was moving through the air. I caught the scrape of cardboard sliding, and my butt hit cool marble. I fell back on my elbows, legs splayed for only a second before Finn stepped between them. We'd been in this position before. I already knew this time was different.

This time, his hands went to the zipper at the back of my uniform dress, dragging it down until the dress sagged in the front, the modest neckline not so modest anymore. Finn pulled at the sturdy fabric until he revealed my breasts in a boring beige bra. Hooking his fingers in the straps, he dragged that down too.

Someone groaned. Maybe me, maybe him. Then he laid me back, my arms trapped at my sides by the dress, my breasts completely bared. Finn followed me down, his lips tasting my neck, my collarbone, dipping lower. I squirmed, the marble cool against my heated skin, slippery as my hips twisted and rolled. Finn's tongue traced the inside of one breast before his mouth closed over my nipple and sucked gently, his tongue soothing, as if warming me up.

I didn't need warming up. I was about to boil over. He nipped with sharp teeth, drawing a gasp from my throat before his mouth closed over the smarting nipple and sucked hard.

The top of my head almost blew off. This time I knew the groan was me. I whimpered, trying to breathe. One strong hand closed around my breast, squeezing, lifting it to his mouth to tease and lick and suck. His other hand slid up my thigh under my dress, closing over the waistband of my underwear and dragging my panties down my legs, moving out of the way just long enough to get them free and toss them to the floor.

My dress was still on, technically, but I was naked everywhere it counted. For once, my sensible, practical side didn't have a damn thing to say. This was where I'd wanted to be ever since that kiss a month before.

No. I was a liar.

This was where I'd wanted to be ever since that first kiss when I was still a teenager.

I wanted to be exactly where I was, spread out on this counter, desperate for Finn Sawyer. I could think about reality later. I wanted to reach out, to fumble with his buttons, zippers, his belt, to get rid of whatever was in my way. With my arms trapped by the dress, it wasn't happening. I squirmed, needing him too badly to care that he knew how much I wanted him.

Finn switched to my other breast, squeezing, tasting, nipping at my hard nipple then soothing the spark of pain with gentle, rhythmic suction. I couldn't take it anymore. He was trying to kill me. This was his revenge for whatever he'd always disliked about me. It had to be revenge, because he was teasing and teasing, and I just wanted—

"Please, please, Finn. Please." I didn't need to say what I was asking for. He knew. The bastard waited, teasing me a little longer. Finally, finally, he slid the hand that had torn off my panties up the outside of my thigh, tracing his fingers to my belly button with a feather-light touch, down between my legs, stroking over my clit, then back to cup my ass.

"Finn, you asshole," I didn't care that I was begging. I

needed that light, teasing touch back on my clit where it belonged.

He chuckled, nuzzling between my full breasts, his breath hot on my skin, the scruff on his face the sweetest abrasion. "You want me to fuck you, Savannah? Because if you don't, now's the time to let me know."

"Yes, goddammit. Yes. Please, Finn." I could hate myself for begging later. Maybe. In that moment I would have done anything. I couldn't remember ever wanting anyone as badly as I needed Finn Sawyer inside me. Like I needed air. Like I needed my heart to beat. His fingertips moved between my lower lips, finding slick heat.

One long finger pressed inside, stretching me more than I would have thought. It had been a long time. Way too long since I'd had anything other than my own fingers inside me, and I don't know if anything had ever felt so good.

Finn's finger withdrew, pulling a moan from me as it moved. My breath caught, head spinning as he replaced his finger with the blunt head of his cock. Yes. This was what I wanted. I knew it, but I hadn't guessed that Finn Sawyer's cock would feel like the best, most perfect thing in the world, pushing inside, filling me inch by inch.

The stretch was almost too much, burning as he slowly moved deeper. That burn was painful, yet so sweet and luscious I had to have more. I rolled my hips into him, the pain spinning into pure pleasure.

His lips found mine in a graze of a kiss, so light all I wanted was another kiss. His mouth was at my ear, his voice a growl. "Savannah, fuck, you feel so good." He jerked his hips in a hard thrust, and another, and I was so full of Finn.

Tilting my hips, I wrapped my legs around his waist and rocked into him. "Finn." It came out on a gasp, all I could say. My brain had shorted out completely. My body glowed with sensation. Everywhere he touched, I was alight, my breasts full and swollen, my pussy so full and slick. The push and pull of his cock inside me had me seeing stars. Every time he filled me and thrust into my clit, I cried out, a whimpering moan I'd never heard before. What was he doing to me? I couldn't do anything but fuck him back and try to breathe.

"Savannah, fuck, you're— I—" He gave up, kissing me instead, his mouth hungry and demanding, an anchor holding us in place. Slipping one hand between our bodies, he pressed his thumb into my clit in a firm swirl.

I exploded, screaming, a primal sound of violent joy tearing through my body. This was so much more than an orgasm. So much more than sex. This came from the marrow of my bones, from the deepest part of me. It was everything.

Finn jerked against me, going stiff, the rhythm of his hips uneven as he collapsed over me with a cry as primal as my own.

He stilled, except for his hips, still rocking in the slightest movement, his chest heaving for breath along with my own. An eon later, he stirred, his lips moving along my jaw, leaving feathery kisses in their wake, his breath harsh in my ear, my own breath just as rough.

There were no words in my mind. I had no words.

Propping himself up on his elbows, he stared down at me, his mossy green eyes guarded. "Well, that was a long time coming," he said, his words so cool they were a slap.

Something inside me jolted and shut off. He wasn't wrong, but did he have to say it like that? He was still inside me.

Drawing on every bit of the ass kicker I knew I was, I gave him an equally cool look. As crisply as I could manage with my heart still thundering and my breath ragged, I said, "Just so you know, I still don't like you."

I didn't expect his answering grin, the shields gone from his eyes, replaced with a spark of humor. "Fine with me, sweetheart." He kissed me again, a short, hard, claiming kiss.

Stepping back, his body disengaging from mine, he was zipping his jeans and striding out the front door before I could free my arms from my tangled dress. I slid to my feet, wobbling as I got my balance and yanked at my dress until I brought it back into place.

I watched him cross the lawn to the Manor through the front windows, his stride determined and swift, with the tiniest hint of a bounce in his step. A thousand thoughts raced through my mind, but mostly, I was thinking, what had we just done? And when could we do it again?

Chapter Twenty

SAVANNAH

Hours later, the sun was dipping in the sky, casting shadows across the winding gravel path back to the Manor. I was in a rush, the path ahead seeming endless, the Manor further away instead of closer.

But no, it wasn't. That was just me being an anxious jumble of nerves because I'd spent too long in the cottage trying to get my head together, avoiding the Manor and the kitchens. I'd hoped that if I could just straighten and organize the things I'd moved to the cottage, maybe somewhere in that process I could straighten and organize my wayward brain.

I had sex with Finn Sawyer.

Why?

What the fuck was I thinking?

It was the worst of all possible bad ideas. I mean, come on. I wasn't a teenager anymore. We had way too much history, most of it awful. I was his boss, kind of. But he was my boss's younger brother. Yikes. I couldn't orchestrate a more complicated mess if I tried.

All that was piled on one side of the scale. On the *oh, hell no, not doing that again* side of the scale. And on the other side was the best sex I'd ever had. By a long shot.

I didn't know sex like that existed. The idea of not doing that again was utterly insane. Because why? Why was I not doing that again?

Oh, yeah. All those very practical, sensible, logical reasons piled on the other side of the imaginary scale in my mind. I thought of my mother's booty calls. Could I?

No. With someone, maybe. Not with Finn.

Sex with Finn was a disastrously awful idea.

End of story.

I straightened and I organized and I hung things up and didn't leave the cottage until I was late for dinner. I still wasn't any clearer on what I wanted or what I was going to do than I had been as I'd watched Finn stroll out the door.

And what if he, I don't know, said something, or did something that gave us away? If my mother had any clue we'd had sex . . . I didn't know if she'd be mad or happy, and I didn't want to know.

Oh god, I did not want to know what my mother would think about me having sex with Finn Sawyer.

Okay. Have to keep moving. I picked up my pace, trying to take deep calming breaths at the same time. Note to self: Rushing and calming do not go together. I yanked open the side door and clattered down the steps, entering the kitchen with a flush on my face and my hair flying out of my braid every which way.

Great. Because if I wanted to have sex with Finn again —which I wasn't going to, but if I did—I really didn't want him to see me all sweating and red-faced.

And oh my god, why did I care what Finn Sawyer thought about how I looked? I wanted to get in my car and disappear for at least a week. A month. Until I could forget the feel of Finn's hands on my hips as he—

No. I had dinner with my mother and two young children, and—oh, shit—also Finn Sawyer. I stood in the kitchen doorway, watching Finn move with smooth coordination between the oven and the counter where he was plating dinner. Kitty worked beside him, loading trays to go in the dumbwaiter.

My mother had Nicky and August at one of the prep sinks, washing their hands. Everyone looked up, gave me a quick glance, and went back to what they were doing. Everyone including Finn. Okay, if he could be grown up and professional, then goddammit, so could I. I was the epitome of grown-up and professional. It was going to take more than Finn Sawyer to shake me.

I could hold it together. It wasn't like this was a big deal. We'd had sex. People had sex. Now we had a job to do. Pretending today was like any other day, I called across the kitchen, "Do you two need help getting dinner set up?"

"I think we're good," Kitty called back, sending a questioning look to Finn.

Finn nodded in agreement. "We've got it. We'll have dinner on the table here in ten minutes."

"Okay, great," I said brightly, feeling weirdly unsettled. I should be glad he had everything under control. And I was. I just . . . I didn't know what part I was supposed to play. I was struggling to be the perfectly efficient housekeeper in this exact moment when what I wanted was to march across the kitchen, grab Finn by the collar of his faded t-shirt, and drag him into the scullery. Which I wasn't going to do for so many very good reasons.

Forget that. I was going to get myself together. Now. I washed my hands, smoothing on lotion afterward more thoroughly than I needed to, buying a little time to look normal while I figured out how to *be* normal.

I turned to my mom, now sitting at a table with the kids. "Sorry, I got distracted over at the cottage," I said. "Thank you for everything in the boxes you brought. Those things already make it feel like home." I pictured the cottage in my mind and smiled. "It's so beautiful, Mom." I sank into the seat opposite her. She reached across to clasp my hand.

"I know, honey. It's absolutely gorgeous." My mom's eyes filled with tears as her smile met mine. "I'm so happy for you. It's a beautiful home. And even more, it's meant to be your home." She let out a sigh. "I worked hard for Prentice, and he paid me well, but I was an employee, and it was a job."

Waving her hand in a circle to encompass the kitchens, and, I thought, the whole of Heartstone, she went on, "This is different. Griffen and Hope made you a home because they want this to be your home."

I smiled back at her as my eyes went a little watery too. "I didn't realize moving to the cottage would make me so weepy," I said quietly.

"I know," my mother said. "Trust me, I was more than happy to get out of that place and move into my cottage in town when I finally quit working for Prentice. And still, I shed a tear or two when I drove through those gates and thought I'd never cross them again. Change is always hard, even when it's good."

I squeezed her fingers before I let go. "I have a wise mother," I murmured.

"That you do," she shot back with a wink.

Turning my attention to the kids, I asked, "Did you boys have a nice day at school?"

"Yeah," August said, kicking his heels against his chair

and bouncing a little in his seat. "We had kickball in gym, and my team won both games."

"My class didn't get to play kickball," Nicky exclaimed with a scowl.

August sat back and folded his arms over his chest, nodding. "I know. Not until second grade. But it's so awesome. I hit Chad in the head with the ball, and I didn't even get in trouble." He stared up at the ceiling, reliving the memory. "It was the best."

They went off into a rambling conversation about sports at school that I didn't even try to follow. It was all I could do to sit there with a blandly polite smile and nod at the right moments.

Finn set our dinner on the table, a gorgeous roasted chicken, loaded baked potatoes, and a green salad with freshly baked buttered rolls. Damn, the man could cook. Someday I would ask him exactly how and when he'd learned to cook like this. Not today. Today I was going to pretend he didn't exist.

Not that I needed to. Finn took care of that as he jumped into the kids' conversation about sports and their argument about whether it should be called soccer or football and, regardless of the name, whether it was superior to baseball. I couldn't possibly have cared less about any of it. I zoned out, keeping my face in a bland mask until I heard, "Savannah!" in a sharp tone. My mother.

"Sorry," I said, sitting up and focusing on her face. "I didn't hear you. I guess I'm just tired." My eyes involuntarily flicked to Finn. His own composure broke just long enough to send me a smug smile, a glint in his eyes that I swear to god made my nipples perk up. Annoying man.

"That's all right, honey," my mother said, pulling my

attention back to her. "Tomorrow is going to be a big day. We should all get to bed early."

I nodded along. "Yes, definitely. Early to bed tonight." A good night's sleep was exactly what I needed to clear my mind.

The second dinner was over, I jumped up to clear the plates, going stiff as Finn came up behind me at the sink, his tall, broad frame engulfing me with heat. "We need to talk. After you put Nicky to bed." Out of sight of anyone else, his lips grazed the sensitive skin just below my earlobe, and I shivered, giving a stiff nod.

I put Nicky to bed, still distracted, giving more absent nods as he chattered away. I guided him from teeth brushing, to pajamas, to a back rub until his eyes finally closed. As soon as I was sure he was out, I changed from my uniform dress into an old slouchy sweatshirt and equally old slouchy sweatpants, just to make a point. We were going to have an adult conversation about adult business. I was not going to seduce him, and the sweats should preclude any chance of me being easily seduced.

The absurdity of that hit me as I headed down the hall to the kitchen. Like ugly sweats would stop Finn if he wanted to get his hands under them. More importantly, I was kidding myself if I thought I'd stop him if he made a move.

Heart pounding at the confrontation to come, I found Finn sitting at the kitchen table, a cup of tea in front of him, a magazine open on the table beside the tea. I spotted a photograph of what looked like a quiche beside tiny print. A recipe. Of course.

"Hey." Finn stood, sliding back his chair silently and crossing the kitchen to meet me. His voice low, eyes intent, he said, "We didn't use a condom."

Ice slid through me for the briefest second. We hadn't used protection. How was that not the first thing I thought of after it was over? What the hell was wrong with me? I mean, it had been the best sex of my life. My head was spun. But still, I never forgot things that important. Never. I was distracted by the upcoming move, and I hadn't been planning to have sex at all, but still. That was no excuse.

Then, the ice slid away as quickly as it had come. "It's okay," I assured Finn. "I have an IUD. I got it after Nicky was born, and the doctor checks it every year. Also," I shifted, suddenly uncomfortable. "I, uh, I was tested for other stuff a while ago, and I— There hasn't been anyone since." I forced myself to finish, awkwardness tangling my tongue.

"Okay, good," Finn said, running a hand through his dark hair. "That's one less thing to worry about. I made an appointment to get tested tomorrow. I'm always careful, but it's been a while since I was tested, so I'd rather make sure you don't have anything to worry about."

"Oh, um, thanks, that's very—" Words ran through my head. Mature. Adult. Responsible. Thoughtful.

In that moment, I had to admit to myself that the man standing in front of me was not the Finn I'd grown up with. This Finn *was* an adult. He *was* mature and responsible. We stood there in the dark, staring at each other, wary and calculating.

Finn finally broke the silence. "Look, I'm sorry for what I said after. It didn't come out the way I meant it."

"How did you mean it?" I asked, cautious. He hadn't hurt my feelings exactly, but I hadn't loved what he'd said. It left me feeling like I was something to check off his to-do list. Finally fuck Savannah Miles. *Check.*

His eyes slid away, then flashed back to hold mine,

something hot and intent simmering in their depths. "What I meant was I've been dreaming of that for the better part of my life. And when it finally happened, it was better than anything I'd ever imagined. And believe me, I have a pretty vivid imagination. What I should have said is, *Thank you. That was fucking awesome. Can we please do it again?*"

"Right now?" I squeaked out, eyes circling the room to make sure we were alone. Relief spiraled through me, my thoughts tumbling through my head. I didn't want to be relieved. I wanted to be pissed off. Were we going to have sex right now? Here? Could we? My previous protestations disappeared, and I couldn't remember a single reason we shouldn't do it again.

He laughed, a low chuckle that had my body at a simmer in a flash. Cupping the side of my jaw with one hand, he dipped his lips and grazed them across mine. "Not right now. You just said it's been a while for you, and you have a big day tomorrow. I don't want you to be sore."

He kissed me again, that smug grin turning up the side of his mouth. Instead of annoying me, it raised the simmer to a low boil.

"So fucking cocky," I whispered, and his grin bloomed into a full smile, brimming with arrogance and satisfaction.

"Yes. Yes, I am. And we are definitely going to do that again."

Finn's long fingers sank beneath my loose braid to cup the back of my head, pulling me close, and he kissed me, long and slow. He kissed me until my brain melted out of my ears like warm caramel, and all I could think about was slipping my hands under his shirt, feeling his warm skin, the shift of muscles beneath.

When he pulled his mouth from mine, I let out a whimper. Finn was the only man who'd ever made me whimper. In that moment, I didn't even care.

"Not tonight," he said. "You need your sleep, and if I get you naked again, nobody is going to be sleeping." He dipped his head for one last slow kiss. "Not tonight," he said again, "but soon." He stepped back and was gone, leaving me wobbling on my feet yet again.

Not tonight, but soon.

How soon? And how was Finn Sawyer the responsible one in this . . . whatever it was? It wasn't a relationship. He hadn't said he wanted to take me to dinner. He said we were going to fuck again. I had no argument there. I didn't want dinner. I didn't want flowers. I didn't want a relationship.

What I wanted was Finn. He'd said he'd been dreaming about fucking me for years. If I was being honest with myself, I'd been dreaming of the same thing. And like Finn, my dreams hadn't come close to reality.

I didn't want a relationship, but I did want Finn. And I was going to have him. Again and again. And when we were done, when this need burned itself out., we'd both walk away satisfied.

Even as I had the thought, I recognized that there was a decent chance this was going to end up biting me in the ass. Friends with benefits in the workplace never ended well.

My brain flashed to the kitchen counter in the cottage. The blinding pleasure, the feel of him inside me. The sound of his groan when he came.

This thing with Finn was going to blow up in my face, and I couldn't bring myself to care.

Chapter Twenty-One

SAVANNAH

One of these days, I was going to come to my cottage without my arms overflowing with stuff, but not today. Today was moving day, the day I'd been waiting for since Griffen and Hope had mentioned updating the cottage and giving it to Nicky and me. Shifting the boxes in my arms and the two duffel bags hanging from my shoulder, I braced the biggest box against the door frame. Finally getting my hand on the knob, I turned it, shouldering the door open. I let the duffel bags slide off my shoulders, and they hit the ground with a thud beside the door. More carefully, I set the boxes on the floor beside them. That was the very last of our things.

It still blew my mind that the cottage was ours.

In the beginning, I hadn't taken them seriously. I hadn't known Griffen or Hope well enough at that point to believe they meant what they said, and I was still living with the echoes of growing up under Prentice's reign, when the staff was treated like children—seen but not heard.

Making his housekeeper comfortable had never been one of Prentice's considerations. He paid my mother well enough, and she'd had a roof over her head. To Prentice, that was more than enough. When I took the job with Griffen and Hope, I was excited about the challenge of running Heartstone Manor and relieved by the salary and good health insurance.

On top of that, I had a gut instinct that Griffen's promises were good, that he would create a working environment that I could, at worst, tolerate, and, at best, grow to love. It pleased me immensely that I'd been right, but even in my wildest imaginings, I hadn't hoped for this gorgeous little cottage. A home just for Nicky and me. It felt like a lifetime since we'd had our own place.

Arms finally empty, I set my hands on my hips and surveyed the main room of the cottage. Everything here was immaculate. I don't know when they found the time, but Kitty and April must have given it a final pass. There was no evidence of drywall dust or leftover tools. The floors gleamed, the counters shone, and the air smelled faintly of lemons and rosemary. It was perfect.

What had been the housekeeper's apartment in Heartstone Manor was now empty except for the furniture. When she was ready, Parker and I would decide how best to transform the apartment into a lounge for the staff and an office for me. But that was a problem for later. Today was moving day, and while it might be quiet for the moment, I knew it was about to get very busy.

A check of my watch told me I'd better get moving. Breakfast in the Manor would be finished soon. Tenn would have already left to drop the kids off at school, and any help Parker had allotted for the move would be showing up any minute. She was a mini drill sergeant, and she had everyone organized.

I looked at the pile of duffel bags on the floor, and

hefted them back into my arms with a groan, crisscrossing the straps over my shoulders until I was surrounded. They bounced against my hips with every step, but I had to get everything out of the way so people weren't tripping over bags while they carried furniture. I headed for the stairs, tossing one of the duffels down the hall to Nicky's bedroom before stomping up the stairs with the rest, awkwardly dropping them in the closet on top of the boxes Finn had deposited the day before.

Finn. A quick flash of memory hit me. Those heated moments on the counter. Somehow, I had not seen that coming, even though I'd thought about it more than I wanted to admit. I'd thought about Finn kissing me, touching me. I'd wanted it. If I was honest with myself, I'd dreamed about it in the dark of night, tucked into my lonely bed. Finn. His hands. His mouth on me. What it might be like with him. But still, I hadn't seen that coming. I wanted it, but I never thought it would happen. Not for real.

Now that it had, I couldn't help but wonder when it would happen again. I didn't doubt that it would. Putting aside Finn's arrogant promise of soon, I knew I wanted it to happen again, ideally within hours. Even as I had the thought, I knew it was ridiculous. For one, I was still sore. The achy twinge between my legs was a pleasant reminder, but Finn had been right about that. Two, today was for moving, not illicit sex with my boss's brother.

I laughed at myself as I headed back downstairs to unpack the coffee maker. The coffee maker Finn bought for me. He didn't get it at the local big box store. They had a decent selection of kitchen stuff, but nothing this high-end. He didn't order it. Packages went through Hawk's team and then came to me. So when had he had time to go into Ashe-

IVY LAYNE

ville? Why did I care? Was everything today going to make me think of Finn?

I hoped not. I pushed that thought away. Finn was complicated, but he didn't have to be. We were both adults. We could handle a little sex. No big deal. But the last thing I needed was for anyone to figure out we were sleeping together. Then we'd have to explain it, and I couldn't explain it to myself just yet.

Neither of us was looking for a relationship. I had no idea what I wanted, but I knew I didn't want a boyfriend, or a partner, or anything like that. I hated the word lover—it felt so old-fashioned, like something my grandmother might have said. Fuck buddy was too casual. I mean, whatever we had was definitely in that territory. It sure as hell wasn't serious, but the word buddy was too . . . friendly. I had a lot of feelings about Finn, for Finn, but none of them were exactly friendly. Friends with benefits? Maybe. But benefits was too pale and transactional a word to describe sex with Finn. Could something that mind-blowing be a *benefit*? It felt more like winning the sexual lottery.

Never mind. I didn't need to label it. And that was all the thought I was prepared to give to Finn Sawyer today. Today was for me and settling into my new house, not for my new friends with benefits/fuck buddy/whatever.

I finished unpacking the coffee maker, stuffing the Styrofoam packing material back in the box and rinsing off the carafe. It occurred to me that I had a brand-new gourmet coffee maker, but I'd forgotten to bring over any coffee, creamer, or mugs. Everyone helping out would want coffee or cold drinks. That was normally the kind of thing I would have taken care of, but I'd been distracted by the details of moving.

I'd stashed cold soda and water in the fridge a few days

before, but coffee had completely slipped my mind. I could run back to the house and get coffee mugs and all the rest of it in a few minutes. First I'd have to run a few pots of hot water through the coffee maker to clean the system out. Might as well get started on that. I had the first carafe of hot water almost full when the door opened and Parker swept inside, a big box in her arms, followed by Scarlett, Sterling, and Hope.

Scarlett held up a grocery bag. "I brought coffee," she said. "I figured you wouldn't have anything set up yet. There's also some half and half in there, and Sterling has a box of goodies Daisy brought home with her last night from the bakery."

"Thank you," I said with happy relief. "I'm glad you were thinking, because it totally slipped my mind."

"Not like you've been busy or anything," Scarlett said with a wink and a smile.

Sterling flipped her platinum hair back off her shoulders and held up a white box that looked like it could have held a cake for at least twenty people. Sliding it onto the counter, she lifted the lid and leaned in to take a deep sniff. It wasn't a cake. It was everything: muffins, croissants, danishes, and cookies. A jumble of deliciousness.

Sterling grinned up at me, her vibrant blue eyes catching the light. "Daisy sent these over," Sterling said. "She's sorry she couldn't help today, but JT has class, and she couldn't leave Grams in the lurch at the bakery. Town is hopping. Quinn has two tours today—leaf season hikers—so she's going to be out in the woods all day, but she told me I could send the phone to voicemail and come help out. I didn't want to miss the fun."

The youngest Sawyer, Sterling, had it rough growing up. Her mother died when she was a toddler, and no one had bothered to parent her since. By the time Prentice died, Sterling had been drinking way too much, a hellion who didn't seem to care about anyone, herself most of all. Griffen refused to put up with her crap, strong-arming her into quitting drinking, getting a job, and most importantly, letting her family love her.

Sterling and I hadn't had the best beginning. When I started at the Manor, I'd been the one in her way most of the time. Griffen declared she wasn't to have her room cleaned by Kitty and April until she'd cleaned it herself first. I still remembered the smell in there. Stale vomit and moldy food. She was cut off from alcohol. She couldn't have access to a vehicle. It seemed like I told her *no* fifty times a day.

She could have been a nightmare about all of it, but Sterling slowly got herself together. I'd gone from viewing her as a potential problem to regarding her with wary admiration as she stayed sober and started taking care of herself. These days she made me smile with pride for everything she'd accomplished, and she felt more like a little sister than anything else. It still surprised me that she seemed to return the feeling.

Parker set the box she held on the counter and turned for the door, calling back over her shoulder, "You might want to unpack that one. I left the other box on the porch. I'll be right back."

Hope eased her way into the suddenly crowded kitchen, pulling open the box Parker had brought with her. "She thinks of everything," Hope said. I looked over her shoulder into the box. Dishes. Dinner plates, sandwich plates, bowls.

"I forgot about dishes," I murmured, grateful yet again for Parker, who seemed to have remembered everything. I was fantastic at that when it came to running Heartstone Manor, but in my personal life, not so much. Moving to help Hope unpack the box, I loaded everything into the newly installed dishwasher.

"It makes sense you'd forget," Hope said. "You've basically been living in Heartstone's kitchen. You didn't need anything for yourself until now."

Parker returned with another box, this one a set of mugs that matched the dishes. "There's more in the Manor. It's with the rest of the things the guys are bringing over, but I thought we'd need the mugs first."

She snapped into drill sergeant mode. "Scarlett, you get the coffee brewing. Sterling, rinse those mugs and see if you can figure out where I put the paper towels so you can dry them off. Hope, you set some of the pastries out on a plate so the guys don't go digging in the box. They'll be here in a few minutes with the first load, and once they've gone back and forth a few times, they're going to be ready for coffee and a snack."

Playing drill sergeant was usually my job, but for once it was nice to let someone else take over. I watched as Parker scanned the cottage with an eagle eye. "Kitty and April did a great job in here. This place is sparkling. If the guys bring everything over the way I set it out, this should go quickly. Rugs first, then furniture. Then artwork and the decorative stuff."

"I don't have any artwork," I said, momentarily confused. I'd sold pretty much everything when we left Richmond. I hadn't had anywhere to go except the guest bedroom at my mom's place in town, and it had seemed smarter to sock away the cash in my savings account than pay for a storage unit.

"Artwork," Parker repeated, lifting her eyes from her

phone, a brilliant smile illuminating her face. "Savannah, by the time we leave here this afternoon, you will be moved in down to the last throw pillow. No boxes to unpack, no clothes to hang, no dishes to wash. We're not leaving until you're at home."

Chapter Twenty-Two
SAVANNAH

I stared at her, dumbfounded. I appreciated the offer of help to move the furniture in. I certainly couldn't have done that on my own. I assumed I'd grab Billy Bob and between the three of us, we'd make it work. But this—this was huge. In the back of my mind, I'd imagined unpacking slowly, my usual day too busy to leave much time for dealing with a home that wasn't the Manor. But if Parker's plan worked, and I was sure it would, I'd get to skip all that. I'd get to enjoy the cottage that much sooner. It was incredible.

"I don't know what to say," I started, my voice threatening to crack with emotion. "I-I know you all have other things to do."

Scarlett gave a hard shake of her head. "Nothing more important than this, Savannah. You spend all day, every day, running the Manor. We"—she swept her hand in a circle to encompass herself, Hope, Parker, and Sterling—"we never have to do anything. We show up to wonderful meals, our laundry is done, the house is clean. It's decorated for the holidays. You think of what we need before we know we need it. You take care of us. Now it's our turn."

Hope cut in. "We know how much you do every day. We talked about it, and we don't want you to come back here at night and have boxes to unpack and pictures to hang. We want you to be at home. So that's what we're going to do. We're not leaving until you're at home."

"You guys—" That was all I got out before my throat choked up. I tried again, but I didn't get a word out before I was enveloped in a hug. Hope's strong arms came around me, her baby kicking against my midsection as she hugged me tight.

"Savannah," she said, "Don't argue. Just say thank you, and let us take care of you for once."

"Thank you," I managed to squeeze out, hugging Hope back. Sterling and Scarlett joined us, wrapping their arms around both of us. Parker caught my eye over their heads.

Smiling, she said, "We've got it all under control. Don't worry."

I swiped away the tears that had gathered under my eyes and sucked in a breath. "I love you guys. So much." My heart hurt with it. It was one thing to like my job, but this was more. This felt like family.

"We love you too, Savannah," Sterling said, giving me an extra squeeze before she let go.

Hope finished loading the dishwasher and started it with the small pack of detergent Parker had brought over in a bag that also included trash bags and a set of silverware. A thought occurred to me as I watched her hit start. "Does Griffen know you're over here? I'm pretty sure he said you weren't helping."

"He says a lot of things," Hope replied with a smirk. "I'm

not going to lift anything. I'm not going to run up and down the stairs." She rolled her eyes. "Trust me, I have no interest in causing any damage to myself." She patted her distended abdomen. "This guy here is doing enough of that on his own. Scarlett brought along some decaf. I'll make coffee and put my feet up as soon as there's somewhere to sit. I promise."

I slung an arm around her shoulder and squeezed. "Not too much longer, and all of us will be too busy hovering over the new Sawyer baby to drive you nuts."

"That'll be nice," Hope agreed.

Scarlett dumped the second pot of hot water and set up the first pot of actual coffee. I'd had a quick cup in the kitchen while getting Nicky ready for school, but that felt like a million years ago. I needed at least one more cup.

"Check this out," Scarlett said, looking at Hope. "It has a single-serve coffee maker on the side with its own travel mug. I can make your decaf while I make regular for the rest of us." She turned to me. "When did you get this? It's very cool. So convenient when you're dashing out the door to the big house."

"Finn got it for me," I said without thinking. Four sets of eyes narrowed in interest, all fixed on me.

"Finn got it for you?" Hope asked with a raised eyebrow.

"Um, yeah, he brought it over yesterday." I didn't mention the fact we'd had the best sex of my life on the counter directly under the pastry box. "I guess he noticed how much I like my coffee in the morning."

That only raised their interest more, but I couldn't think of anything to say to divert them. Buying me a coffee maker was definitely not a Finn thing to do, and we all knew it. I was saved by the front door swinging open. Billy Bob came through carrying a rolled-up carpet, a carpet pad stacked on top.

"This one goes here?" Billy asked Parker, pointing at the front of the main room where the bay window and fireplace made a natural sitting area.

"Perfect, thank you," Parker said, clicking off something on the list on her phone. "We'll get it rolled out before you bring over the furniture."

I had a moment to wonder if I should have paid more attention to Parker and Hope's decorating plans. Maybe I wouldn't like the way they were going to set it up. It didn't matter, I reassured myself. If I really didn't like it, I had all the time in the world to rearrange everything the way I wanted it. For now, I was going with the flow.

Billy Bob disappeared out the door, and Parker turned to the rest of us. "Let's get that carpet pad rolled out, centered on the fireplace. There's a vacuum in the closet across from the powder room." Her eyes flicked to me.

"Gotcha," I said, finding a brand-new vacuum in the small closet just outside Nicky's bedroom. Another Parker gift. I was grateful. By the time I had the cord plugged in, Scarlett and Sterling had the pad and carpet unrolled, centered on the fireplace exactly the way Hope and Parker wanted it. I got to work running the vacuum as Royal and Finn came in, carrying another rolled carpet and pad stacked on top of each other the same way Billy Bob had.

Royal looked at Parker. "Nicky's room or Savannah's?"

Parker tilted her head to the side, studying what she could see of the tightly rolled rug. "Actually, that one goes right here." She gestured to the space between the kitchen counter and the sitting area by the fireplace. "Where the table and chairs will go."

They unrolled the carpet to Parker's specifications and

headed right back out the door. I moved to vacuum the new rug, finishing just as all four of them returned with another set of carpets and pads, one for my bedroom and one for Nicky's.

I'd seen everything during our attic forays to find furniture for the cottage, but at the time, it had been more about the to-do list. Living room carpet, check. Bedroom carpet, check. I hadn't been thinking about style or design. Part of it was that I had my hands full running the Manor, and design wasn't really my thing. When it came to the Manor, I put in the effort, but when it was for me, I was all about function over form.

I could appreciate beautiful things, but I wasn't worried about getting them for myself. And on top of that, the housekeeper's apartment off the kitchen was basic. I think the carpet in there was older than I was. It was clean. That was probably the best thing you could say about the housekeeper's apartment. I wasn't prepared to be picky about the cottage, considering anything was an upgrade.

But now that I saw Parker and Hope's design literally unrolling in front of me, I was a little overwhelmed.

The carpet in front of the fireplace was a Persian design in deep, rich blues and reds, accented by dark gold and flashes of light greens. Everything came together in jeweled harmony, more beautiful than anything I'd expected. Certainly nothing that should be in the housekeeper's cottage. The second carpet, for the dining area, was a tightly woven dark blue. Pretty, soft under my feet, but easy to clean. Perfect for a table that would regularly seat a six-year-old.

I was overwhelmed, yes. And stunned at how perfect it looked. It exactly suited me and my life. How had I missed how well Parker knew me, and how much these people had become my family?

Griffen came through the door, kicking it open gently with the toe of his shoe, somehow juggling two lamps and an end table as he made his way through the living room. "Parker," he called through the lampshade blocking his face. "Where does this stuff go?"

"Right there," she called back, gesturing to the bare floor in front of the bay window. "We'll set those up after Billy Bob brings the sofa and chairs over."

The coffee maker trilled with a noise that reminded me of a robot exuding joy. Even robots loved caffeine. "Coffee is done," I announced.

"I could use some coffee," Griffen said, "after we bring over the next load."

Billy Bob came through the front door, a beautiful antique dresser between them. Billy caught my eye. "Your bed's next. If you want to run that vacuum upstairs first, I'd get to it."

"I'm on it," I said, unplugging the vacuum and lifting it, following them up the narrow stairs at a distance, just in case they lost their grip on the heavy dresser. Behind me, I heard Griffen say, "I thought you were working in the office today."

That must have been directed at Hope. She answered with a laugh. "Griffen, seriously. I'm not sitting in the office while everyone else is here having fun. Do you know how long Parker and I have been working on this?"

"Buttercup," I heard him cajole. "You know you shouldn't be . . .""

The rest of his words faded out as I reached the top of the stairs. I loved that he still called her Buttercup. I remembered him calling her that when I was Nicky's age, a life-time ago.

Billy and Bob set the dresser against the wall, shooting me twin raised eyebrows to confirm it was in the right place. Pretty sure that it was, I nodded. "There's good, I think. If not, Parker will let us know," I said with a shrug, pushing the vacuum over the deep green and gold Berber rug that covered most of my new bedroom floor.

They both laughed. "Never thought little Parker would turn out so bossy," Billy said.

"She's done a great job on this place," Bob added. "She's already got us working on the gatehouse. Looks like that'll be just as nice as your cottage."

I had no doubt it would.

"Be back in a few with the bed," Billy added as they jogged down the stairs.

The noise of the vacuum almost drowned out the chime from my phone. A text message. Lydia again. I didn't want to read it. It had been over a week since I'd last heard from her. I still hadn't replied to her last message. Ignoring her continued to be my favorite approach. No part of me wanted to invite Lydia back into our lives.

I wished we could have bonded in our shared grief over losing Oliver. We could have come together, helped each other get through it. But she'd been so eager to throw blame at me, giving none to her perfect, angelic son. And once she started making noises about taking Nicky and me being an unfit mother, I'd lost interest in bonding over anything.

Really, by the time Oliver died, I was tired of Lydia's martyr act, tired of carrying her guilt for her. I had enough pain, enough grief of my own. I couldn't process hers as well. She'd sworn never to speak to me again, and I'd left. I didn't know what had changed, but she was back, and ignoring her wasn't making her go away.

She's Nicky's grandmother, I tried to remind myself, my finger hovering over my phone screen. All I could see was her name and the first line of the text.

Savannah, I really must insist

She really must insist what? Annoyed that she was intruding on my moving day, a day about family and love and everything good in my life, I stabbed my fingertip at the screen and opened the text message.

Chapter Twenty-Three

SAVANNAH

> Savannah, I really must insist that we meet. I want to see Nicky. I deserve to see my grandson. If you can't drive him here for Thanksgiving. I'll come down and collect him. We'll keep him for the week he has off school and return him at the end of the holiday. You've had him all this time. It's my turn now.

My gut reaction was a big hell no. I wasn't letting her take Nicky anywhere. First of all, he barely remembered her. She was as good as a stranger, and sending him off with her would scare him. On top of that, I didn't trust her. I hadn't for a long time. I just wasn't sure that meant I had the right to keep Nicky from his grandmother.

Three dots appeared on the screen. That was the problem with reading text messages. Now she knew I was on my phone, a captive audience. I wished I'd ignored it, but ignoring her wasn't working.

Hoping to preempt her, I typed,

> I have a busy day today. I can't talk about this right now. I'll think about it and let you know.

I hit send, and the three dots on Lydia's end disappeared. Maybe that would hold her for another day or two until I could think about how to handle this. It was becoming clear that Lydia wasn't going to go away.

Finn and my mother had been right. I needed to talk to a lawyer. Back when Oliver had been alive, and just after he died, Lydia had made noises about going for custody, saying that Nicky deserved better than a single mother raising him. I'd been furious. I'd been raised by a single mother, the best mother on the planet, and I'd turned out just fine. Better than fine. Of all the doubts I had in life, being able to raise Nicky wasn't one of them. No one was taking my son from me.

Winding the cord back on the vacuum, I went back downstairs, spotting the newly unrolled carpet in Nicky's room. I plugged in the vacuum again. Might as well get this one done while I was here. I needed a few more minutes to myself.

I didn't want to deal with Lydia. I didn't want to find a lawyer. But ignoring her wasn't working, and if she got difficult, I couldn't handle her on my own. Everything inside me shied away from the idea of getting a lawyer. It wasn't just the expense, though that was part of it. Lawyers were expensive. Good lawyers were very expensive. And Lydia would definitely get a very good lawyer.

I had a nice savings account. I'd been careful with the money from the sale of our house and belongings, as well as Oliver's insurance and my salary here. If Nicky stayed at Laurel Country Day, the next step would be college, and I would need every penny for that. I was still paying off the last of my own college loans. I didn't want Nicky to have to do the same, so I'd been saving since he was born.

After Oliver's first accident, I'd learned that health insurance was great, but sometimes it didn't save the day, and unexpected expenses could drown you. I liked having a cushion in the bank. My just-in-case money. A lawyer would chew through my nest egg and Nicky's college fund in the blink of an eye. And for what? I didn't know what Lydia wanted yet. Maybe she was going to make a move to get custody, and maybe she just wanted to see her grandson.

More than the money, if I responded to Lydia's request to see Nicky by getting a lawyer, I knew this whole thing would escalate out of my control. Lydia had much deeper coffers than I did, and when it came to anything that had to do with Oliver, she was a little crazy. She was also used to getting her way. If I got a lawyer, she'd get a better one, and Lydia could keep me in court for years as I watched my resources draining away.

I sighed as I vacuumed. I didn't want to be dealing with this, to be dealing with Lydia. My mother had suggested I talk to Harvey, and I could. Harvey liked me. I liked Harvey. We'd known each other my entire life. If I asked him for advice, he would give it, but he didn't practice family law. He could write a threatening letter, or refer me to another lawyer, but he couldn't represent me in this. And even if he did, Harvey wasn't cheap.

I shoved the vacuum over the carpet, pissed off that Lydia was intruding here, tarnishing the sparkle of my new house, of my friends helping me make it a home. She'd tarnished enough of my life, enabling Oliver's addiction until he was too far gone to save, threatening to take Nicky from me, trying to make me believe I was a bad mother.

I didn't want her here. I didn't want anything to do with her.

But what if I were overreacting? Maybe she just wanted to see him. Could I trust her enough for a visit?

It hit me with sudden clarity that this wasn't just about Nicky. If it was, she'd have asked to see him long ago. She never would have written us off in the first place. I believed she wanted to see her grandson, but I knew it was about more. It was about winning, about proving me wrong. Back when Oliver had been drowning in his addiction, she'd been all about what a terrible wife and mother I was. If I'd loved him enough, he wouldn't have gotten hurt, wouldn't have been so lost in the pills.

If she could beat me, it would prove she was right and everything was my fault. And then there was Oliver. If Lydia dragged me into court, all of it would come out.

I'd told Finn about Oliver's death. It still boggled my mind that of all the people in my life, I trusted Finn with the story I'd never wanted to tell. Of course, my mother knew how he'd died. I assumed Hawk knew, because Hawk knew everything, which meant Griffen probably knew. But none of them had ever mentioned it, so I could at least pretend no one knew. I could keep that ugly part of my past private.

I couldn't stand the thought of it coming out, of it being public, of being defined by a past I hadn't chosen, by a man who'd turned my life upside down, broken my heart, and ultimately left me and his son.

I liked being strong, capable, kick-ass Savannah Miles.

Being an object of pity? No. No fucking way. I'd felt pitiful enough when it was all happening. Now that Oliver was gone, I just wanted to move on. I wanted Lydia to leave me alone.

I waited for my phone to ping with a return text. It stayed silent. But I knew this wasn't the end. Unfortunately, I could safely assume from this latest text that she wasn't going to go away.

I pushed Lydia and my problems out of my mind as I finished vacuuming Nicky's room, just in time for Billy Bob to carry in the parts to the adorable oak twin bed we'd found in the attic, with its matching side table and a cute lamp with elephants on it. We'd found the lamp in one of the guest rooms, but it hadn't fit Parker's idea for the room's decor, so she'd switched it out for something else and earmarked it for Nicky.

Leaving Billy Bob to put the bed frame together, I walked back into the main room and stopped short. I'd left with the carpet freshly vacuumed and the rest of the room empty. I'd returned to find the sitting area set up with a graceful, bottle-green sofa and two armchairs upholstered in a multicolored pattern that perfectly picked up the colors in the carpet and the sofa. Everything was angled to face both the fireplace and the bay window.

The side tables and lamps Griffen had carried over were in place, the lamps already plugged in and casting a warm glow over the entire sitting area. Someone had hung an oil painting of the mountains over the fireplace, carried over split logs, and arranged them in an iron holder, a matching fireplace tool set beside it.

Between the sitting area and the kitchen was a rectangular table big enough to seat six, the chairs already pushed in. Daisy's pastries were arranged on a square white platter. Where that had come from, I had no idea. My new blue stoneware mugs were washed and set out on the table.

Finn and Griffen came through the door, hefting a queen-size mattress.

"Looking good in here," Griffen said as they passed through.

I agreed.

Finn said nothing, but his eyes found mine, his intent gaze sending a shiver down my spine. It was not lost on me that the house was filled with beautiful men. Even Billy Bob had their own well-muscled, rustic charm.

But Finn was the only one I saw. His deep, mossy green eyes with that spark of trouble. I was intimately aware of what that spark of trouble could lead to. The best kind of trouble. He wasn't the sullen, jerky teenager I'd hated for so long, but a man who'd laid me out on my kitchen counter and given me more pleasure than anyone ever had in my entire life. I jerked my chin up, breaking eye contact.

"I need coffee," I announced, heading straight to the coffee maker. "Anyone else?"

Scarlett handed me a mug. "Cream and sugar are on the table," she said, her eyes flicking to the stairs where Griffen and Finn had disappeared, then back to me.

"Pretty sweet coffee maker," she said, raising an eyebrow.

I nodded, but didn't take the bait.

"Very nice," Sterling agreed, looking out from where she was arranging throw pillows on the sofa. "It was sweet of him to realize you needed one. He can be a real asshole, but when we were little, he was always sweet. Before his mom died," she added with a wistful smile.

Sterling's own mother had died in a drunk driving accident when Sterling was three. Darcy had taken in the child of her husband's mistress without protest, showering love on Sterling until Darcy, too, died four years later. I could still remember the chill that had fallen over Heartstone Manor when Darcy died. Nothing had been the same after that.

Shaking off her sadness, Sterling narrowed her eyes on me. "You know, I can't quite picture Finn driving into town to buy a coffee maker. He must have had to go all the way to Asheville for one that nice."

I'd been hoping no one else would figure that out.

"He could have ordered it," Hope offered, raising an eyebrow at me. She knew I knew every delivery that came to Heartstone. I assumed she was helping me out because of my obvious discomfort. It was a very Hope thing to do.

Wishing the floor would swallow me up, I shook my head. "I don't know where it came from, but it was nice of him. Where did you find the dishes?" I asked, hoping to divert them. "I love them."

I did love the blue stoneware, the mugs and plates rimmed in a deep cobalt that faded to a pale sky blue in the center. They were gorgeous, but I was ready to toss my mug on the floor if they didn't stop talking about Finn. He was only upstairs and would be back any second. The only thing worse than this conversation would be if Finn was included. I really did not want to stand here while Finn's sisters and sisters-in-law grilled him about the coffee maker he bought me.

Pouring a slug of cream into my coffee, I eyed the platter of pastries and decided against adding sugar. I already knew I'd be eating more than my share of Daisy's pastries today. Starting with the raspberry and cream cheese danish in my hand. I couldn't answer questions if I was chewing, right?

Hope took a sip of coffee, watching me with thoughtful eyes. "After Mrs. Haverty quit, I was pretty sure you and Finn were going to kill each other. When he ended up taking over the kitchens—" She shook her head with an amused half smile. "Griffen and I have a bet going on who'll break first, but so far you both seem just fine." She paused, her cognac eyes narrowing just a little further. "It's interesting. You'd tell me if there was a problem, right?"

"Of course I would," I said automatically, then mentally kicked myself. I tried to recover. "He's annoying, but I haven't poisoned him yet."

"Oh, Savannah," I heard from behind me. "You know better than that. If anyone's doing any poisoning, it's always the chef."

My cheeks flamed.

"Savannah said you bought her a coffee maker," Sterling said with a teasing laugh.

I listened very closely for his answer.

"It's a bribe," Finn said with a grin. He reached past me to snag a blueberry muffin, his body brushing mine. I was sure it was intentional, the jerk. Heat flooded through me. Between my embarrassed cheeks and the rest of my body wanting more of Finn, I was going to combust. And based on his grin, I'd bet he knew exactly what he was doing to me.

Curious eyes flicked between Finn and me. Finn munched his blueberry muffin as if he didn't have a care in the world. Bastard. I was about to crawl out of my skin. This was not a good group of women to try to fool. Every one of them was sharp. No one knew Finn well, not these days, but they all knew me extremely well. And I was not a great actress. I liked things straightforward.

Sipping my coffee, pretending I wasn't desperate for this conversation to end, I thought about making a teasing comment back, like telling Hope not to collect on any bets yet because I might still kill him. But then he'd say something in that charmingly amused tone, and I'd get even more embarrassed, and I'd never be able to fool everyone into thinking nothing was going on. So I kept my mouth shut, gripping my coffee cup like it was my anchor to sanity.

"Savannah likes her coffee," Finn said. "I figure if I keep her caffeinated, I can stay on her good side."

Only Finn and I knew why he wanted to stay on my good side, and it had nothing to do with our working relationship. If he were going to play it cool, I sure as hell wasn't giving anyone else any more evidence there was something to pay attention to. We worked together. We hadn't murdered each other yet. He bought me a coffee maker. That was it. Nothing else to tell.

Sterling broke the silence. "Savannah is pretty patient, but hedging your bets with a coffee maker was smart. You never know when you'll have a bad day and drive her to murder."

"It's been close a few times," Finn admitted with a grin.

"We'll see," Hope said, that thoughtful look still in her eyes. "I have a feeling I'm going to win this one."

I didn't get a chance to ask her which of us she bet on. Hawk appeared at my side, his face somber, as always. "Savannah, do you have a minute?" His tone indicated it would be best for everyone if I indeed had a minute. I was thrilled to give him all the minutes he needed if he'd get me out of this room.

Chapter Twenty-Four
SAVANNAH

"What's up?" I asked, following him to the front door as the others started discussing how to organize my kitchen cabinets.

"This place is great." Hawk swept a glance around the room. "Parker really fixed it up. It looks completely different."

"It does," I agreed. "I love it."

"We need to talk about security. I don't like you and Nicky on your own out here."

Hawk led me out the front door as I mulled over his words.

"But the estate's under guard," I said. "You have people walking the property twenty-four hours a day. Cameras everywhere."

We were all aware of the danger. No one had caught Prentice's murderer, and thanks to Vanessa's notes and everything she'd said before she died, we knew his killer was still out there, still holding a grudge against the Sawyers. Nothing had happened in a while, at least nothing that seemed related to Prentice's murder. I looked at Heartstone

Manor across the side lawn. The winding gravel path looked a million miles long. *It's a two-minute walk,* I reminded myself.

"I've got cameras up." Hawk pointed to the overhang of the porch, first at one corner, then the other.

Realization dawned. Had he seen Finn come in yesterday afternoon and not leave for over an hour?

"How long have those been there?" I asked.

"Put them up yesterday while the rest of you were at dinner," Hawk said. I relaxed. "They're hooked into the system," Hawk continued. "The entire perimeter is covered. Video, audio, and motion detection lights all around. If anything bigger than a rabbit moves near the cottage, the lights will go on, and we'll get an alert. Depending on how interested the deer are, you might need to get good blinds for your bedrooms so they don't wake you up at night."

He stopped, taking in my wide eyes.

"I don't want to freak you out," he said.

"Too late." Though it was good to know that if Lydia made any sudden moves, there was no way she was getting near Nicky while he was on the estate.

"Don't worry, just be smart. It's my job to be prepared for any eventuality, no matter how unlikely. It's your job to be smart. Lock the doors. Use the alarm. Windows and doors are on the alarm. There's a panel at both doors. They work the same as the panels at the house. I set it with the same code you use for the main house." Hawk went back inside, stopping to show me the discreet panel to the side of the door, a smaller version of the alarm panels we had in Heartstone Manor.

"Any questions, let me know."

With that, Hawk left as quietly as he'd arrived. I pushed

away thoughts about the alarm and the reason we needed all this technology.

Back in the main room, Finn was gone, but the women were hard at work, putting things to order. I got to work unpacking the rest of the kitchen things with Scarlett, Hope directing us from her seat at the table where she'd been relegated after Griffen glared one too many times at Parker.

Hope grumbled, but Parker sat her at the table, slid a scone in front of her, and said, "Don't make me fight with my brother. He's going a little crazy with you so pregnant. He's going to drive you nuts when he has a fragile newborn to protect."

"I'm trying not to think about it," Hope admitted. "He's a little overprotective."

Griffen walked by with Finn, heading back to the house for another load of whatever we were missing. The first floor looked mostly done to me, but I trusted Parker's plan. Griffen stopped short at seeing Hope sitting complacently at the table. Dropping a kiss on the top of her head, he met Parker's eyes and said a quiet, "Thank you."

He and Finn left. Billy Bob were gone, and Royal had gone to the Inn to get some work done. All that was left was the unpacking. There wasn't much in the kitchen, just the dishes and silverware Parker brought over and the kitchen supplies from Finn. Scarlett and I had that done in no time. We found Sterling in Nicky's room, halfway done putting his clothes in the dresser. His bed was already made in a cute red and blue tartan comforter and crisp white sheets. Sterling had tucked his worn stuffed Pikachu under the covers as if he were napping.

She looked over her shoulder at us. "Oh, good. Savannah, I left his odds and ends over there by the closet. Can you figure out where you want them? I have almost every-thing else in the dresser. The stuff to hang is on the bed."

The rest of us jumped into action, moving on to books and toys when we were done with the clothes. From there, we moved to my room. It didn't take long to put my things away. Someone had already unpacked my books downstairs, leaving mostly clothes and toiletries up here. My wardrobe wasn't huge, mainly because I'd been wearing a uniform to work since I'd been back in Sawyers Bend, first waiting tables at the Inn and then at Heartstone.

Parker slipped one of my uniform dresses onto a hanger, lining it up with the other four. "I love this dress. It's so pretty, and it looks official, but not boring. Plus, it looks great on you." The black and white A-line houndstooth dress was comfortable, easy to clean, and looked far more formal than it felt. Most days, I wore it with black leggings and black Mary Janes. I could do almost anything in that dress and still feel worthy of the house. Even though Griffen and Hope had said they didn't care about my uniform, Heartstone Manor demanded more than jeans and a t-shirt.

"Thanks," I said. "It's the bonus of choosing my own uniform. And it saves me tons on clothes."

I'd gotten rid of my office clothes when I left Richmond. These days my wardrobe was mostly jeans, t-shirts, and leggings for the rare lazy day at home. I had a handful of nicer things I hadn't worn since I'd come back to Sawyers Bend. Not much. Between the five of us, we finished unpacking the last duffel an hour after we'd started.

Tenn showed up just as we folded up the last of the boxes we'd emptied. He carried an open box, brightly colored spikes poking from the top. When he got closer, I realized they were flowers. Glass flowers.

"You remembered! Thank you!" Scarlett leaned in, kissing Tenn on the cheek and taking the box.

He turned to press a longer kiss to her lips, leaving her eyes bright and her cheeks pink when he pulled away. "I'll be back in a while. Just have to get the kids."

"K," Scarlett said, looking a little dazed. After she watched Tenn leave, she set the box on the counter and pulled out a vase filled with glass flowers, setting it in the middle of the dining table.

"Scarlett, these are beautiful!" I traced a finger over the curve of a purple iris on a vibrant green stem, the curling leaf so perfect it looked real. I knew this was Scarlett's work. She was a glass artist, her studio in what had been one of the pantries down the hall from the kitchen. She made small pieces like these flowers, as well as jewelry and whatever else sparked her imagination. It was an honor to have them, and they meant that much more because they were a gift from her.

Catching her eye, I said, "I love this so much. Thank you!"

"Parker found the vase," Scarlett said, "and we thought it looked perfect with your kitchen and the rest of the colors in here, but it needed flowers. I didn't want you to have to get fresh flowers all the time. I love making flowers, so I thought I'd make you a bouquet you could keep forever."

"Or until Nicky knocks it over," Sterling added.

Scarlett laughed. "I'll just make more. I know all about boys knocking things over."

If anyone knew about boys knocking things over, it was Scarlett. She'd shown up at Heartstone Manor only five months ago, August in tow, handcuffed to Tenn. He'd caught her trespassing at the Inn and was about to turn her in to West, our police chief, when they literally stumbled across a body and Scarlett became Tenn's alibi. It hadn't taken long to see that she and Tenn were crazy for each other.

The surprise had been the way Tenn had taken to Scarlett's boys, eight-year-old August and thirteen-year-old Thatcher. Overnight, it seemed Tenn had become a father and Heartstone Manor a family home. August and Thatcher were good kids, and Nicky had been thrilled to have playmates in the Manor. I'd been happy to make a friend too. Scarlett was funny, tough, and sweet at the same time. Watching her with Tenn always made me smile.

She arranged the glass flowers in the vase, then helped me wash the coffee mugs while Parker and Sterling packed up what was left of the pastries. The knock on the door startled all of us. I looked up to see my mother swinging open the front door.

"We're here for tea," she called out, Tenn behind her holding a tray and a thermos.

"Finn's busy with dinner," Tenn said, "but he thought you guys might want to have tea here today so you could show Nicky and your mom the cottage. The boys are right behind me. They'll be here in a minute."

"Sweet of him," Sterling commented under her breath.

"Very," I agreed, any possibility of further comment cut off by the boys flying through the door, Nicky in the lead.

"Moooom!! This is so cool!" Nicky had seen the cottage before, but it had been empty, not fully decorated down to paintings on the wall and Scarlett's beautiful glass bouquet on the table. He threw himself at me in a full-body hug before careening off and racing down the hall. "I'm gonna show the guys my room!"

August and Thatcher followed, the latter looking a little

sheepish at the younger kid's enthusiasm, as any proper teenager would.

"Looks awesome," Thatcher said as he passed. High praise indeed.

Scarlett smiled at me as he passed. We had three good boys between us. It wasn't a surprise Tenn had taken to them so easily. August hadn't been hard to win over, but Thatcher had been more reserved, torn by his loyalty to his disaster of a father. Tenn had given him space, and more importantly, understanding. Thatcher had warmed up to him faster than I'd expected, and now the two of them shared a bond that was growing day by day.

"Can I stay for tea?" Tenn asked. "After we get a tour?"

"Of course," I said, letting Parker take the lead. At every step, she explained the changes she'd made, and my sense of homecoming grew. I knew part of this was about Parker finding work she loved and excelled at. I loved that for her. But the rest was about her making a home for Nicky and me, and she'd worked her ass off doing it. When we were done, I caught her in a tight hug.

"Thank you, Parker. So much. I love it."

She squeezed me back. "You're welcome. I'm just glad it came out so well."

"It's beautiful," my mother said, reaching to give Parker her own hug.

Scarlett called us to the table, and I poured the tea, using my new mugs for the second time. Something about sharing a meal at the table, even a small one, was the final piece in making the cottage feel like home. It would take me a while to remember where we'd put everything, but I was about as moved in as I could be in one day.

Later, after dinner at the Manor, Nicky and I walked back to the cottage for our first night in our new home. It felt good, but weird, to unlock the door to our cottage and set the alarm behind us, the light from the lamps golden against the falling dark outside.

Nicky took forever to fall asleep, too excited by his new room to settle down. I'd been worried that he would be anxious all alone in his bedroom on the first floor with me upstairs, but once I rubbed his back for a few minutes, he relaxed, chatting to me about his ideas for his new room until he finally ran down and his eyes stayed shut.

Since we'd returned to Sawyers Bend, we'd either shared a room or been separated by only a thin door. I knew we needed our own space, and I was more than ready to have some privacy, but as I turned off Nicky's light and checked for the nightlight in his little bathroom, it turned out I was the anxious one, not him. I was too aware of the quiet around me.

What I needed was a long hot bath in my new soaking tub and an early night.

The soaking tub was heaven, complete with the bath salts I'd been holding on to for ages and had never used. Skin soft, muscles relaxed, I clicked on the gas fireplace opposite my bed and crawled between the smooth sheets, cuddling under the heavy duvet. Tears gathered in my eyes, my heart too full of everything. I loved this gorgeous cottage. My decadent bath, the marble counters in the kitchen, the fireplace in my bedroom. I felt spoiled and loved, so much so that my heart ached with it.

But beneath that, I realized as a tear streaked down my cheek that I was lonely. I was used to being in the heart of the Manor, surrounded by thousands of square feet of solid stone. The cottage was well built, but it was separate. The privacy from the main house I'd wanted so much suddenly seemed lonely. The Manor was so far away, the night dense and dark, the forest so close.

It wasn't that I was afraid. Hawk had eyes everywhere, and no one was interested in the Sawyers' housekeeper. If anyone did get through Hawk's security, I was probably safer here than in the Manor. But with Nicky fast asleep downstairs and me up here in my very adult, private bedroom with a door that actually locked, I felt more alone than I had since Oliver died.

My mind drifted to Finn. I hadn't seen him since dinner, and we hadn't had a moment alone together. I told myself it was for the best. Really. I was exhausted, and he'd been moving furniture all day. I didn't need him.

But I wanted him.

I looked at my phone on my bedside table. If I texted Finn, he'd come. He might have a sarcastic comment or tease me, but he'd come. And then I'd come.

I didn't text Finn. I wanted to, but I was afraid to. Mostly, I didn't text Finn because I didn't like how I felt. Like I wasn't just lonely, I was lonely for Finn.

The first was acceptable. Normal.

The second? That was a problem. Finn was for orgasms. Not for filling my lonely heart. Never for that.

And the sooner I got that straight, the better off I'd be.

Chapter Twenty-Five

SAVANNAH

I was going to break my neck on the attic stairs. Even though I'd been up and down them a thousand times, this time I was navigating them as I brought down dusty plastic bins filled with documents stacked two high. Manila envelopes, stiff and dark with age. Clothbound journals. Scraps of paper, some tissue thin, some stiff, all of them faded. I could have asked for help, but we were stretched thin as it was, and I didn't want to pull April or Kitty away from their tasks just to help me with some storage bins. I'd be fine. As long as I didn't break my neck.

Based on the quick look we'd taken weeks before while going through furniture in the attic, Hope and I thought these were the historical documents we'd been looking for. The housekeepers' records. Receipts, to-do lists, supply orders. Things that would tell us more about what it had been like to run the estate at the turn of the century and through the decades since. While Prentice had used his will to prevent his heirs from opening the house to the public, these documents were still a part of history. My history. I was curious to see how much life had changed at Heart-stone in the last hundred years.

According to my mother, around ten years ago there'd been a leak in the attic roof, and she reorganized the boxes up there, moving anything easily damaged to these plastic storage containers. I don't know how these two had gotten to the part of the attic where old furniture was stored. My mother remembered putting everything back on the shelves, the labeled bins lined up neatly.

The plastic bins were a heck of a lot more secure than cardboard boxes, but they weren't light. Especially when they were stacked on top of each other. I should have made two trips. Any sensible person would have made two trips.

I am usually incredibly sensible, but I was also short on time. I'd been dying to get into these boxes for weeks, ever since Hope and I had stumbled across them, but everything had been far too hectic to take the time to go through old papers.

Until today. Now that Nicky and I were moved into the cottage and completely unpacked, thanks to everyone helping out, I had a little extra time in my day. I wanted to use it on this side project before the next crisis popped up. Hope had already asked me twice this week when I wanted to dig in and see what we could find. I was getting a little worried that she'd try to drag the bins down herself. I remembered well the nervous energy and frustration of waiting in the final weeks of my pregnancy with Nicky, and I didn't want Hope to get any ideas.

Craning my head around the top storage bin, I tried to gauge how close I was to the bottom of the steps. Close? A few more steps, maybe? It was hard to tell. I went slowly, feeling for each step as I went. The last thing I needed was to pitch down the stairs and break something. I did not want to think about navigating Heartstone Manor on crutches.

At the bottom, I thought, I took a confident step toward the doorway and bounced off a wall of muscle. Twisting to see around the boxes, I caught a glimpse of a shoulder. Only an inch or two, but I'd know that shoulder anywhere.

I nudged with the bins, but Finn didn't move out of the doorway. "Could you move?"

"What the hell are you doing trying to carry this much down those stairs?" he demanded. He leaned past me to glare up the narrow staircase. "They're steep, and the lighting sucks. What if you'd fallen?"

Ugh. I didn't like that he was echoing things that had crossed my own mind only moments ago.

"Finn, can you move, please?" My words were polite. My tone less so. "These are heavy, and I want to put them down before I drop them."

"Where are they going?" Finn asked casually, as if my arms weren't about to tear out of their sockets. On the way down, I'd been too focused on the stairs to think about how heavy the bins were. Now I felt every pound. And I knew that tone. Finn was messing with me. Pre-sex with Finn, this would have pissed me off. Now it turned me on. And that pissed me off.

"To my old apartment. By the kitchens," I said through gritted teeth. I nudged forward again, shoving him a little with the bins.

His hands closed over mine. Interesting. Pre-sex Finn would have made me suffer the consequences of carrying something too heavy.

"Let me take them." He pulled on the bins.

Irritation flared. I could carry my own damn too-heavy

bins. "I don't need you to take them. I need you to get out of the way." Why would he not just move?

"Savannah, you carried these all the way down here. Let me take them to the elevator." Was that a laugh in his voice?

He was messing with me, and still, how was Finn the one being reasonable?

"I'm fine," I snapped, yanking hard on the bins.

That turned out to be a mistake. Finn's grip on the bins didn't budge. My backward momentum knocked me off balance until my feet slid out from under me, ramming directly into Finn's. I fell on my ass, sprawling on the stairs, momentarily stunned.

Finn went down like an oak tree, slow and heavy. If he hadn't been holding on to storage bins, he would have caught himself easily. Instead, the bins flew out of his hands as he tumbled back, coming down on his ass, then his shoulder, rolling until his head smacked the hardwood. I winced at the sound, craning my neck until I could see him.

"Finn, are you okay?"

"Yeah. Fuck."

I let out a breath of relief. He sounded more embarrassed than pained.

Propping myself up on my elbows, I looked through the doorway at Finn, still lying flat on his back. The two storage bins had fallen to either side of him, the lids now askew and their contents in a messy pile, mostly on top of him.

Hearing my sigh, he said, "I should have let you carry the damn bins."

"That would have been nice," I agreed.

He sat up, papers sliding off him in waves as he moved. "Everything looks okay. We'll just put it all back in and take them downstairs."

Reason overruled winning. Plus, I could tell I had a bruise forming on my ass from hitting the stairs. "This time I'll let you carry them," I said, getting off the stairs and kneeling opposite Finn. "Try to put everything back in the bin it came from, if you can tell what's what. Not everything in here is dated, so I want to keep things together as much as I can."

Finn scanned the papers around us. What had fallen on either side of him was easy to sort into piles. Everything that landed on top of him was a mess.

"Got it," he said, scooping loose papers on his left side into a pile before setting them in the bin on the left.

I did the same on the right side, doing my best not to look at anything I picked up. Otherwise, I knew something would catch my eye, and we'd be here all day. I'd learned my lesson when Hope and I found the bins shoved behind an old dresser and I came across a journal kept by one of the day maids from the 1930s. I'd sat on the attic floor reading it for a good half hour, Hope beside me engrossed in a ledger, before we realized we were way behind schedule and hadn't cataloged more than a few pieces of furniture.

We'd resealed the lid and resolved to get everything to the apartment once Nicky and I had moved out so we could spread it all out and see what we had.

I had most of the pile on the right side back in the bin when I looked up to find Finn's face barely an inch from mine.

"Sorry about the bins," he murmured.

I started to tell him it was okay, my lips parting to speak until his brushed against them, silencing me. That was okay. I'd rather kiss Finn than talk. I leaned in, feeling his hand come around to cup the back of my head, pulling me close, holding me as he tilted his head and kissed me deeper, his tongue stroking mine, his lips warm and firm, his kiss tasting of Finn.

A door closed down the hall in the family wing, and he eased back. I pressed my lips together, resisting the instinctive urge to follow him, chasing his mouth with mine. I had a million things to do, starting with getting these bins downstairs, but I could have kissed Finn all day. Though maybe not in a hallway where anyone could walk by.

Low enough that no one could overhear, Finn said, "I wanted to come by last night, but I thought you'd be exhausted."

"I was," I said truthfully. I left out the rest.

I couldn't tell him I missed him. That I lay in my new bed, alone, and wished he was beside me. We had sex. Once. I wanted to have more sex. A lot more. And wanting all that sex felt so much less vulnerable than admitting that I'd missed him.

Instead, I said, "I won't be exhausted tonight."

His lips curved in a smile that sent heat blasting through me. "What time does Nicky go to bed?"

"He's in bed by eight, but he isn't really asleep until eight-thirty."

"And what time do you go to bed?" he asked, his voice low and rough.

"By ten. Are you going to tuck me in?"

"Eventually," Finn said, leaning to brush his mouth over mine one last time.

I ducked my head when he turned back to his bin, not wanting him to see my smile. I'd been mulling over how this was going to go. I wasn't usually afraid to ask for what I wanted, but I hated the idea of asking Finn for anything.

I had to get over that. He was turning out to be a good man. As much as his kiss had set me on fire all those years ago, I never would have slept with teenage Finn. He was hot then, and an amazing kisser, but otherwise a total dickhead.

This Finn was still hot, and somehow an even better kisser, but most importantly, not at all a dickhead. I didn't think he'd laugh at me if I told him I wanted him, but it was a relief to know I didn't have to risk it. I was going to get my orgasms, and I didn't have to put myself out there by asking for them. My secret smile might have been a little smug.

I focused on the mess around me. I had most of the loose papers back in the bin. Wedged by my foot, I found a cloth journal beneath a leather-bound ledger. And under that, a dull brown alligator briefcase with brass latches and a combination lock. The latches had popped open, maybe from the impact of the briefcase hitting the floor, revealing about an inch of the interior. Not enough to see inside.

So far, I'd resisted looking closely at anything, but this was different. For one, the suitcase looked modern—at least from the standpoint that it was clearly not from the 1930s—and it had probably been locked. Which meant someone, at some point, hadn't wanted other people to know what was in it. I didn't know the combination, so I couldn't risk closing it until I knew what was inside. I told myself I wasn't wasting time. Looking now, before moving it further and losing the chance to see what was inside, made logical sense.

Moving into a cross-legged position, glad I was wearing leggings under my uniform dress, I pulled the briefcase into my lap. The dull brown alligator skin with the brass latches screamed 1970s. Prentice. No one else would have had something that looked like this. Prentice's father, Reginald, had still been around back then. Prentice hadn't forced him out of the business until the mid-eighties. I never knew Reginald. He died the year I was born, but from what my mother said, alligator and brass was not his style.

The hinges resisted, creaking as I forced the lid fully open. Unlike the haphazard piles of papers in the bins, the briefcase was neatly organized. Inside was a short stack of file folders, the labels faded with time.

Nothing about them said *historic document* to me. I glanced at the two bins beside us. Everything else was old. Pre-1960s old. Curious, I flipped open the top file folder. A contract for something. It was hard to tell exactly what. A partnership agreement? Contracts were not my area of expertise. I'd taken business law in college, but that had been a while ago.

In the first paragraph, I saw the name Sawyer. Not a surprise, given whose house I was in. Skipping the rest, I flipped to the signature page. *Prentice Sawyer for Sawyer Enterprises.* Signed February 23, 2012. The other signature lines had company names, the signatures themselves impossible to decipher. I moved to the next file folder. Another contract, also signed by Prentice, and the same two company names. Some of the pages had handwritten notations in the margins. I couldn't tell if they'd been added later or were part of the contract. They weren't initialed, which suggested they'd been added later, but I wasn't sure.

"What do you have there?" Finn asked. I looked up to see that he was finished re-packing his own bin and was waiting on me.

"Contracts," I said, staring down into the briefcase. "Your father's contracts. I think this is his briefcase. I need to bring it to Griffen. It doesn't belong with the rest of this stuff."

"How did his briefcase get in the bin?"

"That's a good question," I said slowly, thinking. "Maybe when Mom was reorganizing the attic, she threw it in here. I don't know."

Finn dropped the last stack of papers into his bin and snapped on the lid. Standing, he said, "If you take the brief-case, I'll get the bins. We can bring the bins downstairs and drop off the briefcase with Griffen on the way."

"I think that's a good idea." I set the briefcase down, careful not to close it accidentally, and finished putting the last of the papers and journals in the bin so Finn could stack it on top of the other.

Something about the tacky yet modern briefcase and those neat file folders hidden amid the hodgepodge of housekeeper's records felt off to me. My mother could have dropped the briefcase in one of the bins, but how had Sawyer Enterprises contracts gotten into the attic in the first place?

Finn hefted the two bins and turned down the hall to the elevator.

Between the bins and Finn's large frame, the elevator felt too small. I had a moment to wish I had my hands free, that the ride would be longer, and then the door unlocked and we were on the first floor.

Chapter Twenty-Six

SAVANNAH

Finn led the way to Griffen's office, setting the bins down outside and giving the door a quick rap. He opened it without waiting for a response, sticking his head through to ask, "You busy?"

"What's up?" Griffen said in response.

Finn pushed the door all the way open, and we entered. Griffen and Hope sat behind Griffen's wide desk, Royal on the other side, his laptop open in front of him. Papers were spread across the desk between them, an uncapped pen on top.

Hope's eyes lit up when she saw the bins just outside the door. "The housekeeping documents?"

"We're bringing them down to my old apartment," I said. "Which I guess is now the staff lounge. I thought I could spread them out on the table so we can take our time going through them." I shot a look at Finn, and he jumped in.

"We dropped the bins." He paused, raising an eyebrow and tilting his head at me. "Someone was trying to carry both bins at once and wouldn't let me help."

I rolled my eyes. "Then someone else grabbed them, and everything ended up on the floor."

Finn shook his head as if I were the idiot in this scenario. Hope's eyes sparkled with amusement.

"Anyway," I went on. "We dropped the bins, and they spilled all over the place, and I found this." I held out the open briefcase to Griffen. "It looks like it was your father's. There are contracts inside. Way too recent to belong with the housekeepers' records in the bins, and what I looked at was for Sawyer Enterprises. They were signed after you left, so—"

"Thanks, Savannah," Griffen said, setting the briefcase on the desk in front of him and opening the lid all the way. "This was my dad's briefcase. I remember it from when I was a kid. He replaced it. I can't remember when. Maybe when I was in high school."

He opened the first file folder, Hope leaning in to read over his shoulder.

"Partnership agreement," he said under his breath, flipping to the second page, stopping when his eyes caught a handwritten note in the margin. "That's Ford's handwriting."

"You're sure?" Royal asked, leaning in.

Hope nodded. "I recognize it too. That's definitely Ford's handwriting," she confirmed.

As I had, Griffen flipped to the signature page, his eyes narrowing on the date. "2012. Well after my time with Sawyer Enterprises." He flipped back and re-read Ford's notes. "These are notes to himself." His finger hovered over one. "Check source of funds." He flipped back to the signature page. Even from across the table, I could see that Ford had three question marks under one of the company names, the ink dark and thick, grooved into the paper as if he'd been pressing especially hard on his pen.

Royal pointed at the company name marked by question marks. "Isn't that—?"

"I think so," Griffen said.

"Isn't that what?" Finn asked, clearly as lost as I was. I ran Heartstone Manor, but I had nothing to do with Sawyer Enterprises.

Griffen looked up at us. "Yawhood Properties. We think Dad did business with them a few times, but we haven't had any luck tracing anything about it. It probably doesn't matter at this point, but we've been trying to track down loose ends. It's odd to have a party to an important contract just disappear."

"Or possibly not have existed in the first place," Hope said under her breath.

Hope pointed to the other company name. *Chiapas Co.* "I've seen this somewhere."

She closed her eyes, maybe digging in her memory for the name, as Royal shook his head. Opening her eyes, she said, "I know this name. I can't remember if I know it from years ago or if I've seen it in one of the contracts we've gone through in the last six months."

Royal added, "I've been focused on current business, and I don't remember seeing that company anywhere."

"I don't recognize it either," Griffen said to Hope. "So it must have to do with business from back when you and Edgar worked with Ford and Dad."

Griffen moved on to the next folder, scanning the contract inside. "These are some big numbers, but it doesn't say what it's for. Just mentions 'Product.' Same two companies as the first contract."

"That's not sketchy at all," Royal added.

"That's Dad for you," Griffen said with a grim smile. He moved to the next folder. "Another contract. Six months after this last one. Same deal." I could see notes scribbled in Ford's handwriting on this one too. Griffen picked up a manilla envelope and unwound the string sealing it shut. He pulled out a single piece of paper.

"This one isn't a contract," Griffen said absently, scanning the page. Looking over his shoulder, Hope drew in a quick breath and sat up.

"What?" I asked. "What is it?"

"It has Finn's name on it," Hope said.

Finn stepped back, his shoulders rounding forward, shrinking in on himself. If my name had been on a hidden document, I would have grabbed it to see what it said, but Finn had retreated. Did he already know what Griffen was reading? How could he?

Griffen's eyes shot back and forth over the page, the color draining from his face with every line. Finally, he put the sheet of paper down on his desk and looked up at Finn.

"This is a ransom letter. You were kidnapped?"

Kidnapped? Finn had been kidnapped? What the hell was Griffen talking about?

Finn didn't say anything.

"Finn," Griffen said, his voice raising to a shout. "You were fucking kidnapped? In Mexico? What the fuck?" Griffen shot Royal an accusing look. "Did you know about this?"

Royal looked sick, his eyes on Finn, heavy with guilt. "I didn't know until long after it was over. There was nothing I could do by then."

"Explain," Griffen ground out.

Royal kept his eyes on Finn. "Dad told us all that you dropped out of college and joined the army. We tried to call, but your number was disconnected. We wrote but never heard back. Then Tenn and I saw the letter you wrote Dad. When you were living in France. After. We recognized your handwriting, and we knew Dad wouldn't tell us anything, so we opened it. That was the first time we knew anything about the kidnapping."

"And you didn't say anything?" Hope asked.

Royal shook his head, not taking his eyes from his younger brother. "I'm sorry, Finn. Dad told us you were kidnapped in Mexico, that he refused to pay the ransom, just like he would have refused for any of the rest of us. He said you were pissed about the whole thing, that you'd get over it eventually and come home."

"How could you keep a secret like that?" Hope demanded. "Why didn't you tell me or your sisters?"

Royal shifted in his chair and looked at Hope. "Prentice swore us to secrecy. He said Ford agreed with him about the ransom, which was easy to believe. And what would it help if we told anyone?" He met Finn's eyes. "I read your letter. I knew you didn't want to come back here. I figured if you ever did, you could tell your own story. And if you didn't, I didn't want the girls to know what happened to you." Royal swallowed. "Prentice showed us the pictures they sent him. We didn't want the girls to see."

Hope shook her head. "I don't understand this. When, Finn? When did this happen?"

We all looked at Finn.

Through sheer force of will, he straightened, rolling his shoulders back, then jerking one up in a teenage shrug—that angry *fuck off and leave me alone* shrug I knew so well from back in the day.

I wished things were different between us and I could take a step toward him and put my arm around him.

243

Because for all that he was trying to look strong and angry, agony leaked out of every pore.

I stayed where I was. I wasn't sure Finn wanted my sympathy right now. He was practically vibrating with restrained emotion. I wasn't feeling so steady myself. Kidnapped? How could something so big have happened to him, and I didn't know?

Finn's eyes locked on Griffen. His voice when he spoke was so raw, I knew this question had been torturing him. "You didn't know?"

"No, Finn. No, I didn't fucking know," Griffen said, his voice rough and low. "What the fuck happened?"

Finn gave another jerk of a shrug, as if he could fool us into thinking this was no big deal. "I was on spring break. Sophomore year of college. Somebody grabbed me, held me for a couple of days. Dad said he wouldn't pay the ransom. They were going to kill me, but then they got drunk, and I got away."

We stared at him in shock. I'm pretty sure my mouth was hanging open.

His words sank in, and I realized what he was actually saying. "That's—but you never—" I was babbling. I couldn't get the words to line up right in my head. "You never came home. That's why you never came back to Sawyers Bend."

He was supposed to come home that summer. I'd been dreading seeing him, having him around making obnoxious comments and generally aggravating me. I was relieved when my mother told me he had joined the army, even though that didn't sound like the Finn I knew. With the self-absorption of youth, I accepted her story and went on with my life. A wave of nausea hit me. I'd been relieved Finn wasn't coming home, and it was all because he'd been kidnapped.

Finn's eyes met mine for the briefest second before they flicked away, and he jerked his chin up.

"Your father lied," I said, trying to wrap my head around what Prentice had done. "They were going to kill you, and he was going to let them?"

"He told them, 'I don't give a fuck what you do with him. He's worth nothing to me.'" Finn jerked his shoulders in another shrug. "I didn't feel like coming home after that."

"What did you do?" Hope asked, her voice anguished. "You were only nineteen and alone in Mexico. Did they hurt you?"

Finn ignored her last question, but I saw the look in Griffen's eyes. He'd worked with hostages and kidnap victims with Sinclair Security. He knew what happened when people were taken for ransom. He didn't have to ask Finn if they'd hurt him because he knew. My stomach turned over.

Nineteen-year-old Finn had been arrogant, entitled, and cocky. A raging dickhead most of the time. I'd hated him. But I couldn't stand the thought of that snotty boy locked in a dark room. Tied up. Waiting to die. My heart broke for him. No one should be that alone. That scared.

"I called Chef Guérard," Finn said in answer to Hope's question. "He bought me a plane ticket to France. He got me a job, helped me find a place to stay."

"How did you get away?" Griffen asked quietly.

"I got lucky," Finn said flatly. "They were going to shoot me, but they had an idea of how to get some money out of me. I don't know what it was. I don't want to know. They left me tied up and went off to figure out if there was any profit in keeping me alive. I think they were going to move me."

He shifted, glancing at me, then away when he saw the look on my face. I couldn't hide the ache in my heart.

He went on, "My Spanish sucked, so I didn't understand most of what was going on. But they were pissed off, and they didn't tie my hands as well as usual. Probably figured it wouldn't matter since I'd be dead soon and there was nowhere to go. They got drunk, and I had time to get my hands loose and force the window open. Then I walked through the desert until I found the road and a ride back to the city."

Griffen stared at him, gears turning behind his eyes. His phone chimed, but he ignored it. Finally he asked, "Why didn't you say anything?"

My question exactly. Why hadn't he said anything? Why hadn't he told us?

Such a stupid question. What was he supposed to do, just pop it into the conversation? Hey, nice to see you again after all this time. By the way, I left home because I was kidnapped and my dad wouldn't pay the ransom, and I had assumed that all of you were in on it, but I came back anyway.

A flash of pain hit me as another realization sank in. How could *I* not know this? I told him all about Oliver. In some ways, he knew more about me than my closest friends. And I knew nothing about him. And I'd just learned that half of what I thought I knew was a lie. He'd never been in the army. Where had he learned to cook? Someone had said he went to culinary school. Was that a lie too?

It wasn't like Finn and I had engaged in hours of long, deep conversation since we'd both been back. We'd glared at each other more than anything. Argued way too often.

Even now, when we were on very personal terms in one sense, we still hadn't talked much. About meals and the kitchens and Heartstone, yes, we talked plenty. But about ourselves, our lives . . . Not at all.

And I hadn't noticed. I hadn't asked.

It was stupid to feel so hurt. If I wanted to know, I could have asked. It wasn't like Finn himself had lied to me. He just hadn't told us—me—the truth. And I never bothered to ask. Shame flooded through me, so dark and deep my chest ached with it. I never asked. I could hear Prentice Sawyer as clearly as if I'd been in the room.

"I don't give a fuck what you do with him. He's worth nothing to me."

He'd said that about his son. I thought of Nicky. I'd die for him in an instant. I'd do anything to protect him from harm, and Finn's father had left him in the hands of his kidnappers? Men who planned to kill him? I didn't have to ask if Prentice had known what would happen to Finn if he didn't pay. Prentice had known. And he hadn't cared.

I couldn't imagine it. I grew up in this house, thought I knew what a bastard Prentice Sawyer was, and still, I couldn't imagine it. I never knew my father's love. He died when I was too young to remember him. But my mother had loved me enough for two parents, and I grew up knowing that in our brief time together, my father had adored me.

Prentice had left his child to die. Tears welled in my eyes, streaking down my face. I saw Hope wiping her cheek. Griffen's eyes were dry, but dark with pain. Royal's head hung down, hiding his expression. Finn stared out the window to the barren gardens outside, his face blank.

I couldn't leave him there, alone, carrying all that pain. I closed the space between us, sliding my hand into his. This wasn't about sex. I'm not even sure it was friendship. We weren't friends, exactly. I didn't know what we were. But I'd known Finn Sawyer since we were children, and I couldn't stand there and not reach for him.

My fingers closed around his, and I squeezed. Finn glanced down, the blank expression wiped from his face as he took in my tears. "Hey, Savannah, don't cry." Looking up, he saw Hope's tears and grimaced. "I'm okay. No one needs to cry. Really." Now he sounded a little panicked.

Dropping my hand, he paced to Griffen's desk and snatched a few tissues from the box by the monitor. Shoving them in Hope's hand, he grabbed a few more and pushed them at me. "Seriously. It was a long time ago. Dad was a massive asshole, but we already knew that. And I ended up okay. Chef Guérard helped me out. I worked, I learned, I even went to Cordon Bleu. I'm fine."

So he had gone to cooking school. That answered the question of where he learned to cook. I had a million more questions, but now wasn't the time. Finn studied my face until I dried my tears, balling the damp tissues in my fist.

"What I don't get," he said, "Is why there's a file about my kidnapping in that briefcase with those contracts."

"You were kidnapped because of those contracts."

I turned to see Cole Haywood, Ford's defense attorney, standing in the doorway of Griffen's office.

Chapter Twenty-Seven

FINN

Cole Haywood stood just inside the doorway. I hadn't seen him since he delivered the news that Ford was taking a plea bargain for Prentice's murder.

He looked the same, in that every time I saw Cole was like the first time. Cole Haywood was one of those people who was so good-looking you couldn't quite believe they were real. I don't pay a lot of attention to what other men look like, so that tells you all you need to know about Cole. With his chiseled jaw and prominent cheekbones, blue eyes, and dark hair, he looked like one of those models in high-end magazines. He looked like the kind of guy who never wore sweatpants. I wondered if he slept in that suit.

I didn't know him well. He'd had some kind of business with my father going way back. I'd always had the impression that he was a connection of Harvey's. I can't say I was his biggest fan. The way he'd pushed Ford to take the plea bargain didn't sit right with me. With any of us. But at the moment, I wanted to know what Cole knew about my kidnapping. And what he'd had to do with it.

Hawk stepped in behind Cole. To Griffen, he said, "I texted you. I figured you wouldn't mind me letting Haywood in."

Griffen looked at Cole. "Is Ford all right?"

Cole nodded. "As far as I know."

"What do you know about this?" Griffen turned the briefcase to Cole.

"May I?" Cole asked. At Griffen's nod, he picked up the file folders, scanning them rapidly, flipping through the pages with no reaction, as if he already knew what he was reading. As he moved from folder to folder and then finally to my ransom letter, he shook his head. When he was done, he handed the folders back to Griffen and turned to me.

His eyes dark with remorse, he said, "I'm sorry, Finn. You were never supposed to see any of this."

Of course I wasn't. Because I was supposed to be dead. Bitterness flooded me. Cole Haywood could take his remorse and shove it up his ass. I didn't want apologies; I wanted answers. Instead of demanding them, I kept my mouth shut. If I jumped into angry accusations, Cole would go straight into covering his own ass. I needed to know what he had to say if he thought I was buying all of his bullshit.

Cole turned his remorseful expression to Griffen. "I don't know everything. This was one of the first times I worked with your father, and I didn't get involved until after they took Finn."

His eyes cut to me, then back to Griffen, who asked, "What do these contracts have to do with Finn's kidnapping?" Griffen sounded like he had a tight leash on his temper. His jaw was hard, his eyes fierce.

I rarely believed people. People lied all the time. But looking at the rage and anguish on my oldest brother's face, I believed he hadn't known about my kidnapping. And more, I believed Hope hadn't known either. But here was Cole, someone who'd been there, and he knew. I would have thought I'd be angry. I'd been angry for so long. And I was. But now that I was face-to-face with someone who was there, I understood it was a cold anger, and alongside it was curiosity.

I had always known they had kidnapped me because I was a Sawyer. I couldn't complain about growing up wealthy, but it sure as hell puts a target on your back in all kinds of ways. Kidnapping was just the most dangerous. It had never crossed my mind that my kidnapping had been related to a specific business deal. I'd never been involved in Prentice's business dealings. What could I have to do with anything? It didn't make sense.

"These contracts," I said, gesturing to the briefcase. "Griffen said the earliest one was dated 2012. That was after I was kidnapped."

Cole nodded slowly. "Yes, your kidnapping was part of the—" He looked at the ceiling as if searching for a word. "The *negotiation* phase of the deal."

"They kidnapped my brother as a negotiating tactic?" Royal demanded. "Who the fuck does that?"

Cole opened the topmost file folder and flipped through the contract inside. Setting the signature page in front of Griffen, he pointed to Ford's notes. "It looks like Ford figured it out. He never said anything, but this is old news compared to being prosecuted for Prentice's murder. Ford probably forgot about it."

He tapped his finger on the company name by Ford's question marks. "I don't recognize this one. I can't tell you anything about it. But this." His finger moved to *Chiapas Co.* "This is the American front for a"—he paused again as if searching for a word—"gang would be the best description. They operate out of Mexico."

"Gang or cartel?" Griffen asked sharply.

Cole must have understood the distinction he was getting at. "Gang. Not one of the cartels."

Griffen nodded. "Do you know what these contracts are for? The numbers are clear, but whatever they're negotiating over is just referred to as the *Product*."

"Is that even legal?" Hope asked. "Do you know what the Product was?"

Cole shook his head. "It doesn't matter how legal it is. These contracts were never going to see a courtroom. And I don't know what they were into with Chiapas Co." He scanned the room, looking at all of us before going on.

"Look, I'm not going to say my hands are perfectly clean. I've made some decisions I regret, but I wouldn't have gotten involved in anything illegal. Based on the way this contract is written and Chiapas Co.'s involvement, Prentice and Ford had good reasons to keep their mouths shut. I had my suspicions that this wasn't above board, but I don't know anything."

"What were your suspicions?" I had to ask.

Cole just shook his head. "Nothing that matters now. This was all over almost a decade ago." He crossed his arms over his chest. "My guess is that your father was being tight-fisted, as usual, and Chiapas didn't like it, but I can't say for sure. When they found out you were in Mexico, they had a chance for leverage they couldn't pass up."

"Why would Dad have let him go on spring break in Mexico knowing he could be a target?" Griffen asked, glaring at Cole as if he'd been the one to buy my plane tickets.

Cole shifted, his arms dropping to his sides. He shoved

one hand in his pocket, then crossed his arms again. Finally, he said, "Look, I'm your brother's attorney. I also consider him a friend. Your dad was an asshole, but we had business together over the years. I don't feel great talking about this when neither of them is here to defend themselves, but—"

He raised his hand and rubbed the side of his thumb across his forehead. Crossing his arms again, he let out a huff of air. "They called me in after Finn was taken. Prentice and Ford admitted that they'd considered Finn could be a target and that if something happened, it could be an opportunity for them."

The last words came out in a rush, a direct punch to my gut. *An opportunity.* Memories flashed through my head. The raw, bloody stripes on my wrists from the rope. The way the skin had burned, the coarse rope tearing at it every time I moved. The darkness. Hours and hours in the hot, fetid dark. Fists and hot flashes of light.

I'd never been that thirsty or that afraid. Hearing voices I couldn't understand shouting, waving guns at me. How dark and deep the barrel of a pistol looks when it's shoved in your face. When it was all I could see. Waiting, waiting for the bullet. It had been weeks before I could move without pain.

And all of that had been an *opportunity* for them. For what? What was my life worth to my father and Ford?

I was lost in my head, my memories, and then Savannah was there, her arm sliding around my waist. I didn't want to need her. I didn't want her to see me like this, with the worst thing that had ever happened to me thrown in our faces. I didn't want her, want anyone, to hear that my own father and brother had thrown me away.

I didn't think my father or Ford still had the power to

hurt me, but that word. *Opportunity.* The hurt stabbed deep, and I hated them all over again.

Savannah's arm squeezed tight, and she leaned up, her lips at my ear. "Your father was a fucking asshole," she whispered. "On your worst day, you're worth a hundred of him. Easy. At your best, you're in a different universe. Fuck him."

Savannah's words didn't erase the hurt, but they did ease the pain to a familiar dull ache. She was right. My dad was a fucking asshole. And so was Ford. I was worth a hundred of them, easy.

Savannah's arm around me loosened, and I knew she was going to step back. The last thing she wanted was for anyone to think we could tolerate each other. Before she could slide away, I whispered, "Thanks."

"Anytime." Her smile was a flash of sunshine in the tense room.

Griffen opened the other two file folders. "So they used Finn's kidnapping as the opportunity they needed." He raised his eyes to Cole. "For what?"

"To show them they wouldn't be intimidated, even at the risk of losing his son. He said—" Cole's eyes flashed to me in apology. "He said that if he paid for Finn to come home, all his children would be targets, and he'd look weak. He wanted to make a statement."

That tracked. That sounded exactly like my dad's kind of logic.

"Sacrificing your son on the altar of business is a hell of a statement," I said.

Griffen's lips pressed together in a grim line before he pushed ahead. "So they used Finn to show how cutthroat they were, then went back after the kidnapping and made the deal. And two more after that."

Cole nodded. "I didn't know about the other two. Just the first."

"Why did they call you in?" I asked. "The police were never involved. No one ever got prosecuted. Why would they need a defense attorney?"

Chapter Twenty-Eight

Cole cleared his throat, stepped back, and turned a little so he could face me and not Griffen. "Your father was concerned about exposure."

Griffen's light-green eyes flashed fire. "You mean he was worried someone would find out he gave his son up to violent criminals to be killed, and he wanted to know if he could be prosecuted if it ever came out," he clarified, his eyebrow raised, sarcasm dripping from his words.

Cole nodded again. "Basically. He didn't call me in until after they refused to pay the ransom. After Finn escaped. Once Prentice and Ford knew Finn had gotten away, they were concerned the whole thing would come out, and they'd be facing charges."

"And what about Finn?" Hope demanded, leaning forward, clutching Griffen's arm. Her knuckles were bone-white. "Did any of you go looking for Finn? Did you even know he was alive? Did my uncle know about this?"

Cole shook his head vehemently. "No one knew. I only knew after the fact, after Finn got away. I guess it's possible Edgar knew, but I don't see it. Your uncle has his moments, but he never would have condoned something like this. You know how he feels about family."

Hope ducked her head, clearly mulling that over. I knew her Uncle Edgar had taken her in when she was a young child and raised her himself. He wasn't overly affectionate, but he came to the house often for Sunday dinner, and I'd seen the way he looked at Hope. Pride and love and affection. He wasn't cuddly, but he wasn't a man who'd sacrifice a child. Unlike my father.

Cole looked at me. "Your father and Ford were my clients, but I wasn't comfortable with the situation." He shook his head. "That's putting it mildly. What they did to you was beyond the pale. It was a miracle you got away." He cleared his throat. "I went behind their back and got in touch with some contacts in Mexico who did some digging. I verified that you'd been seen back at the hotel alive and that you'd flown to New York and on to Paris. Another contact hunted you down in Paris and learned you'd been in touch with Chef Guérard."

He swung his gaze back to Griffen. "I checked in a month later, and Finn was sharing an apartment in the fifth arrondissement with some students, bussing tables at a restaurant connected with Chef Guérard, so I knew someone was looking out for him."

Cole turned back to me, shoving his hands back in his pockets. "I figured you were better off where you were. The reports I got said you looked happy. Tired but happy. You had friends and a safe place to live. You had a job and an adult looking out for you to some degree, which was more than your father was prepared to do. That far removed from Prentice's sphere and away from anyone involved in his business life, you were as safe as you could be."

I nodded, unable to bring myself to thank him for doing

the bare fucking minimum. He said what my father and Ford had done was *beyond the pale*, but it hadn't been bad enough for him to stop doing business with them. Prentice had been a shit father, but he'd been great at making money. For a lot of people, people like my brother Ford and Cole Haywood, getting their hands on some of that money outweighed any pesky ethical concerns. Like having your own son killed to get an edge in a deal.

"Did my father know where I was?" I asked.

"No. I told him I tracked you as far as New York, and then you connected with a friend who gave you a ride out of the city. The next thing I heard, he was telling everyone you joined the army. I figured you knew where your family was. If you wanted to reach out to one of your siblings, you knew where to find them. After everything that had happened, I didn't think you'd want to be found."

I digested that, rolling Cole's words over in my head, feeling vaguely guilty. After Mexico, I'd never wanted to see any of them again. I'd had plenty of rage to go around. It focused on my father and Ford, overflowing to envelop my whole family. I got on that plane to Paris and didn't look back. At the time, it was the only way I could survive. But later? Later it never occurred to me that I could come home. I'd sent that letter to my father as a final fuck you and wrote them all off.

I'd never been convinced the rest of them had known, but I also never questioned it. They hadn't known where I was, but I'd known where they were. I could have gone the rest of my life never seeing Prentice or Ford again, but the rest of my siblings were innocent, and I'd left them too.

Royal broke into my thoughts. "I'm sorry we didn't try harder to find you. To reconnect. We meant to, but then it had been so long, and we didn't know if you'd want us to—" He shook his head. "I'm sorry."

Royal had been working at the Inn back then. Tenn had been in his last year of college. We hadn't been close before the kidnapping. I was involved in college life, too happy to be away from Sawyers Bend to think much about my family except to be glad they were far away.

"You don't have to be sorry," I said, realizing as the words came out that I meant them. "If you read my letter, I'd have been shocked if you reached out." With a glance at the others, I added, "I'm pretty sure I said something about hoping the Sawyer line died out, Prentice being poison and as good as a murderer, and that I never wanted to see any of my family again."

I'd been so viciously angry. So alone and filled with rage about it. But within months, I'd settled into a new life, working in kitchens, living with roommates who showed me the city, and my anger had slowly drained away. I was free, living the life I'd always dreamed of. I would have been fine never seeing my father or Ford again, but why hadn't I ever tried to see any of my siblings?

"I didn't want anything to do with Dad or Ford," I told Royal. "But I wish I'd figured out a way to stay in touch with you."

"Well, you're here now," Cole said with forced cheer. "Maybe your father actually did something right for once with that ridiculous will." Every eye in the room landed on Cole, none of them in agreement. Reading the mood, Cole said, "Granted, it was another asshole move, but at least the whole family is under the same roof again. You can finally work all this out."

Still no agreement. Cole shifted from one foot to the other, the silence stretching.

Griffen broke it. "These notes of Ford's." He tapped the file folders. "Is this what Dad meant in the will?"

I knew what he was talking about. Our father had left behind a video will. A new one, made six weeks before he died. In it, among other gems, he accused Ford of killing him, saying he knew we were all plotting against him, but that Ford was at the root of it.

Hope closed her eyes and, with perfect recall, repeated my father's recorded words. "I knew what he was up to. Never expected the way he'd screw me over, though. He got me good." Her eyes snapped open, landing on Griffen. "How did Ford *get him*? Did he uncover something?" She looked at Cole. "Could it have to do with this?"

"I doubt it," Cole said. "I know he was poking around in your father's business." He turned to face me again. "A few years after your kidnapping, around the time of that third contract with Chiapas Co., Ford changed. He distanced himself from your father."

I wasn't around to corroborate that, but Hope clearly remembered. She nodded at me.

"They still worked together," Hope filled in, "but he moved out. There was a chill between them."

"He took one of the suites at the Inn," Royal said. "He kept his rooms here. Most of his stuff was here, but he lived at the Inn. I wouldn't say we were close, but he'd come down for dinner a few times a week, and we'd have a beer once in a while. We never talked about Dad, though."

"So there's more," Griffen said. "He never told you anything?" he asked Cole.

Cole shook his head. "I didn't know the details of the will or what your father said about Ford screwing him over, and Ford never mentioned anything about it. Maybe he stirred something up, and one of Prentice's enemies came after him, framing Ford to silence him."

"Then why hasn't Ford said anything?" Royal asked.

"Maybe Ford couldn't find anything, and that's why he hasn't mentioned it," Cole said, shrugging. "These contracts are useless if he was trying to bring Prentice down. Maybe that was all he had, and your father used the video will to throw out a red herring and fuck with all of you."

"I wouldn't put it past him," I said.

Silence fell again. We had too many questions and no answers. There was nothing else to say.

Griffen sat back, the file folders in his hands, his eyes on Cole. "I never asked why you're here."

Surprise flashed across Cole's face. "I forgot. I walked in and saw that briefcase, and everything else went out of my head." He cleared his throat. "It probably wasn't worth the drive from town, but I was headed this way anyway. The DA who was pushing for Ford to get the maximum sentence left the office this week. She took a position in private practice in Raleigh."

"Does it matter at this point?" Hope asked.

"Maybe," Cole said. "She was the reason I encouraged Ford to take the plea deal. She has a real thing about speaking truth to power and putting the privileged in their place, and she was going to make an example out of your brother. Her media presence is powerful, and she could have created a narrative that would not have looked good for him. Ford isn't your father, but he doesn't have an abundance of friends either."

"But Ford already took the deal," Griffen reminded him.

"He did. And right now I don't have anything I can bring to the new DA. The old one wouldn't look at anything short of a smoking gun or a confession. This new one is a little more open-minded. It's not a guarantee, or even a good shot, but be alert. If you can find anything that might undermine the evidence they have, we might be able to work something out."

Not exactly good news, but better than bad news. Considering we didn't have any evidence that supported Ford's innocence, we couldn't do much anyway. I knew West had turned over every rock in the hopes of finding something—anything—that would have proven who really killed our father and had come up blank. Griffen had put the best investigators at Sinclair Security on the case, and they hadn't been able to find anything either. While it was nice to hear that maybe there was a chance of having Ford's guilty plea overturned, unless someone tripped over new evidence, I wasn't holding out much hope.

Cole's eyes landed on the briefcase. "Unfortunately, that's only going to hurt him. His notes on those contracts support the idea that he was working against your father. Still, keep your eyes open. We might have another shot at getting him out. It's a very long shot. But that's better than the nothing we had before."

Hawk and Griffen shared a glance, communicating perfectly without a sound. Hawk stepped back into the doorway, his eyes locking on Cole. "I'll see you out, Haywood."

We all watched them go, an awkward silence settling over the room. Griffen looked at me like he had things he wanted to say. I wasn't ready to hear them. Not yet. I needed a minute. Some quiet. Alone. I needed to think about everything I'd learned.

Ever the peacemaker, Hope looked between us and stood up, bracing her lower back with her palms and rolling her shoulders. "Do you have a few minutes, Savannah? Can we bring those bins downstairs and take a look inside?"

Griffen was immediately distracted. "You're not carrying one of those bins."

Savannah turned to me and raised an eyebrow, silently nudging me to take the chance to escape.

"I've got them. I'll meet you down there in a minute." Ducking out of the room, I grabbed the bins before anyone could stop me. I practically jogged down the hall to the elevator. If the bins hadn't been so awkward, I might have sprinted. Setting the bins on the floor, I closed and locked the elevator door, finally alone.

Everything I thought I'd understood about my family had done a sea change. My father and Ford hadn't just declined to save me; they set me up in the first place. And they acted alone. Those two pieces of information turned everything I knew upside down. I'd spent far too much of my life hating the wrong people too much and the right people not enough.

I let out a gust of air. No, I hated my father and Ford plenty. I didn't want to hate them more. I was done with hate. My father was dead. And in hell, if the universe was just. Hating him only hurt me. And Ford . . . Ford was rotting in prison for a crime he hadn't committed. I didn't need to hate him more. He was already paying a price. Maybe it was enough. I didn't know.

What I did know was that I needed to see him. My father was gone. He couldn't answer for what they'd done, but Ford was still here, and I had things I needed to know.

The elevator doors opened, and I started for the kitchen, hearing Savannah and Hope coming down the stairs behind me. Dumping the bins on the counter, I pulled out my phone.

I tapped open the text message app and pulled up Griffen's name.

I want to go see Ford.

Two seconds later, those three dots popped up on Griffen's end.

And then his answer.

I'll make it happen.

Chapter Twenty-Nine

FINN

The light from Savannah's front porch beckoned through the dark night, leading me down the gravel path between the Manor and the cottage. I'd managed to wait until just after nine. I would have turned up earlier, but I didn't want to look desperate, even if I was.

Okay, not desperate, exactly, but close enough, dammit.

That kiss in the hallway earlier had been just a taste of Savannah. And that fuck on her counter had been more than I'd dreamed, but far too short. I needed more. I wasn't sure exactly how much Savannah would be enough, but I knew I wasn't there yet.

I'd been counting the minutes since dinner, since Savannah had taken Nicky and headed back to the cottage. It was our new evening routine, and I was surprised to find I didn't like it. The kitchen was too quiet after they'd gone. Even though before they moved, Savannah and Nicky retired to their apartment behind the kitchens most nights, and I wouldn't see them again until morning.

Usually, I'd finish cleaning the kitchen, doing any prep

for breakfast, and then I'd leave, heading off to my rooms or to watch a movie or hit some balls around on the pool table. It wasn't like we hung out at night. But knowing she wasn't down that short hall, behind the door to her apartment— that she wasn't under the Manor's roof at all—left me feeling empty. Restless.

It was weird, and I didn't like it. On top of the day I'd had, I hated the deserted feeling of the kitchens. Inside I was raw, still trying to digest everything I'd learned about my father and Ford, about my kidnapping. No one knew what happened except my father, Ford, and Cole Haywood. My siblings had missed me. I'd missed them so much more than I understood. I'd shut off all those feelings, lumping my siblings under the same umbrella as my father and Ford when they didn't belong there.

We were all victims, and I was beginning to understand I wasn't the only one trying to move beyond a painful past. As much as I'd wanted to punch Cole Haywood in the face when he'd made that smugly cheerful comment about how my father's fucked up will had been good in the end, Cole wasn't wrong.

If it hadn't been for the will, I never would have come back here. I never would have found my family again. Not that I was going to be grateful to my father for a goddamned thing. But still, silver linings and all that. I was here, back at Heartstone Manor, and that was something good.

I climbed the steps to Savannah's cottage as quietly as I could, softly rapping on the door. The last thing I wanted was to wake Nicky up. I had plans, and as much as I liked the kid, none of my plans involved a six-year-old.

Savannah pulled the door open, her long sunset curls and waves spilling around her in every shade from dark blond to strawberry to bold red. When had I last seen her with her hair down? Not since she was a teenager. I couldn't think. In her faded t-shirt and leggings, her hair tumbling around her, and a pink flush on her cheeks, she was a goddess.

I shut the door gently behind me, turning the lock.

I didn't want to talk.

I wanted to strip the clothes from her body, lay her out in her brand-new bed, and devour her.

But the tilt of her head and the raise of one eyebrow told me Savannah wanted to have a conversation first. I knew what she'd heard in Griffen's office upset her. Fuck, it had upset everyone. I thought they all knew about the kidnapping. Hell, I thought I knew all I needed to know about my kidnapping. I wasn't sure if Savannah was mad at me or just needed to talk about it.

Either way, she was going to have to wait. The last thing I wanted was more conversation.

Savannah's lips parted. Before she could get out a sound, I stopped her mouth with mine. Savannah could be a bulldog when she had something to say, but I was one of the few people on this planet who knew how to distract her.

Sliding my arm around her waist, I guided her backward to the stairs, kissing, tasting, barely remembering to look up and make sure I wasn't backing us into a wall. We hit the stairs, and I stopped, turning her around and nudging her forward so she went up ahead of me so I could watch the curve of her heart-shaped ass in those tight leggings as she climbed the stairs. God help me if the woman ever put on lingerie. I was about to die just from the sight of her in an old t-shirt.

Finally in her bedroom, I closed the door behind me and turned the lock, stripping Savannah naked my only focus. She was still getting her bearings when I grabbed the hem of her shirt and dragged it up, pulling her arms up with the shirt and whipping it over her head. Her full breasts bounced, eroding what remained of my patience. Hooking my thumbs in her leggings and underwear, I stripped them down her legs, leaving her wonderfully naked.

She bit off a shriek when I scooped her up and dropped her on the bed, watching me with wide eyes as I tore off my own clothes and stretched out beside her. Savannah stared up at me, her eyes still wide and a little shy. "That was fast."

"I've been thinking about this all day," I said.

She paused, and for just a second I wondered if I'd misjudged her and moved too quickly. I knew she wanted me, wanted this, based on how enthusiastically she'd kissed me back downstairs. What I didn't know was what she was thinking.

Then she said, "Me too."

At that admission, I kissed her again. She had the best mouth, full and soft and so mobile. The way she kissed me spun my head, her lips moving against mine, hungry, eager, so full of passion I wanted more. I wanted everything she could give me.

Skin to skin, finally behind a locked door, I took my time, kissing her over and over, savoring the sounds she made, the little moans and gasps muffled by our kiss. She was so warm and soft, her full curves welcoming me as I leaned into her, my thigh sliding between hers, my hands sliding to cup her breast, tearing my mouth from hers to close my teeth on the cord of her neck, savoring her indrawn breath.

Her breast was heavy in my hand, so soft, until I got to the hard point of her nipple. I rolled the stiff point in my fingers, absorbing her moan, loving the way she went rigid, then relaxed, her legs falling apart, the heat from her pussy scalding my thigh.

Her fingertips trailed over my back, the light touches sending shivers down my spine. She was so sweet. I wanted to taste every inch of her. Kissing the strong line of her collarbone, I eased down, sucking lightly on the curve of her breast, making my way to that tight, hard nipple, wondering how it would taste.

"Finn," she breathed, distracting me from her breast. Not an easy feat. "There are condoms in the bedside table drawer."

"Smart woman," I murmured, "but don't rush me."

I was glad she'd thought of condoms. I had a few in the back pocket of my jeans, but distracted by the prospect of getting Savannah naked, I'd dropped my jeans on the floor, the condoms still in the pocket. The bedside table was closer. I stopped by the doctor's office that morning after breakfast, but it would be a few days until I had the results and we could ditch the condoms. I was sure there wouldn't be any issues, but I wouldn't take any chances with Savannah.

Shifting to lie between her legs, I stroked my fingertips over her hip to the dip of her belly button, dropping a kiss there before sliding my fingers down to circle her clit with a touch so light she strained for it. I did it again, just a little harder. And again, and again, each time giving her more, until her hips rocked against me and she dragged my name out on a moan. "Finn, how long are you going to make me wait?"

I didn't answer. Not with words. Leaving her clit, I stroked a light touch along her pussy, the heat and slick moisture making my head spin. I could fuck her now, I knew, and she would thank me for it. *I* would thank me for it. But I wasn't listening to my cock. Not this time.

The first time had been hard, grabbing hands and heat and desperate need. I'd fucked her on her kitchen counter, for god's sake. Nothing about that had been planned ahead of time. Since then, I'd been thinking about this—having her all to myself, spread across her bed, hours alone stretching before us. I would not be rushed.

Shifting further down the bed, I pushed her legs apart with my shoulders, putting myself face-to-face with her pussy. Exactly where I wanted to be. With a jerk of motion, Savannah propped herself up on her elbows, looking down at me with faint alarm.

"Finn," she said doubtfully, "You don't have to—"

I scowled back. "You're so bossy."

"It's just—" She tried to sit up more, but I pinned her hips with my weight. "I don't usually like that."

"How do you know?" I challenged, swiping my tongue across her clit. She shuddered beneath me, her breath catching in her throat.

Her arms trembling, her voice breathless, she said, "I don't— I've never—" She sucked in a hard breath and forced the words out. "The other times I've done it, I haven't really liked it."

I took a moment to silently curse her husband. After everything she'd told me, I wasn't a fan, and this was definitely not a mark in his favor. "That's fine," I said easily. "But you haven't done it with me. Just lay down and shut up for a minute."

Savanah let out a startled laugh, one red eyebrow arching high as she glared down at me. "Did you just tell me to shut up?"

"Yes, I did." Reaching up, I cupped her breast and

272

pushed her back. "Lay down and shut up. Give me two minutes. If you're not having fun, I'll stop. I promise."

"Okay, fine. Two minutes, and I'm not going to fake it if I don't like it." Savannah flopped back on the bed. She squirmed against my tight hold on her hips, and I had to press my face into her inner thighs to hide my grin.

I only had two minutes, but I wouldn't be rushed. I nuzzled my face into her thigh, breathing in the scent of her skin, her arousal. She might not be sure about my mouth on her pussy, but her body was enthusiastically in favor.

"Finn?" I'd never heard Savannah so uncertain.

"Relax, Savannah. I've got you."

My mouth was making her nervous, but she had no problem with my fingers. I needed to get her out of her head, too dizzy with pleasure to think about what I was doing. I pressed the flat of my thumb into her clit, moving it in circles, sliding a finger inside her slick heat. My breath hot on her skin, I fucked her with my fingers, waiting until she rocked up to take me deeper before I replaced my thumb on her clit with my mouth.

My cock jerked at the taste of her. Salty and sweet, I licked and sucked, adding another finger, the tight grip of her body driving me, her moans telling me exactly what she liked. I think the orgasm took her by surprise; her startled cry cut off as she threw her arm over her face, gasping for breath.

Sliding back up the bed, my eyes locked on her face—cheeks flushed, skin glowing, eyes blissed out, She turned her face to mine and kissed me, the taste of her still on my lips.

"I won't be bossy," she said.

I smirked. Savannah, not be bossy? Impossible.

Laughing, she rolled her eyes. "Okay, I'll still be bossy, but I'll trust your judgment. When it comes to this, at least."

I buried my face in her neck, shaking with laughter. We were alone, but we needed to keep it down or we'd have Nicky up here wondering why I was naked with his mom, howling with laughter. When I had myself under control, I lifted my head.

"It was okay, then?" I asked, already knowing the answer.

"I'm not sure," Savannah said, laughter still sparkling in her gray eyes. "I think so, but we should try it again. Later. Not now. Now it's my turn."

Rolling away from me, she reached into the bedside drawer, grabbing a condom and tearing it open. I'd had plans for Savannah, but I was willing to change them if she wanted to take charge. So far, I had been the one to initiate. I'd kissed her in the kitchen. A month ago and ten years ago. The first time on her kitchen counter, it was debatable who'd kissed who, but I'd definitely been the one to lift her onto the counter and pull her clothes off.

This was different. I liked it. With a shove on my shoulder, Savannah pushed me to my back, rolling the condom down my extremely eager cock. Shifting up on the bed, I pulled her over me, letting out my own groan as the scalding heat of her settled over the head of my cock. She sank down slowly, humming in the back of her throat as she stretched around me, falling forward when she'd taken me to the hilt, her breasts even with my mouth. Capturing a nipple, I sucked, my hands loose on her hips, no longer trying to control her movements.

Savannah rocked, the flex of her strong thighs under my hands seducing me further. I was surrounded by Savannah, her taste, her scent, her body, her tight heat on my cock rising and falling, bringing me to the edge far too soon. She teased, slowing when I thrust up into her, making me wait just as I'd done to her, her hips swiveling in the twist that sent a fresh jolt of bliss through my body.

"Fuck, Savannah, so good," I said, my words slurring together, sensation swamping my brain.

"So good," she moaned in agreement, rocking faster. Her breath caught as I cupped both breasts and squeezed her nipples, tugging gently. I thrust up into her, and her orgasm detonated in her body, her pussy squeezing tight. I let her take me with her, Savannah the only thing I could feel.

She collapsed on top of me, her silky hair everywhere, faint tremors running through her, both of us gasping for breath. Too much of Savannah might kill me, but I'd die the happiest of men.

I don't know how long it took us to function again. I wasn't in a rush, the feel of her draped over me warm and close and so welcome.

Welcome. An odd word for that moment, but it was stuck in my head. I'd never felt so welcomed. By her body, absolutely. No question there. But the feeling of welcome wasn't just about her body wanting mine. No, it was in her surrender, her loose limbs and warm breath on my neck. When she slid to the side and cool air hit my skin, I wanted her back. Not sure what to do with that, I rolled out of bed, disposing of the condom in the bathroom.

Chapter Thirty

FINN

I wasn't expecting the fireplace cheerfully burning in the wall opposite the bed when I came back. "Was that on when we came up?" I asked.

"It was," Savannah said with a slight smile. "But we were distracted." She tilted her head to the side. "Are you coming back to bed?"

Good question. I was standing right next to my pile of discarded clothes. I could pull them on and be out the door in a heartbeat. Objective achieved. Savannah had come twice, and I'd come one spectacular time. Libido satisfied. I didn't have to stay.

But I didn't want to go. I didn't want to leave this cozy room with the fire burning, Savannah warm and soft and naked in bed. Slipping into bed beside her, I pulled her into my arms. "I'll leave before Nicky gets up," I said.

She cuddled in, tucking her head into the crook of my shoulder, her breath warm on my skin. I couldn't remember the last time I'd felt this. Welcomed. Wanted. Defenses down, her body languid, Savannah traced small circles on my arm, and in that moment, everything I wanted was in my arms. It was equally comforting and terrifying to find contentment like this with another person. With Savannah. I pushed the unfamiliar feelings away. I was here, and I was happy. That was enough to think about for now.

Savannah drew in a breath, and I remembered her face earlier, when I'd come in. She had things to say, and I distracted her. My stomach tightened. I didn't want to talk. Not about my kidnapping and my father and Ford. Definitely not about anything that had happened in the last hour. Too many new feelings were swirling through me, things I didn't understand yet myself. I wasn't ready to talk about any of it.

Savannah let out her breath in a rush, then drew in a new one. Letting out a sigh of my own, I said, "Spit it out."

"I'm sorry." She eased back, every millimeter of distance too much. Her gray eyes met mine, hers dark with pain, suddenly swimming with tears. "He said you joined the army, and we all just accepted that. We should have asked." A tear rolled down her cheek. Then another. I reached up a hand to wipe them away, my chest aching.

"Hey, hey, it's okay." I hated the sight of her tears.

"It's not okay." Her brows pulled together. "None of this is okay," she argued, her voice rising.

I leaned up and kissed her. "Shh. Don't wake up Nicky. You don't have to be pissed off."

"I am pissed off. And I feel awful that—"

I cut her off with another kiss. I didn't need to talk this out. Not with Savannah. She wasn't the one who owed me answers.

"It was a long time ago. And you were glad to have me gone," I said, meaning to tease. But her eyes filled again. Fuck.

"Not like that, Finn. I hated you, but not like that."

"I know, Savannah. I know it wasn't like that."

I kissed her again, her anger soothing where her tears couldn't. Until this moment, I had no idea it wasn't like that. If you asked me back then, I would have been sure Savannah would shoot me herself if she thought she could get away with it. But holding her in my arms, knowing her so much better than I had back then, I realized Savannah didn't have that kind of hate in her.

Wiping the side of my thumb across her damp cheek, I said, "I'm going to go see Ford."

Her eyes flashed wide. "Really? When? What are you going to say?"

"I don't know. Griffen said he'd set it up. I don't know what I'm going to say. I think I just need to see his face. And I want to know if his story is the same as Haywood's."

Savannah sighed, nestling her head back on my shoulder, going back to tracing circles on my skin. I let my eyes close, sensing that she was done talking. Good. So was I. I just wanted to lay here, her warm body pressed to mine, the firelight flickering on the walls, and drift off, knowing I was exactly where I wanted to be.

We came together again in the dark, Savannah turning into me, her mouth hot on my neck, her hands teasing me awake. Without words, I rolled on top of her, finding her ready, her body welcoming mine, the sound of her pleasure bringing my own yet again. When I came back to bed after dealing with the condom a second time, she curled into me as if we'd been sharing a bed for years, sleepily throwing her arm across my chest and pulling me close.

I woke exactly on time, as I did every morning since I'd taken over the kitchens in Heartstone. The sky outside was dark, the fireplace off, the room chilled beyond the cozy warmth of Savannah's body pressed to mine.

A part of my brain had already clicked into gear, planning the steps I'd have to take to get breakfast on the table. The rest of me didn't want to get up, hating the idea of leaving this bed for my cold clothes on the floor. But Savannah's alarm would be going off soon, and then she'd have to wake Nicky and get them both dressed and ready for the day.

It was time for me to go. I slipped from the bed, something tugging in my chest as Savannah's arms tightened around me. "It's almost time to get up," I whispered in her ear. "I'll see you at the house."

Her eyes flickered open, a smile curving the side of her mouth. I brushed her hair off her face and couldn't resist dropping a kiss to her cheek. "Go back to sleep." Her eyes drifted shut, and she rolled, tugging my abandoned pillow into her arms.

I dressed in silence, creeping down the stairs and out the front door, closing it carefully behind me. It was still dark, sunrise hours away. The cold air took my breath. This time of year—just before Thanksgiving—the days could go either way. Crisp and cool, or warm and sunny, but in the hours before dawn, it was always fucking cold. I quickened my pace, making a note to grab a jacket the next time.

I didn't hear Hawk until his feet crunched on the gravel path behind me, only feet from the side door of the Manor. Stopping, I waited until he caught up, not liking the thunderous expression on his hard face illuminated by the light above the door. Drawing to a halt, Hawk crossed his arms over his chest, glowering at me.

"If you're going to keep this up, you need to get a key from Savannah. It's not safe to leave her door unlocked like that. Locking the knob isn't enough. I want the deadbolt on at the least. The alarm would be better."

Shit. I hadn't thought of that. Or the cameras I belatedly realized Hawk must have on the cottage somewhere. *Fuck*. I wasn't trying to keep this a secret, exactly, but I knew without asking that Savannah wouldn't want anyone to know. Not yet. Maybe not ever. I was surprised by the pinch in my chest at that thought. Did I want people to know?

"I'll talk to her," I said quickly. "Don't say anything to anyone. I don't want you to embarrass her." Savannah would lose her shit if she thought the security team was talking about us sleeping together.

Hawk lifted his chin, managing to look down on me despite us being the same height. "Are you sure she's the one you're worried about being embarrassed?"

"What does that mean?" I demanded, not liking his tone.

"Are you sure you just don't want it to get out that you're sleeping with the help?"

I laughed at the absurdity. Was he implying that I'd be embarrassed if people knew I was sleeping with Savannah? I shook my head, not liking the way his eyes narrowed, but unable to take this bullshit seriously. "Of the two of us," I said, "Savannah is the one who'd be embarrassed, trust me. I'm not sure I'm a step up for her."

Hawk dropped his arms, giving me an incredulous look. "You're a Sawyer."

"Yeah, and have you noticed Savannah giving a shit about that? She grew up in this house. She's not impressed by the name, trust me." A thought occurred to me. "Do you have a thing for Savannah? Are you pissed because you think I'm cockblocking you?"

Something I couldn't read flashed through his eyes before he shook his head. "No. Not Savannah. It's not like that." He shook his head again, something in his words lodging in my brain. Then he distracted me. "I don't have to want to fuck a woman to care about her. I work with Savannah. She's smart. She's funny. She's never a pain in my ass. I don't like the idea of you treating her like a convenience. You're a Sawyer."

What did being a Sawyer have to do with it? And then I understood. He thought I was like my father, who took advantage of the staff just because he could. My own mother had been the nanny before Prentice got her pregnant with me.

"It's not any of your fucking business," I said, trying to keep a hold on my temper. "We're adults who've known each other a lot longer than you've been around. She doesn't need you watching her back. And don't ever fucking imply she's a convenience."

"Then what is it?" Hawk demanded. "Are you two dating now?"

"Jesus, I don't know." I shoved my hands in my pockets. "Look, I don't know you that well. I know you and Griffen are tight, and I know you do a good job around here. But I don't know you. And this isn't your business. Since you care about Savannah, I'll give you a minute of my time to tell you neither of us knows what this is yet. Okay? Please do not go talk to her about this because not only will you embarrass her, you'll fuck it all up. If she realizes anybody has any idea what we're up to, she'll probably never speak to me again. And I know I don't want that."

Hawk just stared at me, his expression blank. Fuck, he was hard to read when he wanted to be. "You know she knows about the cameras."

"I'm sure she does," I said as that realization processed

in my brain. "But either she forgot, or more likely, she assumed you'd have some fucking discretion."

"You're her boss," he pushed, clearly not willing to let this go.

"I'm not her boss. Griffen is her boss, and he told her that if it came down to Savannah versus me, he'd pick Savannah." As I said it, I thought I understood what Hawk's problem was. "If anything, she has power over me, not the other way around."

"She deserves somebody who's going to treat her well," Hawk said, his sharp gaze dissecting me. "If she wasn't stuck here in Sawyers Bend, if she were back in Richmond, she'd probably be married again by now. You're just going to waste her time."

That was it. I was done with this conversation. "What Savannah does with her time is her business. Not mine, not yours. If you know her at all, you know she wouldn't have let me lay a finger on her if she didn't want me to. I'll talk to her about security, and if she's comfortable giving me a key, I'll make sure I use it. The last thing I want is for Savannah or Nicky to be unsafe. But the rest of it, whatever is between Savannah and me, stay the fuck out of it."

Hawk studied me for so long that I almost wanted to squirm. This was the longest conversation I'd ever had with our head of security. I was not enjoying it.

Deciding something he didn't share with me, Hawk nodded. "Don't leave that door unlocked again."

"Got it," I said over my shoulder as I strode past him, praying he didn't talk to Savannah. Last night had been the best thing that had happened to me in a very long time. I wanted it to happen again. And again. The last thing I needed was for Hawk to spook Savannah and fuck it up.

I got to work as soon as I hit the kitchen, the familiar

rhythm of cooking clearing my mind. After, when I was cleaning and setting up for the rest of the day, Griffen strode into the kitchen. For a horrifying moment, I thought Hawk had been to see him and he was here about Savannah.

Instead, he said, "I heard back from the warden at the prison. You want to go for a ride?"

Adrenaline spiked in my chest, but I only nodded. "Yeah, sure."

Was I ready to see Ford? After what I'd learned the day before, I wasn't sure I'd ever truly be ready to see my older brother. But I knew I wouldn't be able to put all this behind me until I did.

"Let's go," I said, flicking off the lights in the kitchen and following Griffen to the garage.

Chapter Thirty-One

FINN

W e didn't talk much on the ride to the state prison Ford had been locked up in for the last seven months. Griffen plugged in his phone and entered the prison's address, asking, "Do you mind?" as he pulled up a music app.

"Whatever you want is cool," I said, not caring what we listened to.

Griffen pulled up a random mix of current hits, and I tuned everything out. Sinking deep into thought, I watched the miles of tall pine trees flash by as we left the mountains and dropped into the rolling foothills.

I hadn't seen Ford since the Christmas before I was kidnapped. We'd never been close. Seven years older, Ford had always acted like a second father, especially after my mother was gone. I'd had more than enough to handle with Prentice. I didn't need another father. Especially not one as judgmental and unyielding as Ford.

Ford had always been the least kind of my siblings. I don't know if it was being so close in age to Griffen, the oldest, without the status of being the firstborn son, or just that Ford was kind of a jerk. Who the hell could guess? My father had fucked up all our heads when we were kids. By the time I was old enough to pay attention, Ford had been set in his path.

He was always a little less affectionate. A little more competitive. I'd been as shocked as everyone else when Ford double-crossed Griffen, taking his fiancée along with his position in the company and the family. But after the dust settled and we had time to absorb what happened, no one was all that surprised at the way things had turned out.

I didn't know what made Ford, Ford. I did know he wasn't one of the people I'd missed in the years I'd been away. But I never thought he'd been behind my kidnapping. Not in a million years would that possibility have crossed my mind.

I'd always thought my kidnapping was bad luck.

I was in the wrong place at the wrong time.

Now that I knew it hadn't been that simple, I didn't know how to feel. Angry? Sure. That was easy. Of course, I was angry. Fresh, bright anger, so unlike the old, calcified anger I'd been carrying around since I was nineteen. That old anger had faded into the background over time. After a while, I hadn't needed it. I had a vibrant, interesting life overseas, filled with friends and work I loved.

Considering I'd barely escaped the kidnappers with my life, I couldn't say they'd done me a favor. But in the end, I liked my life, which was a hell of a lot more than I could say for Ford or my father, at least when the latter had still been alive. My father had been a lot of things, but never happy.

I glanced over at Griffen, his eyes focused on the road, his jaw hard. He was pissed. Still. I don't know why Griffen's continued anger surprised me. I should have known the rest of my family had nothing to do with the kidnapping.

Especially Griffen. Griffen had been exiled years before that, and he hadn't been in contact with anyone. Maybe I thought Harvey would have told him. I'd assumed Harvey had known. And my kidnapping just felt like something Griffen would know, considering his background in private security.

I'd looked up Sinclair Security after I came back to Sawyers Bend. It sounded like they were high-end body-guards, and according to the website, they did plenty of that. But they also worked in hostage recovery, corporate espionage, and anything else their clients needed. Considering they had a whole division of field-trained computer experts and their staff was a who's who of special forces, I got the picture that they handled a whole lot of shit they didn't list on the website.

Despite all that, I thought I understood why he didn't know. I hadn't looked up my family since the day I left. I could have. I didn't. Maybe it was the same for Griffen. Maybe he figured we were all doing just fine without him. I wanted to ask, but the furious look on Griffen's face held me back almost all the way there.

A glance at the screen of Griffen's SUV told me we only had twenty minutes left of the drive. Without meaning to say anything, I found myself admitting, "I don't know what to say to him."

The second the words were out, I worried he'd be pissed that he'd wasted a day driving out here when I didn't even know what I wanted to say to Ford.

"You don't have to say anything if you don't want to," he said after a long moment. "But if you have questions, you have a right to the answers. And I have some questions of my own." His voice was a growl by the end. I wondered what it would take for his formidable temper to boil over. I wouldn't mind seeing it—as long as I wasn't on the other end.

"What are you going to ask him?" I wanted to know Griffen's take on this whole fucked up mess.

"I want to hear his explanation," he said. "We got Cole's story. I want to see how it lines up with whatever Ford has to say for himself." His tone seemed to say that Griffen wasn't expecting Ford's explanation to be any good. I liked that we were on the same page. I couldn't imagine Ford was going to say anything that would make this any better.

"You think Cole lied?" I asked.

Griffen shook his head. "I don't know, but the fact that he worked closely with Dad and Ford for years is a disqualifying connection in my book."

"So you don't trust Harvey or Edgar either?" That had to be awkward, considering he was married to Edgar's niece and Hope seemed to love her uncle.

"Harvey is okay. I'm pretty are there were times when Harvey was the one who tried to talk sense into Dad. I know he fought him over the will. And Edgar—" Griffen shot me a grim smile. "Edgar is tricky."

"Tricky how?" I asked, intrigued by his description. I'd met Edgar a handful of times, but nothing about him had jumped out as interesting.

Griffen shook his head again. "Tricky in ways I'm not free to disclose for another four years and five months. I don't trust him as far as I can throw him, but he loves Hope, and she loves him back, so I'm stuck with him."

I wanted to ask Griffen what he meant about Edgar being tricky, but based on his comment about four years and five months, I could guess that it had to do with the will, which meant I had zero chance of prying it out of him.

We arrived at the prison, and both of us stopped talking.

I knew Griffen had been there before, so I let him take the lead.

Getting into the prison was a weird experience, starting with watching Griffen morph from my slightly forbidding oldest brother into a man who exuded authority. The warden came to greet us, a balding, rotund man with a red face and a thick accent. He fawned over Griffen, who only looked annoyed by the attention.

With a sharp nod and a mention of the time, Griffen got the warden moving, hustling us through the pat down and down one endless concrete corridor and then another. I'd been thrown in local jails a time or two in my reckless twenties, but I'd never been in anything like a state prison, and the contrast made me extremely grateful I'd never fucked up badly enough to end up here.

We ended up in a big room with wide rectangular tables bolted to the floor. Except for us and a guard stationed in the corner, the room was empty. The warden left us after a few more fawning comments to Griffen.

We sat side by side at one of the tables, waiting. Griffen tilted his head in my direction. "I've been out of the bubble too long," he said, too quietly for the guard to hear. "I forgot what it was like to be a Sawyer in the Carolinas."

"And now you're *the* Sawyer," I added. "I bet people trip over themselves to kiss your ass."

Griffen only grunted at that, and I knew I was right.

The room was too empty, the buzz of the fluorescent lights abrasive. I shifted in my seat, wondering what I was doing here. What did I want Ford to say? Did I want denials? Would I believe them? Was there anything he *could* say that I'd believe?

I braced my ankle on my knee, restlessly jiggling my foot before dropping my foot to the floor again.

"Finn," Griffen said, his eyes sliding to me, a shadow of amusement in their depths. His hand came down on my knee, stilling the leg I realized I was bouncing up and down. "It's going to be okay." He raised an eyebrow, and I nodded, swallowing hard, believing him even as I wasn't sure what he meant.

Before I had a chance to think about it, the door clanked open. A guard held it, watching with sharp eyes as Ford passed through, followed by another guard. If I hadn't known it was Ford in that orange jumpsuit, I wasn't sure I would have recognized him.

Ford came to a stop on the other side of the table, facing us. My eyes skipped from him to Griffen and back again, trying to take them in. Growing up, Griffen and Ford had always looked like twins to me. When they were younger, Griffen was always ahead of Ford, the two years between them meaning Griffen was just a little taller, a little stronger.

By the time I was old enough to really pay attention, they'd both gone through puberty and were pretty much identical except for Griffen's blond hair to Ford's dark brown. They had the same tall build, the same broad shoulders, the same sea-green eyes Miss Martha told me they got from their mother. They almost looked like twins.

I could see echoes of the Ford I knew in the man standing in front of me, but only echoes. The Ford standing in front of me wasn't half of a pair. This was a different man entirely. His cheekbones jutted out in sharp blades, and his collarbone was starkly defined against his white t-shirt.

I'd seen too many movies of prisoners doing endless push-ups in the yard. Somehow I guess I expected Ford to be muscled and covered in tattoos, even though the Ford I'd known would never have let a tattoo touch his patrician skin.

This Ford wasn't muscled or tattooed. He was pale, his hair dull, his body far too thin. His eyes, though—his eyes were as sharp as ever. When they landed on me, they narrowed. "Finn. Griffen. What brings you two for a visit?"

As if he weren't in an orange prison jumpsuit, his hands and feet chained, he pulled out his chair and sat, giving me the disconcerting feeling we were in his office for a meeting instead of a prison visiting room.

Griffen didn't waste time. "We found a briefcase yesterday," he said. "In it were some contracts and a ransom letter."

Ford laced his fingers together, resting them on the table, suddenly looking like an executive about to negotiate a deal despite the orange jumpsuit and lack of a tie. He gave a rueful smile that didn't reach his eyes. "Someone finally dug into the historical records."

Griffen nodded.

"And you're here because—" Ford raised an eyebrow for a second, looking so much like Griffen, I got disoriented.

Before Griffen could speak, I heard my own voice. "You and Dad set me up. You were going to let them kill me. Did you even know what happened? After? Did you know what happened to me?"

His facade cracked as he sat back, his gaze catching on the wire-covered window high above. He stared at that bright spot of natural light, the only real thing in a box of concrete and fluorescent glare. The moment dragged. I refused to break the silence, and Griffen said nothing.

"Let it go," Ford said, finally, dragging his gaze back to us, his eyes expressionless.

"What the fuck does that mean?" Griffen demanded, his voice a rough whisper.

Ford stared at him evenly. "Let it go. It was ten years ago." He looked to me. "You're here. You're fine. Let it go."

Griffen surged to his feet and slammed his palm down on the table so hard both guards straightened with alarm. "What the fuck does that mean?" he repeated in a roar.

I sat back, trying to process. I couldn't remember ever seeing Griffen angry. Not like this. Quietly furious, maybe, but now rage burned from him.

He leaned forward. "How could you do that?" His burning eyes flashed to me. "He's your brother, for god's sake. He was a kid. What the fuck is wrong with you? Do you even know what happened to him? Do you know how close it was?"

I thought about Griffen's clenched jaw on the ride here, the exact source of his rage now clear. These were the questions I should have asked but couldn't bring myself to. Griffen had no such trouble. He slammed a fist on the table, the deputy in the corner taking a step forward before Griffen pulled his hand back, shoving it in his pocket. He was furious, but he still had enough control to know we wouldn't get any answers if we were thrown out for assaulting the prisoner.

Ford moved his arm as if to cross his arms over his chest, then realized his restraints wouldn't allow it and dropped his hands into his lap. He looked at me with something that might have been remorse. Maybe. Or maybe it was an act. I wasn't sure I could tell anymore. The memory of him I had built up in my head did not match the man sitting in front of me. I understood that I didn't know Ford at all.

After a moment, he sat up taller, lifting his chin, meeting Griffen's eyes and then my own. "In retrospect," he said, "it was a regrettable decision. I was relieved when I learned you had escaped and made your way back to the States. And when you didn't come home, Dad and I felt it was better to keep things simple."

"So you told everyone that bullshit story about him joining the army?" Griffen asked. "You couldn't even be creative. You just copied what I did."

I was reminded that Griffen had his own reasons to hate Ford, his own anger probably as calcified as my own, and no less real.

Ford didn't react to his taunt. "It worked. People figured Finn was following in your footsteps. And you know, there are so many Sawyers around town, nobody missed one or two."

Griffen was practically vibrating with rage. I watched him, waiting for the explosion. Instead, he relaxed by increments, maybe realizing the futility of trying to get a better response out of Ford.

"We went over the contracts in the briefcase. Found your notes. We know you hid the briefcase in the attic," Griffen said. "What do you know about Yawhood Properties? We've seen it a few times since I took over, but we can't trace it."

Ford shook his head. "I don't know. If you saw the contracts, you saw my notes. Yawhood was a dead end everywhere I looked. It doesn't have anything to do with why Dad was killed."

"How do you know?" Griffen asked.

"I'm sorry for the way things worked out," Ford said, his tone suggesting that he was being very generous in acknowledging mistakes had been made. I didn't even know if he was referring to my kidnapping or his getting Griffen exiled. I wasn't sure it mattered. Either way, it was bullshit.

Ford's eyes slid back to Griffen. "This is all ancient history. It doesn't have anything to do with current events."

Griffen shook his head slowly. "I'm not buying that. If it's not relevant, then why hide the briefcase?"

Ford let out a breath, bracing his wrists on the edge of the table, his handcuffs rattling against the hard surface. "I was grasping at straws, gathering anything I could find. I didn't know it was useless until I looked into things. Just leave it alone."

"What were you up to?" Griffen asked, his head tilted to the side, as if he were thinking, rearranging puzzle pieces in his mind until he got them to fit. Ford didn't answer. "Were you going to try to force Dad out like he forced out Grandpa?"

Ford jerked, a tiny movement I couldn't decipher. Guilt? Surprise? Our father had forced his own father out of the business before I was born. Our grandfather had died less than a decade later, but all accounts indicated that at his death, he was a shadow of the man he'd been.

Ford didn't answer except to say, "Leave it alone."

Griffen sat back, a musing expression washing over his face. "If it doesn't have anything to do with anything, then you won't mind if we do a little digging."

Ford shrugged, the movement loose but his jaw tight. "If you want to waste your time, fine, but I wouldn't think it's worth the risk. Isn't Hope about to deliver your heir? I'd think you'd want to do anything you could to keep your family safe."

"What the fuck does that mean?" Griffen shot back, his eyes blazing again. Even I knew Ford had pressed the wrong button. I figured he meant to rile Griffen, to get under his skin a little. But Ford couldn't have known how Griffen would react to a threat to Hope.

Leaning forward, menace radiating off him, Griffen repeated slowly, "What the fuck does that mean?"

"Is it the baby?" Ford asked, his head cocked to the side, curiosity lighting his eyes. "Is it the thought of a mini you running around? Or is it Hope? Are you in love with Hope Daniels? That's fucking hysterical. Her little crush got you exiled, and now you're in love with her."

"Shut the fuck up about my wife," Griffen growled. "She's Hope Sawyer now, and you're the one who got me exiled. Now tell me what you mean. What risk?"

Chapter Thirty-Two

FINN

"Don't be an idiot," Ford said, the curiosity and amusement draining away until he just looked tired. "Have you all decided that I'm the one who shot Dad?"

"No," Griffen said. "You're an asshole, but no one thinks you killed Dad."

"Then do you know who did it?" The ghost of a smile crossed Ford's face. "If you do, I'd love it if you could pass the info along to the DA. The accommodations here leave a lot to be desired."

"You know full well we have no leads," Griffen said.

"Cole thinks Vanessa knew," Ford said. Vanessa Sawyer, originally Griffen's fiancée, then Ford's wife, had been found dead in the gardens of the Inn, shot in the forehead just like Dad. Hawk's security team made the Manor feel so safe, I forgot—mostly—there was an unknown murderer out there.

"We should have paid her off," Griffen said. Before she was killed, Vanessa made noises about offering information for money. With Ford in prison, her alimony had dried up.

Ford shrugged, no trace of emotion on his face for his dead ex-wife. "Just because you paid her doesn't mean she would have told you anything useful. Vanessa was always looking for a better angle. She would have strung you along. I'm assuming the person whose chain she was yanking ended up killing her. She would have been wise to keep her mouth shut."

"Vanessa wasn't known for her wisdom," Griffen said wryly.

"No," Ford agreed. "And she finally let her greed outpace her instinct for survival." Ford paused and looked Griffen dead in the eye. "Whoever killed her and Dad is still out there. As long as I'm in here, no one's actively looking for them. According to Cole, you've had some trouble, even with me locked up and Dad's murder officially solved."

Griffen gave a grudging nod. "A few attempts on me, one on Royal. Some other bullshit. We're paying Sinclair Security a bundle to keep everyone safe."

"That might be enough," Ford said, sounding sincere for the first time. "I had a plan. Then I poked around without knowing what I was getting into, and now I'm in here."

Griffen leaned forward, his eyes lighting. "Are you saying you found something? Maybe if we—"

"No!" Ford shouted, startling the guard in the corner. In a lower voice, he said, "No. I was looking for evidence of Dad's bullshit. Something I could use as leverage. And something I came across pissed off the wrong person. Or maybe it was just that I was poking around in the first place. I don't know. Then Dad's dead, everything points to me, and I'm stuck with no alibi and the DA gunning for me. If I thought I had anything that could get me out of here, believe me, I'd give it to you. I have no clue. But after what happened to Vanessa, I'd say it's a good bet that if you start digging, you'll end up in here beside me. Just let it go. Let it all go."

"Ford," Griffen started, pain bright in his eyes.

"Griffen," Ford interrupted, "Don't do it. You have a lot to live for. You're king of the manor, just like you were always supposed to be. Knowing Hope, you have a loving and devoted wife. A baby coming any minute. Let things be. Live your life."

"And let you just rot in here?" Griffen asked.

"Let me handle my own life." Ford's eyes flashed to me and back to Griffen. "I've done enough to fuck up everyone else's, don't you think?"

I wasn't sure what to do with that. Ford was an asshole. Beyond an asshole. But did he deserve to rot in prison for the rest of his life? I didn't have to think about that for long. No. He didn't kill Dad, and what he did to me had happened a long time ago.

Griffen sat back, crossing his arms over his chest, studying the brother who'd once been his other half. "So everything Cole said about Finn's kidnapping—that you and Dad set him up to make a statement to Chiapas, that Dad declined to pay the ransom, that neither of you ever tried to contact him—all that was true?"

Ford nodded, the movement sharp and final. "Surely you can't be surprised. You knew what I was capable of when I got you exiled, married your fiancée, and took your place in the family. I sacrificed one brother. What makes you think I wouldn't have sacrificed another?"

"Point taken," Griffen said, pushing his chair back to stand. The second he was on his feet, I was on mine. Griffen met my eyes. "Anything else you want to say?"

I looked at Ford, studying his gaunt face and thin frame.

Ford wasn't sitting in here gloating over all he had done to us. This wasn't a man enjoying his life. This was a man who'd wasted it.

Meanwhile, I was walking out of here, going back to Heartstone Manor, where I had a family I was getting to know all over again. Work I was enjoying. It had been years since I had the time to really play in the kitchen. I might as well have been on vacation.

And there was Savannah. I had a flash of the way I'd left her, cuddling my pillow, a secret smile on her face, her vibrant sunset hair tumbling all over her bare shoulders. I got to go home to that. And Ford was locked in here.

I shook my head. "No, I don't think I have anything to say. Good to know the truth, I guess." I shrugged and met Ford's cold eyes. "You're right. I shouldn't have been surprised. I should have seen it coming. You always were predictable."

Ford didn't say anything, but I thought I saw him flinch.

Griffen's hand slapped my back. "Let's go."

Griffen lifted his chin at the deputy by the door, who made a signal, and the lock clicked, the door swinging open. The guard in the corner moved to stand beside Ford, and the other guard led us out of the room and down the long halls to freedom. We were greeted by a bright blue sky and crisp fall air.

Griffen was silent as we drove down the winding country roads that led to the highway. I was lost in thought, wondering if we'd gotten anything useful out of Ford. I wasn't sure. His version of a non-apology had sucked, but what had I expected? For him to beg me for forgiveness? I should be glad he sort of admitted they might have handled things differently. *Regrettable.* That was the word he'd used. *Regrettable.* Yeah, fuck that, and fuck him.

"I never should have left," Griffen said into the silence.

"You didn't leave voluntarily," I reminded him.

"No," he agreed. "Not at twenty-two, but later. I could have called or written. I wasn't without resources. Even if Prentice wanted to make it difficult. I was angry, and I blamed everyone. I—"

"I know," I interrupted, feeling a moment of pure connection with my oldest brother. "Sometimes I look at Sterling, at Parker, and think about everything they went through. I should have been here."

"I'm sorry, Finn," Griffen said. I knew he meant it. Griffen never would have left me to die. Seeing the way he exploded at Ford and how angry he had been since he learned what had happened, I knew he wasn't Ford or our father. I'd watched him with Hope, with Sterling. Giving Parker a job she loved, encouraging Royal and Tenn with the improvements they wanted at the Inn. The way he watched out for Savannah and Nicky. For everyone.

"You don't owe me an apology," I said. "Or maybe we both owe everyone an apology. I could have come back. I could have called. But I was like you. So pissed at everyone that I never bothered to consider that they might not have all been on Dad's side. I figured they all knew, and nobody came after me, so they could all fuck off."

"You were nineteen," Griffen reminded me.

Echoing Griffen's words, I said, "Yeah, but later, I could have come back." I leaned my head back against the head-rest. "And, you know, it's not the way I would have wanted it to happen, but it worked out for me in the end. I think better than if I'd stayed."

Griffen nodded. "For me too."

I was weirdly at peace. Ford had looked like shit. He wasn't some supervillain, rubbing his goatee and smirking over how he'd beaten us. He was skinny and pale, stuck inside those concrete blocks, time stretching into a future of the same cold monotony.

I was out here in the sunshine with my brother. I was going to make an amazing dinner in my own private kingdom in Heartstone's kitchens. My kitchens. When the day was done, I'd sneak across the grass into the bed of a spectacular woman. All in all, it stacked up pretty well against what Ford had. After that visit, I pitied him more than anything else.

I thought about what he'd said to Griffen. The digs about Hope. We all knew about Hope's childish crush on Griffen when they were kids. Everyone had known, but Griffen had been cool about it, and they'd been friends in a brother/sister kind of way—appropriate considering the age difference. Over time, something shifted. She'd been a mainstay in his life since he was a kid, and now she was his wife. A wife he seemed to love deeply.

"Nothing's going to happen to Hope," I said. He shot me a questioning look. "You're a little overprotective. The day Savannah moved into the cottage, you barely let her get up out of the chair."

Griffen shot me a guilty look. "I know, I know. I'm going insane." He drew in a slow breath and let it out. "Women have been having children for the span of human existence. I know Hope is healthy and strong and she knows her own limits. I know I'm driving her crazy hovering over her. And I know she's a little worried that once the baby gets here, I'm going to turn into a complete nightmare."

"You're very self-aware for a crazy man," I commented.

Griffen choked out a laugh. "Yeah, well, my old boss insisted on a visit to therapy when we had jobs that were—" He paused. "Tough."

I had to wonder what *tough* meant in that context. How tough was the job if afterward your boss thought you needed therapy? They were Army Rangers. Not much was tough for a Ranger.

And suddenly I got it. "You've seen some shit," I said. Griffen nodded in agreement. "And now the idea of a baby is terrifying," I finished.

"Pretty much," Griffen said. "But I also get that I'm being irrational. And I know Hope will be fine. I'm still—" He shook his head. "She's so vulnerable. The baby is so huge she can barely stand up on her own. I don't like leaving her alone. What if—" He shot me another glance, this one sheepish. "I know, I'm working on it. Fortunately Hope's a patient woman."

"Are you going to be crazy when the baby gets here?" I had to ask.

Griffen nodded. "Maybe a little. I'm working on it." He slid another glance my way, this one tentative. "I never imagined anything like this for me," he confessed. "I never imagined falling in love. I never imagined marrying Hope and waking up every morning so fucking grateful she's there beside me. And now there's a baby—"

He rubbed his hand across his chest as if soothing an ache. "Hope, the baby—it's like having my heart outside my body. Maybe if we'd had more time before she got pregnant. More time for me to get used to loving her, to being married. I've seen too many ways life can go wrong. I can tell myself all day that nothing is going to happen to us, but—" He stopped and met my eyes. "Some of it has happened to us. I'm doing my best to not let it take over. When I was on the job, I could just shut it off. But this is different. This is Hope and our child."

Words failed me. I knew Griffen cared deeply for Hope.

I suspected he loved her, but hearing him admit it, seeing the look on his face, the joy and terror, left me off balance. Griffen took care of everything. It hadn't occurred to me that, in this, he might need someone to take care of him. I patted my hand on his shoulder and squeezed, echoing what he'd said to me earlier.

"Everything is going to be okay."

I wasn't sure if Griffen believed me, but his answering smile made me believe, for the first time in a long time, that maybe everything really was going to be okay.

Chapter Thirty-Three

SAVANNAH

I gripped the steering wheel of my car so hard my knuckles were white. Not a great approach to driving on winding mountain roads. Taking a deep breath, I tried to force myself to relax. One hand at a time, I let go of the wheel and stretched my fingers, putting my hands back on the wheel in a relaxed but firm grip at ten and two. Better.

I needed to get myself together. It had been a week since Finn and I had discovered Prentice's briefcase, Ford's notes, and that ticking time bomb of a ransom note. A week since he'd gone to see Ford in prison. I would have expected Finn to be a mess after discovering such a deep betrayal—I was still struggling to understand how Ford could have done such a thing to his younger brother—but Finn had been weirdly relaxed.

I don't think I'd ever seen him smile this much. He joked around in the kitchen, playing along when Nicky asked to help, giving him little jobs that were fun, like buttering toast and sprinkling on sugar and cinnamon, then asking Nicky to taste test.

I, on the other hand, had been growing increasingly more tense as the week went on. Not because of Finn. Considering how he showed up at the cottage every night and what we did behind the locked door of my bedroom, I should have been the most relaxed I'd ever been. Finn was an excellent choice for a fuck buddy/friends with benefits/whatever the hell we were. Every night he came over, I came—usually more than once—and we both passed out, sleeping practically entwined until he crept out before dawn to start breakfast in the Manor.

No, despite my very satisfied body, my rising nerves were all about Lydia. She'd texted almost every day over the last week, growing increasingly demanding, until her final text early this morning just after I got out of bed.

> Savannah, I'm in Asheville. We need to meet. I made a reservation for the Sunset Terrace at noon. I'll see you there.

My heart sank as I read her message. She was here, in Western North Carolina, which meant I had nowhere to run. There was no point in dodging her now. She'd just chase me all the way to Sawyers Bend, and I'd rather face her alone than air our dirty laundry in front of everyone at Heartstone Manor.

I'd been running from this confrontation since her first text, my reasons a jumbled pile of *No*. Not only did I not want anyone to know what a disaster things had been with Oliver, I wasn't sure I trusted her with Nicky. I was still hurt and angry over the way she'd treated me when Oliver lost himself to addiction, and I'd never forgive her for the way she enabled him, hastening his death. So many reasons I was running from Lydia. But it looked like Lydia wasn't going to let me run anymore.

I'd rather deal with her in Asheville than have her come to the Manor and have to explain to everyone why my former mother-in-law had shown up out of the blue. And more than that, I wanted to keep her away from Nicky until I got a feel for what she wanted and how far she was willing to go to get it.

It was a simple matter to take a few hours off in the middle of the day. Griffen raised an eyebrow, but didn't ask for further explanation. Fortunately, Hope wasn't in the room. If she'd been there, I wouldn't have gotten out so easily. She would have sensed my angst immediately and badgered me until I told her. After finishing my morning duties and seeing Nicky off to school, I sifted through my clothes for something to wear.

Even though I was grateful for the way my friends had helped me unpack and organize my closet, I realized this morning that my clothes consisted mainly of multiple copies of my housekeeper's uniform and more pairs of jeans, leggings, and t-shirts than I needed considering I spent most of the week in that uniform. I had a few pairs of khaki pants and shorts and two Heartstone Manor polo shirts for the occasional days I pitched in on cleaning with Kitty and April.

The narrowest sliver of my closet consisted of the handful of dressy clothes that had made the move from Richmond. When I'd quit my corporate job and moved home, I ditched my office wardrobe, knowing I'd have neither the space nor the occasion for those clothes anytime soon. Right now, I would have given a lot for just one power suit.

I finally settled on a gray sheath dress more suitable for slightly warmer weather, a patterned silk scarf Lydia had given me years ago, and a forest-green cardigan with fluttery sleeves. Realizing I was running late, I added tights and a pair of low-heeled booties. I twisted my hair into a low bun, grabbed my purse, and raced for the car. I'd forgotten how long it took to get dressed when I wasn't just throwing on my uniform.

The late morning sunlight filtered through the trees and dappled the mountain road in front of me, doing nothing to alleviate the tight knot in my stomach. It wound ever tighter as I closed the distance between Sawyers Bend and Asheville. The hour-long drive flashed by. It had been years since I visited the historic stone inn Lydia had chosen for our meeting.

Built on Sunset Mountain a decade after Heartstone Manor was finished, the Grove Park Inn had some of the best views in town. When I was a girl, my mother would take me there for the annual gingerbread competition. As I parked my car and walked through the grand reception area, its massive fireplaces burning cheerfully, I decided Mom and I should revive the tradition for Nicky. We could make a day of it. See the gingerbread houses, have lunch, maybe take Nicky to that arcade in West Asheville August and Thatcher had been raving about.

I managed to distract myself with fun ideas for a day in Asheville with Nicky and my mother, putting Lydia out of my mind for the few minutes it took me to find my way to the Sunset Terrace dining room. Gorgeous views, fantastic food. And, unfortunately, Lydia.

Relax, I told myself. *You don't even know for sure what she wants.*

I walked down the long hallway to the dining room, gearing myself up for a fight and not focusing on what was around me. When Lydia came out of the ladies' room, she surprised the hell out of me. When her eyes hit me, her face lit with a bright smile, and she came toward me with her arms spread wide. Not the greeting I was expecting.

She looked the same as ever, her short, rounded frame stylish in red wool slacks and a matching tailored jacket trimmed in pink and red. Her frosted blond hair was sprayed firmly into the same sleek bob she'd had as long as I'd known her.

I leaned down to her embrace, the cloud of her overly sweet perfume clogging my sinuses until I had to bite back a sneeze. Gingerly, I squeezed her back.

"Lydia, it's so good to see you," I lied.

"I'm sure it's not," she said crisply. "I know you've been dodging me and I've been hounding you, but I decided this has gone on long enough."

She pulled back and looped her arm through mine, leading me to the hostess stand, reminding me for a moment of the woman I'd known when Oliver and I had first started dating. Bossy and authoritative, but affectionate and welcoming.

Maybe—

No. Too much had happened, and we couldn't go back. I'd never again be that young girl in love, and Lydia would never be the mother-in-law of my dreams.

I could forgive everything that had happened. Her accusations, the way she'd undermined me and enabled him. I could forgive, but I wouldn't forget. I wouldn't be fooled by Lydia's hug and wide smile, but I could play the game long enough to find out why she was here.

Lydia led me to the table as we followed the hostess, and I sat compliantly in the chair she pointed to. Might as well let her have her way when it didn't matter. I needed to hear what she wanted before I started to push back.

Our waitress came by, and Lydia gave her the same

sunny smile she'd aimed my way, as if she couldn't be more pleased with the world. "It's a brisk day out there, isn't it?" she asked, not waiting for an answer. "A perfect day for hot tea."

"I'll have the same," I said. I needed the soothing familiarity of tea.

The waitress nodded and left. Lydia turned her attention to me, scanning me from the top of my head all the way to my booties, craning to the side to see around the table.

"That scarf looks nice on you," she said finally.

"Thank you," I replied, trying to force a polite smile. "You gave it to me for my birthday. Before Nicky was born."

She hummed in the back of her throat, her eyes locked on my face, studying me so intently I had to resist the urge to wipe my nose and check my teeth. If I hoped wearing the scarf would soften her up, I was out of luck.

"You look tired. Are you still working in that hotel serving food?"

She said it as if she'd never heard of anyone being a waitress before. As if it were slightly distasteful, but she was determined to be nice about it.

"Not anymore," I answered in the most polite tone I could manage. "Do you remember me telling you about Heartstone Manor?" I asked.

"Of course," she said as our waitress set two teacups in front of us, and we selected our tea from a wooden box. After a brief look at the menu, we ordered lunch. I got the lobster bisque, a special I remembered from visits with my mother. Not that I'd be able to eat. Despite my outward calm, my stomach was still a tight knot of tension.

"Heartstone Manor," Lydia said musingly. "Your mother used to be a maid there."

I gritted my teeth, drawing in a slow breath, trying to get

my temper under control. "My mother wasn't a maid. She managed a forty thousand square foot historic home, housing over twenty-five people and a sizable staff," I said stiffly.

Lydia took a sip of tea and didn't comment. I ordered myself to relax. Lydia could poke at me all she wanted. She was trying to get the upper hand. That didn't mean I had to give it to her.

Taking my own sip of tea, I swallowed, inhaling the calming scent of earl grey and lavender. It was the same variety we stocked at the Manor, blended by a local tea company. Remembering that anchored me. Lydia was the interloper here. We might be in Asheville instead of Sawyers Bend, but this was still my place, not hers. I didn't need to let her push me around.

"My mother retired from her position at Heartstone Manor a few years ago," I said. "The family patriarch passed away recently, and his heir offered me her job managing the house. It's been a wonderful challenge," I said truthfully, "And a fantastic working environment. Heartstone Manor is a beautiful house."

"You grew up there, didn't you?" she asked, as if she didn't already know.

"I did." I offered a blandly polite smile. If she wanted to act like we were strangers, I could play along. "I've always loved Heartstone. The Manor was neglected for a few years, and it's been hard work getting it back into shape, but I'm enjoying it."

"I'm sure you are," Lydia said with a saccharine smile, "but what about Nicky? Is Nicky enjoying it? Living there as the son of the help? A second-class citizen?" She gave me a superior look, as if she'd scored a point. As if she understood anything about what that meant.

While being the housekeeper's daughter had stung at times when I was growing up, I didn't think Nicky would have any such problems. Griffen's household bore little resemblance to Prentice's.

I gave a genuine laugh, shaking my head at Lydia as if she was confused and not trying to be a bitch. "It's nothing like that, Lydia. There are other young children in the house, so he has company and plenty to do. The family completely renovated a historic cottage on the grounds for us, and it's absolutely beautiful. Nicky has a lovely room with his own bathroom, but he's just a short walk across the lawn to his friends in the Manor. He's enjoying his first year of real school—"

"I can't imagine the schools there are any good compared to Richmond," she said, tipping her head back so she could look down her nose at me. From my vantage point, she just looked silly.

I thought about her comment and realized she knew nothing at all about our lives. Maybe this whole thing was just that simple. She missed her grandson, and she wanted to be a part of his life again. It's not like she could approach me with an apology like a normal person. I'd never seen the woman apologize for anything in all the years I'd known her. She just maneuvered and manipulated until she got her way.

A little voice—the nice Savannah—prompted, *Doesn't she deserve the benefit of the doubt? At least a little?* I lost my husband. Nicky lost his father. But Lydia lost her son. I couldn't imagine how I could live with losing Nicky. How much worse it would be if I'd tried my best to save him and lost him anyway. She'd loved Oliver so much, and Nicky was the only piece of him left. A part of me despised Lydia, but the mother in me had to give her a chance.

Taking a sip of tea, I answered her question. "Nicky is attending Laurel Country Day School as part of my compensation package."

Her eyes widened, and she sat back. "Laurel Country Day? That's quite a good school. I have a friend in town whose children went there. Her oldest went to Duke, and the other is at UVA. And Nicky's tuition is covered as part of your compensation?" she asked, her eyebrows knitting together.

She looked at me doubtfully, as if I couldn't understand how my own compensation package worked. Did she forget I had a career in Human Resources for years before Oliver died? Probably. Lydia had always seen my true role as a womb-in-waiting for her future grandchildren.

Give her a chance, I reminded myself.

"Yes," I answered. "Griffen and Hope Sawyer insisted."

Lydia's confused look sharpened. "And you're not"—she wiggled her eyebrows—"you know . . . with the Sawyer heir? This Griffen?"

My tea cup froze halfway to my mouth. *What the hell?* With completely false pleasantness, I said, "Did you just suggest I'm trading sexual favors for tuition? With my boss?"

"Savannah," Lydia said in a chiding tone, "You don't have to be so vulgar."

"Oh, is that not what you meant? I must have misunderstood."

Struggling with the whole *give her a chance* thing, I let the silence build for a few seconds. We both knew I hadn't misunderstood anything.

Lydia had the grace to keep her mouth shut.

With another coolly pleasant smile, I explained, "The other boys at Heartstone also attend Laurel Country Day, which is lovely for Nicky. August is a bit ahead of him, and Thatcher is in the middle school, but it made it so much easier than feeling like he was starting a new school by himself. He's doing very well. He's not wild about reading, but his teacher said he's above grade level in math. If you ask him, he'll tell you his favorite subject is recess."

See? I'm being nice, I congratulated myself.

Lydia sat back, seemingly lost in thought, and sipped her tea. Not eager to restart the conversation, I did the same. I wasn't sure what she wanted, other than to be a jerk. I was trying to give her a chance, trying to be kind, but every instinct I had told me to get the hell away from Lydia Harris.

Chapter Thirty-Four

SAVANNAH

Setting her teacup back in the saucer with a decisive click, she said, "Savannah, I came all the way down here because I felt like I couldn't make myself clear through text. John and I just aren't happy with this separation from Nicky. You've kept us apart for far too long."

I wrapped cold fingers around my teacup, doing my best to harness my temper again. I was trying, but she wasn't helping. Not in the slightest. I could put up with a lot, but I was finished with Lydia blaming me for everything that went wrong in her life.

"If I recall," I said as evenly as I could, "you told us to leave and never contact you again. You and John both blocked my phone number." At the time, it had been a shock. I didn't remember much from Oliver's funeral. We'd all been grief-stricken, drowning in pain, and I hadn't understood that they really meant it when they told me never to contact them again. I called and texted later to try to work things out. When I finally realized they'd blocked me, I sat and stared at my unread messages in shock, weeping from the loss.

Lydia let out a tinkle of a laugh and shook her head. "Oh, dear, Savannah. I'm so sorry. You misunderstood. First of all, I never meant that to apply to Nicky. Of course not! I was never angry with my grandson. I was angry with you." Her smile held an edge of triumph, as if she'd been waiting for years to deliver that line.

Maybe she had.

"You were angry with me," I repeated, as if that would make it sound less nuts.

Lydia looked down at the tablecloth, tears filling her eyes. Tipping her face up to the ceiling, she blinked them back with big flutters of her thickly mascaraed lashes. I couldn't shake the feeling that this was all an act. Or maybe I was just angry and inclined to think everything she did was calculated. I couldn't tell. Before I could decide, she went on.

"I'd just lost my son, and you played no small part in that, as you know." Lydia tilted her head to the side and raised an eyebrow, pinning me with a knowing look.

I refused to crumble.

"I *don't* know, Lydia," I said, the cool politeness gone, my tone hardened to steel. "You've insisted that what happened to Oliver was my fault," I said, leaning forward and lowering my voice. "But I'm not the one who kept giving him the pills. I'm not the one who lied to doctor after doctor to get him more. Who lied to me about his sobriety? Who checked him out of rehab early? That was you. I begged you to stop. Over and over. So, I don't understand how you keep turning this around to make it my fault."

Lydia's lips pressed together into a flat line, her lipstick a narrow slash of red. "That's not how I remember it," she said stiffly, sitting back.

I picked up my teacup. "I'm aware that's not how you

remember it, Lydia. It is, however, what happened, and I have no interest in having anything to do with you or John when you insist on throwing the blame for what happened to Oliver on me. I loved him. I did everything I could to help him. If you want to blame anyone, blame Oliver."

"That's a disgusting thing to say about my son," Lydia spat, her face twisting in revulsion.

"It's the truth," I whispered.

A tear dripped over Lydia's lashes, pulling a streak of dark mascara with it. Guilt stabbed at me. My past always brought a messy swirl of emotion—grief and love and guilt and anger and heartbreak and regret. All of it tangled together and clouded my vision. Was this all an act? Was Lydia playing me? Or did she truly believe I was at fault for Oliver's death? She probably did believe it. Maybe that was the only way she could live with the part she'd played.

I smiled vaguely up at the waitress as she slid a bowl in front of me and a salad in front of Lydia. I took a spoonful, letting the rich flavors of cream, butter, and lobster distract me. As good as I remembered. I'd have to come back with my mother and Nicky. I forced down another spoonful, my still-knotted stomach not appreciating the bisque as much as my tastebuds did.

Lydia stabbed at her salad, patting the dressing off her lips as she chewed, her eyes landing everywhere but on me. I'd been here before, during other times when I'd displeased her. She was freezing me out.

Abruptly, I was done playing her games. I didn't need this in my life.

"Lydia, I left in the middle of my workday with no notice, and I need to get back. Why don't you tell me why you're here."

Lydia glared at me, her anger no longer disguised. "I

want time with my grandson. You still haven't given me an answer about Thanksgiving."

"Fine. You'd like an answer? I'll give you an answer. No, you may not have Nicky for the week of his Thanksgiving break. The idea is absurd. You haven't seen him since he was a toddler. He doesn't remember you."

"You could join him," she offered grudgingly.

"After this conversation, do you think I want to spend a week with you and John? Are you crazy?"

Lydia sputtered, wiping her mouth with her napkin, her fork clinking on her plate as she leaned forward. "Don't speak to me in that tone," she ordered.

"I'll speak to you in any tone I choose," I said. "After everything you've said, do you really think I want my son to spend time alone with you? So you can fill his head with lies about me?"

"I wouldn't—"

"Please. You absolutely would."

"Then come with him and make sure I don't," she challenged.

"I don't think so. First, I don't want to. Nicky and I have plans for the holiday, and I don't want to change them. Second, I have to work. I can't just take off an entire week with so little notice."

Lydia gave an exaggerated sniff. "I suppose you can't. For a minute, I forgot you were a servant."

I ignored the last comment, refusing to defend myself to Lydia. I'd had enough of her classist bullshit. I wasn't treated as less than at Heartstone. Manor, and I sure as hell wasn't going to let Lydia make me feel inadequate.

When it became clear I wasn't going to respond, Lydia huffed out a breath.

"Fine," she snapped. "Then John and I will spend

Thanksgiving here. I'm sure I can find a short-term rental or a hotel room. You can bring Nicky to us for the holiday."

"No," I drew in an exaggerated breath, trying not to explode. "I'll repeat, we already have plans. That's not going to happen." Sitting back, I tried for reason. "If you want time with Nicky, we can figure something out. I can bring him to you, re-introduce you. We can do some short visits, and when he's comfortable with you—when I'm comfortable with you—we can talk about more. Not all at once. But gradually."

"If you think you can keep me from Nicky—"

I interrupted her. "This isn't about keeping you from Nicky. This is about Nicky's best interests. He doesn't know you. And I have to wonder, why is that? If you're so interested in your grandson, where have you been? Why now?"

It was clear I'd struck a nerve by the way she tensed up.

"I missed my grandson," she said mulishly.

That was a lie. I could see it in the shifting of her eyes. I could also see she wasn't going to tell me the truth. But something had changed for her, something that made her remember her grandson after all this time. I wasn't sure the why mattered.

I just wanted to get out of here and go home. Hopefully before the boys got back from school so I could change into my uniform and pretend none of this had happened.

"Are you interested in arranging a time to meet Nicky?" I asked.

"I don't need to *meet* my grandson. I was there when he was born."

"But he doesn't know you. Would you like to arrange a time?" I asked slowly and deliberately, my patience frayed to its limit.

"No, I don't want to arrange a time to see my grandson." Lydia pushed her salad away and leaned toward me, her eyes narrowed, menace all over her face. I guess she was done playing nice.

A deep sense of dread settled over me.

"I didn't want it to come to this," Lydia said. "But if you're not prepared to be reasonable, then I have to inform you that I have a lawyer and we will be pursuing some form of custody. Once the judge hears about the drugs and the way you killed Oliver, I'm sure they'll be happy to give me Nicky."

I went still, my lungs frozen, my heart racing.

She said it.

Custody.

My worst fear.

I hadn't heard that word from her since Oliver was recovering from his second accident, and I'd had my hands full balancing Oliver, Nicky, and my job. She tried to take him then, leading to the biggest fight of my marriage. In the end, Oliver had roused enough to tell her to drop it or he'd ban her from our house. She backed down. But now Oliver was gone, and I could see her intentions all over her face. This time Lydia was determined to win.

It was too late to wish I'd listened to my mother and Finn and talked to a lawyer. I'd thought I had good reasons not to, plenty of them, but now that I was staring Lydia in the face, all I had was regret. She was ready for battle, and I was completely unarmed.

On the inside, I was screaming in terror and fury. I gave no sign of my turmoil as I stood, picking up my purse from where it hung on the back of my chair. "I'd like to say it was nice to see you, Lydia, but I'm afraid I can't. You will not be getting custody of Nicky. I don't recommend you try. Any decent judge will laugh their head off."

I moved closer, lowering my voice so only Lydia could hear. "You have accusations, but I have evidence. Emails between me and his doctor documenting my concern about his drug use. My signature on forms to get him to rehab. Yours checking him out early against his doctor's recommendations. Text messages between you and Oliver in which you agree to get him more pills. Pictures of all the bottles of pills, from all the different doctors you found, long after his own doctor said no more. This won't go well for you."

Lydia's chin lifted, and I knew she wasn't afraid.

She wasn't, but I was terrified. I had to get out of there before I broke, and she saw how scared I really was. I knew her. If she sensed my fear, it would only make her stronger.

"Go home, Lydia. You're not getting Nicky." Grudgingly I added, "If you decide you want to be reasonable and start slow with him, we can talk." I was trying to think of my son's best interests. I wasn't at all convinced seeing this woman was in his best interest, but I had time to mull that over.

I dropped two twenties on the table and strode from the restaurant, leaving her sitting there fuming, and drove back to Heartstone on autopilot. Every time I loosened my tight grip on the steering wheel, my hands shook.

Custody. She was going after custody. Did she already have a lawyer? She'd said she had a lawyer, but did she *actually* have a lawyer? I didn't know. More importantly, *I* did not have a lawyer. Not yet, despite both Finn and my mother telling me to get one.

I'd spoken the truth to Lydia. I did have evidence that I'd been trying to help Oliver stay sober and proof that she'd been doing the opposite. But not a lot. Not file folders full of it, just some text messages, pictures, and signatures on medical documents. And Lydia had shown me at lunch how well she could play the grieving mother. If she got in front of a judge and started crying . . .

I couldn't guarantee she wouldn't get what she wanted, at least partly. And the idea of her having Nicky all to herself, the things she would tell him . . . He was only six. Could she poison him against me? I wanted to say no. No, of course not. We had a bond. Nicky loved me. Nicky knew how much I loved him.

But she was his grandmother. I'm sure she was fully prepared to shower him with every material thing he'd ever thought he might want. Between toys, candy, and ice cream, she could go a long way toward gaining his trust. And then . . . I couldn't even think about it.

The last time Lydia invaded my life, it had started like this. Her determined to get her way, me saying no, Lydia pushing back, me saying no again. Over and over, her pushing, me pushing back, Lydia gaining ground until my life crumbled to pieces around me, until Oliver died. I couldn't let it happen again. I wouldn't.

A wave of nausea washed over me, so sharp my mouth watered until I thought I might actually throw up. I'd only had a few spoonfuls of the bisque and had skipped breakfast, too anxious to eat after seeing Lydia's text.

Time ticked by as I sat on I-26, which turned into a temporary parking lot after an accident near the airport, stewing in my fears as it got later and later. By the time I closed the last few miles to Sawyers Bend, I was light-headed, sick to my stomach, and my temples ached. I realized I was clenching my teeth, grinding them together from the tension.

I parked my car and went straight to the kitchens, knowing there was no point in changing. The boys had been home from school for more than an hour. I couldn't play this off like I'd never left Heartstone. By now, I would have been missed. Either way, there were going to be questions I did not want to answer. It didn't matter. I needed to see Nicky.

Chapter Thirty-Five

SAVANNAH

Nicky was at the table munching a cookie when I came in. August and Thatcher had scarfed their tea and taken off, but my mother still sat with Nicky, a cup of tea in front of her as she chatted with him while Finn worked on dinner. Both Finn and my mother took in my unusual choice of clothes and knew something was up. This was not the outfit I'd pick to run errands or see a friend.

Finn's eyes narrowed first. He hadn't liked that I'd only picked at breakfast, asking me if I was okay more than once. I shrugged and put him off, saying, "I'm fine. Everything's fine." That had only tipped him off further that everything was not fine. Now he studied me, knowing for certain that something was going on.

"Where did you go?" my mother asked.

"You look like you're dressed for a job interview," Finn said with a scowl.

"Or a ladies' lunch," my mother added.

"Neither," I said. "It's not important. Everything's fine.

Is dinner on schedule?" I asked brightly. Finn didn't bother to respond.

Dropping into a seat by Nicky, I opened my arms for a hug. "Did you have a nice day at school?" As always, Nicky threw himself into my arms, squeezing as tight as he could and giggling, "Backbreaker!"

Someday he would be big enough to break my back with a hug, but not yet. For now, he was still my little guy. I nuzzled the top of his head, the smell of shampoo and little boy bringing a rush of tears to my eyes. I squeezed back until he shrieked and squirmed away.

"Do you want a cookie, Mom?" he asked, pulling back and showing me the plate in the middle of the table. "I helped Mr. Finn make the cookies. We made them yesterday when I got home from school, and then we put the dough in the fridge, and it got all cold and hard, and then when I got home today, Mr. Finn helped me slice it into cookies, and then we baked them and we sprinkled different colored sugar on top."

He handed me a sugar cookie with sparkly blue crystals on top.

"Nicky, this looks fantastic! I'd love a cookie," I said, my heart squeezing at his pride and Finn's kindness. I knew all about baking with six-year-olds, and it was not for the faint of heart.

Anxiety still had my stomach in a knot, acid bubbling at the scent of sugar. I wasn't sure how I would force myself to eat or drink anything, but I wasn't going to disappoint Nicky.

I glanced at Finn, who watched us with assessing eyes.

"You and Nicky made cookies?" I asked, tears threatening at the warmth in his eyes as he looked over at Nicky.

"He's a good baker," Finn said. "Patient and careful."

His mouth quirked. "Even if he does sample way too much cookie dough."

Nicky giggled again. "Mr. Finn said cookies weren't that hard, so I asked if I could try. And he said sure. So we made cookies. We're going to try chocolate chip next—"

"I thought you would have done chocolate chip first," my mother commented. "Those are your favorite."

Nicky nodded in agreement. "Yeah, Mr. Finn says he has a great recipe for chocolate chip cookies. But then he said he had colored sugar sprinkles, and I wanted to see those, so we decided on sugar cookies. See? I did some in blue and some in green. We ate all the gold. It was sparkly. I did mine with gold and red, and it looked like the fireworks from summer." Nicky grinned and shoved another cookie in his mouth.

My mother slid a teacup in front of me, and my stomach turned over again. I wasn't ready for more tea. I took a small sip and picked up a cookie, taking a bite. Sugar melted over my tongue and went straight to my brain.

"It's wonderful," I said, trying to reassure myself.

Nicky was fine. He was in our home, safe and happy. I wasn't sure how to feel about this little domestic scene. Finn baking with Nicky, my mother watching them and drinking tea. I wanted to wrap myself in the comfort of it all.

Shouldn't I be wary? I was sleeping with Finn, and he was spending time with my son. But we weren't dating, and this wasn't about me. Finn wasn't sucking up to Nicky to get to me. Finn didn't suck up to anyone, and he already had me. The only reason he'd make cookies with Nicky was because he wanted to, and that had my emotions all over the place. I just wanted to crawl into my bed and sleep, to turn off the world and pretend today never happened.

During a break in Nicky's chatter about his school day,

my mother reached out to cover my hand with hers. "Do you want to tell me about your day?"

I shook my head, raising pleading eyes to her knowing ones. "Not right now. We can talk about it later, but not right now."

Her head tipped to the side as she studied me. She might have been thinking, or she might have been using her X-ray mom-vision. Either way, she ended up at the right conclusion. And the wrong one. "You went into Asheville?"

I nodded.

She squeezed my fingers. "Good. It was about time."

I knew she thought I'd been to see a lawyer. She'd reminded me a few times lately to get moving on that. I didn't tell her what I'd actually been doing in Asheville. I would. Later. I didn't want to talk about it yet. I couldn't. I'd fall apart, and I couldn't bear the idea of falling apart. Not now. Later. I just needed to catch my breath. Get rid of this headache, relax, and think without panicking.

"We can talk later," I said again. "I'm exhausted, and I have a headache. I'm just not up for it right now."

"When you're ready, you know where to find me, love bug."

Another rush of tears hit my eyes, and I blinked them away. "Love you, Mom," I whispered.

"Love you too, baby," she whispered back. I could tell she wasn't satisfied, but she was willing to give me space. One of the many, many reasons I loved my mother.

I expected Finn to pry, but he let it go, his eyes thoughtful as they watched me. And then I realized that he hadn't given up. He was just biding his time.

I got to work on the evening chores, got Nicky down, and was just settling into the couch with my thoughts when, as he had every night for more than a week, Finn showed up at the cottage, letting himself in with the key I'd given him.

I was in my robe, face washed, teeth brushed, half convinced I was going to tell Finn I didn't want to have sex, I just wanted to go to bed. Then Finn walked through the door, his dark hair sliding in his moss green eyes, those perfect fucking shoulders stretching his t-shirt just the right way, and all I wanted was sex.

After the day from hell, I just wanted to feel good. To turn off my brain and surrender to my body. I wanted the release only Finn could give me, to fall into the safety and freedom of giving my body to Finn.

Unfortunately, for the first time, Finn was not at my cottage for sex. At least, not right away. He closed and locked the door, stopping just inside, and crossed his arms over his chest.

"What's wrong with you?" he demanded.

"Nothing's wrong," I shot back automatically. It was a waste of breath since we both knew that was a lie.

"Don't fucking give me that bullshit. You've been on edge all day. What the fuck is wrong? What happened? Where were you today? Did you have a doctor's appointment? Are you sick?" His eyes flew wide in alarm, as if that thought had just occurred to him.

Shit. *Shit.* I didn't want to talk, but he looked genuinely worried.

"Lydia came to Asheville," I admitted, the words spilling out before I could think of something else to say. "She texted, and I went to go see her. It was unpleasant. I don't want to talk about it."

He studied my face. "What does she want?"

"I don't want to talk about it, Finn." My voice squeaked

with an edge of hysteria. How could I hold it together for an entire lunch with Lydia, but two minutes into a conversation with Finn and I was already unraveling?

"I don't want to talk about it," I repeated before he could protest. "I just— You didn't come over here to talk, did you?"

He dropped his crossed arms and shoved his hands in his pockets. "I didn't come over here to *not* talk."

"I don't even know what that means," I said, hearing the petulance in my voice. I hated this conversation.

"It means I don't have a problem with talking. You're one of the few people I like talking to. So tell me what's going on, we can talk about it, and then we'll go have sex."

His calm, patient reasonableness suddenly felt very *un*reasonable. I didn't want to talk. Not yet. The whole fucking thing with Lydia had me spun. My head pounded. I felt like I'd been through a literal wringer, and I didn't want to talk about any of it. I just wanted to have sex and go to sleep.

"Why do we have to talk?" I demanded. "I don't want to talk to you." I gestured between us, my hand shaking as I flung it toward him and back at me. "This whole thing we have is about sex, so why aren't we having sex? Since when do you want to talk? This isn't a relationship. It's sex."

Something hardened in his eyes, and he straightened. "That's all this is to you? Just fucking? I'm your booty call, and that's it?" The way he said it made me feel like a royal bitch. I'd had a shit day, but none of it was Finn's fault.

"You don't have to make it sound ugly," I said, rubbing the heel of my palm against my temple. "I just— We know this isn't a relationship. You don't have to hear about my day."

"I didn't think hearing about your day was such a chore," he said in that even tone I recognized from myself when I was holding my temper in line.

"Finn—" I didn't know what to say. I didn't want to talk about Lydia. I didn't want to talk about our relationship, or whatever this was. I wanted to strip off all my clothes, tear off his, and lose myself in his body. And then I wanted to fall asleep with the heavy thump of his heartbeat under my ear. That's what I wanted.

I crossed my arms over my chest until I was hugging myself. My head thumping with spikes of pain, I watched Finn warily, his stiff shoulders and closed expression telling me I'd hurt him. Fuck. Fuck. Fuck.

Finn hadn't done anything wrong, and I'd hurt him anyway. Fuck.

I dropped my arms to my sides. "I'm sorry. I'm sorry, Finn. I'm being an asshole." I wrapped my arms around myself again. "Lydia was worse than awful, and there was an accident on 26 on the way home, and my head is throbbing so badly I think it wants to pop off my neck. I don't want to talk about any of this right now. If I do, I'm going to start bawling, and I won't be able to stop."

Finn's face paled. "Okay," he said slowly, coming a little closer. "I get it. We can talk later, after you've had a good night's sleep and a good meal. You barely touched dinner."

"My stomach hurts." Tears pricked my eyes, and I almost lost it. It had been years since I'd come this close to crying so many times in one day. The compassion in Finn's eyes almost undid me.

"Okay," he said again, taking another step closer. "What do you want? Tell me what you want."

I did the only thing I could think of. I untied the belt at

my waist and shrugged the robe down my arms, baring my naked body. Heat flooded Finn's dark eyes, and the knot in my stomach loosened a fraction. Shaking the robe down my arms, I hooked my finger in the collar and tossed it over my shoulder as I turned and strode for the stairs.

"Are you coming?"

The footsteps behind me told me he was. I made it up the stairs ahead of him, but the second we cleared the door, he shut it behind us, the lock clicking. He caught me in his arms, and his mouth was on mine, fast and a little rough. It was as if he knew that slow and gentle were more than I could take without falling apart.

His hands were everywhere, stroking, squeezing, his palm sliding between my legs to cup my pussy, feeling the heat of my body readying itself for him. He worked one finger inside, the heel of his palm grinding into my clit, sending waves of pleasure through my body. A second finger stretched me, splintering my mind and sending me to that place where all I could do was feel.

Just when I thought I was going to slide over the edge, his hand was gone, and he was turning me to face the bed.

"Bend over," he ordered, a firm hand in the middle of my back, pushing me down. Good thing we'd already discovered the bed was the perfect height for this. "Don't move."

He was gone, moving around the room. I stayed where I was, arms folded on top of the covers, resting my cheek on top. A click and the fireplace came to life, the flicker of flames warming the room. Finn was behind me, tracing a line down my spine, his fingers going down, down, to dip between my legs again.

"So fucking hot, Savannah. Always ready."

The rough hair on his thighs brushed the back of my legs as he fit himself to me, the head of his cock nudging my entrance, his arms coming down on either side of me, his chest pressed to my back.

"Just let go," he said into my neck. "Let go and let me make you feel good."

Then he was filling me, one hand shoving between me and the duvet to cup my breast, the other between my legs to press the heel of his palm into my clit as he thrust.

My brain shut off. I was surrounded, his heat and strength enveloping me, his cock filling me over and over, each thrust pushing my clit harder and harder into his unyielding palm as his fingers cupped the place where we were joined. It was unbearably intimate that he was touching me there, feeling the exact spot where we became one, feeling every inch as he took me and withdrew, the connection between us so much more than merely physical.

I forgot about my headache, forgot my fear, forgot everything but Finn, the pleasure filling me just as he was, chasing everything else far away. I came with a long groan, the orgasm tearing through me, wiping me clean of the day, of everything but Finn, holding me safe in his arms as he followed me into his own bliss.

A minute later, way before I was ready to move, Finn pulled me to my feet, ushering me into the bathroom. He flipped on the water in the shower.

"Hair up or down?" he asked. I stared at him, my mind blank. "Do you want to keep your hair dry?" he repeated slowly.

Oh, I got it. In answer, I grabbed an abandoned hair tie off the bathroom counter, securing my hair in a messy bun. Were we taking a shower?

Steam hit the room, and he pulled me in, his arms around me, the water beating warmth into my tight shoulders. Finn tugged, and I pressed my cheek to his shoulder, holding on, his hands stroking over my back, the tears I'd been holding back leaking from my eyes as I let the water do its work.

I don't know how long we stood there. It could have been a few minutes or an hour. By the time Finn turned off the water, my headache had eased to a dull throb, and my eyes were drooping. He dried me with rough strokes, nudging me to the bed and lifting my side of the covers.

I got in without a word, rolling into him when he joined me, fitting my body to his until my head lay on his chest, one leg slung over his. His fingers threaded through the loose hair at my nape, tugging and stroking, lulling me into sleep.

When I woke, he was gone, as usual. I rolled over, finding his pillow wrapped in my arms, as it so often was since he'd started spending the night. Every morning when he left, I assumed my subconscious prompted me to reach for his pillow, still warm and smelling of Finn, and cuddle it until I woke up, holding him close even after he was gone.

Even as I had the thought, I pushed the pillow away. This wasn't how this was supposed to go.

I wanted to keep a distance from Finn. That was the smart way to do this. Keep it simple. Stay detached. It was sex, not something more. But I couldn't forget the way he held me, how he listened when I said I didn't want to talk, had taken care of me exactly the way I needed to be taken care of.

Aside from my mother, no one had taken care of me in a very long time. Maybe not since I was pregnant with Nicky and Oliver nursed me through morning sickness.

I don't need anyone to take care of me, I tried to tell myself, but it sounded false, even inside my head.

No, maybe I didn't need someone to take care of me. Maybe I could do it all on my own. But did I want to? I'd been so sure the answer was a resounding *yes*. I was a one-woman island, capable of amazing feats with zero help. Grabbing Finn's pillow and snuggling it deeper into my chest, I listened to the soft sounds of Nicky moving below, padding up the stairs to me. I snagged my robe from where I'd dropped it on the floor, sliding it on before Nicky made it up the stairs. This was what was important. Nicky. Our him-and-me little family. This was all I needed.

As a drowsy Nicky climbed into my bed and snuggled in for that last bit of sleep, I tried to tell myself I had all I wanted from life. Great job, a wonderful place to live, good friends, and my perfect, sweet, amazing son. How could I want more? Wasn't all this good enough? It should be. I'd figure out how to handle Lydia, and then we'd be fine. Better than fine. We'd be on the top of the world.

I couldn't stop the flash of memory. Oliver, in the early days, when we'd been so deeply in love. His smile. His laugh when I told him I was pregnant. He'd been over the moon, so excited to be a father.

I'd had *more* once. Once upon a time, I had everything. Losing it had almost killed me.

I didn't need *more*. Not again. What I already had was plenty. It would have to be. I wouldn't survive a loss like that a second time.

I kissed Nicky on the top of his head, resolving to thank Finn for being cool and leave it at that. Just because he was nice didn't mean I had to make a thing about it.

"Come on, baby doll, it's time to get ready for school."

Nicky grumbled, and we fell into our usual morning

rhythm, the cottage feeling empty, even with the two of us there. I told myself it didn't matter. Nicky and I had each other. That was everything we needed. It had to be. I didn't have room inside my heart for anything, *anyone*, else who could leave me broken. Not again. Never again.

Chapter Thirty-Six

SAVANNAH

The woman sitting on the other side of Griffen's desk might just be the answer to our nanny problem. I had my fingers crossed. Paige McKenna was smiling, composed, and calm, her hands folded in her lap, her dark hair in a low ponytail. She had several years of nannying experience, loved children, and had spent the past few years teaching kindergarten. She'd said that while she loved being in the classroom, she missed being part of a family, and she was looking for something more domestic.

Over the years, she'd vacationed in Western North Carolina, loved the area, and was thrilled at the prospect of settling down here. Just as important as the rest of her qualifications, she'd passed Hawk and Griffen's stringent security checks.

"Well," Hope said brightly, "I think I've asked all my questions. Do you have any more of your own, Paige?"

Paige shook her head, her smile cranking up from pleasant to match Hope's happy grin. "This feels like it would be a good fit for me. Are you sure you're all right with me not living in the house at first?"

Hope nodded. "I think that's sensible. I can understand wanting a little personal space, and, to be honest, we're not ready to house you here quite yet." Hope looked to me for confirmation.

"We could put something together if you preferred to be in the house," I said, "But it would be rough. We're still having some issues with the electricity and plumbing in the guest wing. Hope's former apartment in town is charming and cozy and a quick drive from the Manor."

"Sounds like a plan—" Hope cut off as the door to the office opened, and Harvey poked his head in, his rounded cheeks apple red.

"Sorry to interrupt," he said, his eyes lighting with curiosity. "I was looking for Griffen." Harvey's eyes landed on Paige and stopped, his brows pulling together as if he was trying to place her in his memory.

"He's down the hall in the library," Hope supplied.

Harvey pulled his gaze from Paige and nodded at Hope. "I'll find him. We're heading out for a few hours to look at that property we were talking about. Hopefully, the weather holds off." He glanced out the French doors to the barren gardens. The day was gray and overcast, a light drizzle falling to soak everything in damp cold. The tops of the trees swayed with sharp tugs of wind.

"Don't take too long," Hope said. "I don't think we're going to get any snow, but I don't like the look of that wind."

Harvey nodded again. "Agreed." He turned to go.

With a glance at Hope, I said, "Excuse me for a moment. I need a word with Harvey."

Harvey was already halfway down the hall. He turned at my tap on his shoulder, his face brightening with a smile when he saw me. I know what people say about lawyers, but I'd always liked Harvey. He'd worked for Prentice for years, which was not a mark in his favor, but I'd always known him to be honest and kind.

"I need your advice," I said. "Maybe I should come to your office."

"Savannah, what's wrong?" he asked, his smile dissolving into concern after he scanned my face.

"I, uh . . ." I wasn't sure how to start. "My former mother-in-law has been asking to see Nicky. I've been putting her off, being cautious because she doesn't really know Nicky."

At Harvey's confused look, I explained, "She blamed me for my husband's death and refused to have anything to do with Nicky or me after Oliver died."

"Oliver overdosed on prescription drugs, correct?"

I nodded, a little surprised that Harvey knew about Oliver. But I shouldn't have been. I'd had to pass a background check, after all. It's just that no one ever said anything. I guess I liked to pretend that no one knew. Clearly, that was dumb, all things considered.

"Yes, that's right," I said. "I tried to get him to stop, but she was helping him get the pills—" I shook my head. Just saying the words filled me with fear, but I knew I had to spit it out. "I don't know why she changed her mind about Nicky, but she's been asking to see him. Asking me to send him to her for a visit. I met her for lunch the other day, and when I told her we'd have to start slowly, with supervised visits until Nicky is comfortable with her, she got angry and told me she had a lawyer and was going after custody."

Harvey's eyes sharpened. "Have you received any communication from her lawyer?" he asked, his tone suddenly all business.

"No, no, I haven't heard from her or anyone repre-senting her since we had lunch on the seventeenth. Since then, I've called almost every family lawyer in the area but haven't made any progress. Either they aren't taking new clients, they don't return my call, or they want a significant retainer. I have savings, but—"

Harvey nodded again. "You don't want to fork over thousands of dollars if this isn't going to come to anything."

I nodded, relieved he understood. "Exactly. It's not that I'm not taking it seriously, but it's a lot of money. Before I write that check, I wanted to talk to you."

Harvey was silent for a minute. Reaching out, he took my hands in his and squeezed. "Savannah, I'll make a few calls and see what I can do. I'm not a family lawyer, so if this goes further, we'll need to set you up with someone who specializes, but run everything through me for now. If you receive any communication from your mother-in-law or someone representing her, come straight to me. Do not talk to her. Do not answer her texts. Do not engage in any way without discussing it with me first. Understand?"

"I understand," I said, a weight sliding off my shoulders. I hadn't heard from Lydia since I'd walked out of our lunch, and the silence after her threats felt more ominous by the day.

"Don't worry," Harvey said, giving my hands another squeeze before releasing them. "No one is taking Nicky away from you. No one."

"Thank you, Harvey," I said.

"Anytime," he answered, offering me the kind smile I'd liked ever since I was a little girl. Harvey took a step away and then turned back. "Who are you and Hope talking to? Another nanny interview or help around the house?"

"Nanny interview," I confirmed. "I think she's the one. Great qualifications, the kids and Scarlett liked her when they met yesterday, and, most importantly, she passed the security checks."

"What's her name?" he asked.

"Paige McKenna," I said. "Do you know her?"

Harvey gave me a tight smile and shook his head. "I don't, but she looks familiar. Something about her face," he said slowly and shook his head again. "I can't quite place her. I feel like I should know her, but the name doesn't ring a bell. Anyway, I was just curious. I'll track down Griffen and see if we can't look at this land before the weather turns." He headed toward the library, saying over his shoulder, "I heard something on the radio about sleet. I don't like the sound of that," he muttered as he disappeared around the corner.

Satisfied, I returned to the office to find Hope finishing up with Paige. To me, she said, "Paige is ready to start on Monday."

"Fantastic," I replied. Things were looking up. Harvey was going to help me with Lydia, and we'd finally solved the nanny problem.

To Paige, Hope said, "We'll get you set up with a room at the Inn until you can get moved into the apartment."

"If you need help with movers, or anything else, just let me know," I offered as we walked Paige to the front door.

She practically skipped down the steps to her car, seemingly oblivious to the icy gusts of damp wind whipping her ponytail into the air.

"She looks as happy as I am that she's taking the job," Hope said with a grin.

I closed the door firmly against the wind and turned to grin back at Hope. "I was almost willing to take anyone, but Paige seems like the perfect fit. The kids like her. You, Scarlett, and I like her. She has experience, patience . . . She's almost too good to be true."

Hope laughed. "Don't say that! I don't want to tempt fate." Rolling her shoulders, she rubbed her lower back. "I was beginning to think this little one would be in preschool before we found someone."

The wind gusted hard, and the chandelier high above us flickered, going dark for a full two seconds before sputtering back to life. Hope and I locked eyes. "The gennies are fueled up," I assured her. "Billy Bob checked a few days ago when it looked like weather might be rolling in. Hopefully, the power will hold, but we'll be covered if it doesn't."

Hope nodded. We hadn't had to rely on the generators for more than a few hours here and there, but I kept them ready to use year-round, just in case. Between summer storms and winter ice, we never knew when we'd need them.

"With Griffen out and Royal at the Inn, I have some free time," Hope said. "How about you? Do you want to go through some of the historical records?"

"I'd love to," I answered with genuine enthusiasm. My to-do list wasn't empty, but everything could wait if Hope had some free time. I knew she was dying to read that maid's journal from the '30s I'd found, and I wanted to keep organizing the stacks of paperwork. Piles of receipts would probably be mind-numbingly boring to anyone else, but I was fascinated.

Food orders, cleaning supplies, payroll for the staff. Notes between the butler and the housekeeper. In eras past, Heartstone had been like a small town unto itself. It boggled my mind to see what it took to keep the place running, and it left me feeling closely connected to the Manor's history. I'd started jotting things down here and there about my work—notes about the renovations, staff, things that might be interesting to future housekeepers, just as these notes were so meaningful to me.

I stayed close to Hope as we descended the wide stairs to the lower level. She was a little wobbly on her feet these days. I know she was sick and tired of us hovering, but I had to ask. "Are you feeling okay? Maybe you need to—"

"Do not tell me to lay down," Hope ordered, her usually warm cognac brown eyes hot with annoyance.

"I wasn't going to," I lied.

We reached the lower level, and she stopped to rub her lower back again. "I'm sorry. I'm cranky. I didn't sleep well last night because I couldn't get comfortable. The baby's kicking up a storm, and I'm restless and achy and tired. And so sick of being pregnant."

She turned beseeching eyes to me, her guilt clear. I didn't blame her one bit, and I gave her a one-armed hug.

"I know what you mean, sister," I said with a low laugh. "In my last few weeks with Nicky, I tried every trick in the book to speed things up. Eggplant Parmesan. Bouncing on my mini trampoline. Walking. If you'd told me it would make labor start faster, I would have done back handsprings. I already loved Nicky so much, but by then, all I wanted was for him to get out of me."

Hope laughed ruefully. "Yeah, that's it. I feel like he's been in here so long, and I want to meet him. I want to look him in the eyes. And I want him to stop jabbing his feet into my ribs."

"Ugh, I remember that," I commiserated. "Nicky jammed both feet right up under my ribcage all the time. I'd nudge them back, and two seconds later, he'd stretch, and they'd be shoved up under my ribs again. It did not feel good." I smiled to myself. I'd loved most of my pregnancy, but not those pointy little feet poking my ribs. "You're still sure the baby is a boy?"

Hope continued down the hall to the kitchens. "I'm positive he's a boy, but Griffen is just as sure we're having a girl."

"I'm impressed you have the patience to wait and see. You two are so organized. I can't believe you're leaving something so important up in the air." I thought back to finding out Nicky was a boy during an ultrasound. My next stop had been the baby store, where I loaded up on onesies and blankets, not realizing how many I'd get at my baby shower.

Hope stopped at the kitchen door, surveying the clean counters, gleaming stovetop, and the giant pot steaming on the stove. "It smells amazing in here."

Finn looked up at us from the mound of dough on the island in front of him. "Chili and country bread." His eyes focused on Hope's face, taking in her obvious exhaustion. "You look like you need tea." He lifted his chin at the table, a Finn-style order for Hope to sit down.

"We're going to sort through one of the bins," I said. "Do you mind if we do it here? I'll get it out of your way when we're done."

"Fine with me," Finn said. "I just need to finish this, and I'll start tea."

"I can do it," Hope cut in, "while Savannah gets the bin." At my look, she added, "I'm pregnant, not incapacitated. I can boil water and measure tea."

I kept my mouth shut and went to get the bin. The lights flickered again, leaving me in the pitch black for more seconds than I liked, the howl of the wind muffled but still creepy here in the lowest level of Heartstone. I returned to the kitchen to see Finn washing his hands and Hope sitting at the table, a mulish set to her chin.

"Finn made me sit down and rest," she tattled, sounding more like Nicky than herself.

"Take advantage now," I said, nodding at her rounded belly. "Once the Sawyer prince or princess arrives, no one will pay any attention to you."

Hope laughed. "That would be a relief. Now give me that journal."

Chapter Thirty-Seven

SAVANNAH

W e spent more than an hour poring over assorted bits and pieces from the storage bin. Hope was absorbed in the maid's journal and me sorting receipts and notes from the housekeeper to her staff. We finished the tea and devoured more than our share of cookies as the wind rose higher, the power flickering with each heavy gust. I received a text from Laurel Country Day saying they were closing early, followed almost immediately by one from Tenn saying he was taking one of the Inn's SUVs and picking up the boys. Hope checked her phone.

"Nothing from Griffen?" I asked.

"Not yet," Hope said. "I don't like him out there in this weather."

Finn glanced up from shaping loaves of bread and studied the dark sky outside. I expected him to dismiss Hope's concerns, but he admitted, "I don't like it either."

Hope stood and started to pace the long length of the kitchen island, the heels of her palms pressing into her lower back.

"You, okay?" I asked.

"Just restless. I can't sit still." She turned at the end of the island and headed back toward the table. "My back hurts, and I wish Griffen were here," she said peevishly.

Something in her tone, in the way she was walking, tickled my mom's antenna. "Hope, how long has your back been hurting?"

"Off and on for the last couple of months?" she said, sounding annoyed and impatient, two things I rarely heard from Hope Sawyer.

"Hope," I said carefully. "How long has it been hurting like this?"

She shot me an irritated look. "I don't know. Since yesterday, after lunch? I couldn't get comfortable at the desk, so I lay down on the couch, but that didn't help, and then I didn't sleep well. I'm restless, that's all."

I looked at Finn, shaking my head slowly. He caught my meaning and gave Hope an assessing look. We were in that zone where the baby could be another two weeks, or she could come today. Hope wasn't having contractions, but that didn't necessarily mean anything. Every labor is different.

I knew as well as anyone who'd been through it that the last week or two before a baby was born was filled with fits and starts. I'd gone to the hospital more than once with Braxton Hicks contractions, sure it was time, only to be sent home to wait and wait and wait some more.

I glanced at the weather outside, added things up in my head, and didn't like the answer.

"Is it just your back?" I probed.

"Yes," she said, in something close to a snap. Very un-Hope-like.

Abruptly she stopped, looking down at the floor. Liquid

dripped between her feet. "Is that—?" she asked in a thin, hesitant voice.

"Yep," I said, hopping to my feet. Dammit. I liked being right, but not about this.

"I thought it would be a flood," she said, still staring at the growing puddle between her feet.

"Sometimes it is. And sometimes it drips out, and you think you peed yourself," I said. "Ask me how I know." Hope gave me a faint smile.

"Is your bag packed?" I asked.

"It's in Griffen's car," she said.

"Great. He can meet us at the hospital." I slid my arm around Hope's waist. Looking at Finn, I said, "Can you drive?"

"On it," he said immediately. "I think Scarlett is in her workroom. I'll let her know we're going and ask her to take point on things here. Meet me in the garage." Lifting his phone, he added, "I'll call Griffen."

"Thanks," I said, relieved to have all that taken care of. Guiding Hope to the door, I asked, "You okay to get to the elevator?"

I only had my experience with Nicky to go on, but I knew we could be hours away from the baby coming, or it could be a lot sooner than that. We had to get to the hospital.

She nodded. "I'm all wet."

"I know. It happens. I'll grab towels from the linen closet upstairs on our way out. The hospital isn't far."

I didn't mention the sleet. The hospital was a quick drive from town, and in normal weather, Heartstone was a short trip from town. But in sleet, all bets were off. Town to the hospital should still be manageable, but the mountain roads between Heartstone and Sawyers Bend were narrow and steep, with sharp drop-offs on the downhill side.

I pushed out of my head all the ways this could go wrong.

Finn was waiting when the elevator doors opened, a stack of towels in his arms. "Scarlett said Tenn is already on his way back with the kids. I'm still trying to reach Griffen." I took the towels, letting him help Hope to the Jeep. One look at those huge, knobby tires, and I had a flash of relief. Thank god he didn't drive a sports car.

We got the towels spread out in the back seat, and Hope settled in. I slid in beside her. "I'll keep trying Griffen," I said. "Everything is going to be fine. Finn is a great driver, and this is the perfect vehicle to get us to the hospital." I had no idea if Finn was a great driver, but I realized I had complete confidence that he had it under control.

I squeezed Hope's hand as we backed out of the garage, Finn making the three-point turn at a glacial pace. The gleam of the asphalt chilled my gut. Ice. Hope curled forward, her arms curving around her rounded belly, her body suddenly tight. Seconds later, she eased, wilting into me.

"Was that a contraction?" she asked, her eyes a little wild and more than a little scared.

"The first?" I asked.

Hope nodded. "I've had the little ones, the Braxton Hicks, but not like that."

"We've got time," I reassured her, pulling up the clock app on my phone and starting the stopwatch. I flipped back to the phone screen and dialed Griffen. Voicemail. I left a message, trying to sound calm, like this was no big deal.

On the inside, I was worried. What were we going to do

if the baby decided to come quickly? What if we crashed? What if—

I stopped myself. I couldn't catastrophize. I could do this. We could do this.

Finn's eyes briefly met mine in the rearview mirror, concern heavy in his mossy green gaze before he focused back on the slick asphalt. We were still inching down the long, winding drive to the main road, the gates to the estate in the distance.

In my mind, I pictured how far we had to go. We'd been in the car for only five minutes, but the Manor was still in sight. We had to get down the drive to the gates, then down the mountain to town, and then through town and the resulting traffic that always happened when we got weather like this.

We were in the mountains but also in North Carolina, which resulted in a funny crossover of people who had no idea how to drive in the bad weather that we got far more often than our neighbors in the lowlands. Town would be filled with fender benders and traffic. Meanwhile, Hope and Griffen's baby had clearly decided it was on the way.

I tried Griffen again. I'd already left a voicemail, but I wanted to hear his voice, to make sure he knew it was time to get his ass to the hospital. He was going to lose his mind when he found out Hope was making the trip on danger-ously icy roads.

We didn't have a choice. None of us were trained midwives, and Griffen had been adamant about Hope giving birth in the hospital. She hadn't argued, more comfortable with a hospital birth herself. None of us had considered that getting to the hospital might be the most dangerous part of Hope having the baby.

I tried Harvey, hoping I'd have better luck. Voicemail. I

left a short message and tried Griffen again, switching back and forth until Hope's fingers closed around mine in a painfully tight grip.

"Another one?" I asked, switching to my clock app. Seven minutes. I tried to push down the nerves rising in my gut. Seven wasn't terrifyingly close, but ten would have been better. At Hope's nod, I restarted the stopwatch app.

We hit a bump as the drive met the county road into town. Hope gasped in pain. I was very glad for the Jeep's tires, but the suspension left a lot to be desired when we had a laboring woman in the back seat. I gritted my teeth, rubbing my hands over Hope's as I murmured nonsensical reassurances.

I tried Griffen again, almost dropping the phone in surprise when his voice hit my ear. "Griffen," I said, "Griffen! We're on the way to the hospital with Hope. She's in labor. How far out are you? Griffen?"

I caught a crackly sound that might have been Griffen saying, "Hope."

The call died. Hope let out a sound of misery that I thought was as much about wanting Griffen as it was about the pain of labor. "He heard me," I consoled her. At a minimum, I was sure he'd been able to read my texts. In certain places in the mountains, texts were far more reliable than calls.

We inched down the road, drawing close to town so slowly that I thought I might scream. I rubbed Hope's hands, trying not to wince when she squeezed. When I glanced at Finn, he was leaning forward, both hands on the wheel, his jaw tight, his eyes glued to the road, his arms bracing when the wind gusted, trying to shove us to the edge of the road.

I didn't look at the drop-off to my right. The road was

carved into the mountain, with no guard rails between us and the slope straight down. I resisted the urge to ask Finn to hurry and reminded myself that despite being away for years, he knew how to drive in this weather. Slow was the key. Slow was safe. Slow would keep us on the road, unlike the handful of drivers that skidded over the edge every winter in weather just like this.

Finn proved me right moments later as we approached the last big curve before town and a gust of wind grabbed at the Jeep, shoving us to the edge of the asphalt, the Jeep not responding to Finn's gentle press of the brakes.

Hope gasped, bending over her belly, a tear streaking down her cheek. I imagined this was not what she'd had in mind for her labor, and it certainly wasn't what I'd pictured for her. At least she hadn't noticed our slide to the edge of the road. Trying to keep my cool, I reset my contraction timer, holding my breath as Finn calmly downshifted and nudged the steering wheel to the left. The tires caught, and I let out the breath I'd been holding.

"Nice job," I murmured.

Without taking his eyes off the road, Finn said, "So far so good. How far apart are they?"

"Last one was six and a half minutes." Not sure he'd know how to interpret that, I said, "We should be okay. First babies are usually slow." Usually, but not always. Nicky hadn't been slow. We stayed home, thinking it would be hours, and I almost had him in the ER lobby. I kept that info to myself.

The road opened up as we neared town. It was less steep, which was wonderful, but as the trees thinned, the wind kicked up. A gust hit, shoving us to the center of the road. Finn wrestled the Jeep back to our side of the road, only for it to happen again moments later.

"It wasn't supposed to be this bad," Hope said through a gasp. "It was only supposed to rain."

"I know," I assured her. Both of us had lived in the mountains of Western North Carolina all our lives. We knew what the weather station said rarely reflected reality. It could be pouring on one side of town and sunny on the other, snowing here and not there. The mountains made for weird and unpredictable weather patterns.

"Look, there's the Inn," Finn said, relief filling his falsely cheerful tone. I saw right through his smile. By now, I knew his face, knew his moods. Knew when he was lying.

I could see the stone and timber building through the sleet, its bulk a shadow against the gray skies. The Inn at Sawyers Bend was the first sign of town from this direction. I let out a breath of relief, then sucked it back in as Hope's hands clamped down on mine. She let out a low moan that was more of a wail.

"It hurts," she gasped. "I didn't know it was going to hurt this much."

"I know, honey. We're almost there. Finn's going to get us to the hospital, and you can get an epidural if you want one."

My phone beeped with another text. Griffen.

> At the hospital in 5. Where are you?

>> Just got to town. Roads are a mess here, but Finn has it under control. Hope is hanging in there.

> Contractions?

>> 6-7 min

. . .

So far, her contractions weren't speeding up faster than six minutes. That was good. I did not want to deliver a baby on the side of the road in a winter storm.

"Griffen is five minutes from the hospital," I said, wincing as Hope squeezed my hand until I thought my bones might break. God, she had a grip. "He'll be waiting when we get there."

I wasn't sure which of us I was comforting. We made our way slowly past the Inn, and it sunk in that we still had to get from town to the hospital. We pulled into town proper, and, as I'd predicted, Sawyers Bend was a fucking mess. At some point, the power had gone out. Main Street was dark, the stoplights out, cars and trucks parked at odd angles. One intersection had a pileup of five vehicles. It didn't look like anyone had been hurt, but most of the road was blocked.

Chapter Thirty-Eight

SAVANNAH

"**F**uck. *Fuck*," Finn said under his breath, slowing to a crawl as he rounded the rear end of a busted-up pickup truck. "Hang on, ladies," he said, the passenger-side wheels of the Jeep popping up on the curb and throwing us to the left as Finn carefully navigated us around the accident.

The tires dropped back down to street level, sending the Jeep into a slide. Hope screeched in pain as a contraction hit, the seatbelt too tight, the Jeep sliding to the center of the road. With another muffled curse, Finn downshifted, turning just enough for the tires to grab the road, and we slowly straightened out.

"I'm sorry," Hope breathed. "I didn't mean to scream."

"It's okay, honey. Scream if you want to," I assured her. "It's just Finn and me here, and we don't mind."

"You're doing great, Hope," Finn said from the front. "We're past the worst part. It's less icy here, and it's not far to the hospital."

"I thought I was going to do this without the drugs,"

Hope said, her voice thin and breathy, "but I think I need the drugs. This really hurts. It hurts so much."

"I know, honey. I know it does. We'll get you there, and they'll get you anything you want to help with the pain."

I hoped that was true. I'd planned to have Nicky without an epidural, then changed my mind too late. I ended up muscling my way through, and in the way of childbirth, I remembered it all as a fuzzy emotional roller coaster. I remembered it hurt, but then they put Nicky in my arms, and all the bad parts faded into the joy of holding him for the first time.

Sitting here with Hope's grip breaking my knuckles, hearing her cries of pain, I suddenly remembered exactly how much it had hurt. I wanted her to get that epidural. Silently, I urged Finn to go faster. I kept my mouth shut, knowing he was going as fast as he could and still get us there safely. I never thought I'd be in a position to thank god for Finn Sawyer, but here we were. I could focus on Hope because I had no doubt that he would get us there safely. No doubt at all.

"Is Griffen there yet?" Hope asked, her voice childlike.

"He should be there any minute now," I said, checking the screen of my phone for a text. Nothing. "He'll be there soon. Finn and I are here. We've got you. Everything is going to be okay."

Although the roads were clearer once we turned onto the state highway, my worry for Hope escalated. Another contraction hit. Five minutes and forty-two seconds. Too fast, considering we were still on the road. I wanted out of this Jeep. I wanted Hope in the hands of medical professionals.

Finn and I could do a hell of a lot together, but we were not delivering this baby on the side of the road. No way. I refused to acknowledge it as a possibility. I focused on comforting Hope, timing contractions, and checking my phone until the red lights spelling EMERGENCY glowed through the blur of sleet and wind.

"We're here. We're here, honey," I said as Finn pulled on the parking brake and vaulted from the Jeep, racing inside and returning with an orderly pushing a wheelchair.

He opened the back door and reached for Hope, saying, "Stay with her until Griffen's here. I'll park the Jeep and come find you."

Finn and the orderly got Hope situated, Finn giving her a tight hug. "You're doing great, Hope. Griffen will be here any second."

I followed Hope and the orderly into the hospital, checking my phone as I went. Nothing from Griffen. I texted him an update.

> We're here.

Nothing. Not even a read notice. And it had been more than five minutes.

At least we were at the hospital.

Hope relaxed a fraction as we went through intake. She and Griffen had been to the hospital a few weeks before for childbirth classes and had done all their paperwork in advance. The nurse took us to a curtained-off triage room and ran through Hope's information while I helped get her into a hospital gown. We eased her onto the bed, the nurse placing her feet in stirrups for a quick exam.

"Why am I down here?" Hope asked. "Shouldn't we go up to Maternity?"

"We just need to see where you are before we bring you up," the nurse said so calmly I wanted to punch her. She was doing her job, and we needed calm. She was making sure this was the real deal and not false labor before she got Hope set up in a room upstairs. I knew all this and still wanted to demand they bring Hope upstairs ASAP and get her that epidural. I'd never before been tempted to demand, "Do you know who she is?" but the urge to do so now was almost overwhelming.

Hope was the last person to make a thing out of being a Sawyer, but if there was ever a time, it was now.

"Her water broke at home," I said for the second time, in case somebody had missed it. Clearly, the woman was having a baby. Why were we wasting time on paperwork?

As if she'd said it a thousand times before, the nurse explained, "I just need to take a look so I can put it in the chart—" Her words cut off once she took a good look at Hope's cervix. "When did you say her water broke?"

I looked at the clock above the bed. "An hour and fifteen minutes ago." It had taken more than an hour to get to the hospital. It had felt like an eternity, but with the weather out there, it could have been much worse.

"She's at seven centimeters," the nurse said. She straightened and grabbed the phone off the wall, barking orders I couldn't translate.

When she turned back to us, she was all smiles. "Well, Mrs. Sawyer, it looks like you're having a baby. They're getting your room ready, so let's get you upstairs."

Hope looked up at me. "Is Griffen here yet?"

I shook my head. If Griffen was in the hospital, he'd be at Hope's side. "I'll let Finn know where we are and ask him to keep calling Griffen."

Following Hope and the nurse, I tapped Finn's name on the screen of my phone.

"Hope okay?" he answered.

"We're headed up to Maternity. Can you try Griffen and let him know where we are?"

"I'm on it." He hung up.

I held Hope's hand all the way to her room, rubbing her back as a contraction took her in the elevator, her eyes wide and panicked, sweat trickling down the sides of her face. "Just hang in there," I said, "and before you know it, you'll get to meet your baby."

My voice choked up on the last word, memories washing over me. The fear, the nerves, the unrelenting pain. And then Nicky, my baby, his blue eyes blinking up at me myopically, his mouth opening in an irritated cry that had sounded like heaven. All that pain and fear had melted into sheer joy.

We popped out of the elevator to a busy hallway. Nurses were everywhere, someone putting a band on Hope's wrist, another nurse pushing Hope into a room and helping her onto the bed. The doctor strode in, checking a tablet. They were all moving quickly, efficiently, and I was at once glad for their expertise and worried by how quickly they were handling things. Was there something wrong?

"Mrs. Sawyer, I saw you at your checkup a few months ago. I'm the on-call obstetrician from your practice tonight."

"Yes, I remember. Hi," Hope said, breathless.

"Why don't we get you up and walking around?" the doctor asked, handing the tablet to a nurse and murmuring something I didn't catch. Hope and I looked at her as if she were insane. "Do you think you can walk?" the doctor pressed. "You're not pushing yet, correct?"

"No, but—" Hope began.

"Then let's get you on your feet for now. Anesthesiology is on the way up, and we'll see what we can do about getting you an epidural."

"Yes, please," Hope said.

"Once that happens, you'll be in bed, so you'll want to walk now while you can."

Hope shot me a look that clearly asked if the doctor was nuts. I knew the OB was right, and walking was a good idea now that we didn't have to worry about having a baby on the side of the road, but I didn't think Hope wanted to hear that.

"I've got you," I said, helping her back to her feet and winding my arm around her waist. A nurse watched us with sharp eyes until she decided Hope could walk with only my support. Once Hope started walking, she was slow but steady, up and down the long hallway outside her room, stopping every five to six minutes to lean against the wall and weather another contraction.

She was mostly quiet, focusing on putting one foot in front of the other and breathing through the pain. At some point, the anesthesiologist joined us, talking to Hope about what she wanted and assuring her that there was time before she needed the epidural. Hope scowled but agreed when the doctor pointed out that the epidural could slow things down.

We walked some more. The OB passed us, slowing to squeeze Hope's shoulder and say, "You're doing great, Hope. I'll check your cervix again soon. Contractions still around six minutes apart?"

We nodded together. In the Jeep, I'd panicked when Hope had dipped below six minutes, but now that we were here, I thought we were both ready for things to speed up. Instead, Hope stayed at a steady six minutes apart. Never under five and never over seven.

"Why isn't Griffen here?" Hope asked, her eyes pained and worried.

"He's on his way," I promised, wishing I had something more concrete to tell her.

We kept walking. I was very glad I wore comfortable shoes every day. I walked a lot on an average day, and even I was ready to sit down. The OB returned and brought us back to the room so she could check Hope's cervix. She'd progressed from seven to eight centimeters. Two to go.

"Another hour or two at least," the OB said, patting Hope's shoulder again before disappearing.

As she turned a corner, we watched the doctor's white coat flash out of sight. "Why does she keep leaving?" Hope whispered.

"It's okay," I assured her. "When things are going well, which they are, it's mostly you and the baby. She'll be back when it's time. Are you okay? Do you want me to ask the nurses to call the anesthesiologist? Are you ready for the epidural?"

I saw her expression shift, saw the desire to end this part of labor, the boredom, and the pain. Her eyes flicked to the end of the hall and the doors to the waiting room and the rest of the hospital—still no Griffen.

"No, I'm okay. Hungry and tired, and these contractions suck, but I'm okay."

"I'll see if I can sneak you some food later. When I had Nicky, I was so hungry by the time they let me eat, one of the nurses brought me a ham sandwich, and I ate it right in the delivery room while they were cleaning up Nicky."

Hope laughed. "Really? How could you eat with all that going on?"

"I have no idea. I just remember being starving. I would not shut up about it. I told the nurse I loved her when she handed me that Styrofoam takeout box from the cafeteria. She was a saint."

We were giggling when the next contraction hit, Hope doubling over and almost losing her balance.

Then Griffen was there, his face sheet white, his eyes wild. "She's okay?" he asked me, his arm supporting Hope's weight as she breathed through the pain. "Why isn't she in bed?" he demanded, sounding more than a little panicked.

"She's fine," I said. "Doing great, and walking is a good idea for now. They'll want to do the epidural in the next hour or so, and then she'll be in bed. Better to keep moving until then." I straightened and stepped back. "Where have you been?" I demanded.

"We got run off the road by the car behind us. It took a while, but one of West's officers gave me a ride here."

"Are you okay?" I asked, immediately sorry for my aggravated tone as I scanned his face for injury.

"Fine. I even remembered to grab Hope's bag," he said, lifting it up. "I would have let you know, but the signal went down again after we slid off the road."

"Ma'am, Mrs. Sawyer can only have one support person in the delivery room," a nurse called down the hall to me. "Flu season restrictions," she added in explanation. I waved to acknowledge that I'd heard her.

"I'm going to go sit with Finn in the waiting room. We'll be here. You take care of Hope. Before you know it, you're going to be a dad," I said, my voice choking up, tears flooding my eyes. I'd known both Griffen and Hope since I was a child, and now they were going to be parents. I brushed the tears away. All the hormones in the air must be getting to me.

I followed the line on the floor that led to the waiting room. Finn was the only one in there, slumped in a plastic chair, his eyes half closed. I sat beside him, leaning into his side, my head on his shoulder. "You saw Griffen?" I asked.

"He looked like he was about to have a stroke," Finn said, a smile in his voice. "How's Hope?"

"Doing great. Starving and bored and cranky. Ready for the baby to show up." I fell silent, hungry but too drained to do anything about it. "Good driving," I said finally.

"I'm glad you were there," he said. "I could handle the road, but I couldn't have managed that and Hope at the same time."

"You could have," I said, confident that Finn Sawyer could handle just about anything life threw at him. "But it was easier together."

In answer, he dropped a kiss on the top of my head. My eyes slid shut for a few minutes, Finn's arm warm around me. "I'm glad I'm here and not still walking up and down the hallway," I said.

"I've never seen Griffen like that. Freaked out and a little crazed," he said.

"I think that's normal for a first baby," I said, feeling another rush of love and joy for Griffen and Hope, memories of Nicky's birth still swirling in my head.

As if he could read my mind, Finn asked, "You ever think of doing it again?"

"Sometimes," I admitted, the answer popping out before I could think better of it. "Oliver and I planned to have another within a few years, but then—" The words choked off. I couldn't say the rest. "Someday, maybe," I added.

"What about you?" I asked, fatigue dragging me down. The adrenaline rush was gone. Hope was in the hands of medical professionals and well on her way to having the baby. All I could do was sit and wait.

"I never really thought about it," Finn said. "Not until I came home. Hanging out with Nicky, August, and

Thatcher is fun. They're all cool kids. I'm not saying I think parenting is an easy ride, but I can see the appeal. I always thought kids were sticky, loud, and messy. Gross."

I laughed. "They're all of that," I said. "Especially when they're little."

"Yeah, but they grow up into people. Thatcher blows my mind a little. He's thirteen, still a kid, but also kind of an adult already. And Nicky, asking to learn to cook. I figured he'd get bored and wander off, but he pays attention. We have fun. It's cool." After a pause, he added, "Speaking of the kids, it didn't come through until you were in with Hope, but Scarlett texted. Tenn made it back to the Manor with the boys."

I nodded, grateful. I trusted Tenn implicitly with Nicky, knowing he'd do anything necessary to keep all three boys safe.

Finn chuckled. "They stopped at the Inn and got a ride in the salt truck. The boys loved it. Nicky is having a sleepover with August. Scarlett and Tenn are serving everyone chili with cornbread from a box." He wrinkled his nose at the thought of the family eating boxed cornbread.

"They'll survive," I said. Finn's arm tightened around me, and I let my eyelids slide shut.

"Take a nap," Finn said. "We're not going anywhere."

Chapter Thirty-Nine

SAVANNAH

I don't think I fell asleep. Not all the way. I drifted, Finn holding me close. He was warm and solid against me. Being with Finn like this felt so natural. Right. And wasn't that a mind fuck? In a million years, I never thought I'd say something like that about Finn Sawyer.

The last few weeks had been unexpected in so many ways.

Finn came to the cottage every night and left every morning before Nicky was up. We made love and slept tangled together like kittens. I'd always liked my space in bed, but I woke most mornings wrapped around Finn as if he were my favorite pillow. While his presence in my life was almost unobtrusive, so low-key that no one knew what was going on except Hawk and probably Griffen, Finn had somehow become essential to my day. The thought of going to sleep without him, of him not being there, of him not being the person who drove me with a laboring woman to the hospital, was intolerable.

We didn't have long, deep conversations. I didn't bare

my soul to him every night. It was ordinary. Except for the sex. Sex with Finn was never ordinary, which was a delight. But the rest—we talked about our days, always easy since we worked together and had plenty to talk about. And movies, music, places we'd been or wanted to go. Plans for the future. I learned Finn wanted to start his own restaurant and was tossing around the idea of doing something with Avery. Maybe some pop-up kitchen nights at the brewery.

I liked the idea of Finn working with Avery, of him settling here instead of skulking around the kitchens, biding his time until the terms of the will were up and he could escape Heartstone Manor again. I liked the idea of Sawyers Bend being his home again, and I wasn't sure what to make of that.

One Sunday morning, when he wasn't on breakfast duty, he snuck out before Nicky woke up and returned with the fixings for pancakes, the first to cook an actual meal in the new kitchen in our cottage. Nicky had gotten out of bed to find Finn manning the griddle, not the least bit bothered by Finn in our personal space. Instead, Nicky had stumbled into the kitchen, eyes bleary, pajama bottoms hanging off his skinny little boy hips, and said, "Is there cocoa, Mr. Finn?" Finn had told him he could have his cocoa for a price and handed him the whisk.

Together they made us blueberry pancakes, Finn gently nudging Nicky back from frying bacon in the cast iron skillet before he got burned, making sure Nicky put on potholders when they slid a tray of pancakes into the oven to keep warm. They looked at home together, Nicky beaming when Finn gave him a simple "Nice flip" as Nicky successfully turned his first pancake.

Thinking back on the memory now, a puzzle piece clicked into place inside me. When I was pregnant with

Nicky, this domestic scene was exactly what I'd envisioned for us. Laughing mornings in the kitchen making pancakes and bacon and snuggling in bed on a winter night, knowing our child was sleeping nearby. Oliver was gone, and in his place was Finn, the one person I'd never imagined taking Oliver's place.

A part of me shouted, *This isn't how it's supposed to be.* The rest of me told that part to shut up. I was happy. Nicky was happy. Far happier than either of us had ever been with Oliver if I were being honest with myself. What more could we want than this?

I didn't know. I didn't know what to do with this new reality. I just knew I liked it.

With that uncomfortable thought, I drifted off to sleep, my cheek pressed to Finn's shoulder.

My eyes popped open to see Griffen standing in front of us, his blond hair mussed as if he'd been tugging at it. "Did she have the baby?" I croaked, my voice thick with sleep.

"Not yet. She's at nine centimeters. The anesthesiologist is putting in the epidural. They kicked me out for a few minutes, told me to get some air."

Finn smirked at his older brother. "I'm not sure there's enough air in the hospital to fix what's wrong with you."

"I know," Griffen said, sinking into the chair opposite us. "I didn't think about it taking so long. It's always fast in the movies, and there's so much screaming." He shook his head. "This waiting is worse. She'd better be good with this one because we're not doing this again."

He surged to his feet and strode back to the doors, holding up his wrist and the security band the nurses had placed on there to unlock the doors.

Finn shook his head. "He's a mess. You want to get some food? I'm starving."

"Enough to eat hospital food?" I teased.

The hospital cafeteria was surprisingly good. I bypassed all the healthy options, going straight for a burger and a piece of chocolate caramel cake. Finn saw my tray and grinned. "Such a sucker for chocolate and caramel," he said under his breath.

I was, and he knew it. Just days before, he sent me a text with a blurred-out image, typing beneath it NSFW. *Not Safe For Work.* I'd been hit by an overwhelming wave of disappointment. A dick pic? Really? I mean, every woman's gotten one, but I hadn't pegged Finn as the type. Why some men thought an unexpected penis was a good way to get a woman's attention was beyond me. Nothing against penises. I'm a fan, but not in my text messages.

Reluctant but unable to stop myself, I clicked the image and burst out laughing. It was not a dick pic. Instead, it had been a picture of a rich chocolate cake, a pool of liquid caramel in the center, dripping down the sides, topped with a melting scoop of homemade vanilla ice cream. My mouth watered. I could almost smell it.

Those three dots came on the screen, and my phone beeped with another message.

Kitchen. Now.

I dropped what I was doing without a second thought. I met Finn in the kitchen, and he dragged me to the bed in my old apartment, dessert in hand. We were covered in smears of chocolate and caramel by the time we collapsed in the sheets, satisfied in every way.

Sitting at the empty end of a long table in the cafeteria, we ate, Finn watching me with hot eyes as I fed him a bite of my chocolate caramel cake. "Not as good as mine," he said, "But wait until you see what I can do with salted caramel and whipped cream."

I grinned, my imagination running wild.

We finished eating and went back to the waiting room, fielding texts from Heartstone. Everyone wanted to know where the baby was. Nicky sent a picture of the fort he'd built with August and Thatcher for their sleepover. Later Scarlett sent another pic of the fort, all three boys tucked into sleeping bags, out cold.

After what felt like a lifetime, Griffen came into the waiting room, bleary-eyed and beaming. "It's a girl. We have a girl!"

We were on our feet, me jumping up and down and throwing myself at Griffen, Finn settling for a hug and pat on the back.

"Good job, man," Finn said, his eyes bright.

"When can we see Hope and the baby?" I asked.

"No visitors. Too many cases of flu or something," Griffen said, "but we'll probably be home tomorrow afternoon. The next morning by the latest. Royal set you up with a room at the Inn so you don't have to deal with the roads. Should be clear between here and town. The sleet stopped hours ago."

That was Griffen for you. Taking care of everyone else even while he was in the midst of the biggest moment of his life. Belatedly, I realized he'd gotten us a single room. Not two rooms. In case I was wondering if Hawk had spilled the beans, now I knew. I had a momentary flash of embarrassment before it occurred to me that Griffen didn't have a problem with Finn and me, or he wouldn't have gotten us the single room in the first place.

The staff at the Inn was waiting for us, handing us a room key as soon as we got to the front desk. We tumbled into bed and passed out, sleeping until after dawn for the first time in ages. Another time we might have lingered in bed and ordered room service, but the roads were clear, the sun was shining, and we both wanted to go home.

Back at Heartstone, I showered at the cottage and dressed in my uniform before going back to the Manor. School had been delayed but not canceled, and the roads were dry and clear except for downed trees here and there. I saw Finn as soon as I got to the kitchens.

"Griffen called," he said immediately. "They won't be home until tomorrow morning. I think the hospital is being extra cautious with the Sawyer princess. Griffen said Hope and the baby are doing great," he added before I could ask. "But Griffen sounded a little punch drunk."

"I bet," I said, smiling at the news. I was tired, but life was good. Lydia hadn't texted, Nicky was happy and safe at school, we had a new baby in the family, and I was with a very handsome man in a delicious-smelling kitchen. I thought about the new baby, and something occurred to me. "Are you busy?"

"Nothing I can't move around. Why?"

"Hope has a few things for the nursery she hasn't set up yet. They were back ordered and just got in—a glider and changing table. And then there's some stuff up in the attic my mom told me about. She wasn't sure if it was Hope's, but she thought we should look through it. I meant to ask Hope about it, but we ran out of time."

"I can help," Finn offered.

"Thanks. I want them to come home and find everything ready for them," I said.

We had the glider, its footrest, and the changing table put together in less than an hour. We discovered we were both directions readers, which made everything go smoothly, me lining up parts and pieces, Finn following the diagrams and holding everything in place for me to screw in. Hope had done the nursery in a cheerful green accented with yellow. Everything matched, and it was adorable down to the last throw pillow.

"Great," I said, standing up and stretching. "I feel so much better. Thank you."

"Anytime, Savannah." Finn's smile was soft, his eyes gentle, sending flutters through my stomach.

I cleared my throat. "I just want to check the things my mom said were in the attic."

Finn followed me to the attic stairs. "Are they where you found the bins with the historical records?"

"No, not there," I racked my brain, trying to remember where she'd said they were. Then it hit me. "In the corner of the room that has those oak bed frames and bookcases with the steamer trunks from the 1890s."

Finn shook his head in a negative. "Your brain is scary sometimes. Lead the way. You know the attics way better than I do."

He followed as I picked my way through the connected rooms of the attic until I spotted the wood and leather-bound steamer trunks stacked near several disassembled oak bed frames. Three cardboard moving boxes, newer than the furniture surrounding them, were stacked beside the steamer trunks.

"I don't know why Hope would have left anything up here," I said, unfolding the top of the first box. "Huh." I poked through a few things. "This is definitely new baby stuff," I said, catching sight of a video monitor beneath a blanket. "Far newer than anything left over from you or any of the younger Sawyers."

I picked up the baby monitor and turned it over in my hands. "This is weird."

"What's weird?" Finn asked.

"Well, there hasn't been a baby in this house since Sterling, right?"

"Not as far as I know," Finn agreed. "Why?"

"This is the same baby monitor I had with Nicky, except maybe a model or two newer. The screen is bigger, and the whole thing is thinner. But Hope didn't buy this. Her monitor is already set up downstairs, and it's newer than this one."

"Maybe she bought two?" Finn suggested.

I shook my head. "No, this system is expandable. It's why I suggested it. She wouldn't need another one."

I pulled out my phone and hit the internet, searching up the model number and clicking the image search. Immediately I saw a picture of the video monitor I held in my hand. I clicked on it and scrolled down to the tech specs at the bottom of a sales page.

"Three years ago," I said. "This model didn't go on sale until three years ago."

Finn stared at the open box and the monitor in my hand. He shifted the neat stacks of blankets and burp cloths, uncovering baby clothes. Girl's clothes. So much pink. Light pink, hot pink, sparkly pink.

"This can't belong to Hope and Griffen," I said. "They didn't know they had a girl until last night."

"So who—" Finn let the question fade as we opened the other two boxes. More baby things. Cloth diapers, bottles, a breast pump, and two diaper bags. All of it brand new. Only the monitor had been opened. Everything else was still packaged, as if someone had purchased it all to prepare for a baby and then packed it up and put it in the attic.

The implications of that hit me like a freight train, and I sank to the floor, sudden tears rolling down my cheeks.

"What?" Finn asked, alarmed. "What's wrong? Savannah?"

"It's just—" I choked on the words. "Nobody buys all this stuff and then boxes it up unless—" The words caught in my throat, and a sob took my voice. I didn't know what expectant mother these things had belonged to, but she wasn't here, and neither was her baby.

Something terrible had happened. It was the only explanation. There was just too much here for any other option.

I still remembered the joy and the fear of pregnancy so clearly. Wanting Nicky so badly and knowing the many ways things could go wrong. People treat childbirth like it's a given, but it's not. These things represented one of my worst fears. I sobbed, unable to stop myself, still raw from the ordeal of getting Hope to the hospital, memories of Nicky's birth, and the rush of joy that Hope and her daughter were safe and healthy.

"I'm sorry," I sobbed as Finn pulled me into his lap, wiping the tears from my face.

"You don't need to apologize," he said. "This is fucking sad. Even if the baby had turned out to be a boy instead of a girl, they still would have needed the rest of this stuff. My father was a dickhead, but this almost makes me feel bad for him."

Finn's words sparked in my brain, chasing away my tears as information took shape in my mind.

"Finn," I said. "The letters Scarlett found when she was looking for that missing statue. The blackmail notes from Vanessa to Prentice. They mentioned a new Mrs. Sawyer and a secret Prentice was keeping. Vanessa wanted half a million to keep her mouth shut."

Finn nodded, realization dawning.

I went on. "In one of the notes, Vanessa said Prentice was running out of time."

I looked up at Finn, my eyes wide with surprising possibility. "What if the new Mrs. Sawyer was pregnant?"

Chapter Forty

"Let me see those letters," Hope said, her hand out, baby Stella curved in her arm, now blessedly asleep. I'd come in from Savannah's this morning to near-constant wailing, which was the new norm. The kid had some lungs on her.

I handed Hope the stack of blackmail letters from Vanessa to Prentice, wondering what she would see that I hadn't. Once we told her about the baby things we found in the attic, she immediately asked to see Vanessa's letters.

It felt like Savannah and I had found the baby things in the attic a lifetime ago. It was a little nuts that we hadn't managed a family meeting in the past two weeks to discuss what we found, but a newborn in the house had turned routine upside down, and we couldn't have the meeting without Griffen and Hope. I knew if we did, Hope, at least, would have killed us.

I eyed baby Stella with affection. She was mostly bald, with wisps of white hair and blue eyes that looked weirdly monochrome to me. Before I could embarrass myself by commenting, Savannah told me that a lot of babies were

377

born with blue eyes like Stella's, and over the months to come, Stella's eyes would likely shift to their true color.

It had been two weeks since Griffen and Hope came home from the hospital, and so far, they looked both utterly exhausted and completely blissed out every time their gaze fell on their little girl. They'd named her after Lady Estelle Ophelia Sawyer, also Aunt Ophelia's namesake.

I liked the historical reference. My great-great-grandfather William Sawyer met Lady Estelle while studying at Oxford. After bringing his beloved bride home to Western North Carolina, he'd planned and built Heartstone Manor, mainly to soothe his wife's homesickness for England. By all accounts, their marriage had been built on a deep and abiding love. Griffen and Hope wanted to extend that legacy of love to their firstborn. Mission accomplished. Everyone at Heartstone Manor was head over heels for baby Stella.

Since we'd all moved back into Heartstone, the office had never been vacant so often. Pre-Stella, either Griffen or Hope was almost always behind the desk that had been our father's. Later they added Royal to the mix, and he split his time between the Inn and helping run Sawyer Enterprises. Most of the time when I passed by the office, it was two or all three of them in there, laptops open, heads together, finding new ways to grow the family legacy.

But for the last two weeks, it was only Royal behind the desk, doing his best to hold things down on his own while his two partners focused on learning how to parent. The new nanny, Paige, as well as Savannah and Miss Martha, had been working together to give the new parents all the privacy they needed, dropping off trays of food and snacks and leaving with baby-related laundry so Griffen and Hope didn't have to think about anything but Stella.

Since little Stella was feeling cooperative this afternoon and Hope was restless, we decided to meet in the office and dig into the mystery of the boxes of baby things from the attic. After a minute of scanning, Hope shoved Vanessa's letters back at me.

"Still nothing," she said with annoyance. "I keep thinking I'm missing something, but Vanessa kept things to the point in her blackmail letters."

I looked to the door of Griffen's office for Savannah. Not there. She'd been on the way to meet us, then texted to say she'd been waylaid by the electricians and Billy Bob over yet another issue in the guest wing. I knew she wouldn't want us to get too far without her.

On the other hand, I wasn't sure there was anywhere to get. As Hope had noted, Vanessa's blackmail letters were short and to the point. She threatened to tell his secret unless he paid her.

I know who the new Mrs. Sawyer will be, and I know why you're marrying her. 500k or I tell him everything.

And later,

Cutting it a little close, aren't you? You don't have long before you're out of time. Get me the rest of the money, or I tell him all your plans. Once he knows the truth, he'll never let her go.

The final note read:

If he finds out what you did to him, what you stole from him, he'll destroy you. Once he knows the truth, there won't be anywhere you can run that he won't find you. 300k more, and I'll keep my mouth shut. Pay me, and you'll never see me again.

No one had any idea who the mysterious future Mrs. Sawyer was. Prentice had renovated the master suite to prepare for her, and planned to renovate the rest of the Manor, then everything just stopped. He fired most of the staff, Miss Martha quit, and Heartstone began to fall into disrepair.

Rereading the letters now, I thought it likely, from the references to being out of time, that Vanessa somehow knew the mystery woman was pregnant.

It was too bad Vanessa was dead. By the end, she claimed to be ready to tell us everything in exchange for a pile of cash. We hadn't thought she knew anything, only finding the blackmail letters after she'd been shot in the gardens at the Inn.

"Miss Martha," Griffen said. "Can you remember when you first saw those boxes upstairs?"

Letting out a sigh, Miss Martha shook her head. "I wish I could, Griffen. It was after all of you moved back into Heartstone because, at first, I thought they were Hope's. I still wasn't sure when I mentioned them to Savannah. I might have paid more attention if I'd looked through the contents. I wish I could be more help."

Griffen shook his head. "Don't worry about it. Who knows how long it would have been before we opened them if not for you." He looked to the door as I had a minute earlier. "Savannah brought the boxes down earlier but promised not to go through them until we were here. We'll give her another few minutes. I don't want to start without her, considering she helped find them."

I knew Savannah would understand, but she'd be disappointed if we found anything interesting while she was delayed.

"I think—" Griffen began when his phone rang. I'd been around long enough to know that was Hawk's ringtone. Every spine in the room went a little stiffer. Hawk usually texted. "Yeah," Griffen said in answer. "Uh-huh." His eyes flicked up to Miss Martha and then to me. "Hold on. I'm going to put you on speakerphone. I'm here with Hope, Miss Martha, and Finn."

Griffen tapped his screen and set his phone on his desk. "Okay, run that by me again."

Hawk's voice came through the speakers. "There's a Lydia Harris at the gate. She's demanding to be let in to see her grandson. Nicky. She says that if we don't let her in, she'll call the police and have charges pressed against Savannah for kidnapping and murder." There was a pause. "I'm not clear on that last part. Do we have a dead body I don't know about?" Hawk asked, his tone so dry I wasn't sure if he was joking.

I thought everyone in the room knew how Oliver had died—via overdose—but not everyone knew about Lydia's recently threatening texts or the fact Savannah had met with Lydia in Asheville.

I thought back to the night Savannah returned from Asheville when she was so shaken up. Lydia showing up here now made me wonder what exactly had happened that day, what Lydia had threatened. I had my suspicions, and none of them were good.

I frowned. Where was Savannah?

I looked at the door again. "I think Savannah needs to make that decision," I said.

Griffen started to agree when Miss Martha interrupted. "Let Lydia in."

"Don't you think that's up to Savannah?" I asked.

This woman had been terrorizing Savannah. She'd made her cry more than once. The idea of letting Lydia Harris into Savannah's home without Savannah's permission felt all kinds of wrong. Yes, technically, legally, Heartstone Manor was Griffen's home, and he could do whatever the hell he wanted. But it was Savannah's home too.

"I don't think—" I started. Miss Martha gave me a look so sharp I shut my mouth.

"Finn," she said, "I understand that you're trying to protect my girl, and I love you for that. You're a good boy. But she needs to face this woman, and this is the safest place to do it."

Before I could interrupt, she turned to Griffen and continued, "I think Savannah's family has a right to know what's going on."

"She said she talked to Harvey," I said, "The day Hope went into labor. He was going to write a letter for her, look into things."

But Miss Martha shook her head. "Not good enough. This woman has come to her home, Finn. We need to deal with this now. I love my daughter. She is fierce, and she is smart, and she is strong. And for some reason, she's been running from Lydia."

Didn't Miss Martha know? It bugged me that Savannah still hadn't told me exactly what Lydia wanted.

Based on how shaken up she'd been after meeting with Lydia and what I knew of Lydia's texts, I could guess that Lydia wanted Nicky. Visitation? Custody? Didn't Miss Martha understand how painful that would be for Savannah?

Savannah loved nothing more than Nicky, and she carried a mountain of guilt at the way Oliver had died. Savannah would face a hurricane head-on, but she carried so much emotional baggage where her mother-in-law was concerned that she couldn't be rational. I got it. I didn't understand how Miss Martha didn't.

Before I could make my case for Savannah, I was overruled. Griffen looked from me to Miss Martha and said, "I'm sorry, Finn—Miss Martha's right. We need to know what's going on." Looking back at the phone, he said, "Hawk, let her in, but escort her to my office yourself."

"Will do, boss." The phone clicked off.

"I'm going to get Savannah," I said and strode out of the room, hoping she was finished with the electrical crisis in the guest wing. I found her coming down the stairs from the second level on her way to the office.

She took one look at my face and asked, "Finn, what's wrong?"

I didn't sugarcoat it. She had to know the facts. "Lydia is here, and she's making threats. Hawk called from the gate. I tried to stop them, but your mother talked Griffen into letting her into the house. She and Hawk are on their way right now."

Savannah's face drained of color, her jaw dropping open. "Why would my mother do that?"

I shook my head, meeting Savannah halfway on the stairs. Pulling her arm through mine, I guided her down the rest of the way to the front hall. "Let's get to Griffen's office before they come in. I don't want you to run into her on your own."

"I'm not on my own," she murmured. "You're here."

I dropped her arm and slid mine around her shoulders, giving her a tight squeeze as we walked. "Damn straight," I said. "But I'd rather you meet her with an army at your back instead of one loyal soldier."

A thin giggle escaped her throat. It wasn't her usual, robust laugh, but I'd take it.

"It's going to be okay," I promised. I had no business promising something so outside of my control, but I did it anyway. Lydia Harris wasn't going to hurt Savannah. Not again. Not if I could stop her. And she wasn't getting anywhere near Nicky. Not until Savannah decided it was time.

Savannah gave a grunt of acknowledgment. I could tell she didn't believe me. I stopped her in the hall, wasting precious seconds outside Griffen's office door.

"Savannah, look at me."

She raised her gray eyes to mine, hers stark with fear.

"It's going to be okay. Do you believe me?"

She swallowed and nodded. I dropped a quick kiss to her lips and pulled her into Griffen's office, saying to the room, "I just want to make it clear before Lydia gets here that this woman is nuts, and she has it out for Savannah. She's been demanding to see Nicky." I looked at Savannah. "She wants custody, doesn't she? That's why she wanted to meet in Asheville that day."

Savannah went stiff beside me, and her jerky nod told me I was right. Dammit. One of these days, she would figure out that she could trust me. She didn't have to handle everything on her own. Especially not this woman who thought she could take Nicky away.

Hope and Griffen's eyes shot wide. "Savannah," Hope said. "Why didn't you tell us?"

Savannah shook her head, some of the color coming back to her face, her voice tight. "I was handling it," she said. "I didn't think she would get this bad." She shot me a glance, but I couldn't read it. "Finn is right. I think she's a little unhinged. I know she has a grudge against me, but—"

"Don't lie to these people," came a strident, high-pitched voice from the doorway. "It's not a grudge. You killed my son, and now you're corrupting my grandson."

We all turned to face the woman in the doorway. So, this was Lydia Harris. Short, plump, and impeccably groomed. Her hair looked like it wouldn't move in the stiffest of breezes, and her eyes were narrowed in hate on Savannah. I wanted to shift, to block her view, to shove Savannah behind me, away from this bitter, angry, poisonous woman. I stayed where I was. Savannah wasn't a child; despite her fear, she could handle this.

"Watch your tone," Griffen said.

"And your volume," Hope added, dropping her chin to indicate baby Stella.

Lydia ignored them both. "We don't need an audience for this, Savannah. I want to see my grandson."

Savannah drew in a deep breath, letting it out slowly before saying, "If you had any sense, Lydia, you'd know that it's a Wednesday, and Nicky is at school."

Lydia looked momentarily stymied. "I—I thought it was Christmas break already."

"No," Savannah said, "not yet. I believe my lawyer sent you a letter saying that you shouldn't communicate with me directly. The courier said that you signed for the letter. Did you read it?"

That was my girl. Taking no shit, even from her mother-in-law. I rested my hand on her lower back in support, wishing I could transfer strength through that touch, wishing that I could shield her from this.

"I got the letter," Lydia said. "But I didn't read it. You think you can make me go away with a lawyer? I want my grandson. You stole my son. Now you're trying to take Nicky, and you have no right. These people don't know who you are. They don't know what you did. You killed Oliver. Nicky isn't safe with you."

Savannah stood there, back straight, chin up, and stared down at Lydia. "I did not kill Oliver," she said, enunciating each word slowly as if Lydia had a hearing problem. "If you want me to get out my file of evidence, I can. I gave it all to my lawyer after you said you were pursuing custody. Every email, every text message. My lawyer has an affidavit from Oliver's rehab saying that I checked him in, and you checked him out early. Twice. I have the text messages from Oliver's phone where you agree to get him more pills."

Savannah had done her homework. I was impressed, but not surprised in the slightest.

"They should have arrested you," Lydia spit out as if she hadn't heard a word Savannah said.

Savannah said in that same, careful tone, "The police never arrested me because I didn't commit a crime. I did not provide him with drugs except those prescribed by his primary doctors. You did. I did not sign him out of rehab. You did. And I was not the one who provided him with the pills he took when he overdosed. Again, that was you." Savannah crossed her arms over her chest. When she spoke again, her voice cracked. "I am so sorry—" She drew in a breath and forced it out, trying again. "I am so sorry that Oliver died. I am so sorry you lost your son." A tear rolled down her cheek. "I loved him, and I did everything I could to stop it. But I will not let you blame me anymore, and I will not let you take Nicky."

"You're a liar," Lydia spat out. "I have proof. And I'll bring it to court. John and I can provide a stable home for Nicky. You're a single mother, a maid in someone else's house. What if you get fired? All those benefits you told me you had—your housing, school tuition—you won't have any of that. You'll be homeless and broke, and my grandson will suffer. I'm going to get custody. And you can visit him once a month."

"This is insane," Hope said, looking at Lydia as if she'd sprouted horns. "You can't come in here and make accusations like this. And if you'd spent any time with Nicky and Savannah, you'd know that Savannah is a wonderful mother. Not being married has nothing to do with it. Nicky gets everything he needs and then some. As far as I'm aware, Nicky barely knows who you are." Hope's eyes flicked to Savannah. "Is that correct?"

Savannah nodded. "She cut us off after the funeral. Nicky hasn't seen her since he was a toddler."

"That's not the point," Lydia said, her voice rising to a sharp whine. "Those years were meaningless anyway. Now that he's old enough, he's his own person. Now it's my turn. I get him now."

"That's not how this works, Lydia," Savannah said. "Nicky is not your do-over baby. Why don't you go harass Tim?" At my questioning look, she said quietly, "Oliver's younger brother."

"I'm not interested in Tim," Lydia said with a flip of her hair. Except her hair didn't flip. It stayed exactly where it was, sprayed into a frosted blond helmet. She narrowed her eyes again, studying Savannah. I didn't like the look on her face.

I especially didn't like it when she said, "Nicky deserves a male role model. He needs a man in his life. You can't offer him that. He needs his grandfather. John is the only one who can give Nicky what he needs."

And that was it. That was the moment when I snapped.

I opened my mouth and said, "Nicky already has a male role model. Me. Savannah and I are engaged."

Chapter Forty-One

FINN

T he entire room froze, all eyes on me. There was a moment out of time. No one said a thing, and my brain had a second to register.

Had I just announced that Savannah and I were engaged?

Yes. Yes, I had.

And did I mean it? A heartbeat later, I knew I had meant it. Absolutely, No questions. I was going to marry Savannah Miles. I knew jack shit about being a dad, but Nicky and I got along great. I loved the kid. He was fun and smart and sometimes utter mayhem, as any good six-year-old should be. And Savannah . . . I'd have to think about it more later, but I was pretty sure I'd been in love with Savannah since I was a teenager. And this past six weeks with her—falling asleep with her, waking up with her, working with her. All I wanted was more.

Yeah, I meant it. I was going to marry Savannah Miles.

I waited for Savannah to jump in and deny the engagement she hadn't known about until two seconds before.

I waited for Griffen or Hawk, Miss Martha or Hope to

ask me what the fuck I was talking about, but none of them said a word.

The only response came from Lydia, whose eyes zeroed in on Savannah's left hand. "She's not even wearing a ring."

"It's being sized," I lied smoothly. Lifting Savannah's left hand, I pressed my lips to her ring finger. "But she'll have it soon enough."

"And who are you?" Lydia demanded. "What makes you think I'll let you—"

I cut her off. "I'm Finn Sawyer. If your lawyer looks into me, he'll find that I have substantial assets, more than enough to take care of Savannah and Nicky, as well as a successful career and no criminal record." Mentally, I crossed my fingers behind my back. We weren't counting those few arrests in France in my early twenties. I'd long ago grown out of public drunkenness.

"If you're worried about Nicky having a father figure," I went on, "You can let that go. He's going to be just fine. He's a great kid. Not that you would know, since you haven't bothered to see him in years."

Lydia sputtered, looking from Savannah to me. To my surprise, Savannah leaned into my side, her arm winding around my waist. Lydia appeared to be entirely without a response. Of all the things she'd been expecting, Savannah being engaged to one of the Sawyers had not been it.

Then her eyes narrowed again. Whatever was coming next would be more of her poison. "I knew it!" she shouted, pointing an accusing finger at Savannah. "I knew you'd slept your way into your job. You said you hadn't, but I just had the wrong Sawyer."

At Lydia's shout, Stella wailed, angry at her abrupt awakening.

"Okay, that's it," Griffen said, coming around the side of

his desk. "I was trying to stay out of it, but this is my house, and everyone here is my family, Savannah included."

Stopping in front of Lydia, Griffen glared down at her. "You need to have another conversation with your lawyer because you're wasting your time and money with this custody case. No judge will take that child from his mother, with or without a husband in the picture. And, just so it's clear, we couldn't be happier that Savannah will soon become a Sawyer. Hawk will escort you off the property. As you've seen, we have extensive security. If we hear from you again, except through your attorney, I'll get a restraining order. Do you understand?"

Lydia glared back at Griffen, then turned and marched from the office, Hawk trailing behind.

Hawk stopped at the door to say, "I'll get rid of her."

We all watched them go. Savannah kept her eyes on the empty doorway long after Lydia had disappeared. Seconds ticked by, and I waited for Savannah to explode.

It didn't take long.

Ignoring her mother, Hope, and Griffen, Savannah turned to me. "Finn? A word in the kitchen?" She sailed out the door, head high, leaving me to follow.

I thought I heard Miss Martha choke back a laugh, but when I looked up, she was coughing into her fist. Hope had her head bowed over Stella's head, but I saw the curve of her cheek. She was smiling too.

Was no one going to say anything?

They weren't. They were going to let Savannah do all the talking.

In the seconds after I made my insane declaration, I realized that I expected everyone to object, not just Savannah. Looking around the room before I followed Savannah out, I caught Griffen's amused expression. He winked, and I understood that he hadn't just been putting on a show for Lydia.

They were all on my side.

Huh. I'd figure out what to make of that later.

First, I had a woman to talk into marriage.

Savannah was ahead of me, stalking down the hall, then jogging down the stairs to the lower level. She didn't stop until we were in the kitchens, thankfully alone.

Once there, she whirled on me, her eyes hot. "What the hell were you thinking? Why would you tell her that? We're not engaged. We're not even—"

"Don't say we're not even in a relationship," I said.

"Finn!" Savannah protested, throwing her arms in the air. "Why would you say we're engaged?"

"Because I want to marry you."

"You can't!"

"Why not?"

"Because— Because— Because we're not getting married!"

"Why not?" I shot back.

"Because— So many reasons."

I stood there, my thumbs hooked in the pockets of my jeans, leaning against the counter beside the range, and watched her pace on the other side of the island. Back and forth she walked, her eyes sparking gray fire, tendrils of her sunset curls working their way loose from her tight braid, her breasts bouncing wonderfully with her stiff, angry stride. I let her yell for a minute, absorbing it all in silence.

"You've always been so impetuous," she said. "You have to plan. You can't just say we're getting married. You haven't even asked me! I can't do this! I don't want to be played with. I don't want to be the butt of one of your jokes. And

Nicky! What if he hears what you said? He loves you. He'll get excited, and then his heart will be broken."

"Not if we get married," I pointed out, which just caused another enraged growl and more pacing. I paused because one part of what she said was right. "Savannah, I should have talked to you about what I wanted before I announced it to the world."

She stopped pacing and stared at me. I didn't add that I hadn't figured out exactly what I wanted until that moment in Griffen's office. Telling her that now would only make this more difficult. And it didn't matter. Once I knew, I knew. Nothing in my life had ever mattered as much as convincing Savannah Miles to marry me.

Despite what she thought, I wasn't playing with her, and I'd never play with Nicky's feelings like that. Crossing my arms over my chest. I locked eyes with her. "I love you, Savannah. I think I loved you when I was a kid, even though I would have made you miserable back then. I didn't know what to do with it when we were teenagers, so I was a complete asshole. I said those shitty things about you in the cafeteria that day because the idea of that pimply idiot taking you to prom, getting his hands on you made me want to throw up, and I didn't understand why, so I was a complete and utter ass. And I'm sorry."

I dropped my hands to my sides, soaking in the shock in her eyes and, beneath that, the faint light of hope. "I love you. You're the best woman I know. I love your brain and your body and the way you make me laugh. I've never been as happy as I have been since we've been together. I love sleeping with you every night and waking up with you in the morning. And I love Nicky. I even love him when he's crazy and bouncing off the walls. I love cooking with him. That Sunday I made pancakes, I loved seeing him first thing in the morning. I want that to be our lives. I think I make you happy. And I think you love me too."

Savannah stood there, hands at her sides, mouth half open, eyes wide. "I don't—I don't even know what you're talking about. You love me?"

"Where the hell have you been?" I asked, getting a little exasperated. How could she not feel what we had? What we'd built? How perfectly we fit together? "What did you think was going on here? We've been together every night for six weeks."

"That's just sex," she said, but I could tell she had a crack in her armor. She knew it wasn't just sex. She had to.

How could she not get it? We slept together every night. All night. Some nights we didn't even have sex. It occurred to me suddenly that Savannah might not have had a lot of men in her life, aside from Oliver and now me.

"Savannah," I said quietly. "I can count the women I've spent the entire night with on my hands without using all my fingers. If you want the number of women I've spent more than ten nights with, I can do that on one hand. And there's no woman I've slept with all night, every night, for weeks. No one but you. Because you're the only woman I've ever wanted to be with like this. It's more than sex, and you know it is."

I crossed my arms over my chest again, fighting the urge to vault over the island and drag Savannah off so I could show her exactly how much I loved her. But sometimes words are more important than actions.

"You're the only woman I've ever needed," I said. "When you're not around, I want to know where you are. I want to be near you. To hear your voice. To touch you. Hold you. Play with your hair. I don't care. I just want you."

"You never—" She stared at me, her brows pulling together in confusion. "I didn't think—"

"I know," I said, understanding all at once what an ass I'd been. She was right. I'd never said anything. And I should have. "I'm not good at this shit. I didn't say anything because everything was great, and I figured you knew how I felt."

She scowled, and I raised a hand. "Which I now see was stupid because how would you know if I didn't tell you? But now that we're talking about this, I'm telling you now. I love you. I love Nicky. I want to marry you and spend the rest of my life making you happy. Making Nicky happy. Can you look me in the eye and tell me you don't want that?"

She opened her mouth and snapped it shut, then opened it again. "I—I don't—I haven't—"

It was becoming clear that Savannah was not going to be able to put together a coherent response to my proposal. I could let her off the hook for now. Straightening, I pushed off from my stance against the counter and crossed the room. "Hawk has Lydia under control, and you need some time to think."

"I—" she stuttered again.

"I'm going to give you a little space to let this settle in." I rounded the island and came to a stop in front of her. "But before I go, I just want to tell you—" I dropped my mouth to hers, taking her lower lip between my teeth with a gentle nip before I kissed her. "I love you. And of all the dreams I have for the future, spending it with you and Nicky is the biggest and the best. The one I care about the most."

Savannah's eyes fluttered shut as I kissed her again, meaning for it to be soft and seductive, thinking she'd stay frozen, trapped in her roiling thoughts. Instead, her arms wound around my neck, her mouth on mine demanding and possessive. Whatever she couldn't straighten out in her brain, her body—and I thought her heart—knew exactly what she wanted.

I kissed her back, just as fierce, just as demanding and possessive as she was. I drew back before I got too carried away, before picking her up, setting her on the kitchen island, and fucking her there like I almost had all those years ago.

Instead, I slid a final chaste kiss across the highest point of her cheekbone, then her forehead, and I stepped back. "I'm going to go talk to Griffen. I'll see you later."

I left her there, staring after me, her eyes wide and dazed. I jogged back up the stairs, heading to Griffen's office, not surprised to see him, Hope, and Miss Martha waiting for me. They all started talking at once.

"Where's Savannah?"

"What happened?"

"Did you mean it?"

I looked at all three of them. "Savannah needs a little time to process," I said.

Hope snorted with a barely suppressed laugh. "I bet she does. She didn't know you were going to announce you're engaged?"

"No," I admitted.

"Did *you* know you were going to announce you're engaged?" Hope asked, a teasing glint in her eye.

I didn't answer. Hope was a great sister-in-law, but that was none of her business. What mattered was what I said next. "I love her," I said, knowing I needed everyone in this room on my side if I had a hope in hell of convincing Savannah to marry me. "I love Nicky. And if I can talk Savannah into it, we're going to get married. I think I can make both of them happy. I know they make me happy."

I shifted my weight from one foot to the other, shoving my hands in my back pockets. "If anyone has any problems with it, let me know now because we're not doing that thing during the ceremony where somebody stands up and objects."

Miss Martha piped up, "No objections here. She'll come around." She stood to leave, giving me a quick hug on her way to the door. "She loves you too. I know she does. Even if she doesn't know it yet."

Griffen stood, looking down at Hope and Stella. "I think we're going to have to go through those baby things another time."

"That's fine," Hope said, nuzzling the top of Stella's fuzzy head with her lips. "Stella and I are going to go take a nap."

Griffen looked at me. "Finn, I have something for you. Follow me." To Hope, he said, "We'll be on my side of the closet."

A gentle smile, brimming with love, spread across Hope's mouth as she clearly understood Griffen's cryptic statement. I didn't, but I figured I would soon enough.

Chapter Forty-Two

FINN

I followed Griffen up the stairs, through the expansive master suite he shared with Hope, and into his side of the walk-in closet. At the very back, behind a row of suits I'd never seen Griffen wear, he revealed a built-in safe as tall as he was and at least three feet wide. Expertly turning the dial one way, then the other, he swung the heavy door open and began pulling out velvet-lined drawers.

Looking over his shoulder, I saw the drawers were trays of jewelry. I hadn't known anything like this was in the house. "What is all this?" I asked.

"The Sawyer family treasures," Griffen said with a hint of sardonic amusement, another sign he wasn't all about being *the* Sawyer. He was so different from our father; sometimes it still took me by surprise. "I went through all this with Harvey after the dust settled from the will reading and all of us moving in."

He pulled out another tray, scanning the contents, clearly looking for something specific. He opened and closed small boxes until he made a sound of satisfaction and pulled one out. Turning to me, he flipped up the lid, and I blinked.

Sparkly. That was my first thought. I took a closer look and realized it was a ring. An engagement ring. I'm not much into jewelry, but I was guessing the diamond in the center was bigger than a carat but not bigger than two, a solitaire surrounded by a halo of intricate pavé diamond flowers.

Griffen turned the box slightly, and I could see that tiny pavé diamond leaves ran down the sides of the band. It was an old ring. Delicate, yet substantial. And a lot of sparkle without being gaudy.

It would look great on Savannah's finger.

"Where did it come from?" I asked. Griffen set the box in my hands.

"It was your mother's," Griffen said. "Before Darcy, Harvey thinks it belonged to another Sawyer bride. We're not sure who. There's probably a record somewhere in this house, but we haven't found it. It's a Sawyer ring. It was your mother's ring, and as her firstborn, now it's yours."

"Griffen, I—" My voice locked in my throat, and I was appalled to feel wet heat hit my eyes. Was I going to cry in front of Griffen? I stared at the ceiling and blinked.

Griffen cleared his throat, his eyes also on the ceiling. "You don't have to use it if you don't want to, but I wanted to tell you—" Griffen swallowed. "I never understood it because Dad was such an ass, but Darcy loved him. She wore that ring with love. And she—"

He swallowed again, blinking hard. I raised the back of my hand to dash tears from my eyes. Fuck. But I couldn't stop them.

"She loved wearing that ring," Griffen continued. "She loved Dad, and she loved the hell out of you. And Parker,

Quinn, and Brax. If you want it, and you think Savannah would like it, I think Darcy would have wanted her to wear that ring."

I stared at the ring, trying as hard as I could to remember seeing it on my mother's finger. I was ten when she died, old enough to have vivid memories of her, but none included her jewelry. Her smell, the bright joy of her laugh. Her smile when she saw me. Her patience. The strength of her arms when I wanted a hug. I could still remember the way she'd kissed my cheek and nuzzled the top of my head as Hope did with baby Stella. I remembered so many things about my mother, but I didn't remember the ring.

That was okay.

"I think Savannah will love it," I said, taking in the sparkle, the history, the grace, and the strength of the ring. "It suits her."

"It does," Griffen said, clearing his throat again. "And it's your ring now. Yours and Savannah's."

"I just have to convince her to put it on," I said with a smile, closing the box and shoving it in my pocket.

"She's not on board with the engagement plan, I take it."

"I'm working on it," I said.

"You love her?" Griffen asked.

I didn't mind saying it again, even though I'd told him downstairs. "I love her. And I love Nicky."

Griffen nodded. "I can't say I'm surprised. You're not that subtle. She is, but I know her pretty well." He closed and locked the safe, turning to leave the closet. He set a hand on my shoulder and squeezed. "She'll come around. You picked a good woman. And you'll make a good husband and a great dad."

I followed Griffen from the closet, temporarily struck mute by his confidence that I was doing the right thing. I'd expected Savannah's pushback. I hadn't expected everyone else's happy acceptance, and I couldn't deny it felt fucking good.

Just like we'd given Savannah an army to face Lydia, I liked knowing I had my own army at my back. Except my army wasn't in opposition to Savannah. We were just going to help her figure out what she really wanted.

Me.

I hoped it was me.

Savannah was nowhere to be seen when I went back to the kitchens. I didn't search her out, turning my attention to dinner. I still had a household to feed in a few hours. And a plan to make for later.

I was giving Savannah space to think, but I wouldn't let her run.

Savannah showed up to dinner at the last possible second, sliding into her seat, her eyes on Nicky, avoiding mine. That was fine. I could be patient, and she had a lot to digest. I'd had time to think too. When I replayed our conversation in the kitchen, I realized Savannah never said she didn't want to marry me. She'd questioned how committed I was. Wondered if I was messing with her. But she'd never said she didn't want to marry me. I was taking that as a good sign.

Normally Savannah and Nicky lingered over their dinner. Not that night. Savannah finished before everyone else, popping up from the table and pulling Nicky from his dessert.

"Mom, I'm not done," he said, a look of panic in his eyes. Like any other kid his age, Nicky liked his dessert.

Savannah's eyes popped from Nicky to me, then to the half-finished dessert.

"One sec," I said, picking the dish up myself. "Hold on, Nicky. Your mom has some things to do. Let me get a storage container, and you can take it back to the cottage with you."

I slid the brownie and melting scoop of ice cream into a small container and handed it to Savannah. "I'll see you later," I said.

Her eyes flared wide in alarm, but she didn't tell me not to come. She just pulled Nicky out of the kitchen and escaped. I watched her flight with a grin, then looked back at Miss Martha.

She shook her head, smiling at me. "You have a plan?" she asked.

"Kind of," I admitted. "I told her I love her, I love Nicky, and that I know she loves me. She just needs time to get used to the idea. And I have this."

I pulled the ring from the front pocket of my jeans and handed it to Miss Martha, who opened the lid and bit her lip, her eyes welling with tears. "Your mother's ring." She sighed. "Griffen gave you this?"

I nodded. "You remember it?" I asked, wishing I could picture it on my mother's hand.

"Oh, I do. I do. Lord knows why, but she loved your father. And she loved you kids. She'd be so happy." Miss Martha fanned herself, then pinched the bridge of her nose, trying to blink back the tears. "She'd be so happy, Finn. And I'm so happy. I always liked you best, you know."

I gave her a cocky grin, my only defense against more tears. "I know," I said. "That's why you'll be the best mother-in-law ever."

"Well, that's true." She handed me back the ring with a

watery smile. "I'm going to go home and let you talk my stubborn daughter into marrying you."

The hours between dinner and when I usually headed over to Savannah's cottage passed in excruciating slowness, the ring burning a hole in my pocket. When it was finally long enough after Nicky's bedtime that I didn't have to worry about waking him, I let myself out the side door of the Manor for the short walk to Savannah.

In the time that had passed since dinner, I'd come up with a plan, and it didn't involve talking. Savannah was going to try to argue with me. She would use logic and what she saw as good sense to convince me we weren't getting married. Savannah's good sense was one of the things I loved most about her. And she wasn't wrong. I'd done this ass-backward. I was rushing her, and she needed time to catch up.

I didn't know what she was scared of, but I could guess. She didn't fully trust me yet. If she trusted me, she would have told me about Lydia going for custody. And she'd lost her first husband, her first love, in a horrible way, and she still hadn't fully recovered. She had Nicky to think of. I'm sure there was a long list of other reasons she was running from the idea of marrying me. I'd counter them one by one if I had to.

For now, I was going to take this slowly. If I pushed too hard, she'd say no, and that wasn't going to happen. She loved me. I knew she did. There was no way I could feel this much for her, and she didn't feel it back. We'd never be as happy apart as we could be together.

Savannah was an intelligent woman. She'd figure it out —with some nudging from me. Starting with my three-part plan.

I let myself into the cottage, locked the door behind me,

and crept upstairs. Nicky slept like a rock, but I wasn't risking waking him up. Not tonight.

I found Savannah tucked into bed, her hair in a loose bun, her face scrubbed clean. The second I cleared the doorway, she said, "I'm not marrying you."

I shrugged. "Disagree."

"Finn, you can't just announce we're getting married and think I'm going to fall in line."

"You falling in line is the last thing I expect. But we don't need to talk about it tonight," I said.

Her jaw dropped, then snapped shut. "I want to talk about it," she said mulishly, lifting her jaw and glaring at me. "You can't just—"

"Look," I interrupted. "I don't have a shotgun. There's no preacher downstairs waiting. I can't make you marry me, right?"

"No," she agreed carefully, sounding skeptical.

"So don't worry about it," I said easily. "Just relax."

"Because we're not getting married?" she asked slowly, suspicion heavy in her voice.

"No," I answered equally slowly, as if it should be obvious. "We're definitely getting married. Someday. But we don't have to talk about it right now, do we? I can't make you do anything you don't want to do. So if you don't want to talk right now . . ." I shrugged again.

"I don't believe you're giving up that easily," she said, eyes narrowing. "Unless you didn't mean it."

"I absolutely meant it. I don't think I've ever meant anything more," I said, pulling my t-shirt over my head. Her eyes flicked to my bare chest, and I felt a thrill of satisfaction.

Plan engaged.

Before I shoved off my jeans, I pulled the black velvet box out of my pocket.

"I'm not giving up," I said. "I love you. You love me. We're going to get married."

"I just told you I'm not marrying you."

"I know what you told me," I said, sliding under the covers. "And I'm saying we don't have to fight about it. I want to marry you. I love you. I'll make a damn good husband, and you'll be an amazing wife. You're a great mom. I think I have it in me to be a good dad. I never did before, but after spending time with the kids, I know I have it in me. And I love Nicky. I want to be his dad. I'm open to more kids if you want, but I'd also be happy if it's just you, me, and Nicky."

Savannah stared back at me with wide eyes, struggling to take in everything I'd said, clutching the covers close to her chest as if in defense.

I kept talking. "None of this is happening until you decide it is. So, you don't have to worry about it right now. I'm going to marry you, but I'm not going to bully you into it."

"I don't understand you," Savannah said, narrowing her eyes at me. Then her gaze caught on the box in my hand, and they narrowed further. I opened the box.

"Where did you get that?" she asked in a hushed tone.

"From Griffen. It was my mother's. I want it to be yours."

Savannah didn't say a word, her eyes fixed on the ring, then flicking to my face and back to the ring. Finally, she breathed, "Finn." She drew in a quick breath. "Finn. It's so beautiful."

I took her left hand in mine and slid the ring on. It was a

little big, but just a little. It wasn't going to fall off. I held her hand out, turning it so the ring caught the light.

"I knew it would look perfect on you," I said, not hiding my satisfaction.

Savannah studied her hand, turning it in the light, mesmerized by the fire in the diamonds.

"If you decide it isn't your taste," I said, "We can find something else."

"No, Finn, it's beautiful." Her eyes were still caught on the ring.

"You like it?" I asked.

"It doesn't mean I'm marrying you—"

I cut off her words with my mouth.

Stage two of the plan was successful. Time for stage three.

No more talking. Not for stage three.

I loved all the ways Savannah and I came together. Sometimes we fucked. Sometimes we were laughing as much as we were moaning, and sometimes we made love, slow and sweet, dragging it out until both of us were on the edge of begging. Looking back, I realized it was at those times that I knew—this was love. It was so much more than lust or just sex. It wasn't scratching an itch or filling a need. I'd only ever had this with Savannah. I never wanted it with another woman.

I kissed her, a slow, sweet, claiming kiss, her mouth soft and open under mine, her tongue stroking mine. She was wearing my ring, holding me in her arms, kissing me back.

Everything I'd ever wanted was right here, under this roof, and now that I was here, Savannah in my arms, I couldn't believe it had taken me so long to figure it out.

I kissed my way down her body, tasting and touching,

until she shook under my mouth, her clit on my tongue, her cries muffled by her arm so she wouldn't wake Nicky sleeping below. When she got her breath back, she rolled, tackling me with unexpected energy. I expected her to straddle my hips, but she scooted down, running her tongue up my rigid length. Tasting. Savoring. And when her left hand curled around my erection, that ring sparkling in the dim light, it shot straight through my heart. God damn this woman. I never imagined what it would feel like to see my ring on her, but now that I knew, there was no way I was letting her go.

I stopped her before I came, needing to finish inside her. Needing to mark her, claim her as mine in every way I could. I hooked my hands under her arms and hauled her up the bed, rolling to pin her beneath me, finding her slick and ready. I savored her gasp when I filled her, slowly feeling every inch of her body's tight grasp.

Dropping my head, my lips at her ear. I whispered, "I love you. I love you, Savannah."

She was silent, but for the low moan in her throat, her fingers curled over my shoulders, her nails biting in as she rocked up to take me deeper, giving with her body what she couldn't with words. I cupped the curve of her ass, tilting her so I could slide just a little deeper. Just deep enough to grind and rock and wring the orgasm from her body, the tight, pulsing grip of her pleasure taking me with her.

When she could move, she rolled from the bed and disappeared into the bathroom. I heard the water run. She emerged a minute later, tossing a damp washcloth at me. Without a word, I used it to clean myself up, seeing that she'd done the same in the bathroom. She took my washcloth, dropped it behind her on the bathroom floor, and slid under the covers beside me into her usual position.

Her head rested on my shoulder, her arm across my

chest. This time my ring sparkled on the hand casually resting on my chest, the sight of it filling my heart.

"I'm still not marrying you," she said into my shoulder.

"Disagree," I said back, not trying to hide my amusement.

She made a harrumphing sound in her throat, that Savannah sound of irritation I loved so much. I let it go.

We both knew the truth. She may not have said it out loud, but she loved me. And eventually, she was going to marry me.

Chapter Forty-Three

SAVANNAH

The next morning, I jogged down the stairs to the first floor, mentally reviewing my to-do list for the rest of the day. Kitty, April, and I had successfully transformed one of the guest rooms into a usable state, complete with electricity and working plumbing in the ensuite bathroom. It was a small thing, but considering how long we'd been struggling with the guest wing, especially the electricity, I considered it a win. We had Scarlett's family coming for her Christmas Eve wedding to Tenn, only just over a week away. Until this morning, I wasn't sure we'd manage rooms for them. One down, one to go.

Now, I had to find Parker for a meeting on the changes to the space that had been my apartment behind the kitchens. We needed to loop Finn into the conversation. As the cook, he'd likely use the new staff room more than anyone else. He should have input on how we set it up. I glanced down at my left hand and the ring sparkling on my finger. Darcy's ring. My ring.

I couldn't get my head around that. Finn had put an engagement ring on my finger. He wanted to marry me.

The thought still made my head spin. Was I ever going to get used to it? Maybe in a million years. At first, I'd been sure he was kidding. He couldn't have meant it. He was trying to help with Lydia. He didn't want to marry anyone. Especially not me. We'd hated each other for years.

But I didn't hate Finn. I hadn't hated him since I was a teenager. Since this thing between us started, the last thing I felt for him was hate. I admired him. I liked him. I wanted to get naked with him as often as possible.

Did I love him? Finn Sawyer?

I shook my head at the idea. I wasn't ready to think about it. A part of me resented Finn for forcing me to face reality. I'd been cruising along, enjoying the sex, enjoying lying in his arms at night, talking until we fell asleep. Enjoying the simplicity of it all. And then Finn had to slam on the brakes and demand I admit what we had was more than just sex and fun.

It was a relationship. It was real. He wanted me to see him, to treat him as if he mattered.

As the thought took shape in my head, I felt a wave of shame at my selfishness. Too many people had treated Finn as if he didn't matter. As if he were no more than a means to an end. Was I going to be just one more person who didn't truly see him? My heart squeezed at the thought, the ring sparkling on my hand a symbol of all that Finn was.

I could try to lie to myself, to run from what scared me, but Finn deserved better. I deserved better. I wanted to tell myself that the engagement, this ring, was a game, but they weren't. Finn loved me. He wanted to marry me. He wanted to make a family with me. All of that was true and real.

So what did I want?

The answer was immediate. Finn.

I wanted Finn. I wanted him for me because he made me happy like no one else ever had.

I wanted him for Nicky because he was already ten times the father Oliver had been. He loved us. He'd be a good husband. A wonderful father. I knew all of that in my heart.

Still, I couldn't bring myself to tell him yes.

We didn't need this bright future he was dangling in front of me. Nicky and I were doing just fine. We'd lost Oliver long before he'd overdosed, and we'd survived.

But wasn't life about more than survival?

It was. I knew it was. But I remembered the agony of losing Oliver, of watching him leave us a little more every day. In such a short time, Finn had become everything to me. He was light and love, and he filled all my dark places. If he changed his mind, fell out of love, if something happened to him . . . I couldn't. I couldn't go through that again.

Better to survive alone than reach for more and suffer that pain again. Because it wouldn't be *that* pain, it would be so much worse because this was Finn.

Twisting the ring on my finger, I wished I could just table the whole thing until I figured myself out. I couldn't bring myself to say yes, and I couldn't seem to say no. He loved me. I hadn't been able to give him those words, but I hadn't denied them either. I could have told him he was wrong, that this really was just sex, that I didn't love him and never would. I could say all that, but it would be a lie.

And what about his inheritance? Once the clock ran out and he had his money, how long would he be content to stay in Sawyers Bend? I loved living here, loved my work, loved being so close to my mom. Did that mean I wouldn't leave if that's what Finn wanted? I didn't know.

I wanted to reach for that bright, beautiful future he was offering me. I did. But every time I pictured going down to the kitchens and talking to him, I couldn't bring myself to do it. I was chicken. It was humbling to admit it to myself. I was a big, giant chicken. Not willing to say no, too scared to say yes.

What I needed was a distraction. I thought about those boxes of baby things still in Griffen's office. I'd been hoping to dig through them today, but Paige, who'd been a lifesaver with the kids, had told me Stella had been up all night nursing and crying, sleeping in short bursts before wanting to nurse again. Hope and Griffen were exhausted, in no shape to think about anything but Stella and whatever precious sleep they could snatch between feedings. I remembered how that went. And Hope would murder me if I went through the bins without her.

I'd have to find another distraction. My mind flashed to Ford. What if something in those boxes could point us to the real killer? That's what we were all hoping. Shouldn't we go through everything now? We'd already waited two weeks. Really, it had been months since my mother had first seen the boxes.

What were the odds that the answer would be in there? Not good, I had to admit to myself. Those boxes might have been new information to us, but based on the model year of that monitor, they predated both Prentice's murder and Ford's arrest by a few years—old news. We'd get to them soon enough.

Then again, maybe Hope wouldn't mind if I just opened one . . .

My phone rang. Scarlett. She was at Laurel Country Day, picking up the boys from their last school day before

Christmas break. Seeing the time on the screen, I realized she should have been on her way back by now.

"Scarlett, what's up?" I asked.

"Savannah?" She sounded breathless. Scared.

My heart stopped.

"What is it?"

"Nicky's missing, Savannah. I came to pick him up—" She stopped, a muffled voice in the background. Then she finished, "I got here to pick them up, and August and Thatcher were waiting, but no one could find Nicky. His teacher doesn't remember signing him out for pickup. I don't know more than that. They're all looking for him, but I didn't want to wait to call you."

It was like sinking into a nightmare. I was paralyzed, and my brain couldn't keep up with the worst-case scenarios spinning to life in my imagination. My questions tumbled out. "No one knows what happened? He's just not there? How can they not know where he is? What about the sign-out procedures?"

I could hear my voice rising in panic and knew I had to calm down, but I couldn't seem to do it. I'd picked up the boys before. The teachers in charge of pickup always checked the list. Whoever was picking up students had to have an assigned name tag in their car. You couldn't just drive on campus and leave with a student.

"Everything is crazy here," Scarlett said, not sounding much calmer than I was. "The kids' Christmas parties ran late and cut into pickup time, and then they started to rush because the line was backed up and people were honking their horns. They're trying to find who signed him out, but—"

She cut off, and it sounded like she was talking to someone else. Then, louder, she said, "Savannah, I think you should come. I'll call if we find him, but I think you should come."

My heart froze. Scarlett was not a woman given to hysterics. She wouldn't have called if she thought Nicky was just distracted on the playground or messing around with friends.

"I'm on my way," I said, my heart racing, my brain swamped with panic so intense I couldn't think. Oh god, my baby. "I'm on my way," I said again, picking up my pace as I ran down the stairs. "I'll call Hawk, West—"

"You get in the car," Scarlett said. "I'll call Hawk and West. I think the school is outside West's jurisdiction, but he'll call the county sheriff and get his officers moving. You focus on getting here. If anything changes, I'll call you."

I hung up, shoving my phone into my pocket. My mind raced, but all I could think was Nicky, Nicky, Nicky. And then, Lydia. Could she have taken Nicky? She wasn't on the list for pickup. Of course, she wasn't. They weren't supposed to release the kids to anyone who wasn't on the list. But it was the last day before Christmas break, and I knew that sometimes holiday dismissals got a little crazy.

My feet were thudding down the stairs to the first level before I realized where I was going. Finn. Instinct brought me here, and I rounded the corner, skidding to a stop inside the kitchen doorway, something inside me relaxing just a fraction as Finn looked up, took in my face, and straightened.

"What? What's wrong? What happened?"

"Nicky," I said, my words running together. "Nicky is missing. Scarlett called. She picked up August and Thatcher, but no one can find Nicky, and they don't know —" I stopped, breathless. The more I said it, the more terrified I was. Nicky. Where was my baby?

Finn came around the island, his arm sliding around my shoulders, turning me back to the door. "All right, let's go. I'll drive. Have you called Hawk?"

"Scarlett is calling him and West. I came straight to you."

Finn squeezed me tight, dropping a quick kiss on my temple. "You did the right thing. I'll drive. We're going to find him. Everything's going to be okay," he promised.

More than anything, I wanted to believe him. Because it was Finn, I almost did. My phone rang in my hand. Hawk.

"Hawk, did you talk to Scarlett?" I asked, following Finn into the garage and jumping in the passenger seat of his Jeep.

"You're on the way to the school?"

"Just got in the car. Finn is driving."

"Good. Good. I'm on it. I'm calling West. You and Finn go. I'll meet you there."

"Okay." I didn't know what else to say. I wanted to scream, to beg Hawk to find Nicky. Pointless. I knew Hawk. He and West would do everything possible to locate my son. I didn't need to beg or scream. I needed to do something, but there was nothing I could do. I didn't know where my baby was, and there was nothing I could do.

As soon as Finn had the car pointed down the drive, he took my hand, squeezing it tight. "We're going to find him. He's okay." I heard the fear in his words, the slight tremble in his voice.

I squeezed his hand back. "We're going to find him," I repeated.

Any other outcome was unacceptable.

Finn drove with tight control, as fast as he could in the top-heavy Jeep. A half mile before we got to the Inn at Sawyers Bend, Finn swung to the right and took a shortcut loop around town. We hadn't chanced the narrow, steep road in the ice storm, but it shaved a good five minutes off the trip, letting us bypass the traffic in town.

"Do you know where Lydia was staying? In Asheville or Sawyers Bend?" Finn asked.

"You think it's her?" I asked.

Finn's eyebrows drew together, and he shot me a quick look. "Don't you?"

I nodded. "I don't know who else it could be," I said. "I can't see someone showing up in the campus pickup line and randomly grabbing a student. And holiday pickups—" I sucked in a breath, remembering getting the kids the day they let out for Thanksgiving. As usual, there had been plenty of cars in the pickup line, but an equal number of parents and extended family had been on campus, eager to see classrooms and meet teachers. It had been a zoo.

"We met for lunch at the Grove Park Inn in Asheville, but I don't know if she was staying there. I should have asked."

Finn squeezed my hand again, drawing my eyes to his face. "You couldn't have known she'd do something like this," Finn said. "Threatening to sue for custody is crazy, but kidnapping is a whole other level."

"What if they can't find her?" I asked, my voice so small it was almost silent, my worst fears too horrible to give volume. "What if she takes him and just disappears?"

"No, Savannah." Another squeeze to my hand, this one hard enough to hurt, the slight pain pulling me from the well of fear. "Not happening. She can run with him, but she's no match for Hawk, West, and Griffen. West knows every inch of this county, and this kind of thing is what Hawk and Griffen do best. There's no way your mother-in-law can run from them. Not for long."

I nodded, squeezing his hand back as hard as he'd squeezed mine. Flipping my phone over in my lap, I stared at the dark screen, willing someone to call me with good news. I thought about texting my mother to let her know what was happening. I didn't. Not when I had nothing to give her but fear. I'd call her later when I had good news.

Resting on my lap, my phone stayed dark and silent. I wasn't surprised. Cell reception on the shortcut was spotty at best. It rang the second we popped out on the state road that ran from Sawyers Bend toward school. Scarlett again.

Chapter Forty-Four

SAVANNAH

"Did they find him?" I asked, hearing the desperation in my voice.

"No. No, Savannah. I just talked to his teacher. She's distraught, and she's been trying to figure out what happened. There was a substitute, and when they finally tracked her down, she said she released Nicky to his grandmother."

Lydia. It couldn't have been my mother. She would never have picked Nicky up without also getting August and Thatcher, and definitely not without letting anyone know. My heart beat so hard that the rush of it drowned out any other sound. In the back of my mind, I was hoping Nicky was playing hide and seek or had snuck off to the playground; both things had happened before when kids weren't at the pickup line.

"She's sure it was his grandmother? Did she give a description?" I asked. I'd been afraid to let Lydia have private visitation for just this reason, worried that once she had her hands on Nicky, she wouldn't bring him back to me.

"The substitute said she was short. Silver and blond hair. She remembered her silk scarf and a red tailored suit."

"That's Lydia," I said, letting out a breath. "Do they have cameras? Security? Can we verify that it was Lydia?"

"I don't know. How far away are you?" Scarlett asked.

"Ten minutes. Maybe five," I said as Finn flicked his blinker on, slid into the oncoming lane, and passed a truck going the speed limit, the Jeep's engine straining under the increased speed.

"I should have borrowed Griffen's Maserati," he said under his breath.

Another day that would have been a joke. Today, it was a regret. If we'd taken Griffen's car, we'd be there already. It didn't matter that there was nothing we could do once we got there. Nicky was already gone. I squeezed my eyes shut, forcing that thought away. We were going to find him.

"We're out front," Scarlett said. "Pickup is almost finished. I think you're going to beat Hawk and West here."

"Okay," I said. "I'll see you soon." Such banal words. *See you soon*, as if we weren't racing as fast as we could to get to her. I hung up and watched the trees flashing by.

To Finn, I said, "A substitute let Lydia take him. She's not on the list. They're not supposed to let anyone who isn't on the list pick up the kids." My voice was a shriek by the end. I was getting hysterical. I never get hysterical, but no one had ever threatened Nicky before. Not like this.

"We'll fix it," Finn said, his eyes glued to the road as he passed another car, ignoring the blare of their horn as we flew by. "Once we get Nicky back, we'll deal with it. There's a pickup list for a reason. Fucking idiots."

His fury soothed my terror just a little. I wasn't alone. We were going to face this together. We were going to find Nicky safe and well. That was the only outcome I could accept. Anything else was unthinkable. I pulled up Lydia's number and hit the call button. It rang once and went to voicemail. I tried again. It went to voicemail again.

I didn't leave a message. I couldn't think of what to say. After the third try, I set the phone on my lap.

"She's not answering?" Finn asked, his voice tight, sharp, with fear.

"It's going to voicemail. I was going to leave a message, but what if I say the wrong thing? She's obviously unstable. Coming to Heartstone, threatening to sue for custody, and now picking Nicky up at school. I don't know what she's thinking. That she's just going to take him and run? Where? Is John in on it?"

Restless, I flipped the phone over and over in my lap. "It doesn't make sense," I said, babbling all the thoughts running through my head. "I wanted to leave a message telling her to bring my son back, or she'd get arrested, but then I thought, what if I spook her? What if I spook her, and she does something crazy and hurts Nicky?"

Finn let out a held breath. "God, I didn't even think of that, but you're right. If she was willing to listen to reason, we wouldn't be in this situation in the first place. And if you scare her—"

"I don't want her to feel threatened," I said, my blood chilling at the idea of driving Lydia further from sanity while she had Nicky.

"I don't think she's going to hurt him, Savannah," Finn said. "I really don't."

"I don't think she'd mean to," I said. "But sometimes things don't work out the way you plan, and if she panics—" I couldn't bring myself to finish the thought.

"I know," Finn said, squeezing my hand again. "But look, until we have a reason to think differently, we're going to assume that Nicky is fine. Okay? We don't have any reason to think that he's not. Lydia loves him. She wants to spend time with him. She did not strike me as a suicidal woman. Angry, bitter, possessive. A little unhinged. But I don't see her hurting herself or him. Do you?"

I forced myself to think about it, as horrifying as the thought was. I didn't want to believe it was possible. And Finn was right. I had no reason to think Nicky was in danger with Lydia. So I wouldn't. Not yet.

Telling myself not to think about it didn't help. I was sick to my stomach with terror, counting the seconds until we reached the school. A minute later, the turn came into view, a line of cars at the traffic light, ready to leave campus. As we swung onto campus with a screech of tires, I saw that these were the stragglers, and the pickup line was empty. A cluster of people stood by the curb, Scarlett's flaming red hair marking her presence. I spotted August and Thatcher, two women and a man in a dark suit.

The Jeep rocked as we came to a halt, and I shoved open my door. One of the women was Nicky's teacher, her eyes red and swollen. Beside her stood a woman with steel gray hair and a worried expression. The tall man beside her turned to face us, his dour expression tinged with annoyance—the headmaster. I recognized him from his speech at orientation the week before school started. It felt like a million years ago.

Nicky's teacher let out a wail and lurched toward me. "Ms. Miles, I'm so sorry. Clara—" She looked to the gray-haired woman. "She's a substitute, and she forgot to check the list. It was so busy with the holiday parties running late and—"

"You can go, Miss Fletcher," the man in the suit said. "And take Clara with you. I'll handle this."

Miss Fletcher's eyes dropped to the concrete, and she nodded, whispering, "I'm so sorry."

The man turned his attention to me. "Ms. Miles?"

"Yes, I'm Nicky's mother."

Finn shifted beside me, his palm warm on my lower back, letting me know I wasn't alone. He eyed the headmaster and said, his voice grim, "Headmaster Montgomery. It never occurred to me that you'd still be here."

"Finn Sawyer," the headmaster said, his voice dripping with scorn. "It never occurred to me that you wouldn't be in jail."

"Not yet," Finn said, and I remembered he'd been expelled from Laurel Country Day for setting fire to the headmaster's office. That explained the headmaster's rude comment. Finn got right to what was important. "What are you doing to find Nicky? Have you checked the security cameras?"

"Why would we?" the headmaster asked, sounding irritated at the question. "Clara said Nicky's grandmother picked him up. I don't understand what all the fuss is about. You can deal with this on your own. This is a family mix-up, not the school's fault."

I choked back a scream of rage and frustration. "My mother-in-law is not on the list for pickup. She's not allowed to be alone with him. How did this happen?" I demanded, hearing my voice rise in a shriek.

"Ms. Miles, perhaps if you call your mother-in-law, you can sort this out without involving the school. It's the holidays." He shrugged, looking down at me as if I were a minor inconvenience he couldn't wait to brush off. "The last day of school is always busy. We can't be expected to keep track of family issues."

"That's exactly the kind of thing you're paid to keep

track of," Finn said, his voice as hard and cold as I'd ever heard it. "You released Nicky Miles to an adult who is not on his pickup list. An adult who does not have his mother's permission to take him anywhere or be alone with him. Savannah will not deal with this on her own. You're going to do everything you can to cooperate with the police so that we can get Nicky home as fast as possible. Do you understand?"

"The police?" the headmaster asked, raising an eyebrow, the faintest hint of alarm tinging his expression. "Why is it necessary to involve the police?"

"Because my child has been kidnapped!" I screeched.

I wished I could manage Finn's icy, controlled anger, but the headmaster's attitude was too much. I wanted to scream and rage and demand that someone find my child. I did not want to deal with this man's condescending bullshit one second longer. I clung to Finn's hand, hoping he could keep me level before I exploded.

The headmaster's chin rose, eyes fixed behind me, tracking something. I turned to see a police car turn onto campus, lights flashing red and blue, and a black SUV right behind it. West and Hawk.

West jumped out of the police car, leaving the lights on. His eyes caught mine, and he gave me a gentle smile before his gaze moved to land on the headmaster. "Montgomery," he said, in a cold tone that told me all I needed to know about West's opinion of the headmaster.

"Chief Garfield. Turn off those lights. I don't need the community seeing police lights on campus."

"No," West said, turning to raise his chin at Hawk as Hawk jumped down from his SUV. To the headmaster, he said, "This is Hawk Bristol. He's head of security at Heart-stone Manor. He's assisting me in finding Nicky Miles. We need to see the feeds from your cameras to verify the identity of the person who took Nicky."

His tone arctic, Headmaster Montgomery shook his head. "This isn't in your jurisdiction, Garfield."

Before West could say anything, Finn cut in. "Shut the fuck up, Montgomery. You allowed a stranger to kidnap one of your students. Are you going to stand in the way of the investigation and put him at further risk? If anything happens to Nicky, it'll be the end of your career in education. You might not care about Nicky, but I know you care about that."

"If you think you can do anything to me, Finn—"

"Finn won't have to," West said, shooting Finn a look that said *back off*. "Griffen Sawyer considers Savannah and Nicky part of the family. If anything happens to Nicky, he won't be forgiving. Do you understand me?"

The headmaster went pale.

Hawk leveled dark eyes on the headmaster. "I need to see your camera feeds. We need to verify who took Nicky before this goes any further."

After an endless moment, Headmaster Montgomery nodded and turned to lead us into the school. Before I followed, I looked at Scarlett. August and Thatcher stood close beside her as if drawing strength from their mother, their eyes scared, faces drawn.

"You guys should go home," I said. "West and Hawk will find him. There's nothing you can do here."

"You sure?" Scarlett asked. She looked at Finn and nodded in agreement before I could answer. "You're in good hands," she said. Darting forward, she gave me a quick hug. "They'll find him," she said. I wished I was as sure as she was. I wanted to be. I wanted to believe everything would be fine. But it wouldn't. Not until we found Nicky safe and sound.

Still holding tight to Finn's hand, we followed the head-master, Hawk, and West into the school building, down one hall, then another, until we reached a small room filled with monitors, a lone security guard inside.

He glanced up when we entered, nodding at West. "I'm checking the feeds from the halls. We don't have cameras in the classrooms."

Hawk gestured to the monitors. "Put feeds on these two, and West and I can help."

The room fell silent as we watched endless numbers of children and adults smiling and laughing and milling around in the halls. I was livid that the substitute had made such a careless mistake, but watching the crowds, the kids hyper after their Christmas parties filled with cupcakes and candy, parents and relatives chatting as they bumped into people they knew, I could see so easily how one kinder-gartner could have slipped through the cracks.

Chapter Forty-Five

SAVANNAH

After what felt like an eon, we saw her. Outside the classroom door, Lydia was talking to Clara, the substitute. Harried and distracted, Clara looked at Lydia and nodded, nudging Nicky in Lydia's direction. Nicky hung back until Lydia took out something dark and rectangular.

"Is that a picture?" I asked, pointing at Lydia showing it to Nicky.

"I think it is," West agreed.

We watched as Nicky let her take his hand and lead him out of the classroom. When the substitute teacher turned around to look, Lydia and Nicky were gone. It didn't look like Clara fully registered that they'd left. Another parent approached her. She intercepted another student and went on with dismissal.

The security guard noted the timestamp on the feed and switched to other cameras. I was lightheaded with fear as we watched Lydia lead Nicky down a long hall, tugging his hand to hurry him along. My heart pounded as if I were running a marathon. Finn stood behind me, his arm around my shoulders, the only thing keeping me on my feet.

On the monitors, Lydia and Nicky emerged from the building and headed toward the parking lot.

"Fuck," Hawk said under his breath. "We don't have a good angle on the car. Looks like a sedan. Dark. But I can't see the make, and I can't see the plates. Don't you have another camera on that parking lot?"

The security guard shook his head, sending a baleful look at the headmaster who stood beside us, arms crossed over his chest, glowering down at the screens.

"We know we need more cameras in the lots," the guard said in a tight voice. "But I haven't been able to get the funding approved."

The headmaster's jaw flexed, but he said nothing.

"Can we get a view of the road to see which way she turned?" West asked.

The security guard shook his head. "No, we also don't have a camera covering the exit onto the road." He shot another accusing look at the headmaster. "I told him," he said under his breath. "I told him we need more cameras—on the exits, all the doors. He got the board to give him a raise this year, but he wouldn't upgrade the security."

The headmaster seemed impervious to the glares that landed on him at that statement. "Nothing like this has ever happened on campus," he said, as if that was an excuse.

The security guard muttered, "That's a lie."

I didn't have room in my brain to wonder what he meant. All I could think about were Nicky and Lydia. Was he scared? Would she hurt him? Lydia had looked calm and righteous as she walked with him, which told me she felt like she was doing the right thing. I wish I knew what that thing was. Where was she taking him? How did she see this playing out? I pressed my forehead into Finn's shoulder, unable to watch the screens any longer.

A rumble came from Finn's throat. He was done with this bullshit back and forth. "What do we do?" he asked West and Hawk.

West handed the guard a business card. "Can you email this footage to me?"

The guard took his card and nodded.

"I need stills of her with Nicky," West said. "The best shot you can get me of the car. Send it all to me, and I'll get them out to everyone looking."

West turned to face me, his eyes meeting mine, deadly serious and full of compassion. "Savannah, we're going to find him. I promise you, we're going to find him. I want you and Finn to go to my office and wait."

"I can't just sit in your office and wait, West!"

"Savannah," West said, "There's nothing else you can do right now. I've got every officer in the county looking for them. The county sheriff has his deputies on standby. I'll get an Amber Alert posted on the highways and pushed out just as soon as we have Lydia's license plate number. We will find them. I need you and Finn in my office, waiting for Nicky. When we bring him back, he's going to be scared, and he's going to want his mom. I don't want to have to hunt you down or worry that you're out of cell reception. You get me?"

I nodded. I got him; I just didn't like it. I did not want to go to West's office and wait. I wanted to do something. I wanted to find my baby. Finn tugged me out of the room and guided me down the hall and back outside to the Jeep.

"Finn," I said helplessly.

"I know, I know," he said, pulling me into his arms for a tight hug before he helped me into the seat and shut the door. When he was behind the wheel and we were driving, he said, "I don't want to go back and sit in West's office either." He drew in a breath and let it out in a gust of air.

"I hate the idea of doing nothing, just sitting there and drinking his shitty coffee while we wait for someone to find Nicky. Can you think of anywhere Lydia would have gone?"

I shook my head. "I don't know. I don't know if she's taking Nicky to John, and I don't know if he's in Virginia or here. I can't see him agreeing to run off with Lydia and Nicky, and I can't see Lydia abandoning her husband of forty years to take off with a six-year-old. None of this makes any sense."

I tried calling Lydia again. This time it went straight to voicemail without ringing. "She must have turned it off," I said, dropping my phone back in my lap. All the crying I'd done in the last few weeks, and my eyes were bone dry. I couldn't cry. I wouldn't cry. Not until we found Nicky, and I knew everything would be okay.

The alternative was a horror too big for tears. The alternative was a void I couldn't see past. Couldn't see through. There was Nicky in my arms, my baby, safe and sound, or there was nothing. There was no in-between.

"Finn," I said. "What if—?" My voice cracked.

Finn squeezed my hand hard, turning his head to look at me. "No, Savannah. He's okay." Finn blinked hard, and my fear was reflected in his eyes. Nicky wasn't his, but he was.

"He's okay," Finn said again. "He has to be okay. West and Hawk will find him. They will."

I nodded, wanting to believe. Desperate to believe. We pulled into a spot in front of the police station and got out, the thud of the Jeep door shutting heavy and final. This was the last place I wanted to be. I wanted to be home, in our cottage with Nicky and Finn, just the three of us. That was what I wanted. Not this. Waiting, terrified, thinking of Nicky equally terrified and alone with Lydia.

Finn shoved open the door to the station, ushering me in beside him. The dispatcher looked up when we entered, her eyes heavy with worry. We'd gone to high school together and been in some of the same classes. Not friends, exactly, but friendly.

"Savannah, I'm so sorry this is happening," she said. "No news yet. They're looking. West asked me to get you set up in his office." She pushed back her chair, signaling another officer to man the phones.

"They're going to find him," she said.

I just nodded.

"Do you want anything? Coffee? Something to eat?"

I shook my head.

"All right, Just wait here. They'll bring him straight to you as soon as they find him. Everybody's looking for him," she reassured as she disappeared back down the hall.

The clock on the wall ticked slowly, minutes melting into an hour, then two. I sat beside Finn, my head on his shoulder, our fingers threaded together, both of us frozen. I couldn't talk, couldn't think. I just wanted my baby. And Finn. I couldn't have done this with anyone else. Even my mother, as much as I loved her. I needed Finn. His strength. His love. Knowing he was just as worried as I was.

It wasn't the time to talk. I could barely breathe, much less have a conversation—especially the most important conversation of my life. But I knew. I'd known before Scarlett's call, before Finn had dropped everything to get me to the school, before he'd faced down the headmaster.

I was in love with Finn Sawyer. Completely, totally,

head over heels in love with him. I was going to say yes. Of course, I was. There was never another answer. It was always going to be yes. I was just working up the courage.

Now, only a few hours after thinking I was a great big chicken, I understood that I hadn't known what fear was. Fear was my son going missing. Fear was not knowing where my baby was. Fear was losing Nicky.

Telling the man I loved that I wanted to spend my life with him? That wasn't something to fear. That was life. That was love and the promise of the future we'd have together. As soon as we had Nicky back, I was going to tell him. As soon as we had Nicky back.

When it had been so long that I was ready to jump up and scream, my phone rang.

"West?" I asked in a rush after seeing the name on the screen.

"We don't have him yet, but we know where he is, and he's safe."

"What? He's safe? Where is he?" I pulled the phone from my ear and turned on the speaker. "I put you on speakerphone so Finn can hear. Where is he?"

"At a gas station outside of Winston-Salem. We think they were heading to Richmond. He's safe, Savannah. I have an officer on the way to pick him up."

"What happened?" Finn asked. "Are you sure he's okay?"

"The local deputy on the scene said he's fine, just shaken up. You've got a smart little guy there. Nicky told her he had to pee and said he was going to wet his pants. She stopped at a gas station, and the second they were inside, he pulled free, ran to the cashier, and told her he was being kidnapped. He actually gave her my name. How did he know to do that?"

"We, uh, we talked about it," I said, the words coming out in a gasp, breathless with relief. "We talked about what to do if he got lost, how to ask grown-ups for help, who to call. And he remembered."

"He did," West agreed. "He has good instincts. The cashier pulled him behind the counter and called 911. Lydia argued and demanded Nicky back, but the cashier said she'd let the police figure it out. Hold on a sec."

The line went silent, the timer on the call counting up. After a minute, West was back. "One of my officers just got there and confirmed it was Nicky. He's in good shape. Ate a candy bar and drank two slushies. Officer Tucker's bringing him back to Heartstone Manor."

My heart rate slowed down just a little. He was okay. "Can I talk to him?" I asked.

"I'll have him call you from the car once they get on the road. But I promise he's okay. Shaken up, scared. But he's okay."

"What about Lydia?" Finn asked.

West let out an angry grunt. "No. When the cashier pulled Nicky behind the counter and said she was calling the police, Lydia took off. Unlike the school, the gas station had decent cameras, so we know which direction she was headed and the car's make, model, and tags. They'll get her."

"Thanks, West," Finn said.

"You talked to Griffen or anybody?" West asked.

"No," Finn said. "We've just been sitting here. Too worried to talk to anyone."

"I told them not to bother you," West said. "Figured you wouldn't want to talk. But Griffen's livid. Hawk told him what went down at the school. I'll be surprised if Montgomery has a job tomorrow. Your great-great-something

435

grandfather built that school, and even your father kept up with the tradition of hefty donations. Griffen's raising hell with the board. They'll fire Montgomery in a heartbeat rather than risk pissing Griffen off." West laughed. "Wish I could listen in on that phone call. Montgomery has always been an ass. Listen, I have to go. You head home, and you'll be hugging Nicky before you know it."

West hung up. I dropped my phone into my lap, looked at Finn, and burst into tears. "They found him," he said, and I nodded into his neck, my shoulders heaving with sobs.

"He's okay," Finn said, and I heard the relief, understanding how tightly he'd locked his own emotions down. We sat there, arms wound around each other. Hanging on. Letting everything we'd held back wash through us.

Nicky was okay.

The phone rang as we were getting in the car. I answered and put it on speakerphone. "Nicky?" I asked, my heart yearning for the sound of his voice.

"Mom? Mom?"

"It's me. Finn is here too. Are you okay?"

"I'm okay. The lady said she was my grandma, and she showed me a picture of me with you and her when I was a baby, and she said she was supposed to pick me up because there was a problem at the Manor."

His voice got quiet as he said, "I know I'm not supposed to go with strangers, but she had the picture, and she said she was my dad's mom, so I thought it was okay."

My heart squeezed. My poor little boy. He was only six. "I know, honey. I should have told you to watch out for her, but I never thought she'd come to school. She didn't hurt you?"

"She was just weird. Talking too fast, and then she wasn't taking me home and said she was taking me to surprise my grandfather. I asked her to take me home, but she wouldn't, so I told her I was going to pee in my pants and made her take me to the gas station. The policeman said we'd be home soon." A yawn sounded through the phone. All the excitement and sugar were hitting my little guy. The hint of normalcy relaxed me as nothing else could.

Before I could say anything else, a man's voice spoke up. "Ms. Miles? Officer Jim Tucker here. It's good luck West had me watching the roads this far east. Didn't take me too long to get to your boy. I think Nicky here is going to take a nap, and we'll be in Sawyers Bend in about two hours. Chief Garfield asked me to bring him straight to the Manor."

"Thank you so much," I said, sheer relief making my head swim.

"Mr. Finn?" Nicky's voice piped up.

"Yeah, Nicky?" Finn said, his voice rough with emotion.

"Can you make me some cocoa when we get back?"

"Sure thing, Nicky. I'll have it waiting for you."

"K. The policeman had his lights on before. It was cool. But he won't put them back on."

Nicky's voice faded.

"We'll see you soon," Officer Tucker said. "Call this number if you need me in the meantime."

"Thank you," Finn said. "Drive safe."

"Always do," he said, a smile in his voice.

The phone clicked off, and I collapsed back into my seat. Nicky was coming home, and he wanted cocoa.

"I'm not sure he needs more sugar after everything he had at the gas station," Finn said, relief lightening his words, "But I'm making him cocoa anyway."

I reached out for his hand. "We could all use some cocoa," I agreed.

I thought about that on the ride back to the Manor. Finn, in the kitchen at the cottage, making us cocoa before we went to bed. My ring caught the faint light from the dashboard, and I smiled. Some things weren't that complicated after all. We were going home, and Nicky would join us soon, safe and sound.

Earlier in the day, I'd been going in circles, too afraid to grab for what I wanted. And now . . . I looked at Finn's profile as he drove, his eyes on the road, his fingers still curled around mine.

I wasn't afraid of loving Finn. Not anymore.

Chapter Forty-Six

SAVANNAH

Nicky's eyes were drooping, his cocoa only half drunk.

"About time for bed, little man?" I asked, rubbing his back.

He nodded. "I didn't finish my cocoa," he said mournfully, looking into his mug.

"We can have cocoa again tomorrow," Finn said. "Your mom's right. It's been a long day."

Nicky nodded in resignation. "Will you put me to bed too, Mr. Finn?"

"Sure," Finn said, his voice thick with what I guessed was an overload of emotion. He glanced at me as if making sure it was okay. All I could do was smile.

Of course, it was okay. Finn helping me put Nicky to sleep was about the best end to this hellish day that I could imagine. It was early compared to my usual bedtime, but I was exhausted. Despite his nap in the police car, I could tell Nicky was too. We all were.

West had called while Finn was whisking a melting

chocolate bar into hot milk. They'd caught Lydia speeding down a country road that paralleled the highway back to Richmond. She was now in custody, facing charges of kidnapping.

I wasn't feeling overly sympathetic for Lydia, especially after the terror and agony of learning Nicky was missing and the hours of waiting. Still, the idea of my perfect, proper mother-in-law in a jail cell wouldn't process. I wasn't sure she needed jail, but I did know she needed help. Either way, it was out of my hands.

I pushed the problem of Lydia aside. She'd already taken enough of my day, and I had more important things to think about. Already half asleep, Nicky stumbled through putting on his jammies and brushing his teeth. He handed Finn the book we'd been reading before bed, a chapter book about a mystery on a spaceship. Finn made it two paragraphs before Nicky's eyes slid shut, and my sweet little baby started to drool onto his pillow.

Together, we stood, Finn setting the book on the nightstand, and tiptoed out the door. I turned to close it, as I always did, and then looked at Finn in apology.

"I'm going to leave his door open tonight. He seems fine, but he might have a nightmare. Today was—"

Finn nodded. "Leave it open."

I stopped in the hall, not quite in the kitchen, and turned to face Finn. "I, um . . . Now that we're alone, and, um, have some time, I, uh—" My words were tangled in my head. Why was this so hard? It shouldn't be. I tried again. "We need to talk."

Finn's face went carefully blank, his feelings tucked away where they couldn't make him vulnerable. Then the side of his mouth quirked up, and he looked to the stairs, raising one eyebrow.

I shook my head. "Not in the bedroom. I'll get distracted if we go in the bedroom." I wandered into the kitchen and picked up my own half-finished cocoa, staring into the cooling swirl of brown liquid, the whipped cream half-melted on top. I looked up to see Finn standing in the bright light of the kitchen, uncertainty a shadow beneath his deliberately blank expression.

The sparkling fire of the ring on my finger caught my eye. I was doing this all wrong. I'd accused him of screwing up his proposal, jumping the gun, and not thinking things through, but I was no better. More than anyone, Finn deserved my honesty. I owed both of us better than cowardice.

"I love you," I blurted out, relieved at the way his blank expression melted into a cocky grin. "I'm sorry I haven't said it before now. But I love you. So much." I drew in a breath and pushed on, needing to tell him everything. "You fascinated me when we were kids."

"Could have fooled me," he said, raising an eyebrow.

"You fascinated me," I repeated, "but repelled me at the same time."

"Not sure how to take that." Finn leaned against the counter and crossed his arms over his chest.

"Oh, come on," I said, shaking my head. "I was the housekeeper's daughter. You were the bad boy of Sawyers Bend. I got good grades, didn't break curfew, and stayed out of trouble. And you?"

"I was nothing but trouble," Finn admitted.

"Exactly. I couldn't afford to have anything to do with you. I could have gotten my mom fired." I paused, remembering the wild and reckless teenage boy I'd had such a huge crush on, seeing the echoes of that boy in the man who stood before me. "But still, you fascinated me. Maybe a part of me always knew we'd end up here. I don't know. But all these years have passed, and I never forgot you. When you came back, I thought I hated you."

"I'm not the kid I was then," Finn said, arms dropping to his sides, his shrug holding a hint of defensiveness.

"That's not it," I said, wishing I could find the right words. "You could be a jerk back then, but what teenager isn't sometimes? You were a good kid dealing with a lot of tough problems. Your mother died, and your father was the king of assholes. Cut yourself a break."

Finn shook his head. "Everyone else was dealing with the same shit, and I was the worst. By far."

"You weren't," I said. "Everyone coped differently. Ford turned on Griffen. They were best friends, and Ford stole his fiancée and got him disinherited. Griffen ran away, abandoning all of you. Parker and Avery hid by trying to be perfect. Quinn disappeared into the woods, Brax into school and work, and Sterling into a bottle. You were all doing the best you could. And the point isn't the kid you were back then. It's the man you've made yourself into. And the man you are is one I love more than I thought I could love anyone except Nicky."

I looked at the ring on my hand and twisted it so it caught the light, trying to figure out how to ask what I needed to know.

"Savannah, what is it?" Finn crossed his arms over his chest, the grin wiped from his face. "I love you. You love me. Let's get married." He stopped as if something had occurred to him. "Is it Nicky? You know I love him, right? I never really thought about being a dad until I came back here, but we get along great. I'll be a good father."

"I know you will," I said immediately. "It's not Nicky.

He loves you too. He can't wait for tea after school so he can jump into whatever you're doing in the kitchen. I love the way you are together. You'll be a great dad."

"Then what?"

I took another sip of the cocoa, deliciously sweet, even cold. "I want us to be on the same page," I said. "I—"

"Savannah, just spit it out. Whatever it is, we'll work it out."

"Are you going to want to leave after the terms of the will are up and you get your inheritance?"

Finn went stiff, his face frozen in surprise. "What are you talking about?"

"You're here for the inheritance," I reminded him. "You want the money to open your own restaurant. And Sawyers Bend is still the town you grew up in, the town you swore you'd never come back to."

"If I recall," Finn drawled, "you swore the same thing. And yet here you are."

"I know. I never thought I'd come back to Sawyer's Bend. I wanted to be more than the housekeeper's daughter." I shrugged, shaking my head, a smile slowly curving my lips. "Shows what I knew, right? My path back here isn't one I would have chosen, but now that I'm here, I want to stay. I love my job. I love being near my mom. I love working for your family, and I love running Heartstone Manor. And I need to know if your dreams are somewhere else."

Finn was silent for a long moment, studying me. "Is this a deal-breaker?"

I shook my head. "I don't think so. I love you, and I want us to be a family. I want to have at least one more baby if you do too. But before we do this, I need to know what your plans are. I know we can't plan everything. If we could, neither of us would be here." I was babbling. I snapped my mouth shut. Only Finn could make me babble like this. Usually, I knew exactly what I wanted and exactly what to say, but I was in over my head here.

"You'd leave your home for me?" he asked slowly.

I hated the sound of that. I did. Before I gave him the yes that wanted to pop out of my mouth, I forced myself to think about it. Would I leave Sawyers Bend for Finn?

As the seconds ticked by, I knew the answer. Home wasn't a place. It was wherever Nicky and Finn were.

"I love this town and my life here," I said, "but I love you more. I want you to have your dreams, even if they aren't here."

"I'm not here for the inheritance," Finn said. "I was. That's the only reason I came home. I thought I could stick it out for a few years, grab whatever Prentice left me, and take off. Open my restaurant somewhere else."

"And now?" I had to ask.

"And now," Finn shoved his hands in his pockets. "Like you said, I'm not happy about the things that set me on the road I took, but I'm glad I left after the kidnapping. I'm glad I went to France. I had a different life over there. I got to be a different me. Maybe the person I would have been if I hadn't grown up with my father. I don't know."

He pushed off from his leaning position at the counter and stepped forward, close enough that I wanted to throw myself into his arms. I waited where I was, needing to hear what he would say next.

"I do want my own restaurant, but I never had a clear picture of where or exactly what. I just knew I wanted to run my own place. And, yeah, it's a real mind fuck, but I love Sawyers Bend. I love Heartstone Manor. It's not the same house with Griffen and Hope in charge. It feels like the home I always imagined it could be. I love being back in the kitchens. I love being near my family. And this place is like foodie central. Not just Asheville, but Sawyers Bend and all the places in between. Tourists come here looking for good beer and good food. We have some of the best restaurants in the east within fifty miles of where I'm standing. Living in Sawyers Bend won't stop me from running a world-class restaurant."

"Really?" Relief washed through me. I'd been afraid I would have to choose. Home or Finn. I knew the answer was Finn. Would always be Finn. I hadn't truly thought I could have both. Not once the terms of the will ran out.

"Avery and I have been talking about doing some farm-to-table pop-ups at the brewery. She was toying with the idea of adding food but doesn't want to deal with the headache of it on top of running the brewery. And Quinn and I were tossing around the idea of doing a forest-to-table thing during ramp season this spring. She's going to forage, and I'll cook."

"That would be amazing," I said, my mouth watering at the thought of what Finn could do with ramps, the native wild leeks that were prized by chefs and foodies alike.

Finn shifted, dropping his hands to his sides. "I can't promise you I want to spend the next seventy years living in Heartstone Manor. But I can promise that I'm happy here, and I have no plans to leave. And if we ever did, that would be a decision we'd make together. We're a team. I'm not going anywhere without you or Nicky. Ever."

"You're sure?" I asked, needing to push, needing to make sure there was no chance he was placating me. "You could go anywhere."

"I've already been everywhere," he countered. "Here is where I want to stay. It's a bonus that we get to work together, at least for now, and I can watch you run Heartstone like a drill sergeant. I love it when you're bossy."

"Then . . ." I started, moving toward him.

Finn straightened, lifting his chin, and I stopped.

"What?" I asked. He wasn't smiling. I didn't know what that meant. I'd been so busy thinking about my own reservations that I hadn't thought Finn might have one or two.

"I need to know," he asked quietly, "why didn't you tell me about Lydia? About what she really wanted?"

My shoulders slumped, and I stared into the cold cocoa.

"This isn't going to work if you don't trust me," he pushed.

"I do. I do trust you, Finn."

"Then why didn't you tell me?" The undertone of hurt in his voice sliced through me. I should have told him. I wished I had.

"I do trust you," I said again. "But I didn't want to trust you. Trusting you, telling you everything meant I had to face what was happening between us, that I was head over heels in love with you when it was just supposed to be sex. It didn't occur to me that you loved me. I thought I wouldn't get hurt if I kept everything important to myself. Does that make sense? It wasn't you. It was me." I took a step closer, then paused, not sure how to tell him what was in my heart.

"Finn, there's no one on this earth I trust as much as I trust you. As soon as I found out Nicky was missing, I came straight to you. I'm sorry I didn't tell you about Lydia. I can't fix that. But I can promise you it won't happen again."

He closed the distance between us, taking my hands in his. "So this thing's a go? You're going to marry me?"

"Yes," I said, and a wave of relief hit me as the word left

my mouth. "Yes. I can't think of anything I want more than to spend the rest of my life with you."

I pulled my hand from his and framed his face, my eyes locked on his. "You're the most beautiful man I've ever known. Inside and out. I love you so much, and I can't wait to marry—"

Finn's mouth cut off the rest of my words with a fierce kiss. "Thank god," he said when he pulled away. "Waiting was killing me."

"It's only been a day." I laughed. "So impatient."

Finn didn't answer, just kissed me again and pulled me from the kitchen to the stairs.

"We'll be quiet," he said.

"We'll be quiet," I agreed, leaving the door cracked, just in case Nicky woke from a nightmare.

Finn tugged me to the side of the bed, stripping off my clothes slowly, lingering, tracing the curve of my shoulder with his mouth. I wiggled out of his hold and peeled off my bra, tossing it over my head, loving the way his pupils dilated as my breasts bounced.

"I was going to do this slow," he muttered, shoving the dress pooled around my waist to the floor.

"We can do slow later." I yanked his shirt up. His arms raised obediently, and I whipped the shirt over his head. We fell onto the mattress a second after Finn's jeans hit the floor, giggling, rolling, trying to keep it quiet.

For the first time with Finn, nothing was holding me back. No fear, no trying to protect my heart. I'd given it to him, knowing it was in safe hands, as his was in mine.

Once we were tucked under the covers, skin to skin, Finn stopped, holding me still beneath him, his fingers stroking my cheek. "I love you, Savannah," he breathed and proceeded to show me exactly how much.

Afterward, I collapsed back on the pillow, breathing hard. Finn took my left hand in his, curling my fingers so the ring he'd given me caught the light. "How do you feel about short engagements?" he asked.

I turned my head to look at him and smiled. "I think a short engagement sounds perfect."

Epilogue

SAVANNAH

e had intended to start wedding planning
right away. Once I said yes, I found myself
eager to skip from the engagement to the
married part of things. Neither of us wanted to wait,
but we had Scarlett and Tenn's Christmas Eve wedding
only a week after I finally accepted Finn's proposal and a
house full of guests to contend with.

So we waited.

Finn and I were run ragged over the next week, Finn
preparing to feed a temporarily enlarged household on top
of planning the wedding dinner and me working with
Parker and Scarlett to put the finishing touches on the
wedding while I prepared Heartstone for out-of-town
guests.

Hawk stormed around, looking aggravated that we'd
allowed outsiders on the property. He grudgingly acknowledged that Scarlett's family should be allowed to attend her
wedding, but only grudgingly. It helped that both her
parents and the boys' other grandparents had visited over

the summer and thus already passed the security checks. Hawk couldn't really argue, but he didn't like it.

On Christmas Eve, we all stood in the library, a roaring fire casting a flickering golden light that turned the palatial room almost cozy. Parker and I had decorated the towering Christmas tree, adding twinkling lights strategically throughout the room, along with fragrant holly and pine boughs. It was beautiful, but not as beautiful as Scarlett floating up the aisle we'd formed with a white satin runner, her champagne silk gown skimming her body to fall in a glowing pool at her feet. She'd left her vibrant red hair loose, falling down her back in curls and waves, her smile the brightest light in the room. August and Thatcher, one on each side, escorted her to Tenn, who stood at the altar we'd arranged in front of the fireplace, beside Griffen, who'd gotten ordained online at Tenn's request so he could perform the ceremony.

Scarlett and Tenn spoke their vows with quiet conviction, the kiss he gave her at the end sweet and just over the edge of appropriate for a family wedding. They glowed with love. I was happy for them, so happy, and also just a touch envious.

Finn read my mind.

"Have you thought about what you want?" he asked quietly as we watched Tenn and Scarlett turn to walk out of the library, the kids following.

I shook my head, then nodded, then shook my head again, and settled for a shrug. I didn't have a clear answer, just ideas and images swirling in my head. It was almost time for us to jump into gear for the rest of Scarlett and Tenn's celebration, me organizing pictures and Finn racing to have appetizers and dinner ready according to our schedule for the evening. But we had a second or two. The new family would want a moment alone before the wedding festivities got going.

"What kind of wedding do you want?" I asked.

"Honestly," Finn said, his voice low, his mouth at my ear. "I want to be your husband. I want you to be my wife. I want to be Nicky's dad. I could not give less of a fuck about a wedding. I'll do whatever you want to do, as long as I don't have to wait too long."

I snorted at his profanity and nodded. I'd had the big wedding of my dreams, which had been wonderful at the time. This was Finn's first wedding. His only wedding, if I had anything to say about it. If he wanted to go all the way, I would have done it happily. But in the end, we were on the same page. I didn't want the big production. I just wanted Finn.

"I want this," I said, gesturing at the library around us, the picture of the wedding I wanted coming into focus. "I want to get married here in the library. On Valentine's Day. I want red roses, Griffen to officiate, and Nicky to be part of the wedding. And I want to go on a honeymoon for at least a week, just you and me. You can plan that part."

"Done," Finn said.

And it was just that easy.

As the day drew closer, it got easier, which surprised me. Finn insisted on making our wedding dinner, which I thought was insane, but on the other hand, his wedding wouldn't be any fun if he was scowling over the food. And I had to admit, there was something adorable about Finn poring over videos and cookbooks, checking his notes, planning the perfect feast to celebrate our marriage. Aside from me, his life was food, and the time he put into our wedding dinner told me exactly how important the wedding was to him, despite his saying he didn't care.

I put the bulk of my wedding budget into flowers and candles. I wanted the library to glow, a profusion of roses turning it into an indoor candlelit garden. Hope swept in at the last minute and said she and Griffen were paying for everything. I didn't argue, mostly because there wasn't that much to pay for, aside from the flowers and candles and a photographer. We already had the venue, and Finn was catering. Griffen would officiate, as he had for Scarlett and Tenn. All I needed was a dress.

Uncharacteristic of me, I dithered over the dress situation.

I'd had the full-skirted fairy tale dress the first time with Oliver. I loved that dress. It was gorgeous and made me feel like a princess. I didn't want that again this time, but I wanted something special. More than a cocktail dress, but not the full princess gown. Nothing I had in my closet would work. I'd looked in town, driven to Asheville, and shopped online. Nothing was right. As January drew to a close, I was ever so slightly starting to panic.

I considered a last-minute trip to Charlotte or Atlanta to see if I could find something ready to wear. April's mother was a seamstress and had assured me that if I found something, she could do alterations as long as they weren't too complex. But still, the right dress eluded me.

One afternoon in late January, Parker popped into my new office off the kitchens. She'd been working on reimagining the housekeeper's apartment, turning the bedroom into my office and the rest of the small space into a staff lounge. I was thrilled with my desk, file cabinets, and corkboards. I loved how much more room I had to organize everything. Finn laughed when he came in and saw my endless to-do lists tacked up on the corkboards, my desk covered in piles of papers I hadn't filed yet. Parker was still working on finding just the right furniture for the sitting area. I thought that's why she'd stopped by when she stuck her head in and said, "Hey, have a minute?"

"Sure," I said. "Always."

She came into my office and leaned against my desk, her tablet cradled to her chest. "So," she began, "you know I'm still listing my stuff on auction sites."

I nodded. Parker had left her marriage with little more than the clothes in her closet. Determined to provide for herself while she figured out the rest of her life, she started selling the contents of her closet under Sterling's supervision. Sterling had done the same thing when Griffen cut her off from the family checking account, and, at this point, she was an expert at wringing every last cent out of used clothes and accessories.

Parker was blissfully in love with Nash, and everyone knew they'd get married eventually, but for now, Parker wanted to take her time. She was working for Griffen and Hope, managing renovations in the Manor and making a decent salary, especially considering that she didn't have to cover a mortgage or food, and Nash insisted on picking up every bill he could wrest from her hands. Despite all of that, Parker was still selling her things. When I asked her about it, she laughed.

"The truth is," she'd said, "most of those clothes are from my old life. I want to start fresh, so why not sell them? I'm having fun, and I like having my own money, even if it's not a lot. Between that and when Griffen pays me. I like not having to ask anyone for anything."

I'd smiled back. I knew exactly what she meant.

"So?" I prompted.

"So, I was listing a cocktail dress, and I just happened to do some browsing. You haven't found a dress yet?"

I shook my head, my heart leaping in anticipation.

"What do you think of this?" Turning her tablet, she showed me the screen. On it was a wedding dress. Vintage floral lace, strapless, the bodice a graceful curve, dipping to show a hint of cleavage. It was fitted through the waist, flaring below the hips into a train just big enough to look pretty as I walked down the aisle, but not enough to be in the way later. This was a woman's dress, so unlike the princess fantasy the younger me had worn, and exquisitely beautiful. I loved it instantly.

"Oh, Parker, it's gorgeous."

"I saw it, and it looked like you," she said with a pleased smile. "It's elegant, romantic, and exactly the right amount of sexy."

"Is it—" I scanned the text below the picture for the size.

"It's your size," Parker assured me. "It might be a little big, but even with the lace, April's mom should be able to make alterations. And they offer overnight shipping."

"How much is it?" I was afraid to ask. It wasn't new, but this was Parker and Sterling's favorite auction site. It was all high-end fashion; everything was expensive, even if it was used.

Parker clicked the screen dark. "Let me see." I reached for the tablet.

Parker hid it behind her back. "If you like it, it's your wedding gift."

"Parker, you don't need to get me a wedding gift," I said, surprised.

"It's not just from me. Griffen and Hope wanted to give you and Finn the flowers and the photographer and that stuff. But the rest of us, me and Sterling, Scarlett, Avery, Daisy, and Quinn, we want to give you your dress. Please don't argue. We're going to be sisters, and this means a lot to all of us."

"Really?" I squeaked out. "That's so—" I choked up, fanning my face and blinking up at the ceiling. It meant so much to me to hear her say it, even though all of them had said it a million different ways a million times before. "You guys are—"

Parker gave me a tight hug. "We're so happy for you. For both of you. I haven't seen Finn like this for a long time. Not since I was little, before our mom died. He was always so sweet and funny, and then she was gone, and he was so angry at the world. Now he's home to stay, and he's smiling again all the time. That's because of you."

I threw my arms around Parker in a hug. "I love him so much."

"I know you do," she said.

"And I love you. I'm so happy we're going to be sisters."

I let her go, both of us wiping our eyes. Parker clicked the screen of her tablet back on. "I'm buying this right now. You're sure you love it?" She showed me the dress again, and my heart pulsed.

"I'm sure," I said. "I love it."

And that was it. The last piece we had to put into place.

I thought we were finished with hiccups on our way to wedded bliss, but later that afternoon, I got a call from Lydia's attorney. West had been keeping me updated. Lydia's attorney was pushing for court-mandated therapy as opposed to jail time.

If her lawyer had called in the weeks after she'd taken Nicky, I might have hung up on him. The fear had been too fresh. I still didn't like to think about those hours she'd had Nicky. Weeks later, I was still furious at what she'd put us all through and deeply uncomfortable with the level of crazy it had taken for her to think she could kidnap Nicky and get away with it.

If not for Nicky's quick thinking, she might have pulled it off and taken my son from me. But in the months that had passed since Nicky's safe return, every time I thought of the agony of Nicky going missing, of not knowing where my son was, not knowing if I'd get him back, I remembered that Lydia had lost her son. She'd lost Oliver forever. She'd never get him back. Her grief didn't excuse what she'd done, but it made me think.

How much worse was it to know she'd lost Oliver through his own decisions—and hers? I couldn't imagine trying to live with that kind of guilt.

On that afternoon in late January, Lydia's attorney asked me to write a letter supporting his request for therapy for her, instead of jail time. I told him I'd think about it and hung up. That night I lay awake in bed, staring at the ceiling, until Finn rolled over.

"Out with it," he said, nudging my shoulder. "What's keeping you up? Are you still thinking about Lydia?"

I nodded. I'd told him about the attorney's request, but we hadn't had time to talk about it. "What do you think I should do? Am I an idiot if I write that letter?"

Finn stared at me for a long moment and shook his head. "I think you should do what you think is right."

"I can't imagine ever being okay leaving her alone with Nicky," I said. "Not after what happened. But I do think she needs help, not prison, and—" I rolled over, propping myself up on my elbows. "I don't know, Finn. If something happened to Nicky, and I'd played a part in it—" Tears welled in my eyes at the thought of what Lydia must be feeling. "I told her she was going to kill Oliver, and then he died from pills she gave him. I don't know how she can live with that. I think I'd go a little insane too."

Finn rolled me into his arms, brushing his lips over my temple. "Then write the letter. You won't be able to live with yourself if you don't."

I shifted against him, snuggling in, my head on his chest, the reassuring thump of his heart under my ear. The next morning, I wrote the letter. I didn't know how much it would help, but it took a weight off my heart knowing I'd done what I could. I didn't know if we'd ever find our way to any kind of relationship, but if she was willing to work on getting better, I was willing to at least consider it. Later. Now was for me, Finn, and Nicky, and the family we'd make together.

Less than three weeks later, I was walking up the makeshift aisle in the library to Finn, standing beside Nicky, both of them in tuxes, both of them beaming.

I never thought I'd have another chance at love. And more than that, I'd never dreamed I'd have a love like this. Finn took my hands as we faced each other and said our vows. Griffen barely got out the words, "You may kiss the bride," before Finn pulled me close and kissed the life out of me.

I faintly heard Nicky say, "Oh, gross," over August and Thatcher's laughter. A giggle caught me, and I pulled my face back, framing Finn's in my hands. "I love you, Finn Sawyer, and I'm so glad I'm your wife."

He managed one more kiss, and we were dragged off for photographs, then our wedding dinner. Finn had cooked our wedding feast, but he wasn't allowed to serve. This time, Finn and I were seated side by side at the head of the massive table, our family spread out down its long length. I couldn't have imagined a more joyful wedding dinner than this one.

My mother glowed with happiness. She'd adjusted my veil just before I walked down the aisle, telling me, tears in her eyes, "Your father would be so proud of you. I wish he were here to see this." I did too, but the wish wasn't a sad one. Not that day. I was so happy, I couldn't stop smiling. Nicky was running around, too excited to sit still.

The next morning, Finn and I left for the airport. I didn't know where we were going, just that I needed a passport, and the weather would be roughly the same as it was in Sawyers Bend. I'd had to get the passport renewal expedited. I hadn't left the country since before Nicky was born.

When we got to the airport, Finn still hadn't let me see the tickets. It wasn't until we got to the gate that I saw our destination.

"Paris! We're going to Paris! I've never been to Paris. London once after college, but that was it. I've always wanted to go to Paris."

"I know. Your mother told me. I have a friend who's out of town for the month, and he lent us his place. It's in a great spot. We can walk everywhere, and I can show you a Paris you'd never see with anyone else."

And he had. He took me to his favorite restaurants, where he was greeted like a returning hero by his friends and former coworkers. Everyone had missed him. Everyone loved him and clearly respected the hell out of him, which made me happy on multiple fronts. Not only because he deserved it, but it was wonderful to get a glimpse into the life he'd led after he left Sawyers Bend all those years ago.

He brought me to see Chef Guérard, who cooked us an amazing dinner, Finn at his side, taking orders from his mentor with a meek compliance that had me staring in wonder. It was obvious how much he loved and respected the older man and how much Chef Guérard cared for Finn in return. At the end of our night together, he'd slapped Finn on the shoulder and said, "You've done well, mon fils. Come back and bring your new son. We will see what he can do in the kitchen, eh?"

One night toward the end of our trip, when the owner of a bistro stopped by our table to talk, he ended up offering Finn the head chef position at his new restaurant. I could tell by Finn's response that it was an honor and a great opportunity. We both knew he couldn't take it, not without jeopardizing his inheritance, but that wouldn't be an issue forever.

"Are you sure about staying in Sawyers Bend?" I'd asked later when we were alone. "I don't think I fully realized what you'd be giving up."

Finn had smiled and kissed me on the tip of my nose. "Why? Did you suddenly decide you want to live in Paris?"

For a moment, pictures flashed through my head of me and Finn and Nicky living here, in a city I was coming to love. Then I shook my head. "Maybe someday," I said. "For now, I'm too happy at Heartstone to think about leaving."

"Me too," Finn said. "And Laurent is a fun guy to have a drink with, but I've worked in his kitchen before. He's a nightmare of a boss. Micromanaging everything and throwing fits when things don't go his way. Been there, done that. I'd rather run the kitchens at Heartstone and plan events with my sisters. It doesn't matter that they're grown up. If they get annoying, I'll just tickle them until they shut up."

We'd laughed and put aside Laurent's offer. Paris was wonderful, but it wasn't home. We spent our honeymoon like that. Eating fabulous meals and laughing with Finn's friends. We drank a lot of wine and went to bed early every night, sleeping late and making ample use of the privacy and the very comfortable bed.

Love and sex and good food and laughing. It was the perfect honeymoon. I sent Nicky pictures of pastries. He replied with all the junk food my mother was letting him eat while he stayed with her. As much as I loved our time in Paris, by the end, I was a little homesick. I missed Nicky and my mom. I missed the rest of the Sawyers, Heartstone Manor, and our cottage.

Finn had moved his things into the cottage the day before the wedding, Nicky watching with curiosity. "Do I still call you Mr. Finn after you and Mom get married?" he'd asked.

Finn had said, "You can call me whatever you want, bud."

"Are you going to be my dad?"

"I'd like to be," Finn had said. "Are you okay with that?"

I watched with interest to see what Nicky would say.

Nicky didn't have to think. He nodded. "August and Thatcher said Tenn is their stepdad. But their dad's still alive. He never comes to see them, but he's still alive, so they could see him, you know?"

Finn had nodded. Nicky went on, "But my dad's not alive. I can't see him. So, is it okay if instead of stepdad, I just call you Dad?"

I'd watched a tremor go through Finn at that question. He never pushed with Nicky, but at Nicky's request, Finn nodded and choked out, "I'd like that, Nicky. I want to be your dad if that's okay with you."

Nicky had thrown himself at Finn, wrapping his arms around him in a tight squeeze before he raced off shouting, "I'm going to go tell August."

Now, after a blissful week in Paris, we were back in Sawyers Bend, turning onto the long, winding drive to Heartstone Manor, ready to settle back into our cottage and our lives together.

"I miss Nicky," I murmured.

"Me too," Finn said. "I think he's going to like that cookbook I found. I just have to translate for him." We almost pulled past the courtyard until Finn spotted a vehicle in front of the wide steps to the front door.

"Is that Cole Haywood's car?" he asked. Before I could answer, Finn diverted, turning to park in the courtyard behind Cole Haywood's sedan.

"This can't be good," Finn said under his breath as we got out of the car. Finn took my hand. "We'll come back and get our things after we see what's going on."

Already climbing the steps of the house, Cole acknowledged us with a chin lift but said nothing. We followed him inside, the door already opening, Griffen looking past Cole to see us.

Griffen's face brightened. "You're back," he said. "Just in time."

"It looks like," Finn said, looking at Cole and then back at Griffen, obviously hoping for some kind of explanation.

Griffen's expression shifted from happy to grim, but he didn't say anything else.

We followed Griffen and Cole through the entry and down the hall to Griffen's office.

"What's going on?" I asked Hope in a low voice.

She smiled up at me, baby Stella cradled in her arms. "It's so good to see you. We missed you. And I don't know what's going on. Cole called and said he needed to talk to us."

"I'll just get this over with," Cole announced, his tone

461

clipped. Something about the way he held himself put me on alert. Something was wrong.

Everyone fell silent. "I have good news and bad news."

"Start with the bad news," Griffin said, his eyes hard.

"The bad news is that someone tried to kill Ford last night. He survived. He has some stitches and a concussion. He got lucky."

Beside me, Finn went stiff. I leaned into him, winding my arm around his waist, trying to get my head around what Cole had said. Someone had tried to kill Ford? Why? Was it prison politics or related to the murder attempts on the rest of the family since Prentice's death?

"He's going to be okay?" Griffen asked.

Cole nodded, once, his movements brief and irritated. "I told you stirring things up wasn't going to help anybody. But you couldn't fucking listen, could you? You had to dig into things that should be left in the past. You had to go there and see him. He got lucky this time, but that's what it was. Luck."

Griffen and Finn shared a long look. I waited to see what Griffen would say, but he ignored Cole's oblique accusation.

"And the good news?" Griffen asked.

"The good news is that I may have found a way to get Ford out of prison."

TURN THE PAGE FOR A SNEAK PEEK OF WILD HEART, BOOK SIX OF THE HEARTS OF SAWYERS BEND

Wild Heart

SNEEK PEAK

CHAPTER ONE
HAWK

Dawn is my favorite time at Heartstone Manor. Winter or summer, the mornings were misty, the damp air clinging to the edges of the great stone house, the sun barely cresting the vast forest surrounding the Sawyer Estate.

At times like this, Heartstone Manor didn't feel like a real place. More like a movie set. In the back of my mind, I expected a voice to yell *Cut* and a crew to melt out of the scenery. The guy who'd been holding the roses at the perfect angle to catch the light. The prop master who'd arranged the ivy draped over the windowsill just so.

It never happened. As hard as it was to believe, Heartstone Manor was a real place with real people living inside. It was a home, its inhabitants mostly normal human beings, living mostly normal lives.

Kind of. There *was* all that murder and mayhem. The reason I was here in the first place.

A year ago, Prentice Sawyer, the billionaire patriarch of the Sawyer family, had been found sitting at his desk, a bullet hole in his forehead. His son, Ford, the presumed heir to the Sawyer fortune, pled guilty to Prentice's murder. No one had seen that coming.

In a second twist, Prentice's will left everything to Griffen, the son he'd exiled fifteen years before. *Everything,* included the target on his father's back. Griffen hadn't been home long before someone tried to kill him, too.

Griffen Sawyer was the closest thing I had to a brother. We'd met in our first days in the Army and been together through Ranger school, then later at Sinclair Security, where we joined another of our Ranger buddies in the private sector. When Prentice's will forced Griffen back to the home he hated, with an unknown killer gunning for him, I'd been there.

I owed Griffen. While he'd stayed in the Rangers, I'd accepted an invitation to join a team that operated outside the normal boundaries. Off the books. In the dark. I'd been reeling from the loss of my parents in a freak accident, and a change of scenery felt like the only way to shake off my grief. How wrong I'd been.

I should have stayed with the Rangers, with Griffen and Evers Sinclair and work I was good at. I should have stayed in the light. Instead, I'd jumped ship for my new team and sank straight to dark depths I'd never imagined. I thought I understood right and wrong. Good and evil. I hadn't understood how loyalty and lies could twist the world until up was down, and I was pulling the trigger on the innocent as easily as on the guilty.

By the time I dragged myself out of the dark, I was only half human. I can never do enough good to atone for the crimes I committed under orders I should have questioned.

I showed up one night on Evers Sinclair's doorstep, and he let me in. He gave me a job. Griffen gave me a place to live. They gave me time to find myself again. Without them, I would have slipped into the darkness completely.

No one wanted Griffen to leave Sinclair Security for the wilds of Western North Carolina. Even without the threat of murder, I would have come to Sawyers Bend. Putting a guy like me in charge of security is a little like bringing a rocket launcher to a knife fight, but I didn't mind. I slept better here, surrounded by thousands of acres of forest. And I wasn't going to let anyone touch Griffen or his family. Sometimes you need the dark to protect the light.

Standing in the doorway of the gatehouse, my home on the estate, I drank my coffee, watching the mist curl around the Manor, rays of weak winter sun gilding the roof. Heartstone Manor was three stories of warm, gray granite, designed a century ago to mimic the English country estate William Sawyer's bride had left behind. Maybe that was why it looked so much like a movie set. It was a place out of time, on the wrong continent. Now, the day barely begun, the sight of it should have filled me with peace.

Knowing everything that had happened there over the past year, the tranquil image didn't fool me. There was danger everywhere, and it was my job to keep it at bay. Finishing my last drop of coffee, I left the mug on the gatehouse steps and headed out, planning to loop around to the woods on the east side of the Manor, then past the cottage, crossing behind the pool house and formal gardens to the west side of the Manor and the forest there.

I always ended my rounds on the west side. Ever since I'd discovered her sleeping under the trees instead of safe inside the Manor. Late last night, she'd snuck out again, stealing across the lawn in silence and disappearing into the dark woods. I'd bet she was still there, sleeping peacefully, under the illusion of a safety that didn't exist.

I shouldn't care. It was her life. Not my problem. I'd reported the situation to Griffen, and he'd told me to let her be. That should be enough.

It wasn't.

It was March for fuck's sake. Too cold to sleep outside when she had a perfectly good bedroom in the Manor.

Not my problem.

I told myself that a lot where she was concerned. Not my problem. And she wasn't.

I was going to check on her, anyway. I couldn't seem to help myself. Not when it came to her.

Heading out at a slow jog, I texted the team watching the cameras from our base in the lower level of the Manor.

Anything to report?

No, boss. Quiet night.

Doing my rounds. I'll stop by after.

Everything was quiet in the east side woods, the cameras and the perimeter system operating perfectly. As we did every day, I signaled in front of each camera, receiving an acknowledgment from the team at our base. Finished with the cameras, I moved into position and texted my team again.

Triggering Zone One

I deliberately stepped through the almost invisible laser that created the first zone of the perimeter alarm.

Trigger received

I wasn't expecting anything else. We had the woods wired every way we could. No one was getting anywhere near the Manor if I could help it. We'd had more than enough trouble with people who were allowed on the property. I didn't need anyone sneaking up on us.

Between me, my team, and Griffen, we'd reverse-engineered every approach to the Manor. We had a strategy established for every conceivable scenario. Considering our combined backgrounds, that was a lot of scenarios. So far, no one had gotten in. Not since the beginning and that first attempt on Griffen.

We'd still had plenty of trouble. After we added the cameras and perimeter alarm, whoever was after the Sawyers had shifted their attention to the Inn at Sawyers Bend. Sabotage. A knife attack meant for Griffen's brother Royal. Then another murder. Vanessa, the fiancée Ford had stolen from Griffen, then married and divorced. She'd sworn she knew who Prentice's real killer was. Maybe she had, but we'd never know. Whoever was behind all of this had gotten to Vanessa first.

Garden variety theft interrupted our string of murder and attempted murder; A cousin who thought room and board entitled him to walk off with Sawyer heirlooms. After we took care of the stealing, we swung back to murder, this time courtesy of Parker Sawyer's now-deceased husband, convinced he could win back his mother's love if he murdered Parker. Crazy bastard. Shooting him hadn't been a hardship, especially after he almost killed Parker, her sister, and one of my best guys.

The last real excitement we'd had was months ago when Savannah's estranged mother-in-law had tried to kidnap her son, Nicky. Savannah was the housekeeper of Heartstone Manor and practically kept the place running single-handedly. After a chase across half the state, her mother-in-law was in court-mandated psychiatric treatment, and Nicky was doing fine. I'd thought we might have an issue when Griffen got the headmaster of Nicky's school fired for letting Nicky get kidnapped, but he'd left the state without causing any more trouble. Things had been quiet since.

Finished with the east side of the Manor, I followed the edge of the forest, skirting the back of Savannah's cottage. The front door opened, and Finn Sawyer stepped out, stopping to lock the deadbolt behind him before heading to the Manor to start breakfast. He was running late.

Finn had taken me by surprise. At first, I'd thought he was using Savannah. In my world, staff and family don't mix. You never fuck the client. Griffen was the closest thing I had to a brother, but that didn't make me a Sawyer. And Savannah might have grown up in Heartstone Manor, but that didn't make Savannah a Sawyer either. Finn had done that. He'd married her on Valentine's Day, and the look on his face as she walked down the aisle finally convinced me he loved her.

Finn disappeared into the side door of the Manor. I circled around behind the pool house and the barren gardens to check the cameras and perimeter alarm on the south side of the Manor. Everything was functioning normally.

It made my skin itchy. We hadn't had a stretch of quiet this long since I'd been here. Three months since Nicky had been kidnapped, and other than two weddings, life had been calm.

Okay, not exactly calm. We'd gotten word that Ford had survived an assassination attempt in prison. But that could just be Ford pissing people off. I'd gotten the impression that while he was better liked than Prentice had been, he wasn't everyone's favorite Sawyer. Ford's lawyer was convinced his siblings poking into Prentice's murder had made Ford a target. Maybe. Either way, whatever was causing trouble for Ford would spill over onto the rest of his family. If not today, then eventually.

I wouldn't let the quiet make me soft. If I'd learned anything in my former career, it was patience. How to stay sharp through hours, days, and months of monotony. Never lose your edge. Never let the boredom blur your focus. That was how people got killed. I'd lost enough. I wasn't going to lose anyone else.

The west side of the Manor was as quiet as the rest, the woods as still as they ever were. I went through the routine with the cameras and perimeter alarm. All operating as usual.

I didn't see her on my rounds. She knew where the cameras were. I didn't like that she'd chosen to build her nest where we couldn't see her. Couldn't keep her safe. The whole thing made me a little crazy.

It shouldn't. Quinn Sawyer was part of the job. A client. She was nothing to me. In the year since we'd met, we'd had less than a handful of conversations. She was Griffen's sister. Another reason I owed her my best.

My best was ice cold. Detached. Clinical.

Not annoyed, frustrated, and ready to bite her head off.

I'd seen her the night before. I'd been walking the perimeter, as I did on the nights my dreams chased away sleep. Quinn crept out the side door of the Manor not long after eleven, a backpack slung over her shoulder. I didn't know why she snuck out to sleep in the woods. It was a bizarre thing to do, especially for an heiress with a castle to sleep in.

The first time I saw her gliding across the dark grass, lit only by the moon, I hadn't stopped her. I'd followed.

She'd disappeared into the trees at the edge of the woods, and I'd almost lost her. She was alert, her head turning at the slightest sound, as surefooted as if it was full daylight. I had to be careful and quiet, two things I was very good at. Still, I almost missed her hiding spot.

I'd watched from the cover of a rhododendron bush as Quinn pulled a camping hammock from her backpack. She gave it a brisk shake before hooking it between two straps already secured to the trees. An insulated underquilt came next, followed by a sleeping bag that looked like it was rated for subzero temperatures and a rain fly to keep her dry from the damp that would come in the night.

She had the whole thing set up in less than three minutes. She climbed in. I heard the whirr of the zipper on her sleeping bag, the rustle of fabric as she got comfortable, and that was it. Snug as a bug in a rug, as my mom used to say.

I'd been mystified. I still was. We'd never spoken about it. I hadn't spoken to Quinn about much of anything. She was family. I was security. The distinction was important with everyone but Griffen. My job is to keep them safe, not be friends with them, but Quinn is something different.

Quinn is —

I don't know. All these months later, I'm still trying to figure out what it is about Quinn Sawyer.

She didn't sleep in the woods every night, but she was there more than she wasn't. In the coldest bite of winter. In the heat of August. Didn't matter. The nights when I couldn't sleep, I walked the grounds and checked on Quinn.

There had been times, too many of them, when I'd sat at the base of a nearby oak and dozed, my ear cocked for anything that might come too close to the sleeping Quinn.

Nothing ever did. The animals moved past her as if she were neither threat nor prey. To them, she was a part of the forest. I'd seen deer cropping at the undergrowth feet away from her hammock. Fox playing in the clearing. She was like Snow White without the creepy dwarves. I understood the woods and loved the wild. It was part of why I'd been so willing to come here. But I knew the wild wasn't forgiving. And Quinn was defenseless.

It was early, the sun barely cresting the mountains. This time of year, Quinn's guide business was mostly closed down. She wouldn't be up with the dawn, preparing to guide kayakers down the river or hikers into the mountains. Like the wild creature she was, she'd be curled in her nest, fast asleep.

My feet brought me to her clearing, a path I knew better than any other on the estate. It was a few minutes' walk before I saw the dark arc of her hammock against the slowly growing light. No rain fly. Mist wound around the base of the trees, another dark shape moving behind her hammock blurred in the foggy trees.

My hand went to the weapon at my hip as I crouched and moved faster, closing the distance between me and the sleeping Quinn. The shape in the woods moved at a steady pace, splitting into three shapes, one hulking, the other two far smaller, all three dark blobs in the trees.

Goddamned mist. As pretty as it was, it fucked my visibility in the woods. I was too close to call the base and see if they had anything on the cameras. Man or beast, it would hear me at this range.

I reached the hammock. Risking a second to glance

inside, I caught the barest glimpse of dark hair, the curve of a pale cheek, the rest hidden by the sleeping bag. Still asleep. Good. I didn't have time for explanations.

The dark shapes in the trees drew steadily closer. I raised my weapon as they came into focus. A sow and two cubs. Black bears. The female was large for her breed. I'd guess close to two hundred pounds. The cubs were tiny in comparison, which made mama bear very, very dangerous.

In mid-March, this might be the cubs' first foray outside their den. This wasn't the first time I'd seen bears in these mountains. Everyone who lived here spotted a bear eventually, and I spent a lot of time in the woods. The black bears in these mountains weren't aggressive. If you gave them space, they'd give it back as long as you were smart about food and didn't get close to a mama with her newborn cubs.

Fuck. I'd never seen a bear so close to Quinn's hiding place. And this one kept coming. Ambling, not charging, but way too close. Why?

Quinn wouldn't have food. My heart jerked at the thought. Surely she'd know better. Of course, she did. She ran a guide service, for fucks sake. The online reviews of her business were glowing. That wouldn't happen if she was getting tourists mauled because she didn't know how to handle living in bear country.

The sow ambled a few feet closer, finally turning her head to study me. I wasn't fooled. Her sharp nose had already picked me up. The cubs passed her, circling around to wander behind me, far too close to Quinn. The sow wagged her head, lurching forward. On instinct, my gun arm came up, pointed at the sow. At this range, I could get a headshot, but I put odds on the bear's thick skull deflecting the bullet. Especially if she charged.

"What the hell are you doing?" a voice behind me

hissed. The bear's gaze shifted to my left. I couldn't risk turning.

"Be quiet," I hissed back. My gut turned to ice as the sow looked past me at Quinn's hammock. Fuck.

I risked a look back, and my heart thundering in my chest. Quinn was sitting up, her cheeks pink and puffy with sleep, dark silky hair sliding all over the place, her blue eyes bright and alert as they fixed on the mama bear.

"Get fucking down, Quinn."

"No," she murmured. "I don't have anything she wants." In the quiet morning air, her soft voice was musical. Mesmerizing. The sow seemed to agree. She watched Quinn, her gaze only straying to check on her cubs rolling in the scrub beneath the hammock. "I don't have any food, mama. You're just curious, aren't you?" she asked the bear. "Just taking your babies out for a stroll."

"Quinn," I growled. "Shut the fuck up and get down."

"Hawk," she said, the soothing music gone from her voice. "Put that gun away and scare her off. Don't tell me you don't know how to scare off a curious bear."

I let out an annoyed grunt, my gaze moving back to the sow. She was right; I did know how to scare off a bear. I'd done it before when I'd run into a brown bear while fishing in Montana. Sliding my gun back into its holster, I side-stepped between Quinn and the sow and roared at the bear, waving my arms to make myself look as big as I could.

"Get out of here! Go! Get the fuck away!" Ignoring my instincts to run, to shoot her, to do anything but get closer, I stepped forward and roared louder. "Get the fuck out of here! Go! Go! Go! Get lost!"

The bear turned, backing up a hesitant step before her eyes shifted to the right. Her cubs had wandered to the far side of the hammock, no longer cut off from their mother.

With an ursine shrug, the sow ambled away, collecting her cubs and disappearing slowly into what remained of dawn's mist.

"Were you going to shoot her in the eye with that thing?" Quinn asked, sounding amused and not the least bit scared. "Is your aim that good?"

"Yes," I grunted, too annoyed to bother lying. At that range, I could have shot her in the eye. Unless she'd charged.

Quinn sat cross-legged in her hammock, her long underwear rumpled, her eyes sparkling. Why wasn't she afraid?

"Why aren't you scared?" I demanded, my gut still churning at how close she'd come to being a bear snack.

Quinn shrugged. "She didn't want to hurt me. She was just out for a morning walk with her cubs."

"Quinn, there was a fucking oversized sow less than ten feet from you. Her cubs were playing right underneath you. Do you not understand how dangerous that was? You're wrapped up in that hammock like a fucking human burrito. It's winter. They're hungry. How can you be so reckless?"

She shrugged again, sending my heart rate through the roof. I was going to kill her. Or have a stroke.

"Quinn," I tried again. "It's not safe to sleep out here."

She shook her head. "I'm safer out here than I am in the Manor."

"It's safer than it used to be," I said, knowing she had a point. There'd been a murder and more than a few attempted murders inside the manor. Animal attacks? Zero.

"There were bear cubs right under your hammock," I reminded her.

"I know." She grinned, lighting up the forest. "Isn't it cool?"

"No!" I shouted back. I heard myself and snapped my mouth shut.

It was only Quinn who did this to me. Quinn with her pixie body and her bright eyes. She looked delicate. Fragile. The first time I saw her, I wanted to protect her. Ironic because of all the people living in Heartstone Manor, Griffen aside, Quinn needed protection the least.

She knew the woods like the back of her hand. She was fit and strong. She could hike for hours. She knew how to shoot. She knew how to use a knife. The knife was for fileting the fish she caught, not combat, but it was wickedly sharp, and she held it like it had been made for her. I'd seen all of this with my own eyes.

I knew Quinn wasn't weak. She wasn't stupid. She wasn't careless. And here I was, roaring at her like she was the bear I was trying to scare off.

Fuck.

She made things misfire in my brain.

That bear in Montana? I'd faced him down with icy calm, waving my arms and yelling just as I had with the mama bear a few minutes before. The one in Montana had been bigger, a male brown bear who'd wanted our trout for his dinner. I hadn't bothered with my weapon, charging at him when he'd come for us, as calm as I'd been making coffee that morning in camp.

With Quinn in the picture, all that icy calm had burned away. She fucked with my head. I'd seen the bear, seen Quinn sleeping, and let fear take the driver's seat.

When was the last time that had happened?

I knew the answer. The last time I'd let fear make my decisions, I'd fallen into the darkness. I'd destroyed too much. More than I could live with.

I had to hold on to the ice. The control.

I had to stay far away from Quinn Sawyer.

I was here to keep her safe. To keep her alive. Letting her get any further under my skin would only put her in danger. I couldn't allow that.

Quinn Sawyer wasn't for me. I wasn't the kind of man who could have a woman like her. The things I'd done could never be redeemed. Ever.

I wouldn't lose another woman I cared about. Not again. And not this one.

Without another word, I walked away, ignoring Quinn's grunt of annoyance. Good, if she was annoyed, she'd stay away from me. I didn't need the temptation.

If I did nothing else in my life, I was going to keep Quinn Sawyer safe.

Especially from me.

ARE YOU READY FOR HAWK & QUINN'S STORY?

Visit IvyLayne.com/WildHeart
to see what happens next!

Never Miss a New Release:

Join Ivy's Reader's Group

@ ivylayne.com/readers
&
Get two books for free!

About Ivy Layne

Ivy Layne has had her nose stuck in a book since she first learned to decipher the English language. Sometime in her early teens, she stumbled across her first Romance, and the die was cast. Though she pretended to pay attention to her creative writing professors, she dreamed of writing steamy romance instead of literary fiction. These days, she's neck deep in alpha heroes and the smart, sexy women who love them.

Married to her very own alpha hero (who rubs her back after a long day of typing, but also leaves his socks on the floor). Ivy lives in the mountains of North Carolina where she and her other half are having a blast raising two energetic little boys. Aside from her family, Ivy's greatest loves are coffee and chocolate, preferably together.

For More Information:
www.ivylayne.com
books@ivylayne.com
Facebook.com/AuthorIvyLayne
Instagram.com/authorivylayne/

Also by Ivy Layne

Don't Miss Out on New Releases, Exclusive Giveaways, and More!!

Join Ivy's Readers Group @ ivylayne.com/readers

THE HEARTS OF SAWYERS BEND

Stolen Heart

Sweet Heart

Scheming Heart

Rebel Heart

Wicked Heart

Wild Heart

THE UNTANGLED SERIES

Unraveled

Undone

Uncovered

THE WINTERS SAGA

The Billionaire's Secret Heart (Novella)

The Billionaire's Secret Love (Novella)

The Billionaire's Pet

Made in the USA
Las Vegas, NV
29 September 2023

78285533R00272